HAMMERING THE BLADE

BY

FRANK ROCKLAND

A Canadian Expeditionary Force Novel

1915

Forging the Weapon
A Canadian Expeditionary Force Novel
1914

Who knew? In the fall of 1914, Canadians had earned a reputation as hard-drinking and poorly disciplined troops. No one expected much from them. Certainly not the British! All they wanted was a sharp salute as the men did what they were told.

Prime Minister Sir Robert Borden and his Minister of Militia and Defence, Colonel Sam Hughes, had different ideas. Borden had no choice! When England declared war, Canada was automatically at war too. Hughes, however, was eager to get his boys bloodied before the war was over. He would do anything in his power to get the Canadians into the fight.

As the guns sounded in August, the first contingent gathered at Valcartier. Corps of Guide Captain James Llewellyn had trained for this moment, and he was not about to miss out. Gunner Paul Ryan had volunteered to escape his family and to impress a girl. Nursing Sister Samantha Lonsdale had answered the call because she needed a job, and going to war was an adventure.

As the months rolled by, it was at Valcartier and Salisbury Plain that they helped forge the Canadian Expeditionary Force into one of the most formidable weapons of the First World War.

Fire on the Hill

What really happened on the night of February 3, 1916, when a fire destroyed the Centre Block of the Canadian Parliament buildings?

Inspector Andrew MacNutt of the Dominion Police's Secret Service, his wife Katherine, and Count Jaggi know, since they were there in the reading room when the fire started.

Ever since the war began, MacNutt has been struggling to secure Canada's borders against acts of sabotage organized by German military attachés based in New York City. The good news is that the Americans have finally ordered them back to Germany. The bad news is that Berlin has sent one of their best operatives, Count Jaggi, to replace them.

Using his cover as a Belgian Relief representative, Count Jaggi visits Ottawa, where he meets and is attracted to Katherine, who is helping him organize a local fundraiser.

Unaware that Inspector MacNutt has intercepted his secret messages and is hot on his trail, Count Jaggi takes a final trip to Ottawa to see Katherine, with tragic consequences.

Author's Note

Hammering the Blade is a work of fiction. All incidents, dialogue, and characters, with the exception of historical and public figures, are products of the author's imagination and are not to be construed as real.

Where real-life historical or public figures appear, the situations, incidents, and dialogue concerning the person are fictional.

In all aspects, any resemblance to the living or the dead is entirely coincidental.

Author's Note

CHAPTER 1

Sir Robert Borden could hear Sam Hughes' voice when he arrived on the third floor of the hospital. The matron who had been given the rather dubious honour of accompanying him frowned at the disturbance, but she didn't comment as she led the prime minister down the hall to the noise that was emanating from a private room next to the solarium. The solarium was empty, since there were few patients willing at this hour of the morning to take advantage of what was normally a pleasant escape from the demanding hospital staff and what bit of sun was available during the Ottawa winter months. She made a hasty but dignified retreat after she left Sir Robert to fend for himself.

The door was open, and he could see Sam Hughes sitting up in his bed with two male stenographers sitting in white hospital chairs opposite him. They were scribbling furiously in shorthand as Hughes dictated a response to a letter clutched in his hand.

"And further notice…" He stopped when he saw the prime minister in the doorway then continued. "Good morning, Prime Minister."

"Keeping busy, I see," Borden remarked.

"The war effort doesn't stop for any man," he replied with a sour grin. He then the ordered the stenographers, "Take a five-minute recess, gentlemen."

The men flipped the covers of their pads closed as they rose to their feet and left the room to give the two men some privacy. Borden sat in one of the warm chairs.

"So how's the knee?" Borden asked.

"It hurts like a son-of-a-bitch," Hughes replied with a grimace as he rubbed his right knee. It was wrapped in bandages and was raised above the bed. The diagnosis was synovitis. He had banged it when he went home to Lindsay for Christmas. The train had been swaying so much that he had lost his balance and landed on the protruding corner of his berth. He didn't think much about it, figuring he would simply walk the injury off. The veins that surrounded the knee had become inflamed and had swollen it to twice its size, requiring hospitalization. From what Borden could tell, it didn't seem to slow Hughes down much.

"Colonel Carson informed me that he met with you yesterday afternoon?" Hughes stated.

"He did."

"And?"

"He gave me a very thorough report on the conditions at Salisbury Plain," replied Borden. Lieutenant-Colonel Wallace Carson had led the advance party to England last October to prepare for the arrival of the Canadian Expeditionary Force. "I didn't realize what our men had to endure."

"The men have been splendid under such conditions. It's a testament to how well they are maintaining their morale."

"True. That is very true."

"Are you going to push through the order-in-council for the colonel?" asked Hughes.

"I've been considering it," Borden replied reluctantly. Borden knew that Hughes was pushing to have his friend appointed as a special representative.

"He is a good man. Very reliable. I need someone in England to look after our men. I haven't been to happy with the way the War Office has been treating our contingent," Hughes said as he continued to push for Carson, since Borden had not categorically said no.

"I will support you on this matter," Borden replied. Borden then took Hughes' beaming smile away by adding, "I have some concerns, but as long as Colonel Carson's role does not overlap or duplicate George Perley's work in London."

The current order-in-council draft read that Carson was responsible for supplies and other requirements for the contingent in the UK and at the front. Also, he was to be responsible for the supply depots to ensure that the CEF had what they needed to operate effectively. Some of this fell under the authority of George Perley, the acting Canadian High Commissioner in London.

Hughes looked pleased and irritated simultaneously. Borden knew why when he said, "I saw the New Year's list. Some good names were on it."

"Yes, they were," Borden sighed. He knew that it was an opening salvo by Hughes to get on the honour's list. Hughes was peeved that his colleague had been appointed Knight Commander, order of St. Michael and St. George, which allowed Perley from now on to be addressed as

Sir Perley. Borden had made the recommendation, not only because Perley was a close friend and advisor, but because of the tireless and thankless work that he had done as the Acting Canadian High Commissioner in London. Hughes, Borden knew, felt that he was also entitled. If history were any guide, Hughes would not relent until he received the same honour.

Borden tried to change the subject. "One of the reasons I've come is to discuss war supplies, since you couldn't attend the last Saturday's council meeting."

"I should have been there. Damn knee!" Hughes muttered through clenched teeth. "The troops need those supplies."

"I'm well aware of that," replied Borden. "It's a question of efficiency. I would like to avoid some of the problems that have occurred due to haste, such as the boot contracts."

"The damn boots are fine."

"Be that as it may," Borden said, trying to let it slide, but when he saw Hughes become defensive he hastened to add, "I believe that it was a remarkable achievement to raise 31,000 men, equip them, and send them to England in two months. It is unfortunate that the Imperial government has not seen fit to engage them at the front to date. The latest message we received from the War Office indicated that they will utilize them in February."

"It's about bloody time," exclaimed Hughes. He had been frustrated that his men had not yet fired a shot in anger.

"Yes, of course, but to ensure that our men receive the supplies necessary to prosecute the war, we need to put the contracting and administration of them on a more firm footing."

"Exactly!" replied Hughes, excited. "That's why I'm suggesting to you that a committee of prominent businessmen be engaged for that purpose. They will have the knowledge, experience, and know the preferred methods to obtain the best quality for the lowest price for our men."

Borden paused to consider it. "The idea does have some merit." He rubbed his moustache then shrugged. "I will bring it up at this afternoon's council meeting and see what the other members of the cabinet think."

"By all means," replied Hughes.

Borden could see that Hughes didn't like that idea as he rose to his feet. "Well, I must be off. Is there anything I could get you?"

"Yes," said Hughes as he pointed to his knee with his chin, "a new knee, if you have one to spare."

Borden chuckled. "I'm afraid not. I've been using mine praying for the safe return of our men."

PRIME MINISTER'S OFFICE, EAST BLOCK,
PARLIAMENT HILL, OTTAWA

"Son-of-a-bitch!" Borden swore when he read the telegram marked "secret" that George had sent him from London. It was a good thing, too. If his ministers had been aware of it, the cabinet meeting that he had just come from would have been even more exhausting. He had spent most of his time placating their bruised egos. They had been peeved, and a few were offended by Hughes' suggestion concerning the war supplies.

So far, $50 million worth of orders had been placed in Canada, providing work for 300 factories. A British clothing order for $4 million had been awarded to Montreal firms. And more was coming. The difficulty was managing the contracts that were inundating the Department of Militia and Defence. The issues with the boot contracts and others he suspected were only the tip of the iceberg. What was also causing headaches was the lack of coordination with the Imperials. They were under no obligation to inform him of the orders they placed in Canada. This caused snags when the factories couldn't complete Canadian orders, since they were running full-tilt filling the British ones.

That was why George's telegram pissed him off. Hughes had asked his good friend, who he had made an honorary colonel, for assistance with some gun contracts. The problem was the accusations that Allison had been inflating the prices and pocketing the excess profits. It didn't help, after sending warnings to the War Office, to avoid financial dealings with Allison that Hughes had contradicted him by sending a letter defending the man. It didn't leave a very good impression with the Imperials concerning him and his government.

Well, at least he knew where he could find Hughes to give him a tongue-lashing.

CHAPTER 2

"So when do you think we're going to France?" asked Corporal Downing as he dipped a horseshoe into a bucket of cold water near the anvil.

"Everyone says it's going to be soon," replied Paul Ryan, watching the water steam and hiss as it quenched the hot metal. When the farrier saw that it was sufficiently cool, he pulled it out and went over to the nearby horse. He lifted a heavy hoof and placed the steel on it to check the fit. He gave a dissatisfied grunt as he dropped the leg and returned the shoe to the nearby forge.

"Yeah, right! Nobody knows shit!" Downing said. His burly arm flexed as he pressed on the bellows to increase the forge's heat. When the shoe glowed red-hot, he used a pair of tongs to carry it over to the anvil. He gave the steel a couple of blows with a hammer then said, "That should do."

He went over to the horse, raised its leg, and placed the hot shoe on the hoof. It sizzled for a moment, and the smell of burnt horse filled the air. The animal remained placid as the farrier pulled some nails from his leather apron then tacked the shoe in place. "He's done. Next!" the corporal said as he gave the draught a friendly pat.

"Some of the rumours making the rounds are that we're going to Egypt," said Ryan as he brought a second animal into the tent. Corporal Ryan had been tasked with bringing some of the unit's horses for Downing to take a look at.

"Heard that too. It would be grand. Egypt's hot and dry. Need a bit of a rest," remarked Downing as he examined the animal's legs and then lifted each hoof to inspect them. Just above the man's head, Ryan could see the "CA" that was branded into the horse's haunch. Above the animal's rear there were overcast skies. It hadn't rained yet, but it probably would. Since their arrival last October at Salisbury Plain, the horses of the CEF had suffered a higher than normal percentage of hoof ailments such as softening of the hoof, lost shoes, abscesses, seedy toe, and thrush. It had been keeping the farriers quite busy.

"Don't we all? Everyone's getting sick and tired of all of this training," Ryan replied.

Downing snorted. "Yeah, right. You walked past punishment row?"

"I did." Ryan grimaced. About a half dozen men had been tied to a fence, enduring Field Punishment No. 1 for serious infractions; mostly drunkenness on duty or desertion.

"If it's Egypt, it's a long way from your girl," stated the corporal.

"I don't have a girl!" was Ryan's quick response.

"Sure you do," Downing retorted with a leer. "Didn't you go to her ma's place on New Year's Day?"

"So did a half-dozen others," Ryan pointed out.

"Are you seeing her soon?"

"Yeah," Ryan admitted reluctantly, "this afternoon."

"There you go. How many others did she invite?"

"I don't know," whispered Ryan.

"There you go," the corporal repeated with a knowing grin.

★ ★ ★

Ryan got out of the truck with packages in his arms. He had showered, and his uniform was freshly washed and pressed. His cap badge and buttons were brightly polished. He squared his shoulders after he opened the gate and made his way to the farmhouse. His arrival had been announced by the barking dogs. A thin white blanket of snow covered flower and vegetable beds.

"It's you," Maggie's mother snarled when she opened the door. He had been hoping Maggie would get there first. He had met the Thompsons last November when he came over to retrieve a Canadian horse that wondered off and eaten most of her garden. She hadn't been impressed with him then. She hadn't softened much since.

"Is Maggie in?" he asked.

A frown appeared briefly before she yelled, "Maggie, the Canadian is here."

Maggie came into sight from the kitchen. "Ma!" Her tone was an admonishment.

"Don't be impertinent, girl," her mother retorted. "You're still not in my good graces."

"Yes, Ma," Maggie replied with chagrin.

"I brought some maple sugar candy from Canada," Paul said, offering the package to Mrs. Thompson.

She softened somewhat. "Take the young man into the sitting room while I get some tea," she said as she took the packages and headed to the kitchen in the back.

Maggie led him to the sitting room beside the entrance. The room was plain, with several gold-coloured wing chairs with matching settee arranged around a coal fireplace. There were several pastoral paintings on the walls.

"Have a seat," Maggie said, getting the settee so he could sit beside her.

"Are you sure?" he replied. "Your mom seems to be upset."

"She's been crossed with me since New Year," she replied. She had invited him and a bunch of other young men to her house for a New Year celebration. "So when are you going to France?"

"News travels fast," replied Ryan.

"It's to be expected," she stated then added with a mischievous twinkle, "Some of the other lads have mentioned you're going soon."

Paul knew that he gave himself away when he croaked, "What lads?"

"Oh," she replied nonchalantly, "some of the lads from the New-foundland regiment and few from you lot that have dropped by."

That explained some of her mother's hostility. She would have preferred one of the local lads for her daughter.

It was at that moment that her mother appeared with a tray holding a Brown Bess teapot and white china cups. Her frown deepened when he saw that he was sitting on the settee, even though there were several inches of clear space between him and Maggie. He could see her examining Maggie's dress, checking to see that it hadn't been ruffled by wandering hands.

She placed the tray on the table and poured the tea. She didn't show any signs of leaving, especially since there were three cups on the tray. Her presence had put a crimp in his plans.

"So what did you do before you joined the army?" Maggie's mom asked.

"My dad owns a clothing enterprise in Montreal," he replied.

Her eyes brightened. "So he has plenty of coin?"

"I guess."

"Mom!"

"So you'll be taking over your father's concern, eventually," she continued, ignoring her daughter's embarrassed outrage.

Ryan could see the avarice in her eyes. It was something he had seen before, and he knew how to kill it rather effectively. "Not really. It'll be probably go to my younger brother. I have another a career in mind."

"Which is?

"Writer."

"Writer!" Mrs. Thompson said with a start. "Is there much money in that?"

"Not much, I'm afraid."

"Oh." She couldn't keep the note of disgust out of her voice.

Despite Mrs. Thompson's reaction, he still liked Maggie. He decided to bite the bullet.

"I was wondering…" he stuttered, "… if … you were free … Saturday evening. There is a new moving picture in Salisbury."

Maggie gave him a wry smile, then she glanced at her mother.

"Saturday evening?" questioned her mom.

"Mum, I would really like to go the pictures. Angela will come with us with her lad."

"Not without me and Angela's mom you don't," Mrs. Thompson replied tersely. Paul's heart sank. All he needed was a chaperone.

JANUARY 8, 1915
LARK HILL, SALISBURY PLAIN

"So what do you think?" asked Lieutenant-Colonel Currie.

Captain Llewellyn blinked. The commanding officer of the 2nd Brigade was asking his opinion, and it was taking getting used to. His previous commanders were "this is what you are going to do and you are going to do it my way" types. It seemed that his CO was cut from a different cloth.

"Captain?" Currie prompted him again.

"Sorry, sir." The captain saw, from the corner of his eye, the officer beside him giving him a tense glance. He was amused by the look of disbelief that appeared on the man's face that changed when he said, "I think it's a good idea."

"Hmm," Currie murmured thoughtfully as he looked at the two aperture sights for the Ross rifle that he was holding. He lifted one up to his right eye to peer through it and then the other.

"So the suggestion is that we enlarge the aperture to 5/64 inches?" he questioned as he looked around the assembled officers in his command tent. Nearly all the senior officers were in attendance, since the day's training was cancelled — again! The rain that was streaming off the canvas walls didn't appear to be slowing down much.

"That's correct," replied Captain Cox, who was seated beside Llewellyn. He was responsible for the armourer section of the brigade. "Enlarging it will help in acquiring the target faster."

"But there is a loss in accuracy," pointed out Captain Henricks, who was sitting across from Llewellyn.

"That's true," conceded Cox reluctantly. "But at the ranges we are talking about, it will be negligible."

Currie nodded. "The latest reports indicate that ranges are 100 to 300 yards. The average distance between our trenches and the enemy."

Llewellyn was pleased that the colonel was reading the intelligence reports that he had been preparing for the brigade.

"How long will it take?" Currie asked.

A brief look of concern appeared on the captain's face before he said, "It will take about an hour to enlarge each one. It's exacting work. If we go full-tilt, it will take us about three weeks to a month."

Currie frowned at the news. Llewellyn knew why. There were rumours that Lord Kitchener had finally decided to send the Canadian Division to France in the first week of February, but the official orders had not yet been received.

"Can we continue the work if we are sent to the front?"

"Yes," the armourer replied quickly to assure his CO. "It's a relatively simple process. We can adapt them in the field. Still, we're talking about five thousand rifles, so it will take some time."

"I see," replied Currie as he paused to consider the problem. He nodded slightly when he made a decision. "Okay, proceed with the modifications."

"Thank you, sir," the armourer replied with relief.

"Well, now that is out of the way," said Currie. "Let's move on to more important matters — baseball."

"Yes, Colonel," replied Captain Llewellyn. "The men would like to formalize their baseball games. Even start an interunit league between the brigades."

"You mean to tell me that the men still have enough energy to play baseball?" Currie queried with a raised eyebrow.

"Yes," replied the captain.

Currie grimaced somewhat as he rubbed his clean-shaven chin. "I don't know. The men do need some rest and relaxation, I suppose, but I do have some concerns that it does not distract the men from their duties."

"The men and the junior officers have assured us that they will ensure the games are arranged off-duty and will not interfere with their training and assigned tasks."

"Okay. That will be fine. However, if it interferes with the men's work, we will need to revisit it."

"Thank you, Colonel," replied Llewellyn. He added with a grimace, "We're a bit short on baseball equipment."

"Good luck finding that in England," Currie laughed.

Llewellyn sighed. "I wonder what the quartermaster will say when I put in a request."

"Good luck with that," replied Currie. From his tone Llewellyn surmised he wouldn't approve the request if it came across his desk.

"Of course, sir. I was thinking more along the lines of the YMCA. They want to provide wholesome Christian entertainment for the men."

"That will be fine," replied Currie. "Now, concerning Christian entertainment, I've been getting a number of notifications of intention of marriage forms sitting on my desk waiting for my approval," he said as he looked around the officers. Some of the men squirmed in their seats.

"Yes, Colonel," remarked the Captain.

"Please ensure that the form is completed properly before it reaches my office. It seems that some of them are missing the medical officer inspection reports. So far none seem to be in the family way, but I doubt that will last."

Currie glanced outside the tent then said, "It seems that the weather is improving. Let's see if we can get some training in."

JANUARY 15, 1915
NO. 2 CANADIAN STATIONARY HOSPITAL, LE TOUQUET

"I'm afraid that they are not in any condition to answer questions," Samantha informed the major, who was standing in front of her at the entrance of the medical tent.

The major glanced over her shoulder at the five men who were lying and sitting on canvas cots. "They seem to be fine," he remarked.

"Major," Samantha replied as she glanced at the Coldstream Guard insignia on his cap badge, "Are you a medical doctor?"

"No," he admitted, "but I can tell when men are malingering."

"Malingering!" Samantha sputtered. She was tempted to poke the man in the chest with a forefinger, but that would not be politic. "I don't know what your definition of malingering is, but I don't think bullet, shrapnel, and bayonet wounds are part of it."

"But ... but ... the prisoners could escape!" the major protested.

"Not without their pants they won't," she retorted.

"What?" His eyes widened when he finally noticed that the men were dressed in long grey woollen underwear.

"And I don't think that those with a missing arm or leg will get very far," she added.

The major, seeing that he wasn't getting anywhere, finally relented. "Where can I find the senior medical officer?"

"In the main building," she said, pointing to the Hotel du Golf. The three-storey red-brick luxury hotel and golf resort was the current home of the No. 2 Canadian Stationary Hospital. "When the doctor gives his permission, you can come back and interview the prisoners."

"I will. What is your name?" he demanded.

"Lieutenant Samantha Lonsdale. Nursing Sister, Canadian Stationary Hospital."

The major acknowledged with a nod then turned on his heels and stomped toward the hotel.

When she turned and faced the five men, she saw, with one exception, that they were staring at her anxiously. They were also watching the reactions of the man with close-cropped blond hair and blue eyes who was sitting up in his cot. Samantha glanced at the man's left leg, or rather the stump. It was all that remained, and it was covered by a thin grey blanket. He made a comment in German, and the other men relaxed somewhat. They were still anxious, since they were what remained of a German machine-gun unit that the Coldstream Guards had captured during a battle near Cuinchy. About half the current patients in the hospital wards were the results of the decision by the Irish and Coldstream Guards to regain the ground that they had lost to the 2nd Bavarians a few weeks prior.

The Hague Convention required that they provide the same level of care that they provided to their own men. The Germans were being sheltered in the medical tents after their initial treatment and stabilization to avoid any unpleasantness on the wards.

The lack of pants wasn't a deliberate attempt to keep the prisoners from escaping. Rather, it was the result of basic hospital procedure. The clothes needed to be cleaned before they could be returned to the patients. The Germans had half their clothes in tatters when the medics had cut them away to treat their wounds. Ideally, they would have preferred cutting them along the seams so that they could be mended easily. Getting new uniforms was a bit of a supply problem. Besides, they would rather not give them Canadian uniforms unless it was absolutely necessary.

"Thank you, *Fräulein*," he said in perfect English.

"You're welcome," she replied. She had been initially surprised that he spoke such good English. He was around her age, twenty-two or twenty-three, and was a junior officer, a lieutenant. He had been rather reticent about his background, only giving his name, Karl Hartmann, and rank.

When he winced in pain, Samantha asked, "Your leg hurting?"

"My ankle, actually," he replied. "The one that is missing."

"I'll check your bandages," she said. She felt a small butterfly in her stomach when she approached the man. She couldn't help glancing at the medical tent entrance, where she caught the glimpse of one of the guard's arms. When Matron Riley requested volunteers to care for them, she had been rather hesitant putting her hand up, especially when no else had. So far she had been pleasantly surprised at how quite civilized they were.

One of the men on the cot near the black coal-fired stove in the centre of the tent made a remark in German, causing all of them to chuckle. They were silenced quickly when the lieutenant gave them a stern look.

"What did he say?" Samantha asked. She suspected the comment was about her.

"Nothing of importance," Karl replied quickly, confirming her suspicions. He groaned when the pain hit him harder. "*Mein Gott*! I heard patients make complaints about the pain when they had lost a leg. I did not believe it was real."

"You're a doctor?" she asked as she checked the bandages around the stump for bleeding.

He bit his lip. He reluctantly replied, "No, I'm a medical student."

"Really?" Samantha blurted. "Why are you in the army?"

"In Bavaria all the men from seventeen to forty-five are required to serve in the army for two years. If you are in the medical profession, you can serve for one year. Once you have completed your education, you can come back to become a medical officer."

"I didn't know that."

"Is it not the same in your country?" he asked as he watched her work.

"No, in Canada our soldiers are volunteers," she replied. The bandage was still white, which indicated that there was no bleeding.

"That is strange," he answered. He then asked casually, "Are there many of you in France?"

"Enough," she replied as she looked straight into his eyes. She was telling him she knew what he was trying to do. Samantha was about to say not yet, but 31,000 Canadians would be arriving shortly — but then she remembered Captain Llewellyn's admonishment when she'd let slip similar information to him. Also, there was a possibility of prisoner exchange, so the less he knew, the better. She wondered for a moment how the captain was doing. The last she had seen of him was in December when he was with the advance party preparing for their arrival in France.

The German smiled. He seemed to be enjoying the little game they were starting to play. "I would like to visit your country after we win the war."

"After *we* win," she corrected him as she folded the blanket back over his leg stump.

"Ah yes," he said. Samantha could tell he was confident that Germany would prevail.

CHAPTER 3

When Borden saw Laura's face, he knew her trip had not gone well. She was the last one stepping out of the train car with the vice-regal insignia painted on its side. The two flags with identical royal crests hung limply from the poles bolted to the wooden shell. The train car was named the *Alexandra* in honour of the dowager Queen Alexandra, the mother of the current king.

He felt a certain amount of pride when he viewed the train car. It had been built ten years earlier in his native province of Nova Scotia by the Rhodes, Curry & Company out of Amherst. The chairs and sofas in the rear observation salon were upholstered in royal blue, with matching carpets, and the interior was panelled using Cuban mahogany. In the front of the car there were sleeping berths where one could lie down to rest on long trips.

Unless she hadn't gotten any sleep the previous night, she wouldn't have taken one of the berths. It was only a six-hour ride from Toronto. After he had pleasantries with the duke and duchess, who had descended first, he gave his wife a peck on each cheek. They didn't have to wait long for the red caps to arrive with the luggage. The governor general and his wife were whisked off to the waiting cars with royal pennants on the front fenders fluttering slightly in the afternoon wind.

Their chauffeur drove the car to a stop in front of them once the governor general's party had left the white stone station's main entrance. As they settled in the car, he asked, "How was the trip?"

"I don't want to talk about it," she replied tersely. Laura had gone with the royals to Toronto to attend the annual meeting of the Red Cross Society at Convocation Hall. After the four o'clock meeting there was supposed to be a dinner at the York Club afterward.

"Did you walk here from the office?" she asked as she touched her flowered hat.

"Yes," replied Borden. He had spent most of the morning in his office, only five minutes' walking distance from the train station. It was directly across from the Château Laurier.

He managed to get a great deal done. He also finally made a decision to suspend Sam Hughes' Examination Board. It had been a rather easy decision to make when during his meeting with Colonel Smith, the man responsible, he found him to be rather useless in explaining its functions. He had to review documents concerning an increase in the pensions for soldiers on active service. White, his finance minister, was becoming quite agitated with the increase in war expenditures. They still hadn't decided on whether or not to approve a tax on income, which Thomas had proposed as a method to increase revenue. There was resistance from some members of the cabinet, since they felt they might be intruding into provincial jurisdiction. Then he had to deal with middle-men again. Thomas had brought another case to his attention. This time it was about a binocular contract for the militia.

"How was the train trip back?"

She made a face. "Comfortable, but the governor general was not in a good mood."

"Oh? His speech didn't go well?" he asked, wondering if he would have to deal with any fallout.

"Well, enough. But a total waste of my time. I don't know why I bothered going," she answered in disgust. "No, it was just that on the way back he kept complaining about the planned trip to the Panama Exhibition."

The Panama Exhibition was a world fair being held in San Francisco to celebrate the completion of the Panama Canal. Borden was sure the organizers were dismayed that war had broken out. They had spent the last three years planning, issuing invitations, and constructing the facilities for the fair.

"I read the telegram that George sent concerning the fair," Borden replied. "I replied telling him he was to remain in London until the war is over."

"Let's hope it will be over soon."

"So do I," he replied. "So why was the duke complaining?"

"He doesn't want to go."

"Sadly, he is the most senior ranking official available," Borden pointed out.

"That might be. But the duchess is distraught. She's worried that he could be kidnapped or assassinated."

Borden was about to dispute the duchess's claims until he recalled the latest intelligence reports from the Dominion Police's Secret Service. They'd been getting indications that the Germans were recruiting Sikhs and German reservists to sabotage British and Canadian targets. What he couldn't refute was that they were in this mess because of the assassination of the Archduke Franz Ferdinand in Sarajevo.

"Well, at least I have my will done," Borden jested. It was the wrong thing to say, because Laura became very quiet. He had executed his will last Monday and had sat down with her and explained the provisions he had made to ensure that she was well-taken care of.

The war had increased the stress on him and his cabinet. He had to replace several due to illness. The latest was Francis Cochrane, his railway minister, who he might need to replace if he didn't recover from his illness. Borden had been fighting poor health as well, and the latest news from his sister concerning his mother was not good.

"I don't want to talk about it."

"Yes, dear," he replied as he sat back in his seat. His face became somewhat bleak. He was not looking forward to the coming week. His wife wasn't happy, and he was fairly certain he would be spending much of his valuable time dealing with the governor general and his unwillingness to go to California.

JANUARY 29, 1915
PRIME MINISTER'S OFFICE, EAST BLOCK, PARLIAMENT HILL,
OTTAWA

"Seven hundred thousand dollars wasted!" sputtered Sir Robert Borden in disbelief. "Seven hundred thousand dollars!"

Major-General Fiset stood rather uncomfortably in front of the prime minister's desk in the East Block. Borden had a second office in the Centre Block, which he generally used when the House was in session.

"Oh, sit down!" ordered Borden, pointing to one of the two red floral-patterned wooden chairs in front of his desk. The khaki-uniformed officer removed his cap from under his left arm and placed it in his lap when he took his seat. Borden glanced at the row of ribbons on the man's left breast. One of them was the DSO, the Distinguished Service Order, for his service as a doctor in the Boer War. He glanced at the medical serpent insignia the forty-year-old from Rimouski had on his collar. While Fiset carried the title of surgeon-general, Borden hadn't demanded his presence for his medical advice. His private doctor provided him with plenty. No, he had called him because he was the deputy minister of the Militia and Defence department, and he needed to account for the large wastage of taxpayer money.

"Minister Hazen has informed me about the problems with the Oliver valise equipment," he said pointedly.

He could have waited to have this discussion with Hughes, but he was out in BC, ostensibly on a recruiting drive. The real reason he was on the west coast was to deal with recalcitrant militia commanders. During the last several months, the fear of German naval raiders in the Pacific had dissipated, especially when the British Navy had destroyed most of Germany's East Asia Naval Squadron at the Falklands last December, so there was no need to keep the militia there on active duty. It was costing the government thousands of dollars. Orders to stand down had been ignored. What the Conservative apparatus in Vancouver was telling him was that Premier McBride was using the militia to bolster the provincial economy, since it was in a recession.

On the other hand, Borden thought, *I probably wouldn't have gotten a straight answer if he were here.*

Borden wasn't giving Fiset any choice in answering his questions concerning the Oliver equipment. If he were a little sharp with Fiset he would be forgiven, since he had spent most of the past week arguing with the governor general about the San Francisco trip. All he knew was that a Dr. Oliver, a Canadian military surgeon, had designed equipment that allowed a soldier to carry sufficient ammunition, clothing, and rations to support himself in the field for twenty-four hours.

"It's the weather, Prime Minister," stated Fiset. "The men have been enduring unusually wet conditions in England. The water has damaged the equipment to the point that the components have been rendered useless."

"All of it?"

"I'm afraid so. All the shoulder braces, backpacks, haversacks, ammunition pouches, waists belts, and the water bottle carrier are made of leather," Fiset explained.

"Then it's a similar situation as the men's boots," replied Borden with disgust.

"I'm afraid so," replied Fiset as he played with his cap. He had already briefed Borden on the men's boots. A new pattern based on the British hobnail boot was being sent to all the manufacturers. Vigorous inspection procedures were being implemented to ensure that the new boots met the specifications and wouldn't have the same problems the current footwear had encountered. And hopefully put an end to the current political crisis facing his government.

"If it was such an obvious problem, why were they issued in the first place!" Borden demanded as he stabbed his desk with his forefinger.

Fiset smoothed the top of his cap as he carefully considered his reply. "The department has been trying to replace that particular pattern for six years now. We had recommended to the minister no new purchases of Oliver equipment, since we wanted to replace it with the Mills pattern web accoutrements. The department had already purchased two thousand Mills pattern sets for the Permanent Force. We had plans to purchase an additional ten thousand sets per year for five years to equip the Active Militia."

Borden leaned back in his chair as he raised his eyebrows in surprise. "Why wasn't this done?"

"When we submitted a request for an initial ten thousand units shortly after the minister was appointed, he denied the request. The minister stated that he couldn't make his way clear to approve this particular pattern. We had a desperate need for five thousand sets for the men, so we put in a purchase order for the Oliver, which he approved."

Borden blinked his grey eyes. "He approved the Oliver?"

"Yes."

"Was the Oliver cheaper?"

Fiset shook his head. "The web equipment was $5.50 per set, while the Oliver was $8.80."

Borden clenched his jaw then said, "Just to be clear. The minister paid more for equipment which when touched by water is rendered useless, resulting in repurchasing the same said accoutrements?"

"The minister has been very clear that he would only approve purchases that would be in his view suitable and from Canadian sources. We have been trying for several years to get Canadian companies to produce the Mills pattern for us. To date our efforts have been in vain. We also haven't actually received complaints directly from the War Office. It is only the first contingent that is currently replacing the Oliver with webbing."

"Damn," muttered Borden. "So what are the department's plans for the new units being recruited and trained?"

Fiset glanced at Borden and said, "There isn't much we can do until Canadian companies start producing web equipment. We have currently no choice but to continue to use the Oliver in Canada. When we send them to England, it will have to be replaced with Mills. We would like to order webbing from England, but all their production is going to the new armies that Lord Kitchener is recruiting."

Borden turned his head and stared through the window at the West Block directly across the large, snow-covered lawn of Parliament Hill. He turned back to Fiset. "I want a full report on this topic and all messages from the War Office concerning this subject as soon as possible."

Fiset acknowledged, "Yes, Prime Minister. I'll have the quartermaster-general prepare a report for your earliest convenience."

As Fiset was rising to his feet, thinking the meeting was done, Borden said, "Speaking of reports, I reviewed a copy of the report on the ammunition supply that was forwarded to the governor general."

Fiset sat back in his chair with a tired sigh. "I wish that I could be more optimistic, but the report is a fairly realistic assessment of our ammunition supply for the next four to eight months."

"The deficiencies will be that large?" Borden asked in surprise.

"I'm afraid so, Prime Minister. Our current estimates indicate that we need 105 million MK VII rounds for the next four months. The fifty thousand men who are currently being trained need about twenty-five million for upkeep and training. The first and second contingents, when the 2nd arrives in England, will need two thousand per man. That totals eighty million .303 rounds. We currently have in stores eighty million, mainly the MK VI. If our projections are correct, and I think they are, that means by April we will be short by seventy-three million rounds for May to August 1915.

"We are sourcing seven million from other sources. The Dominion Arsenal is currently producing one million rounds per month. By May, we will have only thirty-one million rounds available for all of our forces. That does not take into account the Colt and Vickers machine gun units. They can consume up to twenty to thirty thousand per day, if not more."

Borden's shoulders slumped. "What happens when we run out?"

"That is something we don't want to contemplate. We are trying to economize as much as possible. The report doesn't include the shortages in artillery shells, either," Fiset pointed out.

"Yes, I know, I've read the reports from the Shell Committee," replied Borden in a concerned tone. "So the proposed new plant at the Dominion Arsenal will help with the strain?"

"Yes, Prime Minister. It will take time for that plant to go on stream. Once they get into full production, they are estimating they will be able to produce two million .303s a month."

Fiset gave him a sympathetic look when Borden felt his face turn a little greyer. Borden became more tired at the thought of what might happen if the Canadian contingent didn't have enough bullets to fire at the enemy.

CHAPTER 4

FEBRUARY 10, 1915
LARK HILL, SALISBURY PLAIN

"Crap happens," said Captain Lamb, the commander of the Fusiliers' 2nd Battalion as rain dripped off the brim of his forge cap. "Remember that?"

Captain Llewellyn laughed as he lifted the collar of his greatcoat to prevent water from dripping inside. "God, it seems a long time ago."

"Yeah, nearly four months since Quebec," Lamb replied.

Llewellyn glanced at the company arrayed behind Lamb. He wasn't fooled by the men's nonchalance. He could tell from the slight movement of their hands to their packs and the anxious side glances they gave him that they were hoping he had brought them their marching orders.

"So the men have a day's ration then?" Llewellyn asked with a grin.

Lamb snorted. "They are not likely to let me forget."

Llewellyn recalled the day when the regiment left Valcartier without orders. They had arrived at the Quebec City port nine hours earlier than their scheduled time. All the Fusiliers, except Captain Llewellyn's company, had arrived without rations. Most of the men went hungry until they boarded the *Alaunia*.

He glanced over to Colonel Topham, who was slapping his thigh with his swagger stick as he paced anxiously beside his staff car. It was the lead vehicle in the transport column that carried the battalion's tents, equipment, and supplies. Behind the motorized vehicles, four companies loaded down with packs were lined up in columns of fours, waiting to start their eight-mile march to Amesbury station. The last of the tents were being taken down and carted over to the last of the horse-drawn G.S. wagons in the column.

"So why are you here then?" asked Lamb.

"I just wanted to see you off," said Llewellyn with a shrug. "We're following you shortly."

"Ah," replied Lamb with a cocked eyebrow. "That's what I figured."

The captain knew Lamb had read Lieutenant-General Alderson's orders. It had made it quite clear that he wouldn't tolerate any unit moving without specific instructions from the Division's headquarters at the Ye Old Bustard Inn. Any unit that did start marching toward

21

one of the designated entrainment stations without permission would be replaced by one of the 4th Brigade's units. The 4th Brigade was the Division's reserve and would remain behind in England. Llewellyn had understood the order. Alderson didn't want a repetition of what occurred at the port of Quebec.

Discipline had improved greatly in the last four months, but there were still problems. Last week in the weekly orders the GOC had a paragraph inserted pertaining to saluting senior officers. The Canadians were not sticklers for that particular convention. A complaint had been received from Lieutenant-General Campbell, the GOC of Southern Command, concerning the lack of respect shown by Canadian soldiers to senior officers on the streets of Salisbury.

It was two weeks ago that rumours started to fly that the War Office had finally gotten off their asses and decided to send them to France. They were in earnest when all the senior brigade and battalion commanders were called to London. When Currie returned, he had a spring in his step, and he gave his staff a wry smile before calling a meeting to brief them.

When the four battalion commanders and their staff crowded into Currie's command tent, he informed them, "Gentlemen, we've been ordered to France."

"About bloody time," said one of the men at the table.

"Hear! Hear!" exclaimed several others.

"As you are aware, the 4th Brigade was designated as the reinforcement depot for the Division in mid-December. For the last several weeks they have been moving from the Sling Plantation to the Tidworth Barracks. We will be entraining 18,500 men and five thousand horses for deployment to France.

"The order of battle will be as follows. The Division's mounted troops will be comprised of the 1st Cavalry squadron and a cyclist company. The artillery will bring twelve batteries of 18-pounders, one heavy battery of 60-pounders, and an ammunition column. There will be three companies of engineers and one signal company. Also, two Army Service Corps, three field ambulances, and four communications units will join the twelve infantry battalions that are going."

"The 4th is not going to be happy," Llewellyn pointed out.

"It can't be helped. Someone has to stay behind," Currie replied with a shrug, indicating it could have been the 2nd.

Llewellyn had little doubt that Currie would have been picked to go. So far he had shown to be the most competent and efficient of the Canadian commanders. The only issue that might have raised some doubt was his lack of combat experience. Lieutenant-Colonel Turner, the commander of the 3rd Brigade, had plenty, with a Victoria Cross to prove it. However, the captain had heard some rumblings about how Turner was managing his brigade.

"We currently have a draft plan for the entrainment of the Division. Our port of embarkation is Avonmouth on the west coast of England."

"Where will we be landing?" asked Major Tennison. He had his pipe out, but it was unlit.

"Saint-Nazaire," replied Currie.

"Long way around," the major remarked. When the other officers looked at him, he answered their questions. "Saint-Nazaire is on the west coast of France. We'll be a long way from the front."

"True, General Alderson would have preferred Le Havre," Currie added. "The Germans have declared the English Channel a war zone, so all naval traffic is under submarine threat. We're going the long way around to avoid that. The port of embarkation is not to be discussed with the men. If rumours are spread to the effect it is Le Havre, it would be capital.

"Based on the current entrainment plan it will take four days and seventy-nine trains to move us. The infantry battalions will be sent via Amesbury, while the artillery is assigned to the Patney and Lavington stations. Bulford station will be used by the mounted units and the field ambulances.

"I want all the men's kit inspected and additional supplies ordered. An advance party will be heading for France on the 2nd to prepare the way for us. On the 4th, the king will review the men.

"Any questions?" When no one replied, Colonel Currie ordered, "Well, let's get at it."

Colonel Topham stopped pacing when he spotted a motorcycle churning through the mud toward him. The captain watched as the bike slid to a stop in front of him and the rider handed him a piece of paper. He snapped his swagger stick under his arm and then ripped the message open. He broke into a wide smile and enthusiastically barked, "The order has been given. Let's mount up."

Despite the pelting rain, the men were cheerful. Finally, they were going to see some action.

FEBRUARY 12, 1915
SS *KINGSTONIAN*, BAY OF BISCAY

Paul staggered on the deck of the SS *Kingstonian* as she plowed through the late-morning heavy seas. They had been only a half-day from Saint-Nazaire when the storm hit. The ship's captain was forced to turn his ship into the westerly wind, away from the disembarkation port, to prevent the cargo liner from capsizing. The Leyland company vessel was 467 feet long and 54 feet wide and had a 6,456-ton cargo capacity. She had a single funnel amidships and four king posts, two on the bow and two on the stern, that towered over the hatches. Prior to the war she had sailed the Antwerp–New York run. Now she was part of the convoy that was carrying the Canadian Division to France.

"Start checking the lines," Corporal Ryan ordered. His squad of ten men had harnesses around their waists, which were clipped to ropes strung on the wooden deck. They nervously tugged on them, checking that they were secure.

"Right," replied Paul's friend Reggie, who had transferred back from the Remount Depot just a week prior to embarkation. Paul was sure he was currently regretting his decision, since his face was pale as he led half the men to the port side. The other half remained with him, with Corporal Edwards as the squad leader.

They needed to check the ropes and chains that held the horse stalls locked to the deck. The stresses of the ship as it pounded the waves caused the fasteners to loosen. In heavy seas, it posed a danger to the ship, its crew, passengers, and cargo.

Seasickness had hit the men hard. Most of them had expected a smooth trip, similar to their sailing of the North Atlantic last October to England. No such luck. The medics had tried their best, but they quickly ran out of seasickness serum.

The Bay of Biscay off the west coast of France was pleasant enough, with the occasional rough seas during the summer months, but it was notorious for bad winter storms like the one they were trapped in. They were among the last of the thirty-vessel fleet transporting the Canadian

Division to France. They had lost sight of the other ships when they turned into the wind.

Things even out, Paul thought as he tugged on a cable, testing its tautness. When they had left Salisbury Plain, each battalion had marched the eight miles to Amesbury, where they had boarded a train. No one had known which port they were being shipped to. Most had been betting on Southampton, since it was the shortest route to France. Instead, they arrived at Avonmouth on the west coast of England. Boarding the ship had gone rather smoothly. They had a few hiccups, but nothing like the chaos that had reigned at Quebec City. The entire unit's guns, limbers, wagons, and horses were aboard this ship, so when they disembarked they could quickly be ready for action.

He checked to make sure his squad was still on the deck. He didn't bother trying to yell, since his voice wouldn't have carried far in the crashing waves, the howling winds, and the whimpering of frightened horses. He wondered who was more afraid, him or them. The horses had exhausted themselves during the first hour that the storm had hit. Now they lay listless in the stalls.

When the bow of the ship smashed down on a wave, a cable snapped. The first he knew of it was when one of his men disappeared. When he checked to see whether the man's harness had held, he saw that the soldier had been cut in half. He shoved the three men beside him down as the chain whipped around the deck. It barely missed Reggie's head by a hair. Then a second wave washed the dead man and three others overboard with the horse stalls. There was nothing he could do, since he was holding on for dear life himself.

Paul looked in astonishment as the next wave tossed one of the horse stalls back onto the ship. The cage splintered as it hit the deck, spilling a heavy draught horse onto the cargo hatch. The animal lay stunned until a new wave pushed the steed back into the sea.

"We're going to die," groaned Corporal Edwards.

"Like fucking hell," Ryan yelled back. It took precious seconds for him to get his mind into gear. Then he started shouting orders. He knew his life and his men's were in his hands, the ship's captain's, and God's. He had a job to do, and he was going to do it, damn it!

FEBRUARY 15, 1915
SAINT-NAZAIRE

Captain Llewellyn groaned in agony as the nurse checked the bandages that wrapped his chest. He was lying in a cot in the hospital marquee that was being used as a temporary way station for wounded soldiers before they were loaded on a waiting hospital ship docked at the Saint-Nazaire quays. He interspersed his groans with cursing.

"Now, now, Captain. There's no call for that," she admonished. She spoke with an Aussie accent. Normally, he would have paid closer attention to the nurse who was taking care of him, especially if she were somewhat attractive. She was solid-looking and had a no-nonsense approach to her charges. "Do you need a shot?"

Llewellyn was tempted, but he disliked taking drugs unless he absolutely had to. He shook his head as he replied. "It only hurts when I breathe. Stupid accident."

"What happened?" she asked.

"Wrong place, wrong time. A couple of heavy crates weren't lashed properly, and they came loose. They pinned me against a bulkhead."

"Be thankful you only have a couple of broken ribs and you didn't puncture a lung."

"Yeah, I know. How long will I have to stay here?" he asked.

"Broken ribs normally take four to six weeks to heal," she said with a shrug. "You should be up and about in a week or two. If you behave!"

"Fat chance of that," said Major Tennison as he entered. She humphed as she moved on to other patients in the tent.

Llewellyn did a double take and then demanded, "What the hell are you wearing?"

Tennison looked down at his robust chest that was covered by a tanned leather vest with a greyish yellow fur lining. "They handed these sheepskin fur jackets to us to keep the chill out."

"Really?" The captain looked dubiously at the jacket. He wondered how it would handle mud.

"It's warm," the major replied sheepishly then changed the subject. "I just dropped by to check on how you were doing."

"How do you think?" he replied. The captain immediately regretted it, especially when a sharp pain jolted him. "Damn," he rasped. "Sorry, Alf."

When the major acknowledged with a nod, Llewellyn asked, "How's the disembarkation going?"

"Rather well, all things considered. You missed the parade when we arrived in port."

"Ah, so that was what all that caterwauling was about," stated Llewellyn.

When the 5,861-ton cargo liner *City of Dunkirk* started to disembark the 2nd Brigade, they had been piped ashore by the Black Watch, to the amusement of the small crowd that had gathered on the quay. The citizens of Saint-Nazaire were becoming jaded by the constant arrival of British troops. In September of 1914, the British Service Corps had transferred their headquarters to the port from Le Havre and Rouen during the retreat from Charleroi. They were afraid that the channel ports were in danger of being lost to the Germans. When the crisis had passed, they returned to Le Havre, but Saint-Nazaire was still a vital port for troop ships, cargo vessels, and hospital ships for the British war effort.

The harbour was about 280 miles west of Paris, and its docks and basins could handle thirty-two ships at a time. As well, there was a dry dock to repair and build ships. Just a mile from the docks they had a train station with a double-track railway. The port supported a brisk trade of barge traffic, since it was located at the mouth of the Loire River.

"Yes," replied the major as he pulled out a pipe and a pouch of tobacco. "The weather played havoc with the schedule. They have been arriving in dribs and drabs."

"Have we lost any?" asked the captain anxiously.

"Not yet. We've been lucky. Some of the men have been pretty banged up, and we lost a few."

"Ouch!"

"The horses didn't fare well. We lost more of them in two days than we did when we crossed over last October."

"Shit!"

"That too. I just came from the disembarkation office. Colonel Currie had me over there to smooth over some ruffled feathers."

"Oh?" Llewellyn said curiously. Currie had been promoted to full colonel on February 1st. He had been fit to be tied when one of the *City of Dunkirk* boilers had broken down, which had forced a twenty-four-hour delay. Then they were delayed again as they had to fish out several men who had fallen off the ship into the harbour. They had a tough time hauling them back on board. They had refused to let go of their bottles of whiskey to catch the lifelines. To add insult to injury, the damn ship ran aground in the Saint-Nazaire harbour when the captain decided he didn't need a local pilot to guide his vessel.

"Yeah, supposedly an embarkation officer asked some of our men to help with the unloading of our ships. They told him they were here to fight, not to be goddamn coolies."

Llewellyn tried to prevent a chuckle to save his ribs. "Well, that's our men."

The major snorted. "I'm going to have to read them the riot act. When I find out who they are, they'll be some field punishments."

"Good luck with that," replied Llewellyn. "How are Griffiths and Henry doing?"

"They're fine. Griffiths is conducting an inspection," the major replied casually as he filled his briar pipe and then lit it. Several men in the nearby cots sniffed at the sweet-smelling aroma.

Llewellyn narrowed his eyes suspiciously at the major. "What kind of inspection?"

Tennison gave him a wry smile. "It seems that prostitution is legal in France. They call the local brothels *Maison de Tolérée*. He's over there to determine the selection they have and the quality."

Llewellyn would have shaken his head if it wouldn't have caused him more pain. "Oh well. As long as he doesn't miss the train. When is the brigade entraining?"

"Tomorrow morning. It doesn't look like it's going to be comfortable. They're going to jam us into these forty-men or eight-horse train wagons for the next couple of days to get us to the front."

"Have you heard where exactly we will be assigned?"

"Not yet."

"So I'm going to be stuck here then."

"Not exactly. You're going to travel in style. You're being transferred to La Touquet for convalescence until you feel up to rejoining the brigade."

Llewellyn sighed with relief that he wasn't going to be left behind. His second thought was *I wonder how Samantha is doing?*

FEBRUARY 16, 1915
SAINT-NAZAIRE

"What the fuck?" the private spat. Some of the man's spit fell on Paul's gloved hand that he was holding up in front of the man's chest.

Corporal Ryan would have rather been elsewhere, but Captain Masterley had assigned him to guard duty. When the captain had called him into his command tent on the outskirts of Saint-Nazaire that was temporarily housing the 65th, he handed him a sheet of paper with typed names and addresses on them. "This was provided by the disembarkation officer here. It's a list of establishments with bad reputations. They have advised us that it would be wise to warn our men about them."

Paul had glanced at the sheet and then handed it back to the captain, who gave him an ironic smile.

"We all know how well our men follow orders," he said, which caused the corporal to raise an eyebrow in surprise. The captain continued as he waved the sheet of paper. "That's why we're posting sentries at each of these establishments as a friendly reminder. With a thousand or so young devils with cash in their pockets and stiff pricks raring to go, I think it would be wise, don't you think?"

"Yes, sir," Ryan had replied. He wasn't about to question the captain.

"Good! Let's see what we can do to get as many as we can to the front in one piece, shall we?"

So far it had been uneventful. It was chilly night, and Ryan was wearing his greatcoat, forage cap, and gloves to keep warm. The wool sweater underneath helped, especially when the cold wind blew from the Atlantic. At least he was protected from the brunt of it, being on a side street off rue Amiral Courbet. Amiral Courbet ran straight through the peninsula that protected the harbour from the beach on the Bay of Biscay on the west to the wharf on the mouth of Loire River on the east. The owners of the small bars and cafes that dotted the district were unhappy, since he and the other guards were driving business away. The hookers weren't pleased either. The streetwalkers on this side were not pretty, and some were not very clean either. That was why he was keeping his back to the stone wall as much as he could.

"Why don't you go down the street? They're more respectable places where you can get a decent drink," he suggested.

"I want to drink in this place," the man slurred. Obviously it wasn't the first bar he had been in this evening.

"*Mais oui.* Why not!" exclaimed the bartender, who had just come out of the bar. He was short and stocky, with thick arms. "Beer cheap. *Les femmes....*" he said as he made a woman's silhouette with his hands.

"This place is off limits," Ryan said firmly as he ignored the barkeep.

"Fuck you!" the private exploded as he hauled back with his right fist. Before he could throw the punch, his buddies grabbed his arm.

"Don't!" warned one of them. "You don't want another number one," he said, referring to Field Punishment No. 1.

"All right! All right!" the man replied. When they released him, he glared at Ryan as he bent down to pick up his fallen hat from the cobblestone street. He jammed it on head as he turned on his heels.

The bartender glared at Ryan then flicked his chin at him in disgust as he re-entered his establishment.

One thing that Ryan was grateful for — he was shipping out in the morning with the brigade's advance party. The rest of the unit was being delayed for a couple days. Their train had been reassigned to carry French troops to the front. They had to wait until another one became available.

CHAPTER 5

"Read in the *Citizen* that you announced a special committee on boots," John Ewart said in amusement. Sir Robert Borden and Ewart were in the parlour, where a card table with four chairs had been arranged. A deck of cards was resting on the green tablecloth. There were sheets of paper with a yellow pencil in front of each chair to record the points of each trick. The Bordens had invited the Ewarts for dinner and a friendly game of bridge. Laura and Jessie were freshening themselves up before they joined the men.

Borden sighed. "It would be rather funny if it weren't so serious. The opposition has been hammering us during question period for the last few weeks. The militia department released a report indicating what the issues were with the boots. The opposition is claiming cover-up."

"Understandable, especially now that the contingent is in France. The general public might not understand the finer points of law," said Ewart. Like Borden, Ewart was a lawyer, a rather prominent one. He had been involved in the Manitoba School Question, and he had pleaded cases before the Supreme Court of Canada and the Judicial Privy Council of Canada. He also was one of the dominion's leading constitutional experts. Borden had been friends with Ewart for several years, and they occasionally played golf together at the Royal Ottawa.

"But they do understand that if you paid twenty bucks for a pair of boots, you don't expect them to fall apart a month after you bought them."

"I'm aware of that. That was one of the reasons I had to call the commission. I've spoken with Wilfrid Laurier, and he agreed to appoint three members from his caucus to the committee. Are you looking for work? I didn't think it was in your line."

"It would be a rather amusing anecdote for my clients. Working on a boots inquiry committee. Rather appropriate for a government lawyer."

"Polishing them or giving them one?" jested Borden.

"Now, I know you're a politician," Ewart said, making a face. "What might not be a joke is this proposal for tax on income."

Sir Robert blinked, since White had presented it only two weeks ago. "White's idea. He's suggesting a temporary tax on income to generate additional revenue. We've raised excise and tariffs, but it's not generating enough funds to help us prosecute the war."

"Are the costs that bad?"

"Yes, they've been quite steep. My cabinet is currently divided on the topic. We're hoping that the war will end soon so we will not have to implement it."

"A lot of people are not going to like it. Technically, the *BNA Act* gives you the power to raise funds direct and indirect. The provinces will object. They will argue you're overstepping your bounds," Ewart pointed out.

"It's a political risk," admitted Borden. "But we need to find the money somewhere. It's only a temporary measure until the war is over."

"Talking about political risk, are you still going ahead with the bill to give the soldiers abroad the right to vote?"

"Of course," replied Borden. "It actually wasn't much of a political risk. With thirty thousand men in France now and with the 2nd contingent going in early May, it would mean that there would be nearly sixty thousand potential Conservative voters overseas."

"Do you have the provinces on board? They're responsible for the electoral lists. Based on the current residency requirements, Canadians abroad are not entitled to vote," said John.

"I know, and that is why we need to change the legislation," replied Borden. That was what complicated the issue. The federal governments used the electoral lists created and managed by the provincial governments. Most of the provinces had a one-year residency requirement, except for BC, which was six months. Ontario had additional ones that allowed the casting of votes if they resided in a town for three months or in an electoral riding for a month. This had been enacted not to penalize voters who moved from town to town looking for work. The other requirement was that the person voting had to be male, aged twenty-one or over, and a born or naturalized British subject. With 1.3 million votes cast in the last election, the military overseas represented nearly five percent of the vote. In certain ridings, especially rural ones, it could be the difference between winning or losing.

"The opposition is not going to like granting the soldiers abroad the vote either," Ewart remarked.

"I'm shocked."

"And I heard that you were upset that a British general was appointed to command the Canadian Cavalry Brigade?" Ewart asked.

Borden shook his head. "You're well informed. Yes, General Seely was appointed as the commanding general by Lord Kitchener. I wasn't happy about it, since they did it without consulting me first," replied Borden with a bit of heat.

"What did George say?" asked Ewart.

"He said to let it go for now. Seely won a DSO in South Africa. He is a former British MP and ex-secretary of state for war," Borden replied.

"How long will you keep letting it go?" Ewart demanded. He was well known as a fervent Canadian nationalist. He firmly believed that Canada was an independent nation, and the only tie between Canada and Great Britain was the monarchy. While Borden appreciated his point of view, he wasn't willing to go that far, at least not yet.

"Why don't you cut the cards," said Borden as Laura and Jeannie entered the room, ending the political discussion.

FEBRUARY 20, 1915
TRAIN STATION, HAZEBROUCK

"You owe me a quarter," said the private, with his hand held out to Corporal Ryan.

"Yeah, yeah," grumbled Ryan as he dug into his pocket and handed him two dimes and a nickel. Where the private would be able to spend the Canadian coins he didn't have a clue, and he was too tired to care.

The forty *hommes* or eight *chevaux* boxcar had been extremely uncomfortable for the last two days as they made their way across France. They hadn't been informed of the destination when they boarded the train at Saint-Nazaire. For most of the trip they had to sit with their arms wrapped around their knees, since they had been so tightly packed that they couldn't stretch out. He had to admit, from what he could see through the slats, that the hills and valleys of France were quite beautiful. Ryan had been surprised to see waifs approach the train begging for bully beef when they stopped on occasion to stretch their legs and get rations.

As they made their way, the men made note of the names of the stations and towns they were passing through. They hadn't been issued maps, but the British newspapers had printed general maps of France to give their readers some sense of where the Allied and German armies were fighting. They were using them to determine the general direction they were heading. Since they had time on their hands, they had run a lottery as to which train station would be their final destination. Private Kevin Pratt won ten dollars.

"Right," Ryan said. "Now get your kit."

As the door opened, Ryan was the first to jump down onto the platform, with the rest of his squad behind him. The other men in the car were reinforcements for the British Second Army, headquartered at Hazebrouck. They had picked up the men when the train stopped at Abbeville to be reconstituted to carry the essential supplies and men for the 3rd Corps, to which the Canadian Division had been assigned.

The train station's size had surprised Paul; he hadn't expected it to be so large. When he exited he saw that the station, a two-storey building with wings that anchored it, had a tan brick exterior with large vertical windows. The wing on his left appeared to be a hotel. He glanced at the large clock and the arch with *Chemin de Fer* above the main entrance. The roof was black slate. The courtyard was filled with lorries, horse-drawn G.S. wagons, and hand-drawn Maltese carts that had been tasked to move the supplies to the 3rd Corps' depots. He would later learn that the station was a major train hub for Flanders.

His orders read that he and his men would be met at the train station. He was trying to decide whether or not to go to the hotel. The officer could be at the bar getting a drink. Then he saw Captain Masterley arriving in a truck.

"Looks like you made it safe and sound," he said cheerfully.

"Yes, sir," replied Ryan.

The captain pulled out maps from the haversack that he had slung over his shoulder. "Our billets on these maps are marked. You and your men are to find them and verify that they are adequate. The brigade will be here in a few days. We need to check that they are sufficient for our needs."

"Yes, sir," replied Ryan. He turned to his squad lined up behind him and pointed to the truck. "Let's get at it."

FEBRUARY 22, 1915
NO. 2 CANADIAN STATIONARY HOSPITAL, LE TOUQUET

Samantha had just left the Hotel du Golf when she spotted Captain Llewellyn treading among the vehicles in the hospital's car park as he headed toward the golf course. It was a crisp morning, with the wind coming from the ocean. A dusting of snow had fallen overnight, but it was being quickly melted by sunlight penetrating thin clouds.

She buttoned her collar to keep the wind out as she examined the tall form of the captain dressed in his greatcoat with an empty sleeve. She knew that he couldn't slide his right arm into it. For now, all that he could do was keep it pressed against his chest, preventing the arm from swinging. She realized what he was trying to do and that he was being foolish. Nurse Glover had informed her that he was a very exasperating man, and that didn't surprise her in the least. She had dropped in to see him when she heard he was a patient. They hadn't received many Canadians at the hospital, so he was an object of curiosity for the staff. She did feel a bit of relief that he was only suffering from broken ribs and that he was healing nicely.

That was the problem: the captain had gotten it into his head that a morning constitutional would help speed up the healing process. While a brisk walk the first thing in the morning did wonders to get the blood circulating and clear one's mind, it just wasn't recommended for cracked ribs. But there he was on his morning stroll. How he dealt with the pain she couldn't fathom, since he was refusing to take morphine. He had insisted that the other patients needed it more than he did. She considered him for a moment then decided what to do.

"Good morning, Captain," she said when she caught up to him. "Where are you off to?"

"I was thinking of playing eighteen holes of golf," he said as his footsteps crunched on the gravel path that ran beside the fairway. She hid her smile when she noticed that he had slowed his pace to match hers.

"The caddies would love that, especially the pretty ones," Samantha replied.

He gave her a startled look.

She grinned. "Didn't you know? All the caddies at the resort were women."

"They were?"

"Oh yes, we hired some of them for the hospital for housekeeping, the laundry, and the cooking."

"I can't fathom that. It must be a French thing," the captain remarked as he examined one of the fairways covered with the medical staff's bell tents. "Do you play golf?"

"Oh God, no! I don't see the point of chasing a white ball around the countryside."

The captain laughed then winced. He gulped a few lungs of air to quiet the pain. When his breathing returned to normal, Samantha asked, "And you?"

"I never had the time," he replied. "Are you out for a morning stroll too?"

"I just came from preparing monthly returns on the types of casualties that the hospital has been treating."

"I must be the only broken ribs case," said Llewellyn.

"Yes, and you're at the bottom of the list."

"Ouch, that hurts," the captain replied as he put his left hand over his heart. "So what's at the top of the list?"

"It's between shrapnel wounds and frostbite," she replied. When he gave her a surprised look, she continued, "The shrapnel wounds are relatively straightforward to treat. The men in trenches are being wounded by the artillery shells raining on them."

"That's what I've heard. This..." he indicated the forge cap he was wearing with his left hand, "doesn't provide much protection. That is why parados are being built in the trenches. I did read reports about frostbite. I just didn't think it was cold enough here for that."

"I said the same thing when I first heard it," Samantha said. "Researchers are trying to determine what's causing it. It has something to do with the conditions in the trenches. The latest information is that it's the symptom of the effects of cold weather and constriction of the blood circulation in the feet. The men in the wards have told me that when they were in the trenches they hadn't taken off their boots for weeks. They were stuck knee-deep in wet mud for all that time. They had worn extra pairs of socks to keep their feet warm and kept their boots tight to prevent them getting soaked."

"Were they able to recover?" he asked.

"Most of them. Some had to have their feet amputated," she replied.

Llewellyn winced then asked, "Any prevention?"

"Not at the moment," Samantha answered. "The only thing that comes to mind is to keep the men's feet dry or at least get them out of their boots more often."

"That's going to be easier said than done," the captain replied thoughtfully. Samantha could tell that he was storing the information away for the future.

"Now, we have gone far enough. Let's get you back in bed."

"Oh!" Llewellyn said with a grin.

Men! Samantha thought. "I don't want to get Nurse Glover into trouble."

"I will under one condition," the captain said.

"No!" Samantha replied immediately.

"But you haven't heard my condition!" Llewellyn protested.

"Unless it's medical, I don't want to hear it," she retorted. She then pointed to several husky orderlies who were marching to work. "Do you want me to call them over?"

The captain put up his right hand chest-high in surrender. "All I was going to ask was if you'll have lunch with me in the cafeteria."

She looked at him then replied, "It's a maybe, if you get back to your ward."

"Maybe's good enough. I can work with that," he replied, satisfied as he allowed her to lead him back to the Hotel du Golf.

FEBRUARY 22, 1915
FARMHOUSE, STRAZEELE

"We're shovelling shit, again," groused Private Harris as they entered the stone barn that was to be their billet for the foreseeable future. The barn was a low-slung affair with two-foot-thick stone walls. The ceiling was ten feet high, and thick wooden beams held up the red clay roof. It had been designed to protect the farm's work animals. From what Ryan could tell, the farm was a small one. It was rather early for the season, but this area of France produced sugar beets and potatoes. There was an orchard of fruit trees nearby. He wasn't sure whether they belonged to this farm or the next one over.

The problem with the barn was the horse manure that had been left in the stalls. They needed to be cleaned out and fresh straw laid down to soften the ground when the men went to sleep. The previous occupants were a British cavalry unit. When they had vacated the premises, they were supposed to have left them in the same condition that they found them. Paul sincerely doubted that the place had been this filthy when they moved in. He didn't know whether the Imperials had left it in such conditions due to haste or spite. They hadn't been happy to leave such a comfortable abode.

He sighed. No matter what, he couldn't escape shovelling. A soldier's lot. He glanced at the elderly man who owned the barn. The corporal had seen the gleam of greed in the man's eyes. Staying in the barn was not going to be free. The man might be patriotic, but business was business. Thank God the quartermaster was going to take care of the bills. As far as Ryan was aware, they were only paying for a dry roof over their heads. Other arrangements were being made to ensure that the men were fed.

When he heard one of his men mutter, "What a shithole," Ryan gave him a glance that silenced him. He didn't want to get off on the wrong foot with their hosts. He knew that the squad he was responsible for was not pleased. They were giving him the eye, since they were quite far from the nearest village. It meant that it would take forty-five minutes to an hour of marching before they could find an *estaminet* where they could get a drink or maybe a bit of slap-and-tickle. What he had seen of the land as they marched along the passable roads was that it was crisscrossed with slow-moving streams.

Thank God they didn't have the horses with them. It would have been rather crowded. If there were a choice between the horses and the men, the horses would win. Upon reflection, it would have been better, since one couldn't count on the temperament of some of the horses. Some had a mean disposition.

"*Où est l'eau?*" he asked.

The old man cocked his head as he tried to decipher Paul's French. Paul spoke fluent French but with a Quebecois accent, which the man wasn't used to.

"*Viens*," he finally said as he led him to a well, and he was surprised by the relatively modern pump. The farmhouse was a two-storey affair made of the same stone as the barn. There were two windows on each floor, and the entrance was a solid plain oak door that had seen many years of service. Paul hadn't seen any women, but the old man might have hidden them until he felt that Paul and his men were relatively harmless.

Paul sighed.

"Oh, Corporal!"

"Yes," Ryan asked.

"There's no shovels in the barn," said Private Harris.

Paul turned his head toward the old man, who put on his sly grin.

"I have shovels. I can rent them to you, cheap," he replied in perfect English.

FEBRUARY 25, 1915
PLOEGSTEERT WOODS

"I'm glad to see you're back," Colonel Currie said in a listless tone when Captain Llewellyn stepped off the bus. He had hitched a ride from the No. 2 Stationary Hospital in La Touquet. "How are the ribs?"

"They are fine, sir," he replied cautiously. Well, mostly fine. The 110-mile train trip and then the last three miles on the bone-rattling bus had irritated them. He felt a dull ache when he breathed. Not enough to incapacitate him, but enough to tell that the ribs were still there. That was not what currently bothered him. The colonel didn't appear to be his normal cheery self. The first thought that popped into his mind was *Did I do something wrong?*

He glanced over at Major Tennison, who was standing in the back of a knot of men just outside the colonel's HQ and billet. It had taken some effort, but he finally was able to find the 2nd Brigade HQ. He had flagged the bus driver to stop when he spotted Colonel Currie and his friend. The major gave him a slight shake of his head, which he couldn't decipher.

"Are you ready to get to work?" asked Currie.

"Yes, sir," he replied promptly.

"Good, drop your kit in the office and then catch up with us," the colonel ordered as he turned and marched toward a copse of trees in the distance.

Once he had dropped off his kit at the farmhouse, he caught up with Tennison, who was tailing the 2nd Brigade's GOC. "I hope that my kit will be safe," he said to the major. "Where is everyone staying?"

"The 5th Battalion is at Le Bizet, the 8th is at Doostrove, the 10th at Romarin. The 7th is with us here at FM 29," Tennison replied.

"Okay," replied Llewellyn. He grinned at the major and then asked,

"By the way, did you find those men who didn't want to be coolies?"

Tennison gave him a sour look. "I tried, but no one wanted to admit to it."

"*Quelle surprise,*" remarked the captain. He then leaned over and whispered, "What's wrong with Currie?"

Tennison whispered, "He's been pretty sick with the grippe every since he came back from the trench warfare instruction he attended last Sunday. He finally managed to get out of bed yesterday."

"Ah, that explains it," he replied, glad that the colonel was not pissed at him. "So how are things going?"

"Not bad so far. We're doing well enough to impress Field Marshal French. He will inspect us in a few days."

"Does that mean we'll be assigned a section in the line?"

"That's the current rumour."

"How are the men doing?"

"Fine. We've suffered a few casualties."

"Anyone I know?"

"I don't think so. We've had ten wounded so far, but none killed."

Llewellyn grunted an acknowledgement. "Were are we going?"

Major Tennison grinned at him. "Your old company. They're attached to the 7th Battalion of the 1st Hampshire for instruction."

Llewellyn snorted as he examined the Ploegsteert Woods for the first time as they passed a row of homes on his right. He would learn later they were the Belchier Cottages. The Canadian Division had been assigned here because it was a relatively quiet sector where they could be acclimatized to the realities of trench warfare.

To be honest, he didn't know where he was exactly, since he didn't have a map. When he had earlier been driven through the small village of Ploegsteert, the bus driver who had acted as a tour guide explained that they were in Belgium, about two miles north of the French border. Most of the village sat empty, except for a few diehards who had refused to move, although artillery fire had severely damaged it. The land in the area was mainly farmland. Based on the farmhouses and barns he had seen, they seemed to be raising pigs and cattle. The bus driver informed him that the area was also well known for growing fruits and vegetables.

As Currie and his entourage neared the trees, the traffic on the road became heavier with motorized trucks and horse-drawn G.S. wagons dropping off supplies. The supply people were sorting and repacking them for the nightly run toward the trenches.

At a crossroad that led into the forest there was a sign that read *Regent Street*. Most of the elm and beech trees that flanked the road were denuded. A light covering of snow covered the ground. Visibility was a couple of hundred yards, but when the leaves grew in the spring it would be severely reduced. The captain could see the scarring that shrapnel had done to the trees.

He turned to Tennison and asked, "Does anyone know why this forest is here? I would think they would have ploughed it under by now."

Tennison shrugged. "I don't have a clue."

The road had been paved over by wood planks. The ground on both sides was damp and would get wetter when the light covering of snow melted. They had to make way for a platoon returning with the previous day's empty ration tins and pans.

When they reached Hunter Avenue, they took a right and headed northward, or at least it felt that way to the captain. Everyone stopped for a moment as they watched a burial party gently place a body into a freshly dug grave. Two soldiers waited patiently as the chaplain wearing a clerical stole draped around his shoulders said the prayer for the dead and then made the sign of the cross. Once he had finished, they began to cover the grave. The captain noticed the freshly dug graves next to it.

At a small stand of trees they came to a stop. Two corporals with the insignia of the 1st Hampshire rose to their feet. They had been tasked to lead the party into the trenches. One of the corporals looked up at Colonel Currie, who at six-foot-two was a good half-foot higher than both of them said, "Mind your head, sir."

"Will do," Currie replied, giving the corporal a tired, wry smile. One of the corporals turned, and Currie followed him into the communication trench. The captain smiled when the colonel stooped slightly as he entered it. The trench was barely deep enough for a man of his height. Before the captain entered, he took a quick glance to determine how far the actual firing line was. The area in front of them was relatively flat. The only indicator of a trench was a thin barbed wire fence about seventy-five yards in front of him.

The communication trench was tight and wet. Several men were trying to empty the water using a foot pump. Others were shoring up the sides with sandbags to prevent the walls collapsing.

It was the smell that really hit him when they finally arrived at the main trench line. It was from the body odour of men who hadn't had a bath in a week, rotten food, the urinal smell, and a putrid smell that he suspected came from corpses laid out in No Man's Land. He had to breathe through his mouth to cut out as much of the smell as he could. It didn't help, since it was so strong that he could taste it.

Currie, he saw, had blanched a bit. His being sick for the last several days made an unpleasant situation even worse. After the pleasantries were done, the 1st Hampshire captain in charge of the trench led Currie on an inspection tour of the fire line. They had marched only to the first traverse when Captain Jordan appeared with an upset look on his face.

"What's wrong?" Currie asked the Fusilier officer.

"One of our men was just killed," he stated as his lips quivered slightly.

"Who?" demanded Currie.

"Captain Lamb!"

Llewellyn sucked in his breath.

"How did it happen?" demanded Currie.

"We had roused the men an hour before dawn to prepare them for the morning hate," he replied. The morning hate, Captain Llewellyn knew, was a common practice. To prevent the enemy getting any ideas, at first light the men in the trenches would empty their magazines in the general direction of the enemy trenches. Dawn was usually the best time to launch an attack, because the men were less attentive.

"He decided to take a quick peek over the trench," Jordan continued with a waver in his voice. "A sniper got him. They are bringing him out now."

The men made way for a stretcher that was carrying Captain Lamb coming around the corner. They had to press against the trench walls to let them pass. He didn't hear Colonel Currie's admonishment that this kind of thing had to be stopped. All he could think of was seeing his late friend, with whom he had quite a few beers, pass by with a bullet hole in his forehead.

FEBRUARY 27, 1915
PLOEGSTEERT WOODS

"Another goddam review," Private Edds muttered to Corporal Ryan as he planted branches in front of the small depression used to conceal the C Battery's horses.

"Yeah, what did you expect? You're in the army now!" replied Private Harris as he dumped a bundle of branches beside them.

Edds hopped back a step so the branches wouldn't dirty his greatcoat that hung loosely on his angular body. "How many has it been this month? Four or five?"

Harris looked down at his own greatcoat and brushed off some smudges. He was of medium height, with a rangy build. He used his fingers to count. "Let's see. There was the king and queen, Lord Kitchener just before we left Salisbury. Then there was General Dorrian-Smith a few days ago, General Alderson..."

"I don't know if I want to count the general," protested Ryan. "He was inspecting the billets, not us."

"There's a difference?" retorted Edds.

Harris turned to Paul. "Was that why you made us clean up the pigsty in double time?" he demanded.

Paul shrugged. "What do you think the CO would have done to us if he walked in with the general?"

Harris grunted an acknowledgement as he slogged over to the water cart. "Now it's the field marshal," he snorted as the lead horse slurped noisily from the bucket he had come back with. He lifted the brim of his cap back then asked Ryan, "Are we going to get any forage for them?"

"Well, he's a field marshal; he can do what he wants. What the fuck does he care?" Edds groused as he stuck another branch into the wet ground.

"Just get the screen up," Paul ordered Edds. He turned back to Harris. "Yeah, later this morning."

He understood the grousing. They felt that the inspections were a waste of time. They had to spit and polish their uniforms and equipment. From the dignitaries and COs to the sergeants, everyone was looking for a fault.

Paul glanced at the screen they were building and then compared it with the one in front of the gun pit where the C Battery's four 18-pounders were dug in. The pit had been dug during the night, and it wasn't particularly deep. Just enough that they sat a couple of feet lower than the surrounding ground. There was a slight slope that allowed the guns to be rolled in, and, more importantly, rolled out when they needed to move them. They were pointing in the general direction of the trenches.

He glanced over at Ploegsteert Woods on his left, where they had spent the last few days receiving instruction on the daily activity of a gun battery supporting troops in the front lines. He was trying to recall exactly where the 1st Westminster gun battery was located in the woods. But that was next to impossible. They had been guided by a tough-looking sergeant that they met at one of the intersections on Plugstreet; the men had anglicized the village's name, the corduroy road that had been built in the middle of the woods, and they quickly got disoriented.

The sergeant, a man in his mid-thirties who looked like a bull-dog, had given them a once-over, and he hadn't seemed particularly impressed. He had been standing beside a Maltese car that was had been loaded with 18-pounder shells. He tossed his head at the cart then said to Captain Masterley, "We're low."

The captain looked at the cart then said, "Okay, men, grab one on your way past."

He had passed the order along to the rest of his section. When he reached the cart, he was handed an 18-pounder shell. Their guide led them on a meandering route through the woods as he followed the man in front of him. It had taken a half-hour to reach their designation. His arms ached as he carried the shell pressed to his chest. The half-moon had given some illumination, but it didn't prevent the nearly invisible tree branches from snapping at them as they made their way. The soft ground caused him to stumble from time to time, nearly losing his grip on the artillery shell. There would have been hell to pay if he did. While they tried to march quietly, the woods reverberated with the sounds of horses and men working. They had to avoid the watchful eyes of German observers. Everyone sighed with relief when they finally arrived at their destination.

The sergeant had pointed to a pile of shells being held in place by four thick wooden stakes near one of the guns. "Pile them there," he said. He then turned to Captain Masterley and said, "I'll take you to the CO."

"Lead on," Masterley said.

As they waited, one of the men tending the guns came over and asked, "Do you have a fag?"

"I don't smoke," Ryan replied.

"You will," he said when Harris handed him one of his.

"Canadians joining the fun, eh?"

Paul hadn't known what to say. He was relieved when Captain Masterley came back and started to assign the men to the guns they were to shadow. The number one shadowed the number one gun, number two the number two, etc.

When the grey sky finally lit the gun emplacement, Paul was able to exam it more closely. There were sandbags in front, over which the barrels peaked. Along one of the walls sat a telephone operator listening to a handset. A plank had been set up where he could write notes. A canopy of tree branches had been built overhead and was covered with netting. The netting had bowed slightly with the mass of dead leaves piled on top of it for camouflage. A map was pinned against the sandbag wall, with markings showing the trench lines. An arc had been drawn on it. He assumed it indicated the maximum range of the guns.

Paul was impressed by the men manning the 18-pounders. To be expected, since they had been fighting since August.

The daily routine in the gun pit was different from the normal daily routine that he was used to. Some of it was the same, of course. The men slept among the guns, and at reveille they rose an hour before dawn for the morning hate. The rifle fire that had burst out loudly caused him to duck, to the amusement of the Westminsters. They had stood by their guns in case the German artillery decided to lob a few in their direction, requiring them to retaliate. After that the guns were inspected and cleaned in sequence. Signallers were sent out to inspect the telephone lines that linked them to the forward observation posts for any breaks.

Paul was disappointed that the guns weren't fired during his time there. The weather was bad. While the guns were registered on the German positions, the forward observers couldn't provide confirmation that they were actually hitting their targets. No point in wasting valuable ammunition.

He turned his head when he saw Lieutenant Lash headed his way after conferring with the captain. "Get the men ready. He's on his way," he ordered.

Paul barely had time to yell out his orders when the convoy of staff cars came to a halt on the road next to the field. Out of the car stepped Lieutenant-General Alderson with the CO of the 65th and a man he presumed was Field Marshal French.

He was surprised by Field Marshal French's small stature. He looked as if he barely met the height requirement. He wore the standard walrus moustache, which in his case was white. He was also bow-legged. Paul hadn't known that French was a cavalry man.

French led the inspection of his unit, leaving Paul's gun for last. Paul answered the standard questions senior officers asked such as name, where you came from, and are you satisfied with the work? To which he would give the standard responses the generals wanted to hear, especially the last question. The standard response was "I'm happy to be here, Field Marshal! I want to do my bit, Field Marshal!"

French's face was a mask to the corporal, so he didn't know if he was pleased until after he had left. Lash told them, "I've been informed that the field marshal was pleased with us."

"If he's was happy with us, does that mean we're going to see action soon?" asked Paul.

"Yeah! What else are we here for?" replied the lieutenant.

CHAPTER 6

MARCH 5, 1915
TRENCHES, FLEURBAIX

"In what shape are they in?" asked Captain Llewellyn as he scanned the sandbagged trench.

"We have a lot of work to do," replied Captain Metford as the Cape Bretoner fingered his Royal Canadian Engineer badge on his cap before he covered his balding head with it. "In case we need it for a retirement."

"Which we are not currently contemplating," Llewellyn added quickly when he noticed the squad of soldiers nearby had paused their digging. When Metford noticed the lack of noise, he turned his brown eyes on them. They quickly bowed their heads as they concentrated on tossing wet mud onto the nearby pile. On the other side of the trench was a horse-drawn wagon with two large spools of black wire. Several of Metford's men were pulling telephone and telegraph wire for the trench's communications.

Llewellyn smiled in amusement as a messenger pedalled past with a birdcage filled with passenger pigeons tied to the olive-green bike's rear carrier. The bike was heading toward the trench line, two thousand yards further up and currently occupied by the 1st and 3rd Brigades. His brigade had been designated as the reserve. He knew the men of the 2nd were disappointed, but someone had to do it. They all would have their shot soon.

That was one of the reasons he was here. Lieutenant-General Alderson had ordered all officers to familiarize themselves with the GHQ's 2nd line. That trench line would be the primary position for the 2nd but the fallback for the 1st and 3rd if they needed to retire.

"How's the digging?" Llewellyn asked. He glanced up when he heard the faint drone of aircraft. He spotted them flying below the large pillow-like clouds. From the distance, he couldn't tell if they were friend or foe.

"Not all that great. Every few feet we hit water. The water table is high here. That's why we have to use sandbags to build up the fortifications and strong points."

"The country is pretty flat," Captain Llewellyn stated. The front line ran in a northeasterly direction through the surrounding farmland. It reminded him somewhat of the prairies with its numerous small dips.

"You noticed," the captain snorted. "And they call that creek over there a river?" he said with derision as he pointed in the general direction of the Lys River.

Llewellyn smiled in agreement. The Canadian Division had been assigned six thousand yards of trenches near Fleurbaix. They were relieving the Second Army's 7th Division. Protecting their right flank about three thousand yards north of Aubes was the 8th, while the 6th Division was on their left flank. The first units of the brigades had started moving in on the 28th, and the last units were in place by the 3rd of March. All the men of the Canadian Division were excited and tense at the same time. Finally, they were where the real action was.

"How's your billet?" Metford asked as he took a stick of chewing gum out of a pack he had in his coat pocket. He offered one to the captain, who declined with a wave.

"Eh," was the captain's reply.

"That bad?"

"It's dry."

"Keeping busy?"

Llewellyn shrugged. "The 7th left their intelligence reports, which I'm plowing through to get a feel for what we are up against. I'm also going through the daily reports being sent to HQ. I've been getting copies of the summaries from the 1st's and the 3rd's listening posts and patrols that they have been sending out."

Captain Metford's attention was distracted when a truck stopped to drop off more steel plates. "No, over there," he yelled. He indicated the pile near the trench the men were digging. "We need them for the slit holes."

When he spotted an officer examining the plates, he shouted, "Hey, Gary." The officer looked around, trying to find the voice that hailed him. When he spotted Metford, he smiled and raised his hand in greeting. He had to convert it to a salute when the platoon that was marching past mistook his movement for one.

All three men partially crouched when they heard the bursts of artillery shells landing near a pile of rubble about a thousand yards away. The outline of a half wall was all that remained of a farmhouse that the Germans were using to register their artillery. A few minutes later the divisional artillery returned fire in retaliation. The duel didn't last long, only a few minutes.

"Who issued the invitation?" asked the major as he turned his gaze from the rising black smoke back to Metford and Llewellyn.

"It wasn't me," replied the engineer. He used his chin to point to Llewellyn. "It could have been him. He's a staff officer."

Llewellyn gave Metford a chagrined look before giving the major a salute. "Captain Llewellyn. I'm on General Currie's staff." On March 1st Currie was promoted to Brigadier-General.

"Major Windshift," he replied after he returned the captain's salute rather perfunctorily. That was something that Llewellyn had to get use to. Staff officers were not highly thought of by line officers. They were a necessary evil, which the line officers had to tolerate to get the real job done. It was the same attitude he had before he became one.

"Where are you off to?" asked the engineer.

"Your stores," the major replied.

"Oh?" the engineer inquired.

"Some sections of our trench lines are in bad shape," he replied. "My CO wants some sixteen hundred sandbags, fifty of those steel plates…" He indicated with a thumb over his shoulder at the pile behind him. "A hundred and sixty feet of stakes, a thousand feet of barbed wire, seventy pounds of three-inch nails, and four thousand rounds of ammunition to replace the bad stuff that ordnance gave us."

"That's all?" asked Metford as he chewed thoughtfully.

"We do need seven hammers, four saws, four gallons of rifle oil, and thirty shovels."

Captain Metford grunted. "Didn't you get your allotment?"

"We're supposed to have 115 shovels, but we only got sixty. We can make do with thirty more. Can't dig without shovels," Windshift pointed out.

"I know. What few I have are over there digging latrines," Metford said as he spat out his gum in the latrines' general direction. "I'm going to need more shovels for the men to finish the new works we're planning."

"The colonel has noticed that the Germans are sapping in front of our trench, so we need them as soon as possible," replied Windshift.

Llewellyn interjected, "I don't run stores. But I would talk with Sergeant Cameron over there. He should be able to help you out."

"Will do. Thanks," replied the major.

"By the way, what was that ruckus last night?" asked Metford. "Kept me up all night."

"The colonel was pissed with the battalion on our right last night. Something spooked them, so they let go. Which pissed the Germans off in front of us. Guess they wanted their beauty sleep too, so they let us have it. You've seen how shallow the communication trenches are. We lost a man from one of our supply parties. He didn't find cover fast enough. Real shame. He was a good soldier."

All three men paused for a moment of silence. It was interrupted when a staff car pulled up with Major Tennison in the driver's seat. Before Llewellyn could acknowledge the major, something caught Captain Metford's eye. "What the fuck do you think you are doing? You don't use sandbags for the floor! That is what the goddamn planks are for!" the captain shouted. "Excuse me, I have to see to this, otherwise, they are going to fuck it up."

The major gave an acknowledging nod to both captains and Major Tennison before he headed off to stores.

"Get in."

"Thanks for the lift," Llewellyn said as he slid into the passenger seat.

"Don't thank me. I was looking for you."

"Oh?"

"The Division is planning an attack," the major said with a grin.

MARCH 7, 1915
NO. 2 CANADIAN STATIONARY HOSPITAL, LE TOUQUET

Samantha reread the letter Captain Llewellyn had sent her after he had arrived safely at Brigadier-General Currie's headquarters. She liked his handwriting. It was free-flowing, with a bit of flourish in the swirls. He mentioned he had enjoyed their lively lunches and dinners. There had been additional walks on the golf course. If they had wanted a private moment, it would have been difficult with the matrons and the other nurses keeping an eagle-eyed chaperone. She was pleased that he had been circumspect in his letter. Which wasn't surprising; there was a censor stamp on the envelope that indicated it had been read by the censors, making sure the captain wasn't spilling any secrets.

She slipped it into her skirt pocket as she entered the Hotel du Golf. The lobby looked a bit shabby to her to now. She wasn't surprised, considering the number of patients who had passed through since last November. Standing beside the staircase with three men, two civilians and one Imperial officer, was Matron Riley. When the matron saw her, she motioned her over.

"Gentlemen, I would like to introduce you to nursing sister Samantha Lonsdale. She will be your escort during your visit at our hospital. If you require anything, she'll be at your service.

"Miss Lonsdale, these two gentlemen are from the press. This is Michael Conrad from the Toronto *World,* and this is Dennis O'Leery from the Montreal *Daily Mail.* This is Major Clarke-Chapman from the Footguards."

"Pleasure," Samantha said as she shook the two reporters' hands. She gave the Footguard major a cool nod. She remembered him from when he attempted to interrogate German prisoners under her care.

"These two gentlemen would like to interview several of our guests from the Princess Patricia's," Riley informed her.

"Yes, Matron," Samantha replied. Colonel Shillington and the matron had briefed the staff that newspapermen would be coming and had issued stern warnings about what they could or could not say in front of the pressmen.

"We're here to do a human interest story on the Patricia's," said Michael Conrad.

"Of course," she replied. The *World* reporter was in his mid-forties. His overcoat was open, and she could see a couple of black notebooks bulging from the coat's baggy breast pockets. "If you'll follow me, I'll take you up to the BC ward, where we have placed the wounded Patricia's." Samantha didn't have to explain to the reporters that the Canadian hospital's wards were named after the Dominion's provinces. They were supposed to be briefed beforehand.

"I would follow you anywhere gladly," said O'Leery with a slight leer. The man was in his thirties, with a coat similar to Conrad's. She tried not to wrinkle her nose, since the man reeked of cigarette smoke.

As she led them up the stairs, the *World* reporter attempted to interview her by asking her the five W's: who, what, where, when, and how. When he asked, "How have you been coping with the patients?" she glanced at the reporter and behind him saw the major give her a frown.

"I'm sure that you are not interested in me."

"I disagree," interjected O'Leery. "I think you would make a lovely story. Do you have a beau?"

"Hmm," interrupted the major. "You indicated that you were interested in interviewing wounded Canadians, were you not?"

Samantha's opinion of the man went up a notch.

The *Daily Mail* reporter gave the major a gruff response. "That's right! Since this is the closest that you allow us to the front lines."

When the major didn't reply to the jab, he turned to Samantha and said, "Please lead us on, *mademoiselle*, to the war heroes."

When they entered the BC ward, all the beds were occupied by soldiers of the Princess Patricia's Canadian Light Infantry. The hospital had made a special point of gathering them all together in one place for the interviews.

"Gentlemen," Samantha announced, "these newspapermen are here to interview you for your home papers."

The soldiers looked up at the pressmen with some interest. It wasn't often that a reporter wanted to talk with them. Some of the men showed excitement at the prospect of getting their names printed in the papers.

Both reporters scanned the men. They didn't look particularly surprised that most of the wounded were privates, with a few NCOs scattered in the mix. With the British high command blocking their access, they had to take what they could get. She had heard rumours that Max Aitken, the newspaper baron, was getting involved in the Canadian war effort.

"What's your name?" O'Leery asked the nearest patient. The Toronto *World* reporter stood beside him to ensure he didn't get scooped.

"I'm Private Nick Mason," replied the man after shaking hands with the reporter using his left hand. His right hand was heavily bandaged.

"How did it happen?" O'Leery finally asked after getting the private's particulars. Mason was twenty-eight, married with two children, and had immigrated to Canada from Glasgow.

"We were in the trenches when the Boche let us have it. They're tough buggers, they are, the Prussian Guards and the Saxons. They tried to take our trench."

"We gave them a right lesson," said the soldier in the next bed with a bandage covering his belly.

"Is that what happened to you? They got you too?" asked the reporter.

The man shook his head. "Naw, I was with a work party trying to dismantle German trench wire, and we got unlucky."

"Oh, how so?"

"We had a thick fog, you see. It was so thick you could barely see your hand. We were having a grand old time until the wind came up and blew it away. We didn't know it, but the Boche had sharpshooters seventy yards away, and they started to plink us. The buggers! My buddy got it in the back, and then I got hit. I was out there for most of the day until my sergeant came and got me."

"Are you looking to go back?"

"Sure!" Mason replied enthusiastically. "It beats lying around here or in the billets."

Samantha nearly snorted. She knew that most the men had complained bitterly about the miserable life in the trenches. But then they couldn't tell the pressmen that, could they.

MARCH 10, 1915
2ND BRIGADE HEADQUARTERS, FLEURBAIX

Captain Llewellyn couldn't help glancing at the wall clock on the ground floor of Brigadier-General Currie's HQ. The 2nd Brigade had taken over a two-storey white stone building in the small village of Fleurbaix. When he glanced out the window, he saw a couple of parked staff cars in the small courtyard. Messengers' bicycles and motorbikes were leaning against a white-painted iron railing that was mortared on several feet of red brick. There were several riding horses tied next to them.

When he scanned the room, he noticed most of the men had the same set of nerves as his. They kept glancing at the wall clock or checking the time by pulling out pocket watches.

Currie was sitting at a desk staring at a note. The captain wasn't sure if he was actually reading it or not. Llewellyn wondered how much sleep the brigadier-general had gotten the previous night. The captain himself had tossed and turned for most of it. He wasn't sure what time Currie went to bed, since the brigadier-general had inspected several companies during the evening to verify their preparedness.

Thumb-tacked on the plain wall near Currie, above the wainscoting, was a large map of Fleurbaix. The map extended from Armentières in the north to La Bassée in the south. The trench line that the Canadians were responsible for was marked in blue, while the German trenches were in red. Pins on the map indicated the location of Lieutenant-

General Alderson's and Brigadier-Generals Turner and Mercer's HQs. Also marked were the positions of the divisional artillery and the 2nd Brigade's billets.

A messenger came in and handed Major Tennison a note. When he read it, he grunted then announced, "The mounted troops and cyclists are in position for road control if we need them."

"Are the rest of the men ready?" Currie asked, looking up from his note.

Tennison nodded. "The last of the units have reported in. They're under arms at their billets and are ready to move when the order is given."

"All we can do is wait, then," replied Brigadier-General Currie as he glanced at the wall clock again.

Llewellyn noted that the minute hand was nearly hitting seven thirty. A few more minutes, then the attack would begin. He barely finished the thought when the artillery lighted the morning sky and the window beside him rattled. He could see the frightened horses strain at their leashes.

Everyone had read Lieutenant-General Alderson's *Operational Order 5* issued the previous day. The 6th, 7th, and the Indian divisions were to launch an assault on the German trenches at 8:20 a.m. this morning after the artillery barrage had softened the enemy. The assault had two objectives: penetrate the two trench lines they faced and capture the village of Neuve Chapelle.

The Canadian Division was not directly involved. Their job was to convince the enemy that they were the ones planning to launch an assault. For the last few days they had been conducting aggressive night patrols. In a half hour, all the rifles and machine guns in the 1st and 3rd Brigades would open fire on the trenches in front of them. The Division's guns had targeted the Germans from Fromelles Aubers to the nearby railway crossing, as well as Le Maisnil and the Le Maisnil–Fromelles road. Known and suspected gun positions would be pounded.

The 3rd Brigade was tasked to keep an eye on the 7th Division's right wing, since they would be crossing the 3rd Brigade's left in their assault. They had to be careful that Turner's brigade didn't fire on them while simultaneously preventing the Germans from sending reinforcements when they learned where the actual assault would take place. As well, the 7th battalion was in readiness in case they needed to assault the German trenches. If that happened, the closest units from Currie's brigade would follow and occupy the vacated trenches.

"Well, it started," stated Brigadier-General Currie as he leaned forward in his chair.

65TH FIELD ARTILLERY GUN PIT, FLEURBAIX

Paul's arms ached and trembled slightly. There was a knot in his lower back just above his left hip. He used the left sleeve of his jacket to wipe the sweat from his forehead and then coughed to clear his lungs. It didn't help much. Whoever said smokeless gunpowder was smokeless was lying. The air in the gun pit had a slight grey tinge from the thin trails of smoke from the ejected 18-pounder shells. He spat to get rid the acrid taste in his mouth.

"Hurry it up, McGill," yelled the loader. Paul could barely hear him with the cotton earplugs he was wearing. He didn't bother correcting the bombardier calling him by his nickname. He would deal with the man later. After all, he was a newly minted lance-bombardier.

"Here you go," he replied as he wiped the shell to remove any grit with a damp cloth before he picked it up from the rack and handed it to the loader. The loader didn't bother acknowledging Paul as he shoved the shell into the breech then pulled the lanyard. The gun bucked and then rolled back into position.

Paul was readying the next one when Sergeant Roscoe yelled, "Cease fire! Cease fire!"

"About bloody time," muttered Paul. They were to pound the Fritz trenches for forty minutes. They had started at seven thirty, based on the captain's timepiece. Since he had been rather busy, Paul didn't know the current time. He leaned forward with his hands on his knees before he raised himself erect stiffly.

"You can say that again," replied Bombardier Jenkins as he tossed a spent casing onto an uneven stack on the opposite side of the pit. Beside the pile there were several gallon cans of gun oil to lubricate the 18-pounder's moving parts and recoil system. Near the stretcher there was a cloth head pole used to clean and oil the gun barrel. Their iron rations for the day were at the back of the pit, out of their way.

"How's it going?" yelled Captain Masterley. He had come in a crouching run via a shallow communication trench that connected all four of the captain's battery's guns. The weapons had been arranged in a slightly staggered formation about thirty yards apart so that they couldn't all be taken out by a single shell. The captain frowned when he saw how depleted their ammunition stock was.

"We're doing fine so far, but we need more from the ammunition column," Sergeant Roscoe replied.

"More is on the way," acknowledged the captain.

Paul glanced at what remained in their pit. The fire plan called for four rounds per minute. After forty minutes that meant that they had fired almost 160 shells at the German trenches. At least, that was what Captain Masterley had stated in their powwow yesterday evening. He had given each of the lieutenants a copy of the fire plan for today's show. Guns 1 to 3 were to be active for today's demonstration, while the fourth gun was being rested.

"So how are we doing?" asked the sergeant.

"We got them by the short hairs," the captain replied with a grin. "They're massing their reinforcements now."

"That's a good thing?" blurted Paul.

The captain replied, "Sure is. The 7th division is starting their attack as we speak. We're here just to hold their nose while they kick them in the ass."

When the captain had laid out the fire plan, he had not explained to them what the Division's plan was for today's attack. Plenty of rumours were floating around that said the Canadians would be assaulting the enemy trenches. All the officers were rather tight-lipped about it. Most of the men had only had a couple of hours of shuteye before they reported for duty this morning. Those who had kept watch overnight were in the rest area a couple of hundred yards in the rear with the horses. They were to relieve the active gun crews in about six hours' time.

"Good shooting! The OPs have informed us that we were on target," said Masterley.

The sergeant's face beamed with pleasure at the news. For the last several days, they'd been firing between fifteen to twenty rounds per day to register each of the battery's four guns. They occupied the same areas but not the actual pits that the 8th Division had used. Before the 8th had left, they passed on their range notebooks that the battery commanders had found useful in arranging the Division's artillery.

They all heard the roar of rifle fire to their left. It meant that the British Imperials were starting their attack.

"I better check on the other guns," stated the captain as he returned the sergeant's salute.

After the captain disappeared, heading to the number 4 gun, the sergeant turned to Lance-Bombardier Ryan and said, "You heard the captain; you better get your men and go get more ammo."

Ryan's arms still ached as he tossed the sergeant a salute and scurried out of the pit to the supply dump about three hundred yards in their rear. As he did he wondered how long his arms would last.

CHAPTER 7

MARCH 11, 1915
CENTRE BLOCK, PARLIAMENT HILL, OTTAWA

"Is Sam still sulking?" John Reid asked Prime Minister Borden as they entered the Centre Block's main lobby. The slush streaks that covered the eight provincial shields set in the marble floor were fresh. Question Period was in less than an hour's time.

"Yes, he doesn't want to give up his portfolio, but he wants to command the 2nd contingent," Borden said with a touch of frustration. He hadn't been pleased with Sam Hughes' lacklustre performance nor that of some of his other ministers in the House. The Liberal opposition had been hammering them on the budget. They were accusing his government of excessive expenditure.

Borden was heading to his Centre Block office in the west corner of the building's new wing. He needed to be nearby during Question Period. What added to his frustrations was the firestorm created by Professor Adam Scott, the head of the Civil Service Commission. At a People's Forum several days earlier he had made a statement, not based on facts, that two thousand government officials had been dismissed and then replaced with ten thousand more. For the last several days they had wasted valuable time sorting the mess out. His main concern was how this would affect his truce with the Liberals.

Reid's moustache shook in agreement. "He can't be both. While I like the thought of sending Sam to the front, I don't think it would be wise to inflict him on the Imperials. What I heard is that he doesn't think highly of General Alderson."

Borden glanced at Reid as they took the steps on their left that pointed toward the House of Commons. They heard the buzzing of MPs as they hung their coats in the wooden lockers that lined the corridor that led to the Green Chamber's main entrance. They were eager for the three o'clock Question Period.

"I agree. If he doesn't listen to me, I doubt that he would fare much better under the general."

"That would be all we need. Sam being court-martialled for disobeying orders," stated Reid.

"God help us," replied Borden.

"Has he sent you those reports you requested?" Reid asked as they turned down the corridor that led directly to the prime minister's office.

Borden snorted. "He's been dragging his feet. I specifically informed him that I wanted him to be prepared. Also, he has to interest himself in the Boots Committee. I have not been liking what is coming out of there. I'm also extremely annoyed that millions of dollars of military equipment was left behind when the Canadian Division went to France. All of which had to be replaced."

Reid grimaced. "Well, at least the Canadian Division has distinguished themselves so far."

"I've read Perley's telegram to that effect," replied Borden.

"When is the 2nd Contingent sailing?"

"Sam is supposed to send an encrypted telegram to the War Office informing them of the early May sailing. Arrangements still have to be made to receive them."

"Good! That brings up the question about the elections," replied Reid. "Have you decided yet?"

"No," Borden answered. "I've spoken with Thomas. He doesn't think that it is the proper time. There could be fighting in May or June, which could impact the elections."

"That's possible," replied Reid as he bobbed his head in agreement. "At least Parliament will be prorogued after Easter."

"We all need the rest. I'm a bit surprised that the Liberals are looking so tired."

"That's exactly where we want them," Reid answered. "I've talked with Francis. We both agreed that we are in very good shape in Ontario."

"I know. He let me know yesterday. But I heard rumours that Gouin is running federally in Quebec." Borden was referring to Sir Lomer Gouin, the Quebec Liberal premier. He had supported Canada's entry into the war. Borden knew that he and Laurier had not initially gotten along, especially when Gouin was instrumental in removing the former Liberal leader. Since then they had buried their differences. But the only reason Gouin would enter federal politics was to lead the Liberal Party. As far as Borden knew, Laurier had not indicated any willingness to step down.

"That will cause us problems," replied Reid.

"We can lose fifty-five seats in Quebec and still have the majority that we need," Borden said confidently.

"True. Now, if we can give the soldiers the vote, that would be of help."

"Agreed," Borden replied.

"If the Liberals in the Senate don't block it," stated Reid.

Borden shrugged. "They are not going to like it, but if they object to giving the military the vote, it will cost them."

"We can only hope," replied Reid.

"Now, can you give me an update on the negotiations you're having with the CNR?" asked Borden as they entered his office.

MARCH 12, 1915
2ND BRIGADE HEADQUARTERS, FLEURBAIX

The captain's sandwich crunched when he bit into it. It was not the crustiness of a fresh French baguette. Rather, it was that of several days'-old stale bread that had been allowed to harden so it was less susceptible to green mould. The 2nd Brigade bakeries were making bread for four thousand men daily, but they couldn't still keep up with the demand.

The thin slice of bully beef and cheese didn't do much to soften it. He didn't ask what kind of cheese it was, and frankly he didn't want to know. It was what the orderlies had brought. At least the coffee helped somewhat to wash it down.

He shifted in his chair to ease the stiffness in his right rib. For the last several days he had been reading the incoming message traffic that detailed the progress of the attack. He didn't wander very far from his desk, because he was afraid he would miss something. There was a notepad with several pages folder over and blue-black ink bleeding through the paper. Similar handwritten notes were visible on the messages that lay scattered on the thin plywood. Some of them were nearly indecipherable scrawls. Part of his duties was to prepare an intelligence summary for Brigadier-General Currie. He was expecting it by ten o'clock this evening.

His jaw stopped grinding when he read the latest order that had gone out to the divisional artillery and engineers. The order stated that the GOC was ordering the Canadian Division to attack the salient in front of the No. 1 subsection.

Precisely a half hour before the assault, the artillery would subject the salient to rapid and concentrated fire. When the Division's assault began, the artillery would increase its range.

The infantry would not wait for the artillery fire to end. They would launch their attack precisely at the appointed hour, which would be communicated once it had been determined. Two reserve battalions would provide the Brigade support. One of the reserves would take the place of the assault battalion once it went over the top.

Work parties were to cut passages through the Canadian wire to allow the infantry to pass through. Grenadiers and work parties would accompany the line to cut the German wire.

To overcome ditches and other obstacles, the men would carry planks. Also they were to carry empty sandbags.

Once a trench was captured, the men must prepare for a counter-attack. Men would be detailed to start digging a communication trench back to the lines. Others should press the attack and clear the trenches in front of them and on their flanks.

Llewellyn snorted when he read the line that all successes had to be communicated to the troops on their flanks and to Divisional Headquarters.

He was so focused on reading it that he didn't see Major Tennison rise from his tan canvas chair and stretch his lower back. He manoeuvred through the large room that had several desks staffed with officers who were monitoring the incoming messages. The bulk of them were status reports on the readiness and positions of the 2nd Brigade units that were to support the 3rd in their planned assault when the order came down.

"Things are looking good," the major said as he moved a tan canvas chair in front of Llewellyn's desk.

"I guess. The Indians have captured Bois du Biez, and hundreds of German prisoners have surrendered, so the rush is on," said Llewellyn as he set his sandwich on his plate.

"That it is," the major agreed. "I think we're ready as we can be. By the way, did you read what the 3rd Brigade scouts found?"

"I did. It was a good idea to send them out," agreed the captain. "No one knew about that ditch in front of the German trenches they found. It would have slowed us down when we launched our attack. Also, our men have been making good use of those telescopes they borrowed."

"It made sense. The signallers weren't using them," acknowledged the major. "The German snipers haven't been happy since."

"I've read the reports," replied Llewellyn. His forehead wrinkled slightly.

Tennison registered that Llewellyn was concerned. "Problem?"

"I don't know, Alfred," replied Llewellyn truthfully. "It's just a feeling. I've been reading them...." He indicated the papers on his desk. "Everything seems to be going well. But the Indians stopped when they reached their objectives. They didn't restart until about an hour or so ago. It gives the Germans time to recover."

Major Tennison rubbed his cheek. "They had orders to stop and wait for new ones."

"I know. What I'm reading is several hours old. Most of the messages I'm getting are from the runners."

"Telephone?"

"Not much," conceded Llewellyn.

"If they are pushing forward, maybe the engineers can't keep up," said Tennison.

"I suppose." The captain paused when he heard the tempo of the artillery fire change. He raised an eyebrow.

Tennison answered, "I was expecting it. We got a message from the 4th Corps to provide them with returns on our artillery supply."

The captain grimaced. "Is it that bad?"

"I have no idea," replied the major. "Let's hope not. In the meantime, we're to get ready to support the 3rd when they go over the top tomorrow."

Llewellyn picked up a yellow pad and a fountain pen. "Well, I better get back to it and get this report done for the general."

The major grinned. "You're a wise man."

MARCH 21, 1915
RIDEAU HALL, OTTAWA

"My condolences for your loss," said Prime Minister Borden. "I was saddened when General Gwatkin informed me of Colonel Farquhar's death."

"Thank you, Prime Minister. It's very kind of you," replied Princess Patricia. She was a tall, attractive woman in her late twenties. She was seated on the settee in a sitting room beside her father. The princess's eyes were slightly reddened by the tears that she had shed. The duke, dressed in khaki, seemed distraught at the news of the colonel's loss. Lieutenant-Colonel Francis Douglas Farquhar had been his military secretary before he was given the command of the Princess Patricia Light Infantry that Montreal businessman, Captain Andrew Hamilton Gault, had raised last August.

When Farquhar approached the princess to name the regiment in her honour, she had been delighted. The princess also had designed the regiment's colours and insignia. Borden had to admit that it was a stroke of genius. Patsy, as she was known to her friends and a name he would never use, had been taken into the country's heart and was extremely popular.

Borden felt awkward about what to say. He had the occasional meeting with the late Farquhar on military matters, but Hughes mainly dealt with him. He had seen Farquhar at the Royal Ottawa Golf Club, and they had played matches against each other. From what information Major-General Gwatkin could provide, the Princess Patricia's had been relieved of trench duty in Saint-Éloi, and Farquhar was showing the replacement CO a communication trench that needed to be finished when he was killed by a German sniper.

Lieutenant-Colonel Farquhar was the third officer from the duke's household to have been killed to date. The other two were captains Rivers-Bulkeley, his former controller, and Captain Newton, his former ADC and a Princess Patricia who had been killed by an artillery shell in January.

"Please offer my condolences to the duchess," Borden said as he rose to his feet. He knew that the parade of mourners would be arriving shortly. He had glimpsed Gwatkin when he had entered. The chief of staff had phoned him at home, where he was getting some much-needed rest. Laura had been upset, since the colonel and his wife Lady Evelyn were a popular couple in Ottawa high society. Lady Evelyn had followed her husband back to England shortly after the PPCL sailed. She was now living in London. He would be sending her a condolence telegram.

This was a bit close to home. From what his senior advisors had been telling him, the war would last another eight to nine months. That was what he was afraid of. How many more letters would he be signing?

MARCH 27, 1915
TRAINING FIELD, FLEURBAIX

Captain Llewellyn was standing against the trench wall. In front of him, guarding the corner, was Private Kershaw. He was holding his bayoneted rifle at the ready. The oiled blade gleamed when the sunlight hit it. Beside the captain, Corporal Duval was holding his own in a similar fashion. The corporal released his left arm and made a throwing motion. Llewellyn watched as two grenadiers pulled the pins from the bottom of the grenades they were holding.

The grenades were a percussion type, which meant they detonated when the top of the grenade hit the ground. A ribbed cast iron ball encased the brass cylinder containing the plunger and detonation charge. A sixteen-inch wooden handle with a couple of cloth streamers attached was screwed to the bottom of the brass. The streamers were there to help the two-pound grenade land on its head.

The two Fusiliers leaned back and threw them over the trench. The intent was to clear the section on the other side of the traverse. The trenches were not built in a straight line. Corners jutted in and out to prevent the enemy simply shooting down an alley and killing every man in sight. It gave the defenders a great advantage but made clearing the trenches a complex operation. Complex usually translated into dangerous.

Captain Llewellyn followed the grenades as they left the men's hands. One flew perfectly. With a flutter of streamers, it stabilized as it sailed into the next section. The second one didn't fare as well. When the soldier released it, one of the streamers snagged on the man's webbing and hit the top of the trench. It tumbled backward to land head-first in front of the captain.

"Fuck!" swore Llewellyn.

"You're dead, Captain!" yelled the instructor, who also wore captain's stars. "And the corporal and two grenadiers. The rest of you lot. Go! Go! Go!"

The squad squeezed past him as they rushed to the next section. It was tight, since two of the men wore bandoliers that dragged with the tied grenades. The rest of the ten-man squad, now reduced to six, also carried besides their rifles, shovels, picks, and half-filled sandbags. The sandbags were to be used to create a protective bulwark against a counterattack.

Following them was a couple of soldiers with stretchers. The first question they asked cheerfully was, "Who bought it?"

The captain reluctantly raised his hand. "Figures," muttered one of the body snatchers as he hustled the captain onto a stretcher. To ensure that he didn't fall off, they took the unusual step of strapping him tightly to the pole and canvas. As a former Fusilier and now a staff officer, he had become one of the lowest forms of life. They banged him along the trench walls until they emerged from the communication trench. Thankfully, the trench was a short one. Once out, they dropped him beside the ambulance wagon, where a medic started his routine to check for wounds.

"Don't bother," said one of the men who had carried him out. "He's dead."

"Imagine that," replied the medic, who made the imaginary motion of removing his identity disk from around his neck. He then attended to Corporal Duval, who was being carried out fireman-style.

"My, my, you're in a fine predicament," said Major Tennison as he peered down at Llewellyn.

"Leave me alone," Llewellyn replied. "I'm dead."

"How did that happen?"

"One of the grenadiers had butterfingers," he remarked as he tugged at the straps.

"Let me," said the major. He unstrapped the captain and helped him to his feet. "Besides getting killed, how's the training coming along?"

"It's coming along," repeated Llewellyn, listening to the cacophony as the squad continued their attack.

The training was partly the result of the lessons they had learned during the Neuve Chapelle attack. To the great disappointment to the 3rd Brigade, if not the entire division, they had received orders to stand down. The 8th and the Indian Division had an opening. Unfortunately, because of a combination of poor communications and the Germans digging in, the door had been slammed shut. Field Marshal French wanted to continue the attack, but he had to call it off because the artillery had depleted their ammunition. The captain had seen the recent orders that the guns' rate of fire be reduced from fifteen shells to three shells per day per gun.

"Where's Currie?" asked Llewellyn.

"He's with General Alderson, getting a briefing," replied Tennison.

"Oh!"

"The latest rumour is that they're transferring us to the Ypres Salient," he replied.

Before the captain could ask about the transfer, the instructor marched over. "Well, Captain, are you finished with your dilly-dallying?"

"I'm dead."

"Well, I just resurrected you. Get back into the trench and do it again."

"Yes, sir," said Llewellyn as he scrambled back into the trench.

"And this time don't get yourself killed," ordered Major Tennison.

CHAPTER 8

APRIL 12, 1915

PRIME MINISTER'S HOME, GLENSMERE, OTTAWA

"**I** want a divorce!" declared Laura.

"It's not that bad," replied Borden defensively.

"If you actually looked like … like … this," she pointed dramatically at the three-foot-tall polished marble bust of him that rested on top of the desk. On the floor beside it was an open packing crate with straw spilling out onto the area rug that covered the hardwood floor. "I wouldn't have married you in the first place!"

"But he's the best sculptor in Canada," Borden protested.

Alfred Laliberté had finally delivered the completed piece. It had become a tradition that a likeness of the prime minister was created in paint or marble to preserve his features. The best artists in the country were commissioned for such work by the party in power, and the money was privately raised. Once completed, the objects would be donated to the government. The project had been given to Montreal artist Alfred Laliberté, who had gained fame nearly fifteen years earlier for his life-size sculpture of Sir Wilfrid Laurier. With Laurier's support and encouragement, Laliberté went to Paris, where he attended the École nationale supérieure des Beaux-Arts. When he returned in 1907, he set up his studio on rue Sainte-Famille in Montreal.

For the last several weeks Laura had been complaining about the bust. They had seen the preliminary work two weeks earlier when they stopped in Montreal after his mother's funeral.

He still couldn't believe that she was now gone. He had managed to get to Grand-Pré in time. With his brother and sister he had sat beside her until she passed away at three o'clock in the morning.

The funeral was held at the old Covenanter Church. He was pleased that the church, which had been sitting empty for nearly a decade, had been taken over by the local Presbyterian diocese a few years before. The memorial service was conducted by an Anglican and Presbyterian minister from the nearby Wolfville parishes.

The church had been filled with memorial wreaths from the locals and from those who had come up by special train from Halifax, mainly his friends and colleagues from the Nova Scotia Conservative associations. The local telegram office was overwhelmed with the flood of condolences that arrived from across the country, England, the States, and the rest of the Commonwealth.

He could still hear the mourners singing "Lead, Kingly Light," "Peace Perfect Peace," and "All Hail the Power of Jesus' Name."

It had snowed four inches the previous night. By the time the service was over, it had melted and the path they took to lay Mother to rest beside Father had turned to mud. It was somewhat fitting that she passed away fifteen years to the day that Father did.

"So where are you going to put this monstrosity?" she demanded, breaking his train of thought.

"On the Hill, of course," he replied as he regarded the sculpture. Last week Laliberté had come up to Ottawa to finish the piece. The artist had stroked his Van Dyke beard as he observed Borden working in his office. Laliberté said he had come to capture his *'puissant'* and his *'virile.'*

"Good, I want it out of the house. It makes you look to stern and disagreeable."

Borden sighed. Obviously, the artist hadn't succeeded in his task, or at least not with his wife.

APRIL 15, 1915
2ND BRIGADE TRENCHES, YPRES SALIENT

Captain Jordan of the 2nd Battalion, Richmond Fusiliers, was berating Corporal Duval when Llewellyn came around the corner of the newly dug traverse in the trench designated 1A. "If you do that again, I'll bust you back to private. Now get back to your section."

Llewellyn wasn't particularly surprised that Duval was in trouble. He was amazed that he had kept his corporal stripes so long, especially under a by-the-book captain such as Jordan. Duval saluted the captain, and as he passed Llewellyn he gave him a wink.

When the corporal was out of earshot, Llewellyn couldn't resist asking, "What was that all about?"

"I'll show you," Jordan said as he stepped onto the fire step, a wooden plank set against the trench wall. The fire step was needed in deep trenches to allow the men to fire over the top. Jordan motioned for Llewellyn to look through a fire slit. The loophole was covered by a steel plate that hung from cords embedded in the sandbags. He moved the plate slowly to the side, ensuring that his head blocked the light. The Germans kept a close eye on the trenches, and it was not wise to attract their attention.

What he saw through the hole was a brand-new barbed wire fence that was nearly three feet high. This was one of the reasons he was in this trench section. It abutted the French Algiers division on their left, and the Canadians had been busy improving them ever since they had taken them over from the French.

He had attended an intelligence briefing a few days before at Lieutenant-General Alderson's headquarters at the Château des Trois Tours in Brielen. The HQ was about six miles behind their lines. He had arrived for the meeting after sunset. Daylight movement was severely restricted, as they didn't want the German observers to identify their key positions. That was one thing you needed to get used to in the Salient. During the daytime, it looked empty and devoid of life, although there were twenty thousand men living in the trenches, with an equal estimated number of Germans on the other side.

When he arrived, several Jack Johnsons had landed near the château, chewing up some of the hedges near the moat. He had seen work parties crossing the walk bridge. They were to make improvements to the communication trenches and the dugouts to which the headquarters staff could retire to if the château came under heavy bombardment.

He arrived late, as he had underestimated how long it would take to clear the guard detail. He should have known better. What had held him up were the messengers who arrived on various modes of transport and had priority. Then he had to find the Canadian Division's intelligence office, which he finally did on the ground floor.

When he entered, Major Mills-Martin glanced at the clock and then back to him with some annoyance, sending him a clear message. There were two other officers in the closet, Captain Lagrove, a Grand Prairie native with the 1st Brigade, and Captain Lockhart, from Almonte, with the 3rd Brigade. They occupied the only two canvas chairs in the room, and that meant Llewellyn had to stand.

"Let's begin," said the major. Llewellyn didn't know him very well. He was a new addition to the Division, in his early thirties, trim, with a standard moustache. The man's hairline was beginning to recede. There was a scar running along his left cheek, the result of a shrapnel wound. He was on loan from the 5th Corps and like most of Lieutenant-General

Alderson's staff officers was British-born. Some were men that the general had brought with him when he took command — men he knew and trusted. Others were on loan to fill the gaps. Llewellyn knew there was grumbling among the Canadians that most of the staff positions went to Imperials. The problem was that there were very few Canadians that had taken and passed the staff officer course.

"We have been receiving a preliminary report on the condition of the trenches. It doesn't look good," Major Mills-Martin said. "The French have a different doctrine. They prefer to lightly defend their first-line trenches. When the Germans attack, they retire to their second or third line and then counterattack to drive them out.

"As you are aware, General Alderson has clearly indicated that we do not give up any of our trenches to the enemy. If one is taken, we are to counterattack immediately and forcefully. To that end, that is why I have called you here," he said with a thin smile.

"I've seen the conditions of the trenches in our section," said Captain Llewellyn. "It would be difficult."

"This is true," added Captain Lockhart. "The trenches in our section are nothing but mounds of mud. We have work parties shoring them up with sandbags and building fire steps. In some sections they don't have parados to protect the men from the artillery. The water level is two feet high, and we're having a devil of a time trying to drain them.

"The most unpleasant problem for the men is the decomposing corpses in front of their trenches. They are finding the smell hard to take."

Captain Lagrove nodded in agreement. "Not just in front of the trenches. The work parties have been finding bodies in them that have been previously interned."

"We have been finding the same thing," Llewellyn added. "It slows down the men, as they have to remove the remains and rebury them in the cemetery."

The major grimaced. "General Alderson has asked one of the chaplains to talk with the local mayor about acquiring a plot of land as a last resting place for our men."

There was a moment of silence.

The major then asked Llewellyn, "Are the trenches in your section in the same condition as the 1st and 2nd?"

"Pretty much," acknowledged Llewellyn. "In some cases there are no parapets and the communication trenches rather shallow. We've lost several men already as they attempt to cross them. Also, there are only a couple of strands of barbed wire and coils of French wire about seven feet out in front. Most of which are rusting, and some have collapsed."

"That's pretty much what we've seen all cross the lines," the major replied with a sigh.

"The biggest problem is not only the poor souls that are decomposing, but the trenches and shell holes have been used as latrines," said Lagrove.

"We're aware of that. A large quantity of disinfectant has been ordered, and it will be the sanitation officers' job to make the trenches safe for the men," replied Mills-Martin.

"We're working as hard as we can, but we need time," Captain Lockhart pointed out.

"That's understood. That's why we need to send the scouts and the patrols out each night. We need to verify the intelligence reports that the French have been supplying us, but we also want to discourage the Germans as much as we can," said Mills-Martin.

"I heard rumours of some kind of asphyxiation gas attack?" Llewellyn asked.

The major nodded. "You shouldn't believe all the rumours. But in this case we've gotten reports from the French that they captured a German soldier from the 234th Regiment of the 26th Corps. He said that an attack was being planned for today or tomorrow. As you can see, it hasn't happened yet."

"Does anyone know how they're planning to spread this gas? If it exists, wouldn't it kill their own men?" Captain Lockhart asked.

Mills-Martin shrugged. "He did have a gauze mask that is supposed to be dipped into some kind of liquid. We don't know much more than that. We don't even know if his story is fanciful or not. That's why we need to get the scouts out. We need to find out what the Germans are up to."

"If it's true, how are we going to protect the men?" asked Llewellyn.

"Let's hope that the medicos can come up with something," replied the major. "Meanwhile, we need to know if they have increased the number of men in their trenches and if they have new equipment. Some of our planes have spotted indications that they were moving their artillery. Let's get to work and find out," the major said, dismissing them.

Now, when Llewellyn turned his head toward him, Captain Jordan said, "See what I mean."

"All I see is barbed wire. Pretty good job," answered Llewellyn.

"That's German wire in front of our trench."

"German!" Captain Llewellyn exclaimed as he re-examined the wire through the loophole. "How the hell did they do that?"

"They didn't. Corporal Duval and his squad did. I was complaining that we couldn't get any wire from the quartermaster. I sent the corporal out on a patrol last night. The Germans seemed to be rather more forceful than usual at this morning's hate. I thought they were preparing for an assault. When I looked out to see what had agitated them, I saw that their wire was gone."

"Duval stole their wire!"

Jordan was not pleased that Llewellyn appeared to be trying hard not to laugh. "It ain't funny. There are proper channels and procedure. This is highly irregular."

"Well, Captain," Llewellyn said, waving at the wire, "what do you want to do? Give it back?"

APRIL 21, 1915
2ND BRIGADE TRENCHES, YPRES SALIENT

"Well, Corporal Duval, I understand you're going out on a little midnight stroll?" Llewellyn enquired.

Corporal Duval snorted. "You could call it that ... sir."

"Don't use that tone again, Corporal!" snapped Captain Jordan.

Jordan was sitting in a canvas stool along the half-wall of the dugout. Standing beside the black-curtained entrance was Sergeant Booth. He hadn't seen the sergeant since he had been unceremoniously dumped last November by the Fusiliers' CO, Colonel Topham. He had recruited the sergeant last August in Toronto. One of the best. He appeared to be a bit stiffer than normal, and he was keeping a wary eye on Captain Jordan. Llewellyn had a fair idea what the issue was, but there was nothing he could do about it. Sooner or later the efficiency of the company would be examined. If found wanting, it would be investigated to find the cause.

"Yes, sir. Won't happen again, sir!" replied Duval as he snapped to attention. A mist of sand cascaded when his head brushed the log ceiling that had been built to protect them against shrapnel.

"I would like to join you this evening," Llewellyn stated.

"Sir?" Duval replied as he swivelled his gaze to him.

The captain leaned forward, placing his elbows on his knees as he looked into the corporal's eyes. "General Currie has been very pleased with the reports that you and your men have been providing. Especially the detailed mapping you have done of the German trenches in this sector."

Duval's face softened. There was a touch of pride when he said, "We've been going out with compass and rope to get measurements, Captain."

"Ah," Llewellyn answered. "I just want to stretch out my legs a bit. Been sitting all day at a desk."

"Yes, sir," Duval replied. Llewellyn was pleasantly surprised that the corporal hadn't replied with a touch of derision. Most of the privates and NCOs thought the staff officers were somewhat touched in the head. Sometimes they weren't wrong.

"What time is the patrol scheduled for tonight?" Llewellyn asked Captain Jordan.

"Midnight, sharp," Jordan replied as he gave the corporal a pointed stare.

"I'll be here by ten, then?"

"That would be fine, Captain. I'm glad to have you along," stated Duval.

Captain Llewellyn doubted that very much as he watched the dismissed Duval leave. The captain would have loved to be there when Duval informed his section who was accompanying them and why.

★ ★ ★

"Here you go, Captain," said his guide as they stopped at a black-curtained opening in the trench wall. The captain didn't know exactly where he was. He was fairly certain that the private had taken him the long way around for his own amusement. That staff officer thing again. He was supposed to lead him to the 4th Company.

The private pulled the curtain open and once the captain was in quickly closed it to block the feeble light from a candle that was set on a small, battered table. Shadows danced on the grim faces of twelve men who stared at him.

The cubbyhole was freshly dug, as the shovel marks could attest.

The roof hadn't been strengthened. A near miss would cause the ceiling to collapse and bury the men in three or four feet of dirt.

"Grab a seat, Captain, if you can find one," said Sergeant Booth.

"Thank you, Sergeant. By the way, how is the missus?"

The sergeant appeared to be pleased that he remembered. "From the letters she's been writing to me, she seems to be doing fine," he replied with a shrug that indicated women were women.

When one of the men moved over, the captain blinked when he recognized it was Father Stoats who had moved aside to make room for him on the dirt floor.

"Don't tell me you're joining us?" demanded Llewellyn.

One of the men beside him snorted, which brought a smile to the chaplain's face. "If you think that I could be of service..." he teased.

"Try that and we'll sit on you till you get some sense," retorted the private who had snorted.

"Is that any way to speak to your chaplain?" Stoats demanded.

"Damn right. If God doesn't like it, he can punish me with a number one." The man looked up at the ceiling. When nothing happened, he raised his hands and said, "See."

When the men stopped chuckling, Llewellyn asked, "How did you get to France? The last I heard, most of the chaplains were being left behind at Salisbury."

"The War Office did try to insist that only five chaplains come. They said that was the authorized allotment for a British division."

"How the hell — sorry — did you convince them that you were needed?" asked the captain.

"We made a conjoint argument that with all the trouble the contingent caused at Salisbury, letting us lose in Europe without moral guidance might not be a good idea. They finally saw the wisdom in allowing us to come," said the father with a straight face. "Besides, technically I was still the Fusiliers Intelligence Officer, so I would have come over regardless."

Llewellyn laughed. He had appointed the good chaplain to the position temporarily last October, because there wasn't a slot for a chaplain in the battalion's table of organization. This allowed Father Stoats to draw pay and rations while the Battalion sorted out the mess. Captain Jordan had replaced the Father as the intelligence officer. He wouldn't have been the Llewellyn's first choice, but then it was none of his business.

When the curtain opened, Corporal Duval slid in and quickly closed the curtain behind him. "Let's get started," the corporal said as he placed a circular black object on the table.

The captain was quite familiar with it, since it was a standard fifty-foot surveyor's tape. There was a steel pull tab that dangled from the front edge. In the centre there was a brass recessed handle that had been blackened.

"Okay, I want to go over our plan for tonight. We're going to go over the top at the sentry post in section one, and our return route will be via section five. The sentries have been informed. I hope that they won't shoot at us like they did two nights ago."

"Fucking buggers," muttered the man beside Stoats.

"Well, if they do it again we'll give him a new asshole," replied the corporal.

"Language, language!" protested the Father.

"Yes, Father," replied the corporal then continued, "Our job tonight is mapping their trenches across from sections one to five. Take a look at what new defensive works they have been putting up. Unless we are fired upon, we want to get in and out as quiet as possible."

"The corn stubble out there is going to be a bit of a problem," said one of the men.

"And those willow trees won't help much either," replied another.

"We're going to take it nice and slow. We have a job to do. Okay, make sure that you don't have any papers or documents on you when you go over the top. Hand over your pay books to Sergeant Booth. You'll get them in the morning."

One of the regulations was that the men were required to carry their pay books in their right breast pocket at all times. The captain knew it was standard procedure to remove their papers to deny the enemy valuable intelligence if they were captured.

"Now, all of you are familiar with the terrain..."

"Mud, mud, and more mud," the men chanted.

The corporal then glanced at Llewellyn, and he made a note of the .45 on his right hip and his Ross rifle. "We go over with fixed bayonets."

"Okay," replied the captain as he pulled out the bayonet from the sheath on his left hip.

At the sight of the shiny blade, the corporal said, "Better put some mud on it. We don't need that to give us away. You'll need to hood the breech to keep the mud out. If you don't it, will become useless out there."

"Good, we're all set then?" Duval asked. When no one said anything, he turned to Father Stoats. "Father, you want to give us a prayer?"

"Of course," Stoats replied. "May God keep you safe..."

★ ★ ★

"Halt — who goes there?" demanded a voice that then fired a shot at Captain Llewellyn. A bullet actually whistled past his ear.

"You fucking idiot! Give us a fucking chance to give you the fucking password before you fucking shoot at us," yelled Corporal Duval, who was crouching beside him.

Suddenly, German flares lighted the night sky. The captain, Duval, and the rest of the patrol froze so that they wouldn't give themselves away. They all hit the dirt when the distinctive pop-pop of German machine guns opened up.

"Fucking idiot!" cursed Duval as he spat out mud.

Bullets whined overhead as they thudded into the sandbags six feet away. They were inside the wire now. The trench was so close but so far away. Llewellyn tried to scrunch further down as German searchlights lit and began making a slow, arcing path of visibility toward their location.

Until now, their mission had gone reasonably well. Duval had placed him in the middle so that he couldn't get lost, although the moon was in its first quarter and was providing some illumination. The noise from the various cursing working parties on both sides covered any noises they might have made. The German curses were just as colourful as the English ones.

They had used ladders to climb over the top. Then they had made their way through the lane in the barbed wire and the French coil wire in front of their trenches. The wire was quite effective for slowing down an enemy attack, but it presented a serious problem for their patrols getting in and out. Lanes had been created for that purpose and their use alternated so they couldn't be given away. After all, if one could get out, one could get in.

Once they were out in No Man's Land, they crawled to their start location for their mapping exercise. Duval would take out his compass and pop open the lid. The compass he was using was the standard issue Verner Mark VII. The lid contained a thin, radium-painted filament that glowed in the dark. Once he fixed and sighted a landmark, he pressed the transit lock bearing on the compass to lock the needle in place so that he could read the dial. He would take one reading of a landmark on the German trench and then repeat the process, looking to their own lines. This would provide a focal point for their calculations.

Then Duval would hand the tongue of the tape to one man and crawl with three other men as it slowly unwound from the container. They would stop when they ran out of tape. Duval would glance back to see if the tape was relatively straight. He then took another bearing of both trenches. At this point, calculating the distance was relatively simple geometry, since the length of the base was known, fifty feet, and the compass bearing provided the tangent angles. As a surveyor it was basic stuff, and he could do most of the calculations in his head. The hard part was converting the compass degrees to tangent angles. An old-timer had once told him to simply multiply them by 0.017.

Right at this moment, though, the captain wasn't exactly calculating tangent angles. What he was calculating was how long it would take to crawl the last six feet of mud with a nine-pound rifle that now felt as if it weighed fifty.

All he could do was to take a cue from Duval. What worried the captain was that the morning hate was coming in an hour's time.

So will it be a German or a Canadian bullet? was Llewellyn's thought.

CHAPTER 9

APRIL 22, 1915
SAINT-JULIEN, YPRES SALIENT

"Have you assigned men to assist the farmers with repairs to their fields?" asked Lieutenant-General Alderson as he pointed to a farmer and his farm hands getting a plow ready. The land was beginning to dry out, allowing them to use heavy farm equipment for the spring planting. "We want to remain on good terms with the locals."

"Not yet, sir," replied the captain after a slight hesitation.

"Why not?" demanded Alderson. He wanted to see what sort of excuse the captain would use. The order had been issued by his artillery commander the previous day.

"No excuse, General," replied Masterley.

"Well, see to it then," ordered Alderson.

"Yes, sir," replied the captain as he saluted crisply before hurrying away to comply.

Lieutenant-General Alderson had just completed an inspection of the 3rd CFA Battery concealed about a thousand yards northeast of the small village of Saint-Julien. It was part of his regular inspection rotation to keep his men on their toes. He knew too well the negative impact of slackness, especially with the Canadians. While they were still considered green, they had come a long way in terms of discipline. He reconsidered that thought as he watched a German Albatross reconnaissance plane fly overhead.

The aircraft was painted grey, with black crosses on its wings and tail. It was one of the newer types. It had a ring-attached machine gun for the observer who sat behind the pilot. The observer, however, was staring intently at the ground with a bomb in his hand.

Alderson's eyes narrowed when he saw that the plane's engine had attracted the attention of the nearby gun crew. They had stopped working and had moved to the edge of the camouflage netting to get a better view. Aircraft were still a novelty. Despite strict instructions, the men were not to gather when they saw an aeroplane. He watched some of the men wave to the others to come take a look. They didn't bother to take cover when the observer finally released his bomb.

The black cylinder wobbled for a moment then stabilized as the streamers took hold. When it landed it detonated in a small cloud of dirt and dust. The reaction from most of the men was amusement at the show.

Alderson turned his head, searching for Captain Masterley to reprimand him for the behaviour of his men, when the German artillery barrage increased significantly in volume from the low background he had been hearing for most of the day. It was so heavy, he could feel the ground vibrations, even though the trench line was two miles away.

At this point, Masterley rushed over to him from the nearby command post. "General, the Germans have launched an attack against the Algerians."

"What kind of attack?" Alderson asked as he turned his head to the northeast, although he couldn't see much. Artillery shells were starting to land near his position. Dotting the sky were more German aeroplanes, and he could see the arrival of several French planes to scare them off.

"The report we received indicates that they released some kind of gas cloud, sir. It looks like they have launched a major attack."

"Understood," he answered. "Find the CRA and inform him that we need to get back to La Tours as soon as possible. We'll pick up horses at Wieltje. Let my HQ know that I'm on my way."

"Yes, General," replied Masterley.

Before the general turned to leave, he said, "In future tell your men to keep their heads down when there is an aircraft in the vicinity."

Captain Masterley blanched at the reprimand.

ALDERSON'S HEADQUARTERS, CHÂTEAU DES TROIS TOURS

When Lieutenant-General Alderson finally arrived at Le Château des Trois Tours, he headed directly to the reporting centre, where he found his most senior general staff officer, Colonel Romer, staring at the map of Ypres. The forty-six-year-old colonel, who had close-cropped hair and a moustache, was a recent addition to his staff. In late February, Alderson had received a request from the 3rd Corps to exchange GSO1s. His previous GSO1, Colonel Hearn, had gone to the 5th Division, while Romer moved over to take his place. The colonel had plenty of experience. He had served in the Boer War. He also had been with the 5th during the retreat at Mons and been at the battles at Le Cateau, Marne, and Aisne. The colonel was still adjusting to the Canadian way of doing things.

"What are the French doing?" he asked.

Romer understood that Alderson was referring to the French 45th Algerian Division that was guarding their left flank. The French Eighth Army was responsible for nearly five miles of trenches from Steenstraat, where they abutted with the Belgians to the Ypres-Poelcappelle road, where the Algerians met Brigadier-General Turner's 3rd Brigade. "Everything seemed rather quiet until five o'clock. Then we started to get reports that a green vapour cloud was seen drifting toward the French."

"I saw the cloud when I was inspecting the 12th Battery. It was moving toward Langemarck."

Romer nodded in acknowledgement. "That was what the 3rd Brigade reported before we lost touch with them."

"When?" demanded Alderson.

"About ten minutes ago the lines went dead. German artillery cut our telephone and telegram lines. The engineers have been ordered to repair them. Our communications circuits to the 2nd Brigade seemed to be working. They reported that their trenches are being heavily shelled.

"What concerns me is we are getting unconfirmed reports that the French are retiring from their lines. If true, it is going to cause problems with the 3rd Brigade's left. I have orders prepared." He indicated by pointing to the manila *Messages and Signal* pad that was holding down the corner of map. He could see the colonel's neat handwriting on the lined five-column form. It was standard practice that GSO would write and sign the orders that the GOC wanted to issue to his command. "Our divisional artillery will support the French by shelling the German lines directly in front of the 45th. The 3rd will provide them with rifle fire support."

Alderson skimmed the order. "Agreed. Also, order the reserve battalion to their positions."

Romer glanced at the wall clock and then put 6.00 p.m. in the *Time* box just below the *From* box already filled in with *1st Canadian Division*. He then tore the page off the pad and handed it to the nearest orderly, who rushed off to the communications centre.

"Where is the 1st Brigade presently?" Alderson asked. The 1st had been designated as the Division's reserve brigade.

Romer looked up from the order he was preparing and replied, "They've been spending most of the day training at Vlamertinghe. They were scheduled to provide work parties for the engineers to improve the 2nd Brigade's trenches."

Alderson frowned slightly. The 1st Brigade was currently attached to the 5th Division as a reserve in preparation for an attack on Hill 60. "Inform 5th Army HQ that there appears to be some kind of gas attack on the French. We'll keep them abreast as we receive more information."

"Yes, sir," Romer replied as both men turned toward the echoing booms of the German artillery.

2ND BRIGADE HEADQUARTERS, POND FARM, YPRES SALIENT

Captain Llewellyn woke up with a start. He was lying on his cot fully dressed. It took a moment for the drowsiness to clear. After glancing at his watch, which read five thirty, he realized that he had slept for an hour. He groaned in disgust. He had only sat down for a minute to rest. He had felt fine when he returned from the previous night's patrol. He had prepared a report, a rather thin one, on what he had learned. He then spent the better part of the morning collating an intelligence report on the current order of battle of the 3rd Landwehr Brigade that was their opposite number. After he had completed the report, he went to his quarters to clean up. Mud got into some of the most awkward places. He finally realized it was the artillery that had woken him. It was louder than usual. It was amazing what one could learn to sleep through.

When he stepped out of his canvas tent into the afternoon sun, he saw that a small crowd of refugees was parked near the pond. Most of them wore faded black. There were more carts than horses, which told him they were pulling them themselves with all their worldly goods loaded on them. A couple of tired grey horses were drinking from the pond. Some of the kids, dressed in rags, were bringing nosebags for the horses. The refugees had been passing through for the last few days as some of the farmers finally decided to abandon their property. The Brigade tried to help where they could by providing them with food and water. They were a standoffish lot, but he suspected that they were getting a better deal from the Canadians than from their compatriots.

He glanced down the gravel road and saw that more refugees were coming. Mixed in among them were khaki uniforms. This was a surprise, since troop movements were forbidden during the day.

A door behind him banged, and when he turned his head to see who it was, he stiffened. Brigadier-General Currie headed toward him. When he had stopped beside Llewellyn, a frown appeared as he stared at the German planes buzzing overhead.

"General." Llewellyn greeted Currie with a salute.

"Captain," Currie replied as he returned it. "Rather violent demonstration, don't you think?"

"Yes, sir."

"They have been bombarding the French for an hour, and now it seems they have turned their attention to us."

"Our trenches are being hit?" Llewellyn asked as he glanced up at Currie. The general was taller by several inches.

"Yes, they've been bombing our rear areas intermittently."

"I see some troops are moving to their battle positions," stated the captain as the khaki uniforms moved closer to them. They didn't seem to be marching with much discipline.

The general examined them for a moment and then exclaimed, "They're French!"

They were close enough now to see that they were indeed French troops. Based on the fez headgear, they were Zouaves. The only Zouaves Llewellyn was aware of in the area were with the 45th Algerian Division covering the 3rd Brigade's left flank.

"Ask them what the hell they are doing here!"

"Yes, sir," replied Llewellyn as he stepped onto the road and put his hand up to stop an officer on a brown bay. "*Lieutenant, qu'est-ce qui se passe?*"

The young officer, barely out of his teens, couldn't look him in the eye. "*Gaz, du gaz,*" he croaked as he bowed his head in shame.

Several of the Zouaves who shuffled past added, "*Beaucoup de morts! Asphyxiés!*"

The captain noticed that several them were not carrying their rifles. Only a handful of the men appeared to be wounded, a couple seriously enough to be supported by their comrades. Others were coughing harshly as they were trying to catch their breath. He did notice that most of the men had red eyes, and there appeared to be angry burn marks on their exposed skin. The other thing that perplexed him was the irregular yellow splotches on their mustard khaki uniforms. It looked if someone had been careless with bleach.

Everyone crouched when a Jack Johnson freight train was heard. When the shell landed in the field a hundred yards away, the horse bolted. The officer started yelling, "*Les allemands arriveront! Tout est perdu!*"

The captain quickly got off the road to avoid being trampled.

"What the hell happened to them?" asked Currie. "They're supposed to be a crack unit."

Currie's right, thought Llewellyn. The Zouaves were famous for their fighting skills. Their distinctive white balloon pants, blue jackets, and fez headgear had been copied by several militaries around the world. Then Currie's next statement caught the captain's attention. "If they are here, who's guarding our left?"

⋆ ⋆ ⋆

"Anything from the 3rd Brigade?" Currie asked when Captain Llewellyn entered the room with a raft of messages. The room smelled of stale coffee, and the air was thick with tension strengthened by cigarette smoke. The smoke had nowhere to go, since the lone window was covered with a black curtain to prevent signalling to the Germans their location. The room was lit with oil lamps, since electrical power was unreliable.

"Not yet," replied the captain as he took a seat at the table. Normally, the seats were filled with staff officers, but they had stepped out of the room to send orders to Currie's battalion commanders. The only other officer in the room was the newly acting Lieutenant-Colonel Tennison. They all stared at the map of the Ypres Salient. On the map were fresh red and blue pencil marks indicating the latest positions of the Canadians and the Germans.

"These are from the 5th and 8th battalions," Llewellyn stated as he placed them on the table.

"Do they have anything new to report?" Currie asked.

"It's relatively quiet at the moment," he replied.

When Currie frowned, Tennison said, "We've heard nothing since we forwarded the message from the 85th Brigade that they had placed their machine guns in position at Wieltje Farm. They said that their right is touching with the 3rd, but they have a gap between them and the 10th on their left." The 85th was part of the British 28th Division that had been rushed in to help support the 3rd Brigade. They had been temporarily transferred to Lieutenant-General Alderson's command.

"That is what worries me. How long ago was that?" Currie asked.

"About an hour or so," replied the Lieutenant-Colonel.

"Are our lines still down?"

"The engineers are working on them," Tennison replied.

"I need to know what is happening with the 3rd Brigade's left. The last report we received was that Turner's left had been pushed back," Currie said as he rubbed the back of his neck.

Llewellyn understood the general's frustration. Based on the reports that they had received, the 3rd's left had been pushed back to the GHQ Line, their second line of defence. At their urgent request for support, Currie had ordered the 10th Battalion, commanded by Lieutenant-Colonel Boyle, to report to Brigadier-General Turner and comply with his orders. The 10th had been initially assigned to work party duty when the Germans launched their attack.

That was what worried Currie and his command. The German gas attack had surprised them all. No one had expected the French collapse. It had opened a breach that the Germans were taking advantage of. If they knew how well they had succeeded, and if they could push enough troops through the gap, they could cut across the salient and surround the Canadian Division. That really worried everyone. What alarmed them was they didn't have answers to two questions: were the Germans still capable of launching another gas attack, and what could be done to protect their men against it? The medical people were looking into it, but they had no answers yet either. In the meantime, Currie's staff was working hard trying to lift the fog of war that had descended on them.

"Have the 7th Battalion reached Locality C yet?" Currie asked as he brushed aside the ashtray filled with cigarette butts from the map.

Llewellyn had visited Locality C. It was a two hundred-yard support trench on the western part of Gravenstafel Ridge that the French had dug. They had built it on the skyline in their usual style, with a few strands of barbed wire in front. The Canadians hadn't made many improvements there, since the priority was trenches 1 and 2 held by the 5th and 8th Battalions about 1,200 yards in front of Locality C.

As if he had read Llewellyn's mind, Currie said to Tennison, "Let the engineers and stores know. Make sure that they get what they need to strengthen their defences."

"Yes, sir."

Then Currie turned his eyes on Captain Llewellyn. The captain could see that he had made a decision. "I want you to go to Turner's HQ in person and report back to me on their situation. I need to know what's happening with the 3rd Brigade. And I need to know where the Germans are and what the hell they are up to."

"Yes, sir," Llewellyn said as he rose to comply with the order.

CHAPTER 10

APRIL 22, 1915
MOUSE TRAP FARM, YPRES SALIENT

It took Llewellyn nearly an hour and half to get to Mouse Trap Farm. He could have cut across the fields, since Brigadier-General Turner's headquarters was only a mile and a half as the crow flies. He decided against it, since his horse could easily break a leg in the dark, and he didn't want to be mistaken for a German officer. The men would be bound to be edgy with all the chaos.

He turned his horse instead onto the Wieltje-Fortuin road and headed in the general direction of Wieltje. The road was a narrow gravel lane that the farmers used to move their livestock from one field to another. In certain sections he had to move off the road because it had been blocked by cursing farmers herding their cattle away from the battlefield. In others he had to walk his horse, since there were troops double-marching to their battle positions. Traffic was heavy in both directions as the quartermaster wagons headed toward the front lines filled with food, water, sandbags, barbed wire, and, most importantly, ammunition.

Sometimes his horse would shy from one of the tall trees that intermittently dotted the lane. When he peered down to find out what the problem was, the faint light from red Very flares outlined the dead bodies of French soldiers. He had seen ambulance wagons filled with wounded trying to race down the road get stuck in the heavy traffic.

The first traffic warden he saw was when he finally got to Wieltje. They were trying to unsnarl the traffic congestion at the fork that the tiny village surrounded. It had a dozen or so houses belonging to those who worked on the nearby farms. Nearly all of the buildings had been taken over by the Division's quartermasters. The rest were being used as billets. It had taken a pounding, since most were smouldering hulks.

He avoided the fork by following a company cutting across the backyard of one of the houses to the Wieltje–Saint-Julien road. He only travelled a half mile when he found the guard unit at the entrance of the narrow lane that led to the 1st Brigade Headquarters at Mouse Trap Farm. He was familiar with the road, since he had been there several times to share intelligence.

The courtyard was packed with cars and trucks revving their engines and whinnying horses pulling SAA-filled carts. Grooms were trying to steady several horses. Beside them, messenger bicycles leaned against the main red-brick wall below white-shuttered windows. Three A frame-style buildings surrounded the courtyard. The stable's large arched doors were open, revealing men saddling horses and loading carts with boxes and crates. The servant quarters were now the HQ's billets. A moat surrounded the property. The locals called the farm Château du Nord. When the Imperials were here they had called it Shell Trap Farm. For reasons Llewellyn didn't know or actually care, it had been renamed Mouse Trap Farm.

The guards at the main entrance recognized him and were about to let him in when Major Garnet Hughes stepped out.

"Brigadier-Major, may I have a word?" asked Llewellyn.

Hughes glanced at him coolly then said, "If you must."

The captain kept his face expressionless. He was well aware that Major Garnet Hughes and Brigadier-General Currie had a recent falling out. Exactly why was not clear. From what he could gather from the rumour mill, it seemed Currie didn't think the major had what it took to be a battlefield commander. He had been quietly transferred to Brigadier-General Turner's outfit. It was a delicate situation since Garnet Hughes was the one who had convinced Currie to volunteer in the first place. Garnet was also Sam Hughes' son.

"General Currie sent me to get a situation report, since your wires are down."

Garnet's moustached frown deepened. "The situation is serious. The French have retired, and we have the Boche behind us."

"Where?"

"Kitchener Woods."

"Shit," muttered Llewellyn.

"That is where I'm going. I have orders for the 10th Battalion to clear them out of there."

"Dear God," exclaimed the captain. "How bad is your left?"

"Our left is still in place," Major Hughes replied.

Captain Llewellyn gave him a startled look. "But the reports that I read before I came here stated that your left was being pushed back to the GHQ Line."

"No, it has not. There is a gap between us and the French that the Germans took advantage of."

"Currie has set up his brigade based on the information that your left has been turned," the captain exclaimed.

"He'll have to make adjustments then."

"What about the bridges across the canal? Did they blow them yet?"

"No, but engineers have them mined, and they are ready to blow them if necessary."

The captain grunted. At least Brigadier-General Mercer could prevent the Germans crossing the Yser canal, since the Canadian Division was responsible for two wooden bridges that crossed over it. That is, if the Germans didn't bring bridging equipment with them.

"Okay, I'll inform Currie," Llewellyn said.

"You do that. I now have to get the 10th to clear out Kitchener's Woods. We need to get the Germans out of there," Major Hughes answered as he headed to a waiting staff car. He left Llewellyn to make his own way back to Brigadier-General Currie's HQ.

APRIL 22, 1915
CASUALTY STATION, YPRES SALIENT

Samantha watched as artillery shells bracketed the ambulance that was charging fiercely along the Wieltje–Saint-Julien road. The men on the road had heard the shells coming in and had scattered off into the ditches and fields. For a moment she thought the ambulance had managed to escape unscathed, since it continued moving. It wasn't until it stopped in front of her with the engine clicking that she realized it hadn't. The driver and the man in the passenger seat slumped forward, gushing blood. Shrapnel had decapitated both men.

Technically, she shouldn't have been there, since nurses were normally assigned to hospitals located miles behind the front lines. Samantha had been transferred to the Ypres Salient from the Hotel du Golf a couple of days earlier at the request of Captain Moore, the Richmond Fusiliers' senior medical officer. She had worked for him at the Toronto General, and he had written a very flattering recommendation letter to the Nursing Service when she volunteered. She had been happy to see the good doctor again but noticed he had lost some of his pudginess.

Upon her arrival, Dr. Moore had insisted on her accompanying him on an inspection tour of the casualty stations.

They were at the fourth one when the first wounded French soldiers started to arrive. It was set up in a stone cottage with a wooden table set in the largest of the two rooms. Most of them were dark-skinned Moroccans who had been suffering from chemical burns and wracking coughs. They couldn't do much for the men's lungs, but they could treat the burns.

"This is inhuman," Captain Moore had said after he and Samantha stepped outside to get a breath of air. One of the Moroccans had died on the operating table. They had to make way for the orderlies to remove the body.

"I know."

"Asphyxiation gas!" the doctor had spat out in disgust.

"I know," repeated Samantha. She felt the same way. "It has to be in a high concentration. Otherwise it would not have this effect." She indicated the men lying on stretchers outside the farmhouse with her hand.

"Oh?"

Samantha sighed. "In Sudbury we are used to clouds of sulphur gas rolling in from the mine smelters. We had to water the gardens to avoid the acid damaging the vegetables."

It was then that she was interrupted by the artillery. Samantha grimaced at the damaged ambulance and then wondered whether any of the men in the back had survived. She was surprised when she heard groaning.

"Let's get them out of the back," she ordered the two lightly wounded Moroccans sitting nearby. They didn't understand English, but they got the gist of what she wanted.

"Get those poor souls out of the front seat," Captain Moore commanded one of the orderlies who had come to help. The captain then followed Samantha.

As Samantha passed the cab, she stumbled when from the corner of her eye she saw one of the men's heads staring at her from the front seat. She focused her gaze on the late evening light that peered through the truck's ripped khaki canvas with the red cross painted on it. When she arrived at the back, she saw men piled on top of each other. She could only guess that the blast had thrown them to the floor. A soldier with a bloody head bandage that covered his left eye stared at her in puzzlement.

"I'm in Hell, and the devil is punishing me with a beautiful woman," he croaked.

Samantha snorted. "You're not in Hell yet."

APRIL 23, 1915
SAINT-JULIEN, YPRES SALIENT

Paul Ryan had pissed his pants. He couldn't help it. Dirt spurts were popping out of the sandbags, and the 18-pounder's shield was pinging.

He glanced over at the four bodies lying in the shallow depression that they were using as a gun pit. Three were unmoving. Bombardier Harris had a hole just above his left eye, while Bombardier Edds was lying on his back with stitches across his chest. Beside him lay Sergeant Hasson with a leg missing. It had been cut off when a shell landed near him. The shrapnel peppered Bombardier Calderwood, who was groaning in pain. A bullet had ricocheted off the shield, hitting Calderwood's right hip, adding to his woes.

Suddenly there was a lull as Paul loaded a shell into the breech and pulled the lanyard. When the gun recoiled, the shield hit him, knocking him back a few feet. Then the bullets started whining again.

"It's getting a tad hot, don't you think, Corporal?" yelled Henderson, who was about to toss him another shell.

"Yeah," replied Paul as he picked himself up. He was grateful that Henderson didn't notice his wet pants. He would hate to have that on his casualty report. He shoved the shell the bombardier had tossed to him into the breech and stood back a half step when he pulled the lanyard again. When the gun settled, he peered over the gun shield. There wasn't much he could see in the dark. Hours earlier he was uncomfortably ensconced in the battery's forward observation post on the 2nd Brigades' right flank, looking for targets and relaying their positions back to Captain Masterley. He had about a couple hundred yards of trenches to keep an eye on, and he really hadn't seen anything unusual.

It was around seven o'clock that Captain Masterley rang him up and commanded that he come back to the gun pits. They had been ordered to support the 3rd Brigade and had to move their guns to a new location and get them re-laid.

By the time he had gotten back, the guns and limbers had already been hitched to the horses, and they were on the move to their new positions at Saint-Julien. Some of the men gave him dirty looks, since he had arrived after they completed their work. The support wagons were being loaded with their gear and the extra ammunition.

While they had tried to hustle, the traffic on the roads was brutal. When they finally arrived at Saint-Julien, C Battery's four guns were emplaced in a shallow depression with some sandbags and branches in front for some rather pathetic protection.

Over the noise Ryan heard some shouting. "Let's go get them boy … Push them back … Push them back…" A couple of hundred feet away he could see the muzzle flashes from Ross rifles as a platoon was attacking the Boche in front of him.

Ryan snapped his head when he heard noise behind him. He reached for his Ross that was lying beside Bombardier Harris. When he saw Captain Masterley beating a path toward him with four replacements, Ryan relaxed somewhat.

Masterley frowned when he saw the casualties. His frown deepened when he saw what was left of their 18-pounder stock.

"Good job, McGill," he said. The men behind him had their lips pulled down in grudging respect.

"Yes, sir."

"I want you to take Calderwood back to the casualty station."

"I would rather stay," replied Ryan.

"I need you to get more shells. We're going to need them."

Ryan opened his mouth to protest, but it closed when he saw that the captain wasn't about to brook disagreement. The only thing he was grateful for was that the captain didn't notice his stained pants. A couple of the replacements did, and they smirked at him.

"And McGill," the captain ordered, "better keep your head down."

"Good idea, Captain," Ryan replied as he helped pick up a groaning Calderwood and place him on a stretcher.

APRIL 23, 1915
SAINT-JEAN, YPRES SALIENT

"Well, well, Captain Llewellyn. What are you doing here on a dark and stormy night?" said a deep voice as he was passing a military bus laden with troops. A captain stepped off the bus and greeted him. "You're going the wrong way."

"Who let you out!" said the captain. He recognized the young officer. His name was Oliver Cox, and he was a company commander with the South Kent, nicknamed the Bluffs. They had met a few times at intelligence briefings and at a friendly boxing match that the Canadian Division had with the 28th Division the previous week.

"This is most disagreeable. I don't know who I'm most annoyed with, the Germans or you Canucks. I was planning on having a pleasant evening with a smashing young woman," said Cox.

"Well, we do our best to accommodate," the captain said dryly as more bus loads of men were driven by. "Who did you bring with you?"

"Who didn't we bring? Besides us Bluffs, we have 3 Middlesex, the 5 KOR Lancaster and York, and the Lancaster Regiment," answered Captain Cox.

"Problems?" a colonel asked when his car stopped beside them. The captain stood to attention, as did Llewellyn.

"No, Colonel, just jawing with Captain Llewellyn. He's the 2nd Brigade's Intelligence Officer," stated the Bluffs' captain.

"You're a staff officer?" asked the colonel, turning his attention at Llewellyn.

"Yes, Colonel, I'm on General Currie's staff," answered Llewellyn.

"What are you doing here?" he demanded.

As most junior officers did over a pint, they discussed their COs. The 2nd Bluffs officer had spoken highly of his CO, Colonel Augustus Geddes. The colonel sitting in the car waiting for his reply looked as if he were in his late forties. From what Llewellyn remembered Cox telling him, Geddes had served in the Boer War and had been severely wounded. What had piqued Llewellyn's interest was that Geddes had been a staff captain in the War Office's Intelligence Department. Since August, he had been in command of the 2nd Battalion of the Bluffs. They had arrived at the front only in mid-January.

"The general sent me to assess the situation and to consult with

General Turner. I'm returning to my HQ to give the general my report," he informed the colonel.

"Hmm," Geddes murmured thoughtfully then said, "I need a good staff officer. And you are it!"

"Sir?" Captain Llewellyn blurted as he blinked in surprise.

"Brief a runner, and he'll get a message to General Currie," he ordered. The captain realized that he just had been conscripted. Geddes continued, "Captain, the situation is here is in flux. I'm in command of several regiments from different divisions. Plus we have been picking some of your Canadian stragglers. I need to reorganize those Tommies, and you're going to help me."

What could Llewellyn do but salute and say, "Yes, Colonel! What are your orders?"

CHAPTER 11

APRIL 23, 1915
OBLONG FARM, YPRES SALIENT

"We have to take out that Hun machine gun," said Captain Llewellyn as he studied the farmhouse through his binoculars. He had seen the occasional flashes and heard the distinctive sounds of an MG 08. He knew the specs of the machine gun all too well. It was kind of ironic that the Maschinengewehr 08 was a direct copy of the Maxim machine gun. The Maxim was named after its British designer, Sir Hiram Stevens Maxim. He had tried to sell it to the British army, but they viewed the weapon as unsportsmanlike.

The version he was facing fired the 7.92 Mauser round at roughly 450 rounds per minute. It weighed nearly 140 pounds, sixty for the gun itself and eighty for the sledge-type mount. Some were mounted on wheels for easy mobility. It was normally manned by a four-man crew: a gunner to carry the gun, a soldier for the mount, an ammunition hauler, and another man to carry water and tubing to keep the barrels cool.

"We could try to get across before he spots us," whispered Sergeant Booth, who was lying beside him on the small ridge as they observed the farmhouse below.

Captain Llewellyn glanced up at the sky. A thin grey line was starting to appear on the horizon. He moved the metal whistle that hung around his neck to a more comfortable position then replied, "We'll have to do it soon. If it is still dark, we might risk it. I don't want what happened to the 10th and 17th to happen to us."

Booth didn't reply. The word had gotten around that the 10th and the 17th Battalions had been mauled when they attempted to reclaim Kitchener's Woods. From the scattered reports it seemed that they had lost most of their senior officers and about half their men in the assault, and now they were in a tenuous position. Their attack had created a bulge in the freshly dug German lines. If the Huns managed to encircle the two Canadian battalions, they could be wiped out. The captain wasn't in any position to help, although he desperately wanted to. He knew most of the senior officers were trying to get support to them. His orders were clear. They were here to plug the gap between the Oblong and Turco Farms.

"Any signs of gas?" he asked Sergeant Booth.

"Not yet," said the sergeant as he kept his eyes on the farm.

It seemed that he couldn't get rid of the Richmond Fusiliers. He was beginning to feel that they were like a boomerang. No matter how far you threw it, it always came back. After Colonel Geddes conscripted him, he had dragged him to Saint-Jean, where he had set up his headquarters in a house on the south side of the village. It was on the road there that they had run into the Fusiliers. How they managed to get lost and this far out of position was anyone's guess. Llewellyn wasn't sure if Geddes was disgusted or amused. The Bluffs' CO had immediately assigned Llewellyn as the company's CO, since Captain Jordan had been run over by, of all things, an ambulance and was carted off by the same ambulance to an aide station. No one knew where Colonel Topham was, but Llewellyn had sent word to the 2nd Brigade, letting them know where what remained of the Fusiliers were.

He had helped the colonel set up his HQ when Geddes received an order from Alderson that they needed to fill a gap in the lines, and fast. The word was clear, but what was not clear was where was the gap? How wide was it? And what was going to oppose them when they tried to close it? Llewellyn had been impressed by how Colonel Geddes quickly gained control of his improvised detachment. Since Geddes had never worked with most of the units, he had to quickly assess the temperament of each CO and decide if he needed to cajole, swear at, or flatter each one to get them to do what he wanted.

Geddes had assigned Llewellyn, since he was the intelligence officer, and his Fusiliers to reconnaissance to gather the information he needed.

"Did the runner get off?" asked the captain. The runner was to tell Geddes where he was and what he was planning to do.

"Yes, sir," replied Booth.

"Captain," said a quiet voice. The captain turned his head and saw Duval kneeling behind him on a knee. He had sent him out to scout what lay in front of him. Behind him was a soldier he hadn't seen before being prodded with a rifle. They had been picking up stragglers most of the night as they moved forward. Another one just got added to the list.

"Hey, take it easy," said Paul Ryan rather loudly.

"Quiet! Do you want the entire German army to know we're here?" ordered Llewellyn in a quiet tone. "What are you doing here, Corporal…"

"Corporal Paul Ryan, 65th Artillery, sir."

"Where did you hide your 18-pounder? In your pocket?" asked Corporal Duval derisively. The men arrayed alongside them grinned and nudged each other. It relieved some of the tension they all felt. This wasn't a training exercise.

"Where's your rifle?" asked Llewellyn.

"Dunno," replied Ryan. "Lost it, I guess. I was the FO when our trenches got shelled." When he saw their grim faces, he added, "You have a spare?"

"Sure do," answered the captain as he pointed to the slope in front of them littered with bodies. "There's plenty out there you can grab."

Paul turned then started toward the plowed field.

"Where do you think you're going?" asked Corporal Duval.

"To get me a rifle," Ryan replied. His statement brought shaking heads from the men.

"We'll have to knock out that machine gun first," Llewellyn said tersely. "Forget the rifle. I'm assigning you to the 4th platoon. When we rush, I want the 4th to recover as many of the wounded as we can. Is that understood?"

"Yes, Captain," replied Duval as he led Paul away.

"Sergeant Booth, get your men ready."

"Yes, Captain," he replied as he scurried away.

Once the platoons were lined up in attack formation, the captain blew his whistle and yelled, "Follow me!"

APRIL 23, 1915
SAINT JEAN, YPRES SALIENT

The man was screaming in pain when the orderlies placed him on the surgery table. They had to hold him down when Samantha gave him a shot of morphine to dull the pain. It would have been better to put him to sleep using ether, but they were pressed for time. Samantha could see the fear in his eyes as she stroked his forehead in a vain attempt to soothe him.

Dr. Moore gave her a glance then examined their latest patient. They didn't bother counting the shrapnel wounds that the man had suffered. She could see a twisted two-inch piece of metal embedded in the man's ankle. While it was the most obvious one, it actually wasn't the most serious. The metal actually closed the wound, reducing blood loss. It was the chest and the lower body wounds that concerned them the most. He didn't appear to have any head wounds, which was the majority of their cases. The shrapnel air bursts were devastating. He did have an upper chest wound that had penetrated the lung. A medic had taped a cotton gauze bandage on three sides to keep it clean. The bottom was left loose to allow the wound to drain. It would have to hold until they got the man to one of the clearing hospitals, where the surgeons could take care of it.

From the small table beside her she took a bottle of antiseptic and proceeded to clean the wounds. Once she had finished, Dr. Moore used a sterile scalpel to probe and remove any metal fragments. Each one clinked in the white-coated ceramic bowl she held for him. When he was satisfied he got all of them, he put in a couple of stitches to close the wounds, which she then covered with bandages.

He sighed when he took a look at the ankle. He motioned to the two orderlies that were standing near the entrance. "Hold him down," the doctor ordered as he wrapped a tourniquet around the leg. He turned to Samantha and said, "Saw."

She couldn't help seeing the man's eyes widen when she handed the doctor the bone saw. The patient started to struggle, but he passed out from shock after the first couple of strokes. But it only took a few more for the foot to detach. The doctor loosened the tourniquet to ensure the blood flowed freely then bandaged the stump.

"Next," Doctor Moore said.

Samantha stepped aside as the orderlies removed the man to the recovery room. There were three other tables that they'd managed to fit into the surgery. Along the walls were several orderlies treating the walking wounded seated in chairs. They tried not to jostle each other, but it was difficult in the cramped quarters.

She glanced through the open doorway to the courtyard, where more wounded were waiting. The flow had slowed somewhat. Not because the fighting had stopped. She could hear and feel the vibrations in her feet from the German artillery. The Huns were shelling the roads to prevent reinforcements and supplies getting to the front. This meant that it was simply too dangerous for the ambulances to travel.

She had lost count of how many patients she had treated since yesterday. She didn't feel anything at the moment, but she knew when night fell more men would be brought in with holes in them that she could put her fist through. There would be more with wounds she would have to clean that had been filled with dirt, pieces of equipment, and clothing.

APRIL 23, 1915
ALDERSON'S HEADQUARTERS, CHÂTEAU DES TROIS TOURS

"Where are the French?" demanded Alderson.

"Two battalions of the 45th Division are to launch their counterattack against Pilchem in about a half hour," replied Romer.

"Has Mercer acknowledged yet?"

"No. We didn't give him much time to get his men into position," Romer pointed out. It was the French who wanted to launch the attack to regain the ground they had lost earlier in the day.

"It can't be helped. Have the CFA been notified to provide support?"

"They have been ordered to commence firing right about now," Romer replied, pointing to the clock, which read four thirty.

"Good. Have we heard from the 10 Battalion?"

"They have reported that they have cleared the woods and their lines from V25a to C.16.a, and they are entrenching."

"Losses?"

"We haven't received that as yet, but they seemed to be severe. I have received confirmation that Colonel Geddes' detachment is on the march, and they will be linking with Turner's brigade to fill the gap. The Fifth Army has indicated that they will release another four battalions if we need them."

Alderson grunted an acknowledgement. Geddes' detachment would provide additional stiffening for his men. Of the three brigade commanders, Turner was the most experienced, but it was his brigade that had gotten the brunt of the German attack. They had been taking a pounding ever since Turner's left had been turned, even with Currie having released his reserve battalions to the 3rd Brigade. So far, Currie's 2nd Brigade had escaped relatively unscathed. Mercer had been designated as their reserve brigade, but those men were no longer available, since they had been assigned to helping the French.

"Let's hope that Mercer and the French meet their objective." They had been assigned to recapture Mauser Ridge.

Alderson returned to studying the map. He had been training his men since they arrived in October, and this was their major test. *Will they hold?* was the unspoken question that the Fifth Army headquarters had. *Will the Canadians hold?*

APRIL 24, 1915
YPRES SALIENT

Captain Llewellyn's hand went to remove his cap when he realized he wasn't wearing one. He thought his mind was clear and his thinking logical. He was fairly certain he had one when this brouhaha started — regulations. Where and how he had misplaced it was cause for concern, since he couldn't remember. Maybe the lack of sleep; it had been thirty-six hours, and it was finally catching up to him.

"Captain, here's your cap," Corporal Duval said as he handed him a battered and dirty forge cap. Or at least he thought it looked dirty. It was difficult to tell, since it was two o'clock in the morning. The sky over the Ypres Salient seemed to be well lit with star shells providing floating illumination and artillery shells passing each other.

When he tried the cap, it fell down to his ears. "It ain't mine," Llewellyn said.

"It's the only one we got, Captain," Duval answered.

He tightened the inner band and replaced it on his head. He glanced at what remained of his former company of Fusiliers. They were lying along the hedgerow that followed the dirt road. An occasional Jack Johnson landed in the field a couple of hundred yards south. The men were so exhausted, they didn't bother even to look. They were veterans now. If it wasn't close, it didn't bother them.

But they were looking at him, waiting for him to tell them what to do. Captain Jordan had been killed in the first hours of the attack, and so had Lieutenants Vernon and Troope. The other two were so badly wounded that they had to be sent to the nearest casualty clearing station. The sergeants had replaced the missing subalterns as the platoon commanders. And the No. 4 platoon had lost their sergeant an hour earlier. He had been a good man.

To give himself time to think, he pulled out his pipe and packed it with what remained of his pipe tobacco. He accepted a light from the corporal. After a couple of puffs, he finally said, "I'm promoting you to Acting Sergeant, Corporal. I want you to lead the 4th platoon."

"Yes, Captain," he replied as he stood taller.

"So what are we going to do?" asked Sergeant Trevor, a Moncton native. "The last orders were to retire."

"Were they now?" the captain replied calmly.

"Stands to reason," said Trevor. "We don't know where we are, and the Germans are everywhere. Best to find our own lines. No point in getting ourselves killed."

Captain Llewellyn continued to puff on his pipe as he assessed the men. They were near the breaking point. They had lost close friends and buddies, and their commanding officers. That they had stayed this long together was remarkable. Whether they had much more to give was the question. He could always use the .455 Colt still in his holster on his right hip or the Ross that he had slung over his right shoulder. But then he would have to watch his back. He knew what he was going to do just he was trying to decide what the best approach would be. Their lives were in his hands. He tried to straighten his shoulders, but it weighed on him.

He glanced at Corporal Paul Ryan, who looked at him with a pale face. He had a rifle on his lap and two bandoliers, one half-empty, wrapped around his chest. At his feet was a bulky telephone. Pointing at it with his pipe, he asked, "Are you able to get anything with that?"

"If I can find a telephone wire that I can splice into," Ryan replied. His voice had an exhausted tone. They would have gotten rid of the damn thing if it weren't for that possibility.

Captain Llewellyn jerked his head when a sentry fifty feet south of their position yelled out, "Halt, who goes there?"

"I'm a bloody Canadian, you dolt," said the female sitting in the front seat of the horse-drawn ambulance with a sergeant beside her holding the reins. *How did they get this close without making any noise?* was his first thought.

"It's a bloody woman," exclaimed the sentry.

The captain stared at Samantha Lonsdale in disbelief. "You!" he blurted. "What the f..." he nearly blurted out then changed it to be more polite, "hell are you doing here?"

She stared at him for a moment than said, "I'm looking for a man."

"What?" he blurted as the men behind him chuckled at his discomfort.

One of the men rose to his feet then said, "You found him, dearie. I'm right here."

Samantha tossed her head to him then looked him up and down, sniffed, then said, "I'm not your dearie. And you'll address me by my rank," she told him.

"Yes, ma'am," he replied quickly. "No offence, ma'am."

"Men," she said as she returned her gaze back to Llewellyn.

"Miss Lonsdale, what the hell are you doing here?" he repeated. He could feel the men turn their eyes to stare at him.

"Orders," she said. "My orders are to collect the wounded along the road."

"You know where we are?" he demanded.

"Well, of course. I've got a map," she replied.

"Can I see it?" he asked. They had been without a map for the last eighteen hours, and they weren't sure where they were.

"Do you know where the Germans are?" he asked as he pointed his torch at it.

"Yes, we're here. And the last reports are they are there," she said as she indicated a spot on the map.

"Okay," he replied as he examined the map closely. He then folded it and put it in his pocket. "Now, I want you to turn around and go back where you came from."

A determined look appeared on her face. "Men will die out there if I don't tend to them."

"I can't allow that."

"Is that an order?"

"Yes."

"Well, I'm not in your chain of command. And I have my own orders."

"Goddamn it," the captain roared. "Sergeant, turn that wagon around."

The sergeant looked at the captain then at Samantha. "I'm sorry, Captain, but she's in command."

"For God's sake. I can't spare men to protect you."

"I didn't ask. I have a job to do, and I'm going to do it," she replied as she clambered back into the front seat. The sergeant flickered the reins, and the horses moved forward.

"So what do you want to do, Cap?" asked acting Sergeant Duval as they watched the ambulance disappear down the road.

"Damn it. I can't let her go by herself," he muttered. "She's going to get herself killed. I have no choice."

"Well, Captain," Duval said, "there is the easy way and the hard way."

"I know the easy way is to haul her back to the casualty station."

"Then there is the hard way."

"Yeah, we can try to stop the entire bloody German army."

Sergeant Trevor chuckled. "You got it wrong, Captain."

"I have?"

"You've never been married, have you?"

"No," the captain replied with a shrug.

"Sooner or later we're going to make peace with the Germans. If you drag her kicking and screaming back, she will never forgive you. Nor ever let you forget it."

Most the men nodded.

Llewellyn sighed. "Okay. Let's do it the easy way. Let's go and stop the bloody German army," he said as he hitched his shoulders and started marching down the road. The rest of the company rose to their feet and followed the captain.

CHAPTER 12

"Go! Go! Go!" yelled Captain Llewellyn as his first section scrambled out of what remained of their trench. They had spent hours fixing it up. They had torn up duckboards to create a firing step and laid sandbags in a brick pattern to give the walls strength, stability, and protection. Now the trench was practically unrecognizable since the Germans were intent on filling it, using their artillery as their shovel. They were being pushed back to Locality C, but he would make them pay every step of the way.

Just as the first section had scrambled out, a shell landed in front, chewing up the defensive barbed wire. The concussion threw the captain back against the trench wall. He bounced off and hit a nearby private. They hit the dirt together, and the soldier humphed when the captain's weight landed on top of him. Clods of dirt and wire rained down. Over the noise he could barely hear Private Kershaw yell, "If they wanted us to leave, they could have asked."

Llewellyn shook his head to clear debris from his hair and ears. He had lost his forage cap again. He picked up his Ross and checked to see if the dust cover was still in place over the breach.

"Well, we won't invite them for supper, shall we," he shouted to make himself heard over the din caused by the subsequent explosions.

Suddenly the shelling stopped. That was not good, not good at all. He glanced left and right. Some of the men were relieved that it had stopped. For many it was getting on their nerves. A couple of the men were beginning to withdraw into themselves. Then there was Private Kershaw, who seemed to become more comical under the stress. Most of them had been in a sombre mood, since they lost one or more of their buddies.

When he tried to step on what remained of the fire step, he nearly tripped over one of the water buckets that had been strategically placed in the trench to help against a possible gas attack. When he peeked over the jumbled sandbags, what he saw didn't surprise him. There were men in grey uniforms massing for their assault. He took another quick glance to get a clearer picture. He could see two machine gun teams being set up on both of his flanks.

"They are going to hit us again," the captain said to Sergeant Booth, who appeared at his right elbow. "Let's stick with the plan."

"Right, Captain," he acknowledged. He turned his head and yelled, "Okay. Let them have it." Some of the men did the sign of the cross before they climbed on to the fire step as Booth turned and laid his rifle on the top of the sandbags.

"Rapid fire!" Captain Llewellyn shouted as he fired. He felt a certain exhilaration as grey shapes began to fall. As he reloaded, slamming a charger into his Ross, the captain noticed that a couple of his men were struggling with the bolts on their rifles. He didn't have time to think about that, because when he saw the German line falter, he ordered, "Second section! Go! Go! Go!"

Every second man dropped from the fire step and scurried past him down the communication trench. The last squad ran past with a box full of hand grenades. They were a mixture of the standard Mark 1s and improvised hand grenades they made using the empty thirteen-ounce apple and plum jam tins that came with their rations.

"They're at a hundred yards," said Sergeant Booth. Suddenly, the sergeant straightened when a bullet hit him in the throat, splashing the captain with his blood.

"Fuckers," yelled the captain as he emptied his rifle at the Germans. "Fuck! Fuck!" he said as he checked the sergeant. There was nothing he could do. Booth was dead.

"Captain! Captain!" Duval tugged at his arms, trying to get his attention. "He's gone," he croaked as Duval glanced at the sergeant lying against the sandbags. "We have to go!"

"Fuck," said Llewellyn as he punched the nearby sandbag. "Grab the sergeant and let's go," he ordered.

He was the last man out of the shallow communication trench. It ran straight for about fifty yards or so. When he arrived at the end of it, he saw that Paul Ryan was peering over top with binoculars.

"Have they reached it yet?" the captain asked.

"Yes, sir," he said.

"Okay. Let the fuckers have it!" the captain ordered.

All the men beside him had been armed with jam tin grenades. Duval was among the first to let fly. Some of the Germans had seen the lit grenades coming and started to scurry out of the trenches. Llewellyn emptied his clip at them and was happy that several went down. Then he ducked below the trench face as the grenades started going off.

When men screamed and cursed in German, it was a satisfying feeling. Captain Llewellyn knew he couldn't stop them, but he could make them pay for each step.

"Okay," said the captain as he recharged his Ross from the bandolier that crossed his chest. "Let's do it again. And let's do it right this time," he said as he glanced at Sergeant Booth's body beside him.

"Yes, sir," Duval replied with an evil grin.

APRIL 24, 1915
2ND BRIGADE HEADQUARTERS, POND FARM, YPRES SALIENT

Paul Ryan's right foot caught the edge of the road, dumping him face-first into the ditch as he did a running dismount from his bicycle. It was exactly where he wanted to be, but he wished for a fleeting moment that he had done it with some grace. That passed when the four incoming shells started exploding around Brigadier-General Currie's HQ. Shrapnel sliced through the bike's frame in two places, and the seat flew away to disappear into another shower of dirt.

They weren't direct hits, but metal whined off the stone walls. It didn't take long for a Jack Johnson to plunge through the roof and detonate. He wasn't surprised, since flying overhead and directing them was a German spotter plane. He could see the observer in the front seat watching the farmhouse. Ryan knew the pilot had a wireless with him and was relaying targeting information back to the Hun batteries. There wasn't a damn thing he could do about it. His Ross was clipped to the bicycle's frame only few feet away from him. It wouldn't matter, since the plane was out of range.

He glanced back to the farm. He still hadn't seen anyone. Either the senior staff was dead, or the HQ dugout that Captain Llewellyn described was deeper than he thought. When black smoke started billowing out from the back, he spotted men exiting the building via the front doors and windows. Obviously the Albatross above saw them, because more shells started bracketing the only road that led into the farm. They had no choice but to jump into the pond on the other side of the building to escape.

He groaned when he rose to a crouch. The fall had nearly knocked the wind out of him. His ribs ached, but he just added it to the catalogue of aches and pains he already had. He suspected that he would be adding a few more before the day was done. He had very little choice. If he stayed where he was, one could drop on him. When the last of the four shells landed, he got up and sprinted. He knew that he had about two minutes before the next barrage landed. He sprang the leather straps holding the rifle that was supporting what was left of the bike. In the last few days, he had learned that you never knew when you would need one. He looped the rifle around his shoulders as he ran toward the smoke, hoping it would obscure him from the damn plane. At least that was his thought.

Once past the corner, he saw the water was already filled with splashing senior officers as they made their way to the other side. *A nice day for a bath* came unbidden as he made a dive into the water. Shells started to land in the building, and wood splinters cascaded into the pond. When he came up, he saw a large chunk give a glancing blow to a lieutenant-colonel, and he fell face forward into the water.

Ryan swam-walked through the shallow water to the officer and then dragged him to the bank on the other side. Someone helped him drag the body out of the pond. "Are you okay, son?" asked the voice.

Ryan coughed, spitting out dirty water in reply, and when he saw who it was, he nearly choked. It was Currie who had helped him. "I'm fine, thank you, sir."

"How's Colonel Tennison doing?" Currie asked with concern when he recognized the man Ryan had rescued.

"I don't rightly know, sir."

"Don't you think we should find out?"

"Yes, sir," replied Ryan as he checked the lieutenant-colonel. His scalp was bleeding, but the man wasn't breathing, which was the priority. He used the standard resuscitation technique of pressing the man's hands on his chest to force the air in and out of his lungs. After a few presses, the man began to gurgle then started throwing up. Once he had finished retching, his breathing came back to normal.

"Good," said Currie. "I would hate to lose a good staff officer. They don't grow on trees, you know."

"Yes, sir," Ryan said. Brigadier-General Currie had already lost three of his four battalion commanders.

"Damn," said Currie when he saw the fire take a firm hold on his HQ. "General Currie, sir. Captain Llewellyn sent me!" said Ryan, getting his attention. When Currie faced him, Ryan said, "The captain has sent me to inform you that our left flank at Locality C is up in the air."

APRIL 24, 1915
LOCALITY C, YPRES SALIENT

Captain Llewellyn was trying to assess the latest reports from his lookouts. He had placed them at strategic locations in the trenches they were currently occupying at Locality C. He had to, since the 3rd Brigade had retired to the GHQ lines several hours before. He still hadn't received word from Paul Ryan, who he had sent to Brigadier-General Currie's HQ to inform him of what had transpired.

The retirement by Brigadier-General Turner had caught them all by surprise. Then he was hit with another blow when, after he had sent the runner, he discovered that Brigadier-General Currie was missing, presumed dead. Command had devolved to Colonel Lipsett, who was located at the Apex.

"When are we going to get some grub?" asked Private Kershaw, who was sitting beside him.

The captain shrugged as he glanced at the notes in his hands. "Soon, I hope." He lifted the handwritten notes to get better light so he could read the pencil scratchings. His mind was still sluggish. He still hadn't slept much during the last two days, and he had a fierce thirst. They all needed water, and soon. He glanced down the trenches, where buckets of water had originally been set up to wet pieces of cloth they had managed to scrounge. They were using them to cover their mouths and noses to help protect them from the gas that the Germans were using. He glanced down at the black rubber facemask they had taken off a dead German that was lying at his feet. At the first opportunity, he was going to pass it down the line for the medical and quartermaster people to examine.

"How's our ammo?" the captain asked.

"Not that bad. We managed to get everyone the standard 120 rounds or thereabouts," Kershaw replied. "We have to strip the dead and the wounded. But we got plenty of spare rifles."

That was true. Some of the men had doubled up their rifles, using them as spares in case one of them jammed. Their ammunition supply was not great. The Huns were pounding the Apex to push them back. It took him a while, but the captain finally realized that the Germans were trying to straighten their lines.

"I heard that General Currie is dead," Kershaw stated as he checked the action on his rifle.

"Where did you hear that?" asked Llewellyn sharply.

"Word gets around," Kershaw replied in a resigned tone.

"He was reported missing," stated Llewellyn as he read the man's face. He had just confirmed that Brigadier-General Currie was dead. They had received word that the 2nd Brigade's reporting centre at Pond Farm had to be moved. The speculation was that it had been overrun by the Germans.

Both men looked up when a German aircraft flew low and slow over their trench. Kershaw pulled back on the bolt, putting one up the sprout aimed at the aircraft then emptied his magazine.

"Feeling better?" asked the captain as the aircraft continued on its way.

"Much," replied Kershaw as he leaned back against the trench wall.

"So what are the Germans up to now?" asked the captain.

Kershaw turned and raised his head slowly and carefully to peer over the trench. "They've got their work parties out."

"Okay," said the captain as he scribbled in his notebook. When he saw movement in the communications trench, he put his hand on the trigger guard of his Ross. His eyes widened when he saw who it was. "General Currie!" he exclaimed.

"So this has been where you have been hiding," Currie said with a tired smile. The Brigadier-General had deep bags under his eyes, and he had a couple of days' growth on his chin.

"Yes, sir." The captain then blurted, "I heard that you had been killed."

"Well, the day is still young," Currie replied sardonically. "I figured that you needed some help, so I brought you some." He indicated with a toss of his head. Behind him, men were making their way from the communication trench.

"Thank God," muttered Kershaw.

"What is the current situation?" Currie asked.

"Fine now that you are here. We should be able to hold them. But we desperately need rations, water, and ammo."

"I know. They won't able to bring much until late tonight. You'll have to make do till then."

Captain Llewellyn acknowledged with a nod.

"Ah, Mister Ryan," Currie said when Paul Ryan appeared with a Ross slung over his shoulder. In his hands he carried an ammo box. "You can stay with the captain. I don't have further need of you."

"Of course, General," replied Paul.

"Good. I've got to go. I need to direct where the men are needed. I've sent word that I want all the unit commanders to meet in a few hours. Gentlemen, carry on," Currie ordered as he disappeared down the trench heading south.

"You've been busy," said Llewellyn to Ryan. "When I heard that the general was missing and I didn't hear from you, I thought you had bought it."

"I nearly did a couple of times," replied Ryan when he put the ammo box down and sat on it. "When I found the general, he insisted that I drive him to the GOC of the 27th Division to get more men."

"He did what?" Captain Llewellyn said incredulously.

"Yes, Captain. We had to stop a couple of times to ask the units where they were heading, but it took an hour or so to get there."

"What did General Snow say when you got there?" Major-General Snow was the GOC of the 27th.

"I don't really know. I stayed in the car. I heard some arguing, and when General Currie came out he was pissed. He kept muttering about how rude the general had been."

Llewellyn winced. He could imagine what Major-General Snow thought.

"Where did he get the men?"

"Units here and there," Paul Ryan said. "Will it be enough?"

"I really don't know. All we can do is wait and see," the captain said with a sigh. "You better get some sleep — you're going to need it."

CHAPTER 13

Samantha felt herself being dragged out of a deep sleep. "No, no," she protested weakly, but to no avail.

She kept her eyes shut, hoping she could still tumble back into the abyss. She jerked upright when she realized where she was. A grey woollen blanket fell off her onto the gritty floor of the dispensary. It was a place where she normally didn't sleep. She recalled that she had made her way there, holding on to the walls. She vaguely remembered feeling woozy, and her mind was in a deep fog due to lack of sleep. All she had wanted to do was to sit quietly for a minute until she finally felt better before returning to help the surgical teams. She had looked at the chair but decided that the thin mattress in the corner was more inviting. Several days without sleep, food, and water finally wrestled her down and pinned her.

Someone clearly thought she needed rest, since they had covered her with a thin grey blanket. She groaned when she rose to her knees then to her feet. She didn't bother to stretch, since it would ache too much. She unstuck her tongue from the roof of her mouth and ran it over her dry lips. She needed water.

In the corridor, she paused to check on some of the men waiting for transport to the nearest casualty station after their surgery. The sound of the artillery seemed to have lessened somewhat. She hoped that meant they would be able to bring extra supplies in; the dispensary was nearly empty.

She spotted Dr. Moore sitting in a cupboard office. He was dressed in his surgical gown, splattered with blood, and his facemask hanging from his neck. His back was bowed as he rapped a hard biscuit on his plate. She swore it had put a ding in the tin. When he spotted her, it took a moment for him to realize who she was.

"Ah, you're finally awake," he said as he pushed the biscuit around some kind of brown gravy on the plate.

"How long have I been out?"

"Only a couple of hours," he informed her as he finally let the biscuit soak.

"Sorry, Doctor."

The doctor stared at her for a moment as he tried to figure out what she was apologizing for. Then he took his time thinking up a suitable answer. When he finally found it, he said, "No reason for that, my dear. You lasted longer than most of the other doctors and orderlies have. Much longer. I was frankly amazed that you lasted as long as you did."

"Did you get any rest?"

"Humph," was his reply.

"Did you get any rest?" she repeated.

"Soon. I have too many patients," he replied as his eyes briefly closed. "And more are on their way."

"More?"

"Oh, yes. Orders from Trois Tours. We're going to counterattack at three thirty this morning. Which means a lot of young men will be arriving here soon."

"Okay," she replied tiredly. "I hope the supplies arrive by then."

"Yes. We're going to need them."

"And Doctor, you're going to need some rest."

"I'll sleep when it's over," he replied sharply.

"Doctor Moore! You won't be much use to us if you collapse," she stated. "There's a fine mattress in the dispensary that is nice and comfy," she insisted as she tugged him to his feet. He swayed slightly as he struggled to maintain his balance.

"You're a bossy young lady," he complained.

"That's why you hired me," she answered.

APRIL 25, 1915
ALDERSON'S HEADQUARTERS, CHÂTEAU DES TROIS TOURS

"Why the bloody hell did you retire to the GHQ line?" demanded Alderson as he glared at bespectacled Brigadier-General Turner standing before his desk. He hadn't requested Turner's presence, but here he was. Since he was here, he would have a few words with him. That was why he had asked Turner to shut the door when he ordered him into his office.

Turner tried to interject, "Colonel Romer..."

Alderson overrode him. "When my wish was that you utilize the two York and Durham Brigade battalions to strengthen your line and to hold."

"If the general would let me explain," Turner attempted again.

"Then you didn't have the courtesy to inform my command of your decisions. I had to find out from the Fifth Army Corps who was being informed of your movements by General Snow!" Alderson shouted.

Brigadier-General Turner's face blanched at the news.

"The GOC of the 27th Division is better informed concerning my command than I am!"

Turner opened his mouth then closed it again.

"And you failed to keep General Currie informed of your troop movements. You left his left flank in the air! If it weren't for the two battalions from the 150th Brigade, the East Yorkshire, and the Green Howards, the Germans would have cut off the 2nd and 27th Divisions."

Lieutenant-General Alderson leaned back in his chair and scowled at his subordinate. "General Plumer had quite a few words to say about the ground that you lost today when he telephoned me. He wants a counterattack. A strong counterattack toward Saint-Julien. We are to retake it and push the Germans as far north as possible. General Hull and his 10th Brigade are to launch their attack at three thirty.

"You are to provide as much support as you can to ensure that his operation is successful. Do I make myself clear, General?"

"Yes, sir."

"How did you get here?" asked Alderson.

"On a motorcycle," replied Turner.

"I would suggest you get back on it and return to your command as soon as possible. You have a lot to do."

Brigadier-General Turner gave Alderson a terse salute. He snapped a sharp about-face then marched out of the office.

★ ★ ★

When Brigadier-General Turner barged out of Trois Tours, he spotted the motorbike that had transported him to Alderson's headquarters. The bike's rider hurried over from a group of gallopers on the other side of the courtyard. Before the rider could say anything, Turner ordered, "Start the damn contraption and let's get going."

The rider shifted the Harley-Davidson upright. The machine was an early 1914 model with an eleven-horsepower engine and had a top speed of sixty-five miles per hour. He used his heel to tap the kickstand up and then pumped the step-starter a few times until the engine caught and roared to life.

Turner couldn't help giving the château an angry glare. It had been a waste of his time. He had come from his command because he needed to know who he was actually reporting to: Lieutenant-General Alderson or Major-General Snow. Both of them were sending him orders. Well, at least that had been cleared up, even though he didn't actually pose the question.

His main concern was with his command. He had pulled back his men after his telephone conversation around noon with Colonel Romer. It had been clear to him, at least at the time, that the retirement was what Alderson wanted. He had tried to explain that his brigade's position in the afternoon was untenable. They were exposed to direct German artillery, rifle, and machine gun fire. Some platoons had reported that they were being hit from the rear. The GHQ line gave his men a solid defensive position to halt the German onslaught.

His Brigade-Major was supposed to have sent regular reports to Trois Tours, Currie, and Mercer. But the Germans had been deviously effective in disrupting their communications. Many of their dispatch riders hadn't gotten through. The engineers have been slaving away at repairs to the point that they were collapsing from exhaustion. It made coordinating not only his four battalions but Colonel Geddes's detachment as well as two other battalions that had been transferred to his control frustrating. Half the time he didn't know exactly where they were and what their orders were.

As he took his seat, he knew that he had to get control back so he could provide Major-General Hull with effective support. The only good thing about being on the back of the motorized contraption was that it would keep him awake. That was if he got back to his command post in one piece.

CHAPTER 14

APRIL 25, 1915
LOCALITY C, YPRES SALIENT

"Where the fuck is our artillery?" Sergeant Duval yelled above the ra-ta-ta of a German machine gun that was peppering the sandbags of their trench again.

"How the fuck would I know?" replied Corporal Ryan, who was seated beside him. "I must say they are beginning to annoy me."

"Do tell," replied Duval. "At least the artillery has let up."

"Yeah, they sure have a lot of it," Ryan agreed as he glanced at the bodies of four Fusiliers lying in the trench. An air burst had caught them. They had been good soldiers. It bothered him that he couldn't remember their names. The Germans had been pounding them all day. It had been especially intense around five o'clock as they seemed to have taken a liking to their trench. It was obvious to everyone that they couldn't stay there, but the officers had a different opinion. They were not in any mood for arguments. What really impressed Ryan was the German artillery. He knew what the ammunition situation was with the Canadian Division. That the Germans could continue the rate of fire they had since Thursday told him that not only were they extremely well stocked, they also had a hell of a lot more guns than the Canadians. At least double or triple.

The sergeant peered carefully through a slit in the sandbags. The one thing about the Germans, they were smart. They had set up a MG 08 to harass them, and they had placed snipers around it to prevent the Fusiliers from getting any ideas. In the distance, he could see the damaged buildings of Saint-Julien. It left a sour taste in his mouth. They had lost it yesterday.

"What do you have?" asked Captain Llewellyn when he kneeled beside them. The captain had lost his cap again. The one that he was wearing had fallen down, covering his ears.

"It's going to be tough to get to it," replied Duval. "We might be able to take it out when it gets darker. But in daylight we're going to lose a lot of our guys."

The captain frowned as he examined him and what remained of the company. If he was going to order them to do it, they would try to take out the machine gun. Especially since he was more than likely to lead the attack.

"How did the counterattack go?" Ryan asked.

"Not very well," Llewellyn reluctantly admitted. The captain was running a very fine line, Duval knew. He needed to keep up morale by fibbing to them from time to time, but he also needed to maintain the men's trust and respect. He knew that the captain couldn't tell them everything, but what he could he would. "They didn't jump off until nine thirty, and they lacked artillery," he said, giving Ryan a glance. "They got chewed up pretty bad."

Some of the men who overheard gave resigned shrugs. What could you do?

"We're going to hang tight for now," Captain Llewellyn said.

"I heard that we're going to be relieved?" said Ryan, which cost him a glare from Duval.

"You did, did you now?" the captain replied with a snort. "When I find out you'll be the first to know. Now let's get back to work, shall we."

APRIL 26, 1915
CASUALTY STATION, SAINT-JEAN, YPRES SALIENT

"Take it easy with him," Samantha ordered after the wounded man yelped in pain.

"I know how to transport a patient," Corporal Beck retorted as he dropped the stretcher rather harshly into the back of the Ford ambulance.

"You stupid bugger!" the soldier swore as the corporal gave the man a smirk before he slammed the door shut. As the ambulance drove away, he made a show that his back was bothering him from all the heavy lifting by running his knuckles down his lower spine.

"Corporal Beck. You could have opened the man's wounds," Samantha warned him. She didn't particularly like the orderly from Waterloo. He was a whiner and a slacker.

"Yeah, they'll fix him when they get him to the base hospital."

Samantha crossed her arms and stared at him. The other orderlies tried to look busy. "Corporal, gather some men and get those supplies into the dispensary. The food to the kitchen."

The convoy of ten ambulances that had arrived to transport the wounded to the Vlamertinghe dressing station had not come empty. They had been loaded with medical supplies and rations for hospital staff and patients.

"I ain't no coolie," he replied.

Samantha took two steps forward and stared up at the man, who stood several inches taller than her. "It's ma'am! Or sister! Or lieutenant!"

She continued to stare at Beck, who finally backed down when he saw the other orderlies sniggering at him. "Yes, ma'am," he finally conceded.

"Then get to it."

"Yes, ma'am," he replied with a salute.

The salute, Samantha thought, had a touch of insolence in it, but she decided to let it go. She knew that she had won a skirmish in a battle, but it was a start. When she turned to enter the station, she nearly collided with Dr. Moore. He had his head buried in papers he was reading. He gave her a raised eyebrow when he saw Corporal Beck cursing some of his men. Beck wasn't the good doctor's favourite either. "I see that the last of the current patients are on their way."

"Yes, Doctor."

"And the supplies are being squared away."

Samantha simply shrugged a blue-uniformed shoulder. "Catching up with the paperwork?"

"I finally have some time before we get the next set of patients."

"Another counterattack?" asked Samantha. They finally were able to get some rest, although Dr. Moore's uniform still looked rather baggy and wrinkled.

"I'm afraid so. I've just gotten an alert from the Lahore Division."

Samantha gave him an indifferent look. She didn't know who they were. All she was certain of was that her wards would be filled again. "I'll get the wards ready."

"Actually, I have a special job for you," he said, stopping her from entering the building.

"You want me to do the paperwork?"

Moore snorted. "I wish. I have to estimate the number of men that have come through our hands and the types of wounds we treated. I'm afraid we don't have an accurate count of the French, the Imperials, and our own men that have passed through. I do recall we treated a fair number of head wounds," he said with a frown. "We'll have to do something about that. Forge caps aren't much protection against steel balls."

"Don't forget all gas casualties."

"How can I forget? The Imperials have confirmed Dr. Naismith's finding about the gas that the Germans used," he stated with a slight roll of his eyes. The British didn't want to take Dr. Naismith's analysis without having their own experts confirm it. "The gas was chlorine mixed with bromide. They agreed with his suggestion that using a padding soaked in hyposulphite of soda will help protect the men."

"That is good news," replied Samantha. She was familiar with the chemical, a white crystalline powder that dissolved easily in water. It was a common treatment for arsenic and cyanide poisoning. Also, it was used in the textile industry to remove excess chlorine during the bleaching process.

"What we are planning is setting up a manufactory nearby to make face masks for the men. We've ordered cloth and the soda. So we want you to start creating as many face masks as you can for the men."

"Me, sir?" replied a surprised Samantha.

"Yes, we need someone reliable to supervise and to ensure it runs smoothly. Your name came up, and I wholeheartedly agreed. It will be temporary, since we sent to London those face masks that we captured from the Germans. Once they have been examined, I'm sure that suitable patterns will be developed for manufacturing."

"Yes, sir," replied Samantha, pleased that he thought of her for the job.

"Good. We've already assigned Corporal Beck and his platoon to assist you. Also, we will be hiring some of the locals as well." Misinterpreting the look on her face, the good doctor said, "I'm quite confident that you can handle it."

What could Samantha do but nod in agreement.

APRIL 26, 1915
SAINT-JEAN, YPRES SALIENT

Shit, thought Captain Llewellyn when he jumped off the back of the truck that was kind enough to give him a lift to Brigadier-General

Currie's new headquarters. The 2nd Brigade had been pulled out of the trenches during the night and had been reassigned as the reserve.

He had seen the Lahore Division march past on their way toward their start line between the two farms that had been designated Irish and Wieltje. They were to launch their attack in the afternoon. He frowned when he spotted a German observation balloon in the distance. The Germans were up to their old tricks, that was confirmed when the sound of artillery starting a duel began.

The Fusiliers had finally been able to get some sleep. Well, at least a few hours more than they had gotten in the trenches. Some of the fog from his mind had been cleared, but he still felt numerous aches and pains. He had finally managed to transfer command of the company back to Colonel Topham. Understandably, Topham was pissed. The colonel had assumed that the company had been wiped out. He suspected that Topham would have preferred dead heroes to live ones. He would have to explain to Brigadier-General Currie how the hell he managed to lose an entire company. The one thing that the captain was fairly certain of was that the senior officers would be analyzing the Canadians' performance. They would be weeding out those who had not lived up to expectations.

He had hoped to talk with some of Brigadier-General Currie's staff to determine his mood, but here he was talking with an armourer sergeant. When Currie spotted him, he waved him over. The sergeant saluted him then turned his attention back to the general.

"Like I was saying, we've been ordered to pick up any discarded rifles and ammo," the sergeant said with a sour note.

The captain glanced at the back of the horse-drawn wagon. It had been filled with rifles, but he saw ammo boxes and bandoleers mixed in as well. Most of them were Rosses and Lee-Enfields, but he saw some Labels as well. He had seen them being carried by the French, but he hadn't been able to examine one close-up. Designed in 1886, the Label was fifty-one inches long and weighted nearly ten pounds. It had a ten rounds capacity, eight in the tube magazine under the barrel, one in the transporter, and one in the breech. It fired an 8 mm round. It was a reliable rifle, but one of its weaknesses was the tube slowed reloading during rapid fire.

"What are we going to do with them?" Captain Llewellyn asked as he placed the Label back into the cart.

The sergeant glanced at Currie and then back to Llewellyn. "The Labels and the Lee-Enfields, we'll be sending them back. We'll let their quartermasters sort them out. As for the Rosses, we'll be checking the serial numbers to determine who they had been assigned to and then sort it out from there."

Captain Llewellyn winced at the news. If the soldier wasn't dead or wounded, he would need a damn good explanation how and why he had lost his weapon.

"Any ones that have been badly mangled will be used for spare parts," he said. "I want them all checked to ensure that they are serviceable. I've been receiving reports from my commanders that they jammed." Brigadier-General Currie had previous expressed some concern about the Ross's serviceability.

"Did you see of them jamming?" Currie asked Llewellyn.

Llewellyn glanced at the sergeant and replied, "Yes, I did. I just put it down to bad ammunition. Some of the British ammo is not very good."

Currie pursed his lips. "It's been happening much too frequently, and we need to get to the bottom of it. I don't want my men to be put in such a position again."

The armourer stayed silent, as the discussion was above his pay packet. Instead, the sergeant pulled out a rifle from one of the piles and asked as he handed it to Currie, "What do you want done with the Mausers?"

Llewellyn had been briefed on the Mauser. Designed in 1898, the rifle was forty-nine inches in length, and it weighed nearly a pound less than the Label. It fired a 7.92 mm slug. Like the Ross and the Lee-Enfield, it had a five-shell box magazine that could be loaded with chargers.

Currie flicked the safety catch on the back of the straight bolt. He then pulled it up and out, opening the breech. Currie glanced inside and then handed it to Llewellyn for his inspection. To his eyes, the block was very simple but well made. When he slid the bolt shut, it felt very solid.

"Keep a couple," Currie ordered. "We'll want to test them on the range." He then dismissed the armourer. "Very good, Sergeant, please continue."

Then Currie turned his gaze on the captain. "Good to have you back."

"Where do you want me to start?"

Currie examined him for a minute, making him wonder if he were in serious trouble. "We have much work to do reorganizing the brigade. Orders have been sent to Shorncliffe for replacements."

"How bad were we hurt?"

"We're down to 1,200 effectives," was Brigadier-General Currie's reply. Llewellyn grimaced. Five days ago they were nearly four thousand strong. "When the replacements come, we have to bring them up to standards as soon as possible. This is what I want to do...." Currie said as he led them into his HQ.

CHAPTER 15

The captain had nearly missed the message that Sergeant Booth's body had finally been found and recovered. Considering the number of returns flowing through the brigade's headquarters detailing the fighting strength of each battalion, company, and platoon, no one would have faulted if the name of a lowly sergeant didn't stand out.

When he arrived at the appointed time, it took a few minutes to locate the Fusiliers, since there were many internments taking place in the plot of land that had been assigned to the Canadians.

He finally spotted Father Stoats dressed in khaki with his minister's stole draped over his shoulders. Behind him the pallbearers were carrying the body of Sergeant Booth to a freshly dug grave. They were being followed by what was left of Booth's platoon. Acting Captain Wayne had taken over the No. 1 company to replace the late Captain Jordan. The captain had been buried yesterday a few plots over. The other senior officers weren't present today, but then he didn't fault them since they needed to re-organize the Fusiliers to make them once again combat-ready.

The captain gave him a thin smile when Llewellyn fell in. They had first met during the transfer of the 1st Company's command, just after the roll call was conducted. It had been hard as Sergeant Duval called the name. When a name that was called was met with silence, he could see the men glance back and forth down the line. The lips of a few trembled in grief when they heard the name of a dead buddy.

Acting Sergeant Duval would dutifully mark the name in the book. Each of the names that were missing needed to be accounted for as to whether they had been killed, wounded, or taken prisoner. Any identity disks that were found were matched with the man's service record. Also, the circumstances of how they were killed or wounded would be recorded and put into the service jacket as well.

The funeral didn't take long. Captain Llewellyn watched Captain Stoats' eyes water slightly when the bugler sounded taps. The chaplain had been quite busy, and his day wouldn't be ending any time soon, since there were several other interments scheduled. With the funeral over, the platoon was dismissed.

He couldn't help taking a good look at the men. He had just learned that they were being transferred to Festubert.

APRIL 28, 1915
5TH CORPS HEADQUARTERS, ABEELE

Lieutenant-General Plumer was pleased that they were able to move his headquarters relatively smoothly. A 15-inch German gun had been lobbing 1,700 pound shells into Poperinghe. It would have taken only a lucky shot to knock out his headquarters.

Abeele was about three miles west of Poperinghe. The village of about fourteen hundred souls straddled the French and Belgian border. It actually ran down the centre of the main street. The custom station had suspended operations for obvious reasons.

He glanced at his divisional commanders, who had arrived at the small Catholic school for his meeting. His most senior commander was Lieutenant-General Alderson. The others were major-generals: the 4th Division's Wilson, the 5th's Morland, the 27th's Snow, the 28th's Bulfin, the Northumbrian's Lindsay, and the Lahore Division's Keary. All of them were giving each other side glances, and their small talk was practically nonexistent.

It had been a hectic five days, and all of them had suffered losses. He had already seen the numbers, and they were not good. The Canadian Division had taken the brunt of the attack. They had suffered 766 killed, 2,373 wounded, and 2,586 missing. The other divisions suffered losses almost as bad. The 27th suffered 230 killed, 1,042 wounded, and 140 missing, and the 28th had 359 killed, 1,686 wounded, and 494 missing. He hadn't received the latest figures, but the estimates were that the Lahore had lost over two thousand dead, wounded, and missing.

With a catastrophe of this magnitude, there was a strong possibility that heads would roll. Actually, it had already happened. He had received orders from Field Marshal Sir John French that he was to command the newly created *Plumer Force*. True, the name wasn't original, but he wasn't the one who had chosen it. His orders were to contract the British trench lines to a more defensive position, as the current ones were too exposed to German fire. The plan was essentially the same one that Lieutenant-General Smith-Dorrian had proposed several days previously. Field

Marshal French had not been pleased by the suggestion and had moved to strip Smith-Dorrian of his authority. That the two men disliked each other and didn't get along didn't factor much in the decision.

"Thank you for coming. I will be keeping this brief," he said as the men relaxed somewhat. Their jobs were safe for now was their first thought. "We've had a hectic week, and I'm afraid that things will continue to be hectic for the next little while. After my discussions with Field Marshal French, we have decided that we will need to withdraw from the current trenches. The engineers are currently digging a new one. To minimize losses, we will need to pull back. We've lost too many good men. The number will only increase once the Germans provide us with the names of the men they have captured," stated Lieutenant-General Plumer.

His corps had lost too many officers, which they couldn't afford. Colonel Geddes was one. The report was that he had been killed when he went back to his car for a map and a shell landed nearby. What a waste.

"Once the reinforcements have arrived to replace our losses, there are several deficiencies that I would like to address. The first is communications. The Germans were able to target our telephone lines, and the dispatch riders were severely hampered, resulting in excessive delays of messages.

"I would like all officers to attend courses of instructions in the appropriate manner that reports and orders are prepared," he stated. He couldn't help give Lieutenant-General Alderson a pointed glance. "It is essential that orders be clear and concise to avoid misinterpretation."

Major-General Snow grunted in agreement. He had already expressed his displeasure with Brigadier-General Currie when he arrived in person to his dugout requesting reinforcements in the heat of the battle. He had indicated to Plumer that if Currie had been under his command, he would have relieved him on the spot. Currie and Turner were items that he needed to discuss with Alderson after the meeting. Both of them had made serious mistakes during the battle. The question was who was available to replace them.

There had been serious doubts as whether the Canadians would fight. That had been put to rest quite emphatically. All they needed now were good officers to lead them.

"Now, we have to discuss how we will withdraw our men without the Germans noticing. I estimate we will need four days..."

APRIL 29, 1915
PARLIAMENT HILL, OTTAWA

When Sir Robert Borden felt the raindrops, he looked up at the pale blue-grey sky. It was just a small shower passing through. He could see that the sun was struggling to pierce some of the weaker cloud strands. The farmers, he knew, would welcome rain since the local rivers and streams were lower than normal.

He glanced up at Lieutenant-Colonel Herridge of the 5th Princess Louise Dragoon Guards standing behind a draped makeshift altar. Members of the Governor General's Foot Guards band had created it by piling their drums into three tiers. As the senior Ottawa chaplain, Herridge would be leading the memorial service honouring the men who had died at Ypres. So far nearly two thousand, and the numbers kept rising as new casualty lists arrived at the Woods Building.

The stone steps that led from the lawn to the Centre Block were crowded with members of his cabinet, their spouses, the Supreme Court justices, the Ottawa City Council, and the governor general with his family and entourage.

Behind them, in the centre of the hollow square created by the assembled troops, stood Major-General Hughes with his headquarters staff arranged in rows. On the east side were the 8th Canadian Mounted Rifles and the 7th Artillery Brigade. On the south were the Foot Guards with the 38th Battalion. The Foot Guards were dressed in their scarlet uniforms, which contrasted sharply with the khaki-uniformed troops. Near the West Block stood the Dominion and Ottawa Police detachments, as well as the Ottawa Fire Department representatives.

He tried to locate his cousin, Matron Jessie Jaggard, who was leading the local detachment of nursing sisters. He had a pleasant supper with her the previous night as he and Laura got caught up with her. They wouldn't be seeing much of Jessie, since her detachment of nurses would be leaving for England soon.

Beside the nurses were the student cadets from the local public schools who had been granted a half-day vacation to attend. Outside the military square were the local townsfolk who had come to honour the men who had been killed and to offer their condolences. Some of the widows of the fallen were in attendance.

Herridge's next words caught his attention. "We are proud of them, proud of the honour they bring to Canada, proud of the heroic stand which saved the fortunes of the day."

He was giving an excellent speech, but Borden could tell that his words weren't being carried very far. But he was sure that the reporters, photographers, and the moving picture camera were capturing the event for posterity.

When the chaplain finished, the Foot Guard and the 38th Battalion bands began playing "O God, Our Help in Ages Past." Borden and Laura, standing beside him in mourning clothes, joined the crowd as they started to sing the hymn.

The start of the national anthem indicated the end of the service and that the assembled troops were to march past the governor general for his review. Borden knew that initially the cadets were not included, but when the duke expressed his wish that they participate, they had been added to the ceremony.

He stood beside the governor general as the units marched past then headed down Metcalfe Street to be dispersed to their barracks. It was difficult watching them, knowing that he was responsible for some of them not coming back.

It also confirmed his decision to delay indefinitely the elections that the members of his cabinet had been pushing hard for. There were ballots for the soldiers stacked in the corridors of the Parliament Buildings. Public opinion had been running against the idea, and now he knew that the Canadians were united in one thing: trash the Germans.

CHAPTER 16

MAY 9, 1915
ECHO BEACH LAKE, QUEBEC

"**A**re you sure you want to open them?" Joseph Irwin asked Borden. Irwin had just come out of the kitchen with a cup of coffee. He was dressed in his fishing outfit: a duck suit with cuffed khaki pants, a Norfolk-style jacket, a white shirt, and tie. Borden was similarly attired.

"Not particularly," Borden remarked as he fingered the green Grand Trunk Railway envelopes that had arrived earlier this morning. They had to be urgent for Blount to have sent them. Dr. Kidd had ordered him to take a couple of weeks rest after Borden was barely able to get out of bed for several days. He had packed his fishing rods and lures and headed for the lodge Echo Beach Lake Fishing Club had leased two hours north of Ottawa on the Quebec side of the river.

When he opened the first telegram, he saw that the two-page message was in cipher. He was familiar enough with the basic cipher key to get the gist of the message. It was from George Perley in London. It looked like Italy was planning to declare war on Germany and Austria. He was tempted to share the news with Irwin. Ever since the Echo Beach Lake Fishing club had been formed by the former Postmaster General, Gouin, in the 1870s, only members of the Ottawa elite were invited to join. Irwin was the managing director of the International Portland Cement Company. It was a piece of good news. He hoped that Italy's help would shorten the war.

The fishing trip was what he needed. Yesterday, he and Irwin had gone to Deer Lake, where he had caught over sixty red trout with his favourite fly lure. Last night the gang had a very pleasant evening playing cards and telling each other fish stories.

It was when he read the second telegram that Joseph asked him in alarm, "What's wrong?"

Borden handed him the telegram for Irwin to read. "I don't believe it. Nearly 1,200 passengers dead?"

"That is what Blount has written. A German submarine put two torpedoes into the *Lusitania* on Friday afternoon around two thirty. They were near the coast of Ireland when it happened. They're looking for survivors, but they found only seven hundred so far," Borden said as he felt his stress returning. "It's nothing less than cold bloody murder."

Irwin winced. "The bad news keeps coming."

Borden nodded sadly. "I'm still getting names added to the casualty lists."

"Nearly sixty-five hundred so far, the last I heard."

"That's about right, and more are being added daily."

"Is that why you formed the War Purchasing Commission?"

"I had very little choice in the matter. The Liberals have been raking us over the coals with the findings from the Boots Committee."

Irwin gave him a wry smile. "Who knew that Sam had eight thousand friends?"

Borden frowned in annoyance. "That and having one of my own MPs profiteering."

The Boots Committee had uncovered that the militia department had a patronage list of eight thousand approved contractors. Naturally, all of them were Conservatives. It had put him in an awkward position, since he actually had been trying to get rid of the patronage list ever since he was elected. It proved to be more difficult than he thought, since everyone said it was simply the way that things were done. "I'm getting Kemp to head the commission." Edward Kemp, MP for Toronto East, was a minister without portfolio in his cabinet. "I'm also appointing George Gault and Henri Lapointe to it."

"They're good men. The commission should save the government a lot of money," replied Irwin. Borden wondered for a moment if the commission would have an impact on Irwin's company profits. They were in the cement business, after all.

"I hope so. But some members of my caucus are unhappy about it."

Irwin snorted to indicate that it was politics as usual. "So what do you want to do? Stay or go?"

Borden paused to consider the question, as they had planned to go to the nearby Rice Lake. Part of him wanted to go back to work, but if he did he knew what was waiting for him. It was important that he got some rest. It would do him good, and the country needed him. "Let me get my rods and lures."

MAY 10, 1915
WOODS BUILDING, SLATER STREET, OTTAWA

"You're still here," stated Major-General Fiset as he stood in Gwatkin's office door dressed in his trench coat. The corners were encased in shadows, since the office light and the desk lamp didn't quite reach there.

Gwatkin gave him a tired smile as he glanced at the bulging briefcase that the deputy minister was carrying in his right hand. Fiset tapped the briefcase gently against his leg. He was bringing work home too. "The minister wants the 2nd Contingent to be equipped with the new Oliver equipment," Gwatkin stated as he pinched the bridge of his nose. He had started work at seven o'clock this morning. "I wanted to make sure that they actually got on board one of the cargo vessels."

He wasn't surprised to see Fiset grimace slightly. The likelihood that the updated Oliver equipment would suffer the same fate as the old Oliver was high. The modification was simply the addition of a canvas sack and improvements to the leather ammunition pouches. However, the main strappings were still made of leather, which hadn't fared well in the trenches. Sam managed to convince the cabinet to agree to it, he suspected mainly on the minister's claim that it was superior and cheaper than the Imperial webbing.

"I'm sure that we'll find room on one of the cargo vessels," Fiset said with a grin. "We've been planning it long enough."

Gwatkin gave him a slow nod. "When will the *Missanabie* disembark the 2nd Division HQ at Liverpool?"

"The other half of their HQ will be departing Montreal in five days. At least it isn't quite as chaotic as the first contingent's."

"Agreed, I would have preferred to have shipped them in February," replied Gwatkin as he leaned back in his chair.

"Couldn't be helped," Fiset said. "The War Office said they didn't have room for us."

The real reason, Gwatkin found out from a friend of his at the War Office, was that there simply wasn't enough space because of Kitchener's new armies. When they started moving to France, the Canadians could be sent over. They hadn't decided where they would be accommodated, but it wasn't likely to be Salisbury.

"Well, they finally settled in Shorncliffe," Fiset said. "Have you been there?"

"I'm afraid not," stated Gwatkin. "Sadly, General Carson's reports concerning the conditions at Shorncliffe are not favourable."

Fiset leaned against the doorframe. "I know Carson in his last message indicated that the War Office has stopped building huts and are keeping men under canvas."

"He did, didn't he," Gwatkin replied. The message resulted in Hughes sending a note stating that the poor conditions at Salisbury were having a detrimental effect on recruiting. It didn't seem to matter much to Hughes when it was pointed out to him that the Imperial troops were labouring under the same conditions.

Gwatkin frowned as he shifted papers on his desk. "I've got a request for tents here.... Ah, here it is. The War Office requests that the 2nd Contingent bring tents."

Fiset paused to consider. "We'll have to see what we can do. The 2nd Contingent has been short some of their major equipment. The minister has been in my office complaining about the truck contracts. They've been tied up in the subcommittee. They are arguing about which truck is the best for the CEF. Everyone has an opinion."

"I was under the impression that General Alderson had left his trucks behind for the 2nd Division?"

"Good point. I'll send a message to General Carson to find out what happened to them," Fiset said as he stopped to drop his briefcase on the floor and take a notebook from his inside pocket. "I'm hoping with the newly formed War Purchasing Commission that will improve our supply situation."

"Agreed," said Gwatkin. "Our current methods have not been very efficient."

"There's always room for improvements," Fiset remarked. Both men knew that the Boots Committee hung dangerously over their heads. The news so far from the committee had been damning.

"At least the order-in-council came through for acquiring sixty thousand rifles and bayonets for the militia."

"Good, current estimates indicate that we'll have 150,000 men in the field by the end of December, when the third and fourth become available. My concern is the ammunition situation. The supply of the Mark VII has not improved significantly despite our best effort."

"I'm afraid that the preliminary reports from Ypres on usage by our troops has exacerbated the shell situation. Our artillery used twelve thousand rounds in five days. The Shell Committee still is not meeting production requirements, although it has been rising."

"True, but my concern is the state of our 18-pounders. They are rated for twelve thousand rounds. I didn't expect them to reach that so soon. The CFA is still waiting for their equipment promised by the War Office."

First snapped his notebook shut. "According to the latest indicators, the 2nd's CFA won't arrive in England until August. I hope the equipment will be there by then."

"The shipping schedule is the problem. The Admiralty needs to free up the cargo liners and the escort vessels. They prefer that they sail singly or in pairs. A cruiser will meet them once they reach the designated rendezvous point to be escorted for the final leg of the voyage."

"It makes planning for their arrival at Shorncliffe difficult, since they don't know which units and the dates they will be arriving until the last minute."

"You can't really blame them, especially with what happened to the *Lusitania* last week. I'm sure that they're reviewing their operations," Gwatkin pointed out. The Admiralty had major concerns about large convoys.

"Unfortunately, you're correct," replied Fiset. "We got another gram from the War Office concerning Captain Janey and Lieutenant Sharpe." Gwatkin frowned as he recalled that last September Hughes had authorized Captain Janey to buy an aircraft for reconnaissance and artillery spotting. Janey had spent $5,000 buying a used Burgess-Dunne float aircraft from the US Navy. "It seems that they still have not been able repair their aircraft that was damaged on the voyage over."

"Let's clip their wings, shall we."

"I'll let the War Office know," Fist replied. "There's a bit of good news. I guess."

"What?"

"I received a cipher from London concerning the Ross Rifle Company. They don't have a problem with them supplying the Russian government with one point five million rifles if it does not impact their hundred thousand-rifle order."

"And our order of sixty thousand?" Gwatkin asked with a frown. "How did they get the contract in the first place?"

"It seems that a Ross company sales rep approached the Russian attaché in Washington with an offer, and they accepted."

"When you inform the minister, I'm sure that he will be pleased with the news."

"That he will be." Fiset nodded in agreement. "You're leaving shortly?"

"Once I clean the papers off my desk."

Fiset snorted in disbelief as he picked up his briefcase. Gwatkin didn't watch as Fiset disappeared down the hall.

CHAPTER 17

MAY 10, 1915
STEENWERCK

Samantha couldn't help noticing that the building that housed the Deputy Director of Medical Services of the Canadian division on No. 1 Rue d'Armentières was bustling with activity as her truck drove up to the main entrance. She hadn't heard of any new plans, but then she had spent most of the previous week with the wife of the mayor of Nieppe, Madame Vanuxeem. She had been gracious enough to offer her home for the sewing factory. They were producing face masks for the Canadians to help protect them from the poison gas that the Germans had used at Ypres. She had been so busy that she had missed the inspection by Surgeon-General Jones of the three field ambulances on his visit from London. She hadn't been one of the recipients of the gifts he had brought from the queen consort, Queen Alexandria.

When the truck stopped at the car park, she thanked the driver as she got out. Samantha retrieved the bundle wrapped in kraft paper and tied with twine. After asking several orderlies, she finally managed to find where Dr. Moore's tent was.

On her way to his tent, she wrinkled her nose when she saw several men digging a shallow latrine. She couldn't help pitying the poor men. She remembered vividly the latrine she and Major Creighton had inspected when they were at Valcartier. It seemed a long time ago. One thing she had to admit: the army took latrine duty very seriously. She had seen a recent memo from the First Army Surgeon-General concerning the proper use of a latrine trench. It had been brought to the general's attention that the men were not straddling the trench correctly when they were relieving themselves. The memo, several pages long, detailed the proper procedures that were to be followed. It even included graphics illustrating them. She was glad she wasn't one of the sanitation officers.

"Knock, knock," she said when she finally arrived at Dr. Moore's tent. The doctor looked up from his writing desk and smiled at Samantha. "Busy?" she asked.

"Just clearing up the correspondence that has piled up," he stated. He glanced at the bundle she was carrying. "Is that what I think it is?"

"Yes," Samantha replied as she placed the bundle on his desk. She untied the knots and removed the paper.

"Ah! They look very good," he said as he examined face masks similar to the one he regularly wore during surgery. In this case instead of thin cotton, it was made of a heavy muslin pad. "So how has the production been coming along?"

"The mayor's wife is a godsend. She managed to get twenty-five sewing machines into her home and fifty women working in shifts. These are the first batches. They are producing about seven hundred a day. We should have about three thousand for our men in a few days if our supplies last."

"I understand. We're seeing if we can't get additional supplies. The French and the Imperials are beginning to produce their own. The 27th got hit by gas recently, but they suffered minimal casualties."

Samantha sighed. "That's good to know."

"Any problems?"

"My French is pretty rusty, and those sewing machines make a real racket. The women are complaining that their feet ache after pedalling them for a couple of hours. But they aren't grousing too much since they appreciate earning the extra centime that we are paying them," she answered.

"Well, it's only temporary, until we developed a more permanent solution," Dr. Moore stated.

"Yes, sir," replied Samantha. She had enjoyed the challenge of getting the manufacturing up and running. "How long do think?" she asked; while she had enjoyed it, she still preferred nursing.

"Another week or two," he replied. "We've received orders that we are being assigned to the First Army."

"What are you going to do about the patients that are convalescing?" she asked.

Dr. Moore sighed. "We have about 150 that will be fit for duty in five days. If we can't bring them with us, we'll have to turn them over to one of the casualty clearing stations at Bailleul."

"Can't we find a more suitable place?"

"The CO is looking into it. But we won't have much time."

"What about me?" Samantha asked.

"You'll remain here for a week or two until the last of the face masks are completed. I'll make sure that orders will be sent for you to join us."

"Thanks. I appreciate that," replied Samantha.

MAY 12, 1915
CAMC HEADQUARTERS, 13 VICTORIA STREET, LONDON

"I, Jessie Brown Jaggard, do make oath that I will be faithful and bear true allegiance to his majesty King George the fifth, his heirs and successors in person, crown, and dignity, against all enemies, and will observe and obey all orders of his Majesty, his heirs and successors, and all general and officers set over me. So help me God," she declared with her left hand on the Bible and the right hand raised.

Matron Macdonald gave her a warm smile when a major, who was also a justice of the peace, said, "Please sign here and here." He indicated with a finger as he handed her a fountain pen. In the paragraph she noted that he had scratched out the *hes* in black ink and replaced them with *shes*.

Once she had signed he said, "Welcome to the Canadian Army Medical Corps."

"Thank you," replied Jaggard.

"If you have further need…." he asked Matron Macdonald.

"Not at the moment," she replied. "Thank you, Major."

"Madame," he said as he gave her a salute before leaving her office.

"Please have a seat, Matron Jaggard," she said, indicating one of the wooden chairs. Her office was a simple one with a wooden desk in front of beige-painted walls. Pinned to the wall behind her were two maps. The one on her left was a detailed map of Northern France and Belgium with markings indicating the location of the Canadian Division. The second one on the right was a map of Italy's lower boot, which also included Greece and Turkey. On her desk there was a wire in-basket on one corner and on the opposite corner there was a wicker out-basket. A candlestick black telephone sat beside the wicker basket. A couple of glass inkwells, lined up with a dark red vase filled with ostrich feathers, were placed in front of the blotter. "How was your voyage?"

"Pleasant, except for the boat drills," Jaggard replied sourly.

Macdonald chuckled. She had gone through the same drill when the contingent sailed to England last October.

"And the hotel?"

"The Thackeray Hotel is quite adequate," she answered. Macdonald acknowledged with a nod. She had instructed that rooms be booked for Matron Jaggard and the ninety-five nursing sisters that had accompanied her at the temperance hotel. She was well aware of the minister's views on alcohol. He hadn't been pleased that Lieutenant-General Alderson allowed wet canteens. That the hotel was directly across from the British Museum didn't hurt.

"Good, I'm pleased," replied Macdonald. "I'm glad that you're finally here. Your skills and experience will be invaluable." From what she had heard, the forty-two-year-old matron was a hard worker and had a keen interest in her nursing staff. She could have used her sooner. Jaggard had volunteered last fall and been accepted. However, due to personal circumstances she hadn't been available until now. Like her, Jaggard had received most of her nursing training in the States. She started at the Massachusetts General. She also had been the superintendent of nurses at the Morristown General Hospital and the University Hospital in Philadelphia until she resigned to marry her husband, Hebert Jaggard, a prominent railroad executive. She had one child, a son who was near military age.

"I'm ready to get to work," Jaggard replied.

"Good," replied Macdonald. "I'm afraid that you'll have to spend a few days here in London as we arrange transport. We've assigned you to the 3rd Stationary Hospital. They're part of the 2nd Canadian Division who arrived late last month. As of May 2nd they have been assigned to the Moore's Barracks Hospital at Shorncliffe."

"Not Salisbury Plain?"

"I'm afraid not. All the stories you heard about Salisbury are true. Though they are now suffering a drought. Finding sufficient potable water for the men is proving to be difficult," Matron Macdonald said with an ironic shrug. "Shorncliffe is now our main training base. The CO of the 3rd Hospital is Lieutenant-Colonel Casgrain. Do you know him?"

"I'm afraid not."

Macdonald shrugged. "While you are here, we'll give you a brief orientation and what we expect from you. Also, we're transferring some nurses from France to provide you with some experienced staff."

"I've read the newspaper reports. Were the casualties at Ypres that bad?"

"They were horrendous. We don't have enough nurses to meet the demand. The Belgians and the French have also put out calls for experienced nurses. We're supplying what we can. That's one of the reasons why we're bringing some of them back to England to give them some much-needed rest. The Imperials have requested nurses for Malta, to which I'm currently assigning some sisters. They are to ship in the next week or two."

When she saw Jaggard raise an eyebrow. "The War Office has opened a second front in the Dardanelles. Malta is home to their main hospitals in the Mediterranean, except for the bases at Alexandria."

"The Mediterranean!" Jaggard exclaimed.

"I know, we're a long way from home, aren't we?" Macdonald stated. Jaggard acknowledged with a knowing smile. Both she and Jaggard had similarities besides getting their nurse's training in the States. They were born within 120 miles of each other in Nova Scotia. Jaggard was raised in Wolfville, near the Bay of Fundy, while Macdonald was born in Bailey's Brook near the Northumberland Strait across from PEI. There was another prominent figure born in Wolfville, and Matron Jaggard knew him quite well, since they were cousins. His name was Sir Robert Borden

CHAPTER 18

MAY 14, 1915
ENGINEERING TENT, NIEPPE

Curiosity got the better of Captain Llewellyn when he passed one of the engineering tents on his way back to the 2nd Brigade HQ at Merris. The Canadian Division had moved to the Nieppe region of France for rest, recuperation, and rebuilding. Essentially, licking one's wounds — they had been pretty deep.

He had just come from another of Lieutenant-General Alderson's inspections. Alderson had come to praise the brigade for their performance during their battles at Ypres and to pin medals on the survivors. Llewellyn had seen some of the reports recommending Victoria Crosses for some of the men. The three that had stood out were machine gunners Lance Corporal Fredrick Fraser and Lieutenant Bellow from the 1st British Columbia, and Sergeant-Major Frederick Hall, who was killed as he tried to save wounded comrades under heavy fire. He had written recommendations that Sergeant Booth be awarded a Distinguished Conduct Medal. He had put Corporal Duval, Kershaw, and several others of the Fusiliers up for Mentions in Dispatches. They were going up the line for approval.

What had caused him to stop was the captain with the engineer's badge on his cap. He looked familiar. He was talking with a Winnipeg Grenadier lieutenant, one of the recent influx of replacements from Shorncliffe. They were standing beside a pile of empty jam tins spilling from burlap sandbags onto bales of guncotton.

The captain was of medium height, with a chiselled face and a premature grey moustache that was currently scowling. "Yes, I understand," he said in a patient tone.

"I'm just relaying the wishes of my CO," said the lieutenant.

"I said that I understood," snapped the captain, which caused the lieutenant's lips to thin. The officer gave the engineer a stiff salute and then gave Llewellyn the same courtesy before he marched away.

The captain continued to scowl when he demanded, "Can I help you with something?"

"Did you work the CPR line in northern Ontario?" Llewellyn asked.

The captain blinked and cocked his head as he stared at him. "Sure did...." The light finally came on. "You were the surveyor."

"Yes, and you were the engineer laying track," replied Llewellyn as he shook his hand. "We're a long way from home."

"Sure are. I'm Ry Tottman."

"James Llewellyn."

"That's right. Sorry about snapping at you. That young lieutenant got my goat."

"Oh?"

"Yeah, it seems that I made the mistake of calling our bombers 'grenadiers.' The Grenadiers didn't like it."

"Ah." Llewellyn nodded in understanding. The Winnipeg Grenadiers were understandably touchy how their unit's name was being bandied about.

When the captain again stiffened, Llewellyn glanced over, expecting the Grenadier lieutenant again, but instead he saw Brigadier-General Turner and Lieutenant-Colonel Garnet Hughes riding past. They returned the salutes that both captains gave them.

"He's on the outs with Alderson, isn't he?" remarked the engineer as they watched the senior officers' horses disappear.

"What makes you say that?" asked Llewellyn.

"Turner's brigade didn't come with its field ambulance or engineer company."

"I heard about that," replied Llewellyn. It was standard procedure that they accompany the brigade to provide medical and engineering services.

"You noticed they were on horses instead of riding around in a staff car?" While it sounded petty, he was sure that Turner had taken the lack of a motor vehicle as a deliberate slight. Currie and Mercer had been assigned one. A staff car was proving to be a time-saver for a busy general and his staff.

"Watch yourself!" the captain warned Llewellyn as a soldier nearly collided with them. Llewellyn stepped aside as the private carried a coil of barbed wire scraps into the tent. The captain continued, "The scuttlebutt is that both Turner and Currie's heads were on the chopping block."

"I heard that," replied Llewellyn as he watched the barbed wire man use a pair of shears to cut the scraps into smaller pieces. "Old Sam will have a fit when he finds out." At their level Alderson would need Sam

Hughes' approval to remove them. That was unlikely, since Turner was one of his favourites.

"Yeah, I heard that too. Currie's on the outs because he ordered a retreat three times. He then stayed in his dugout, never showing himself in the trenches."

"What the hell are you talking about?" demanded Llewellyn. "I saw him in the trenches."

"You did?"

"Yeah, with my own eyes."

"That's not what some of his men are saying."

"Are you talking about Lieutenant-Colonel Currie the CO of the 15th Battalion?" Llewellyn asked.

"You mean there are two of them?" the captain said in disbelief.

"I'm afraid so. Colonel John Currie is the CO of the 48th Highlanders." Lieutenant-Colonel John Allister Currie had been one of the four captains who had created the 48th Highlanders. The regiment had served in the Boer War, and he had been its CO when the regiment volunteered last August.

"Well, one of them needs to change their names, otherwise there's going to be trouble," the captain stated.

Llewellyn didn't bother to inform the captain that Currie had already changed his name from "Curry" to "Currie." And from what he was hearing about J.A. Currie's performance during the Saint-Julien battle, it was likely he would be sent home soon.

Changing the subject, Llewellyn asked, "You're busy with the jam tins?"

The captain nodded. "Orders from the Division. We need to make as many bombs that we can. We've set up a Ford line. You want to take a look?"

"Sure, I can learn a thing or two for next time."

"You made some during the fighting?"

"Yeah, they got the job done, but were not very reliable."

The engineer grunted an acknowledgement. "Not surprising. Mine are better, but until we get manufacturers to come up with something, we have to make do." When he saw the men had slowed down to listen in on his conversation, he barked, "Who told you you can take a break? Get back to work!"

The process of making the jam tin hand grenades were pretty simple.

The men would fill the tin with scrap metal, in this case cut-up pieces of barbed wire, then stuff guncotton into the centre of the tin. A lid, centre-punched and fitted with a fuse cord, would be placed on top and wrapped with some thin wire to keep the contents fixed inside.

Llewellyn picked up a completed one and hefted the weight. "It looks good. Three-second fuse?"

"Yeah, it seems when you light the fuse, the men want to get rid of it rather quick."

Llewellyn chuckled mirthlessly. "I know. It happened to me a couple of times. The Boche tossed them back at us. I lost a couple of good men because the fuse was too long. Have you tested them yet?"

"Sure have, the men are getting a great charge out of them."

"Good," Llewellyn replied. "They look very good. I think we are going to need them."

The latest rumours were that General Haig would be launching an attack in the next few weeks. If they were true, they were going to need every one of them.

MAY 18, 1915
65TH ARTILLERY, NIEPPE

"Oh, shit!" swore acting Sergeant Ryan.

"What's the matter?" asked Lieutenant Haddon Tait, who was trying hard not to appear nervous. The officer from Swift Current had arrived a week before, one of the replacements from the reserve brigade in England. He still had the spit and polish from the Shorncliffe training depot. He was rather disapproving of the sandbags that Ryan had wrapped around his ankles to keep the mud out of his boots. It had been raining intermittently all day, but the observation post that they had set up near the Orchard was relatively dry. Private Craine, manning the telephone, the third man in their three-man team, had a sandbag draped across his shoulders to give him an additional layer of warmth. Even though it was May, the weather was chilly and damp.

"Take a look," said Ryan as he pointed to his left. When the lieutenant glanced in the direction, he indicated four extended lines of men, fifty yards apart, moving toward the German lines.

"Are they crazy?" the lieutenant exclaimed. "Don't they know about the ditches?"

The muddy field in front of a small copse of trees they had been observing for most of the day was pocked by water-filled shell holes and draining ditches that meandered through the featureless terrain.

"Not if they have the same maps that we do, they don't," answered Ryan with a sinking feeling. Why hadn't they done a reconnaissance first? They should have known that the maps were wrong. Correcting them was one of the tasks that Captain Masterley had assigned to them when he called them to his billet at five this morning.

"Reporting as ordered," the lieutenant had said as Ryan watched the officer salute the captain.

"Lieutenant," the captain replied after he acknowledged him and Private Craine with a nod. "I will be sending you into the forward lines as a FOO for the battery."

"Yes, sir," the lieutenant said eagerly. Paul had been with the captain long enough to recognize the slight embarrassment that had been caused by the lieutenant's enthusiasm. A lot of that had been lost in the last few weeks. They had gotten some rest since being assigned to Lieutenant-General Haig's First Army's reserve. It had given them time to reorganize and replace men and equipment. While they had become more serious, the 65th's morale was undiminished. Ryan watched Tait turn his head toward the sound of an artillery shell landing nearby. The Boche were retaliating to the First Army's bombardment of their trenches. When the lieutenant's head turned back to them, he noticed that neither he nor the captain had turned their own heads.

"Good, I need to brief you before you head for the observation post. The 1st Canadian Brigade is going to attack trenches N.14 to M.10 starting at eleven o'clock tonight." He handed the lieutenant a map and continued. "General Turner's objective is to gain a foothold, and he will be using his bombers to clear the nearby trenches.

"We're to support his attack. We will be planning to defend the K.5 trenches that General Currie will be attacking." Ryan had noticed that the lieutenant was engrossed with the map. When he glanced up to Masterley, the captain gave him a smile. "Problem?"

"Sir, there's something wrong with this map," he had said, showing it to the captain.

"You noticed," Masterley replied.

"Yes, sir, the same symbol is being used to indicate hedges, ditches, and tracks." When Captain Masterley raised an eyebrow, the lieutenant said sheepishly, "I'm a surveyor's apprentice."

"Did you notice anything else about the map?"

After he had examined the map for a few minutes, he whistled. "South is at the top."

"Well done. Unfortunately, this is the only map that is available. As you have noticed, there are questions concerning the accuracy of some of the landmarks. One of the tasks that you will be performing is surveying the immediate area in front of your observation post. We need the info to lay and register our guns."

The lieutenant nodded.

"We'll need them before we are to start the bombardment at 5:00 p.m. this afternoon. It will be a slow, deliberate fire at the New House. The 5-inch guns will fire at trench M.10 to reduce German resistance. The 4.5-inch will target M.10 to N.14. The 18-pounders will clear the obstacles and wire in front of the New House. When the assault begins, we will drop our rate to slow fire.

"Now that you know what your tasks are, get to it," Masterley had ordered.

"If we can see them," said Paul now as he put his binoculars on the men. Some of them began to cluster together in one of the shell holes as they tried to seek cover when a German machine gun opened up. A few had only taken a few steps before they stumbled and fell. Even with the spurts of wet dirt around them, they didn't make any further movement.

"Where the hell is that machine gun?" cursed the lieutenant as he scanned the field.

Paul continued to watch. He saw a squad pause at a ditch. One of the men slipped on the mud near the edge and fell in with a splash. A couple of his comrades leaped in after him, but the water was up to their necks. They didn't try jumping across, since it was too wide and they didn't have any bridging equipment.

"Get on the phone quick," the lieutenant ordered. Craine began cranking the phone.

It was too late. German heavies started landing among the Montrealers.

"The poor buggers," moaned the lieutenant.

Paul didn't look away as the explosions tore the men apart.

MAY 20, 1915
2ND BRIGADE, K.5 TRENCH, FESTUBERT

"Father, can you bless my shovel?" Captain Llewellyn overheard Sergeant Duval ask Father Stoats.

"You want me to bless a shovel?" asked an incredulous Father Stoats.

"Why not!" Brigadier-General Currie jumped in. "It's holey, isn't it?"

Llewellyn nearly laughed, since Father Stoats was stuck not knowing what to say. The men in the Fusiliers work party chuckled politely, not only because the jest was made by the general (you had to laugh politely when a general attempted to make a funny), but because it was true.

The shovel that Duval held did have a hole in it. It was one of the innovations that Major-General Hughes had introduced. Officially, it was known as the Macadam Shield Shovel. The most polite term that the men called it was the Hughes shovel. Llewellyn was surprised that the corporal was using it, since it weighed five pounds. Five pounds didn't sound like much. But your arms tired in a hurry after carrying it all day then throwing dirt for several hours. It wasn't that bad a shovel if the dirt was dry. Digging in waterlogged trenches was a bit of a problem. The hole, designed for a soldier to fire his rifle through, poured water, spraying the men as they slung mud over their shoulders.

"What are you doing with that shovel, by the way?" demanded the general. "I thought we had replaced them all when we left Salisbury."

"These were the only ones that were available in stores," replied Duval.

Llewellyn watched as Currie inspected the rest of the work party that was standing in the communication trench. The Fusiliers were assigned to help consolidate the K.5 trench after the 10th Battalion captured it. The men carried picks, shovels, sandbags, coils of barbed wire, stakes, and wooden planks, which would be used to construct obstructions to block any German counterattack. They were waiting for the order to move forward.

Currie snorted. "Carry on."

"Yes, sir," replied Sergeant Duval as he saluted.

Llewellyn gave the sergeant an amused head-shake as he passed Duval, following the general. Duval returned it with a shrug.

143

About a hundred yards down the trench, they were forced to duck into a dugout to allow stretcher bearers to pass. They were trying to hurry, but their boots kept slipping in the mud. The dugout was the standard pattern. It was dug into the side of the trench, where the men could get out of the rain. Since it was filled with eight men and their equipment, it was cramped. Lying on boxes of .303 ammunition stacked in the middle was a 1914 model Colt machine gun. Llewellyn was surprised to see that attached to its muzzle was a Northover flash absorber. It was designed by a Winnipeg gunsmith, Harry Robert Northover, to hide the flash and dampen the sound of the machine gun, making it more difficult to spot. The men had been squatting silently, smoking cigarettes. They all wore a couple of sandbags draped across their shoulders. They rose to their feet when they saw the brigadier-general enter.

Currie waved them down. "At ease, men."

"We're ready to give them hell, General. Just give us the word."

"You'll have it soon," replied Currie. When the last of the stretcher bearers passed he said, "Good luck and give them hell."

It took them another ten minutes to get to the 10th Battalion's command post. When they entered, they could tell from Major Percy Guthrie's face that the attack had not gone well.

"How bad is it?" Currie asked the acting commander of the 10th Battalion. The thirty-year-old New Brunswicker was of medium height with a haggard, rounded, moustached face. He had been given command of the 10th after the loss of Lieutenant-Colonel Boyle and most the battalion's senior officers. Nearly two weeks before, the battalion had received eighteen officers and 236 men as reinforcements to replace the losses they had suffered at Ypres. The battalion still hadn't been up to its full strength when they were given their latest assignment. Major Guthrie had placed his A, B, and C companies in the fire trenches with D company as support.

"Most of Lieutenant Tozer's bombers didn't get out of the communication trench. They just died in their lines when the machine gun opened up," the major said bitterly. "Tozer has been severely wounded. I ordered a halt to the attack. I saw no point in losing more good men."

Llewellyn could tell that Currie hated being right. He had come out a couple of hours earlier to take a look at the battlefield. One of the problems he had was identifying the location of the K.5 trench. The map had a circle to indicate where it was supposed to be. There was a redoubt there that jutted out in front of the trenches. It was a strong point, bristling with machine guns, constructed out of concrete with sandbags on top. They had assumed it was the K.5.

When Currie reached his headquarters at Rue De L'Epinette, he had gotten on the phone with the Division HQ and told them they needed to delay the attack. He informed them that it was impossible to move from the K.1 and K.3 trenches without being seen. Once the work parties had done their work, they would be able to deploy more securely. The general's face was grim when he hung up.

The latest rumours were that General Haig wasn't pleased with Alderson. He had been given the Imperial 47th Division as well as the Canadian Division to carry out the attacks. The new force had been named *Alderson's Force*. It seemed to be Imperial practice to name temporary formations after their commanders. Just the day before, the *Barter Force*, named after Major-General Charles Barter and composed of the 47th and the Imperial 1st Division, had been dissolved. Llewellyn knew that the Imperials were engaged in a major attack near Vimy to help relieve pressure on the French, but he wasn't privy to those plans. The word from Division HQ was that the attack had to go as planned. The plan had been that Lieutenant Tozer's bombers would lead the attack, followed by the 10th Battalion's A company.

"I agree. No point in losing more good men," replied Currie. "But we still need to take K.5."

"Yes, General," replied Guthrie with a note of resignation.

Now, Currie turned in the general direction of K.5, although he couldn't see anything at this time of night. He turned to Captain Llewellyn and ordered, "Send the scouts out. I want reconnaissance done of the terrain between us and the K.5 trench, and let's prepare a proper plan. I want to launch another attack tomorrow morning to take that trench."

"Yes, General," both men replied.

"Good, let's get at it," said Currie, dismissing them.

MAY 21, 1915
2ND BRIGADE, K.5 TRENCH, FESTUBERT

Captain Llewellyn was standing in a trench looking over the top with a pair of periscope binoculars. Beside him, Brigadier-General Currie was doing the same with a similar pair. Llewellyn could see the tension and anxiety in his face as he waited for the 10th Battalion to renew their assault on K.5.

Llewellyn passed the glasses to Lieutenant-Colonel Tennison, who was standing beside him. As Tennison took them, the captain examined the shallow trench with walls built up with sandbags so they could stand upright. They couldn't dig deep because of the water table. This section had been picked because it was still intact, despite German efforts to shell it. It had been their original line until they had withdrawn. Other sections weren't so lucky. They were now simply holes in the ground.

He glanced at the sky. Based on the current light, they had maybe an hour of daylight left. It had been a long, frustrating day. Currie had wanted the 10th to attack at 5:00 a.m. this morning after a two-hour bombardment had chewed up the wire defences and had taken out the German machine guns. Delays resulted in their attack launching at this late hour. The 2nd Divisional Artillery had been pounding the German lines for several hours now.

"The bombardment doesn't appear to have had much of an effect," stated Currie.

"I know," replied Llewellyn. "They've been using shrapnel."

Currie grunted an acknowledgement. The shrapnel shell had been designed to disperse a cone of steel balls to take out massed infantry. It had limited effect on fortified positions, except for forcing the enemy to keep their heads down.

When Lieutenant-Colonel Tennison tapped him on the shoulder, he passed the binoculars back to him. When Llewellyn peered again over the trench, he spotted the first elements of the 10th emerging from their trenches.

"General, the 10th is on the attack," said Llewellyn.

"I see them," replied Currie as he stiffened.

Llewellyn knew well the plan that Brigadier- General Currie and Major Guthrie had prepared after the major visited Brigade HQ several times before the assault. Llewellyn had supplied them as much intelligence as he could from the reports he had received from other scouts and Major Guthrie's patrols. The terrain was still sketchy. They finally decided the attack would be led by the 1st Brigade's grenade company. A and B companies would lead the assault. One company would assault the K.4 trench while the other would take out K.5. One of the company's section would be using the same communication trench from the previous night.

In the fading light Llewellyn saw the rest of the two companies emerge as planned. They had made exits at various spots in the overhead parapets and wire. It didn't take long for the Huns to spot them as they formed up. Men started falling into the mud as the Boche guns opened up again. Here and there sections took cover in shell holes. When they tried to clamber out to press the attack, machine guns swept them down.

Everyone in the trench was silent. Llewellyn barely heard the whispered, "Damn!"

MAY 22, 1915
2ND BRIGADE HEADQUARTERS, FESTUBERT

The third time's the charm, Captain Llewellyn thought as he stood in the same trench where he had witnessed the ill-fated 10th Battalion attack on K.5. They did somehow manage the capture one of the nearby trenches, but they had to endure constant counterattacks from the Germans who were trying to reclaim it.

Despite their all their efforts, the 10th's attack had been a complete failure.

That was why he was again standing in the same trench with Brigadier-General Currie and his senior staff. Their orders were clear: they had to take K.5. That message had been delivered this morning when General Haig visited Lieutenant-General Alderson's HQ. The captain hadn't been privy to the actual conversations, but the rumours were that Haig hadn't been pleased that *Alderson's Force* didn't capture the trench. Haig then stripped Alderson of the 47th Division, dissolving the force. It might have been a blow to Alderson's ego, but then it had only existed for four days.

"What's this?" Lieutenant-Colonel Tuxford had asked earlier this afternoon as he pointed at the revision marks on the sketch map. Llewellyn had looked up at the forty-five-year old former rancher from Moose Jaw, a tall man, just short of six feet, with a light complexion, brown hair, and blue eyes.

"Major Guthrie had confirmed that the J1 to J3 trenches were actually ditches before he was wounded," he replied.

"How's the major doing?"

"Swearing, but he'll recover," replied Brigadier-General Currie. "As far the 10th..." Currie had left the rest unsaid. The 10th had been mauled, again, suffering nearing 250 casualties. That was why Tuxford and the 5th Battalion had been selected to take K.5.

"Did he indicate how wide they were?" Tuxford asked.

"About ten feet or so was the estimate," replied Llewellyn.

"Shallow or deep?"

"They're deep. You'll need something to cross over," replied the captain.

"How accurate is this?" asked Tuxford. Most of their losses had been due to the bad maps.

"We've been surveying the terrain," replied Llewellyn. "They're as accurate as we can make them in the allotted time."

Tuxford frowned. He was looking for any advantage that he could get, especially since the Germans were expecting their attack.

"I'll get one of my subalterns to gather as many ladders as he can to get us across."

"So we have agreed to the basic attack plan then," Currie stated. Everyone in the room nodded in agreement, although some still had reservations, especially when the first two had failed. "Let's review the plan so everyone is clear on what needs to be done.

"The 5th's A and B companies under Major Edgar will launch the attack at two thirty tomorrow morning. Your men will need to be at the start line at the K.4 trench at one thirty."

"My men are billeted nearby at the Orchard getting some rest," replied Tuxford. "I'll assign Lieutenant Madoc platoons to gather as many ladders as possible. We'll use them to get us across."

"As long as he gets it down by one thirty."

"Yes, sir," said Tuxford. He continued, "The companies will form in two lines, with two platoons from each company in the front. The right section will provide bayonet men to protect the bombing company, who will be attacking from the communication trenches.

"A FOO will accompany them and will direct artillery support once the trench has been taken. The two Colts will then be brought forward. I'm fairly certain that the enemy will not be pleased with our presence." A couple of men chuckled, but mainly a few grins flashed under the moustaches.

"Once your men have taken the trench, send up three flares," said Currie. "If it's daylight, use the blue flags. Get the work parties in as fast as possible and the water parties to bring in as much of the supplies as they can. I want your men to be ready when they counterattack."

Llewellyn glanced over the trench with the binoculars. With the half-moon and the cloud cover, they couldn't see much. It had been relatively quiet until the attack was launched, and gunfire flashes sparkled in the night, punctuated by bright grenade flashes. Everyone waited anxiously for the news.

Around quarter after four, three flares lit up above K.5.

Llewellyn felt a sense of relief that it had finally been taken. In the dawn light, he could see that Currie was worried about the butcher's bill. A few minutes later, German artillery started to land on top of K.5. Currie shook his head. "I think we will need more artillery to keep the Germans off our backs once we have taken a trench."

"Yes, General," Llewellyn replied. "You can't have too much artillery."

CHAPTER 19

"It's getting stiff," remarked Sergeant Duval as he pulled on the Ross's bolt.

"Can you manage a few more rounds?" asked Captain Llewellyn as he watched the sergeant struggle to open the breech. The round finally ejected, to join its fellows that littered the wooden test bench and the ground.

"Sure," replied Duval once he cleared the breech. He fired a couple more rounds, then it froze for good. He glanced sourly at Llewellyn then used a wooden club to pound the breech open.

"So that's round 1,872," Llewellyn said as he placed a mark on the test page in a letter size notebook.

"I concur," replied the major, standing beside him. The officer was in his early thirties, with wire-framed glasses. His ordnance insignia gleamed in the early morning sunlight. He glanced farther down the range at the other rifles that were being tested today: three Ross MKIIIs and two Ross MKIIs.

Llewellyn turned his head when someone behind him cursed. Ten yards away, a bank of test benches had been set up for the Lee-Enfields. The private that had been firing had encountered problems as well. He and a sergeant were examining the rifle's magazine. "It could be a weak spring," he overheard the sergeant say to the private, "that could be what's causing it to jam."

In one sense Llewellyn was pleased that the Lee-Enfield was having similar problems to the Ross. The task he had been assigned was exceedingly dull. Each rifle had to be examined prior to the test. Precise measurements had to be taken of the breech bolt, the chamber, and the muzzle. Any abnormality was noted. During each stage of the five thousand-round endurance testing, the rifles were examined to ensure that the weapons were functional and still safe for the operators. The last sequence resulted in the sights requiring retightening, since they had come loose. Cracks were appearing in the wooden stock under the barrel as well.

"That seems to be the second rifle that has failed," stated the major as he looked up from his pad.

"Yes, I know," replied Llewellyn. He flipped pages until he found the previous testing report. "Hmm. It seems to have failed with the British ammo."

"Really?" questioned the major as he glanced at his test reports. "You appear to be correct. Let me look at the cartridges." The major lifted the lid off one of the ammunition boxes that were stacked safely out of range of the flying brass. There were four piles organized by manufacture. Variations in .303 rounds by the different factories could impact the weapon's performance. The major lifted the lid off a box with *Dominion Arsenal, Quebec, Canada,* stencilled on its side and pulled out a couple of rounds. He went to the next stack and did the same.

He lifted them and then peered at them intently. The major then rolled them in his hands. "Offhand, they appear to meet the specifications." He stepped back toward Duval's bench. He reached down, picked up a spent shell, and examined the casing. He frowned then said, "I think we need to do a metallurgical test to determine the quality of the brass."

"You think there are differences?" asked the captain.

"We don't know until we do a test," said the major.

His attention was drawn to troops on the other side of the Saint-Omer range. They were from the camp located on the hill behind him. The range had been built on leased French farmland. It was four hundred yards long, with targets that popped up when a wire was pulled. There were two wings that were offset from each other, although they pointed to the same targets. It was designed to help soldiers practice overlapping angles of fire so that two units could provide each other with mutual fire support.

There were a number of other ranges in the Saint-Omer area. Several officers that he had temporarily billeted with on this assignment were attending the machine gun school, where they were learning the same topics that he had been taught at Hayling Island. He had taken the course last December and learned about direct and indirect fire in tactical situations, barrage fire, working fire problems using trench maps, night firing, and the ever popular how to administer a machine gun unit.

He'd rather be on the course. It was fun squeezing the trigger and emptying a full belt on the range. At least no one was shooting at you.

But no, he had been asked by Brigadier-General Currie to supervise the testing to determine the suitability of the Ross as a combat weapon.

At Ypres, there had been a significant number of reports that the rifle had jammed. His had performed flawlessly, as did those of most of those of the men he commanded as they held off the German assaults. However, in other units it had been a different story. They had lost confidence in the Ross. About a third of the brigade's five thousand men had discarded their rifles in favour of Lee-Enfields, which were easy to find since they littered the battlefield.

Orders had been issued that the British rifles were to be returned to the Imperials. Many had been slow in complying. Some muttered, quietly, that it would be taken from their cold, dead hands. Which many were starting to feel was more likely if they used the Ross.

Unofficially, he had been tasked to ensure that the testing was conducted fairly, although Currie had doubts about the Ross's efficiency. But he didn't want the British to skew the results against the Ross simply because they didn't like it. Too much of the Canadian equipment had already been replaced by the equivalent British pattern.

Llewellyn couldn't help the feeling that he was simply going through the motions, and the decision had already been made. Still, he was determined to ensure that the testing was conducted fairly. In either case, it wasn't his decision to make.

To be honest, he was glad that it wasn't, because if the findings went against the Ross, he was certain Sam Hughes' screams of indignation would be heard across the Atlantic.

JUNE 6, 1915
FINANCE MINISTER'S OFFICE, EAST BLOCK, PARLIAMENT HILL,
OTTAWA

"So what do you think?" Borden asked.

"I don't think that it would be wise," answered White, who was sitting behind his desk.

"Oh?" Borden had dropped by White's office on the second floor of the East Block. The Finance Department had offices scattered throughout the building. They would have liked to have consolidated on the second floor, but with all the other departments, it had proved to be difficult. Some of the offices couldn't be moved since they were responsible for the vaults in the basement of the building that contained the government's gold supply.

"You'll be out of the country for what, nearly two months? If we weren't at war, there wouldn't be any question that you should go to England. And you have to consider how the Liberals are hammering us. Besides that, who will replace you while you're gone? Hughes?"

Borden snorted. He then rubbed his moustache absentmindedly. "George sent me a message that Bonar Law requested my presence."

"It's risky. Look at what happened to the *Lusitania*."

"You do have a point," Borden conceded. "Laura wouldn't happy with me going."

"That's as good an argument as any."

"Okay," conceded Borden. "So you're in agreement concerning the Australian trade proposals?"

"Yes. If it isn't advantageous for us, then I agree we shouldn't be doing it."

"Good. We'll write up our response and send it to them. Are you working with the income tax proposal?"

"Yes, we are. Our revenues for May were nearly the same as last year's. Seven million for Customs and $1.8 million for Excise. We're only down for $300,000 from last year. We need extra revenue to feed those men you and the governor general reviewed recently."

Borden knew that he was referring to the 49th Battalion that had marched on Parliament Hill a couple of days before. "They were a fine body of men."

"That they were," White replied. Both men knew that some of those fine young men would not be coming back.

Borden scratched his head. "I wish there was another way to raise money."

White shrugged. "Some of my officials are looking into plans for a subscription."

"Would there be sufficient interest for one?"

"I really don't know," White replied with a shrug. "They're suggesting beginning with $50 million to start with to see the public's reaction."

"It might something to consider. We can discuss that when I get back," said Borden as he rose to his feet. "Now, I have to speak with Hughes. The duke complained to me about him again."

"Good luck."

"Yeah. Maybe I should take him with me when I go."

"That would make my day," White said with a pleased look. "Two months peace and quiet."

JUNE 10, 1915
NIEPPE

"Were you drunk when your rifle butt was damaged?" demanded Captain Llewellyn, testing the private standing at attention in front of him. He wanted to see if the man made up an excuse to avoid the hammer that was going to fall on him.

"No, sir," replied Private Olsen, a twenty-two-year-old from Pictou with close-cropped hair and a jagged scar running down his left cheek that marred his baby face. The cap under his left arm displayed the Richmond Fusiliers badge. Llewellyn wasn't familiar with the private, since he was a reinforcement after he had left the Fusiliers. He did look sober. His brown eyes were clear and bright. But the story of how the rifle was rendered inoperable matched the colour of his eyes. Not the bright part.

Well, he was bright enough not to admit to being drunk. It would have made matters worse.

"You testified that you were sitting on a fence when your Ross slipped from your hands, falling on the macadam road, damaging the rifle butt," he stated, reading from the incident report before him.

"Yes, sir. That's what happened."

"Bullshit," interjected Sergeant McCormick, the Fusiliers' armourer.

"You have something to add to the inquiry?" the captain asked McCormick.

"Yes, Captain. There's no way that a fall would have caused that kind of damage." He pointed to the gouged metal plate that was dislocated from the walnut stock. Cracks of unpainted wood radiated toward the trigger guard. "He had to deliberately struck the butt against something with awful lot of force to break it," he said as he glared at the private. The sergeant disliked having his rifles abused.

"Would you like to change your story?" asked Captain Llewellyn.

"It was like I said," Olsen replied, then added, "Sir." The private was sticking doggedly to his story.

Llewellyn turned to Sergeant Duval, who was standing beside the private. "Did you witness the incident?"

The sergeant shook his head. "I was on fatigue duty when Private Olsen reported it."

"Hmm," replied the captain as he flipped a sheet in the report. He raised an eyebrow and glanced up at the sergeant. "Your section seems to have a lower than normal replacement rate."

"I wasn't aware of that," replied the sergeant. "You need to keep your tools in good shape."

"Quite!" Llewellyn replied with a slight grin. The sergeant was many things, but an abuser of his equipment wasn't one of them.

Llewellyn turned his attention back to the private. "Did you have any problems with your Ross prior to this?"

"The action was stiff, and it had jammed a number of times," replied Olsen reluctantly.

"Did you bring it to the attention of the armourer?"

"I did."

"And?"

He hesitated and then said with a bit of heat, "Nothing was done!"

Llewellyn glanced over at the armourer, who had the decency to blush. "It was on my list."

"I see," grunted the captain. "I suppose you've heard rumours that the Ross is being replaced."

"News to me." Olsen shrugged. He couldn't help himself as he blurted, "Are they?"

Caught you, you liar, thought the captain. He had a fairly good idea what had happened. The private had deliberately cracked his Ross so that he would be first in line for a Lee-Enfield. The men had heard the rumours that Brigadier-General Currie was planning on replacing the Ross.

That problem needed to be nipped in the bud before it got out of hand. Besides, the rifle was government property. And that had been his thankless job ever since he got stuck with it. It served him right for arriving late to the meeting to find out that he had volunteered. The government expected that the rifle be returned in the same condition that it had been issued. With, of course, the normal expected wear and tear. If the rifle had suffered damage, it needed to be documented and accounted for. Someone needed to be charged for the repairs. Manufacturing defects meant that the Ross Company would pay for it. Battle damage and accidents the government would pay. If there were evidence of mistreatment and abuse, the man to whom the rifle was assigned to would be docked.

Most of the problems that Llewellyn had seen up to now were such things as the rifle not being seated properly in the bed and small pieces of stock missing or cracking after firing. In one case, two riders collided and their rifles were damaged after their horses stepped on them. Some were the result of shrapnel and bullets striking the weapon. Blowback from bad ammunition was another one.

"You seem to have a good record up to now," stated Llewellyn. "So I will take it easy on you this time."

"Yes, sir."

"You'll be docked a week's pay to repair the Ross and one week of Field Punishment No. 2. Dismissed!"

The private's shoulders dropped slightly at the verdict. "Sergeant McCormick will issue you a new Ross to replace the one you damaged." He definitely wasn't happy with that bit of news.

"Next!"

The private looked as if the captain had passed a life sentence on him as he made his way out of the tent. The captain didn't bother to let him know that Brigadier-General Currie was planning on replacing the Ross. It was unofficial, so it needed to be kept quiet, for now.

JUNE 13, 1915
GIVENCHY

When the sunlight to the entrance of his dugout was blocked, Captain Llewellyn looked up from the small desk that was made from a couple of overturned crates with several duckboards on top. He put out a hand, and Sergeant Duval put a sketch map in it.

"Did you check this against the maps that we were given?" Llewellyn asked. He was impressed by its quality. It had been done by a fine hand.

"Yes, Cap, the Imperial maps here are pretty good. Not the shitty maps they gave us at Festubert," Duval replied as he shifted the rifle slung over his left shoulder.

Llewellyn nodded in agreement as he examined the trench map that the scouts had drawn of the Givenchy sector. The Canadian Division had been reassigned to the First Army and were given responsibility for a small trench sector that ran through the battered village of Givenchy-lès-la-Bassée. It had seen some heavy fighting last December, and what was left standing were frames of wood, stones, and bricks. At least the captain's feet were relatively dry here. The trenches were on a slight rise above the enemy, which helped hide some of their activities from the Hun observers. This time around, the Canadian Division had decided to create their own maps. There were plenty of men like Captain Llewellyn who had surveying experience, so what the brigades had been doing was sending scouts out surveying No Man's Land to see what obstacles they would face, what the enemy trenches were like, where the fortified positions were, and where the damn machine guns were located. He had set up an office near the trenches to collate the reports that were coming in.

"Good, I'll get these up to General Currie," stated the captain. "I want you boys to take a look at this section here." He indicated on the map.

"Yes, Cap," Duval acknowledged.

Llewellyn frowned when his eyes fell on Duval's Ross. "I thought that you were supposed to get rid of that."

The corporal tightened his grip on the leather sling. "She's a good rifle. I want to keep her."

The entire division was finally being re-equipped with Lee-Enfields. The preliminary test report that he had prepared might have had some influence on the decision. But then Currie had developed a dislike for the weapon, and he wanted it gone. Still, he wouldn't have gotten his way if Lieutenant-General Alderson and General Haig hadn't wanted it replaced as well. They had used the rationale that some of the Canadians in the division had thrown away the Ross in favour of the Lee-Enfield. There were many in the division who felt that was just an excuse. The Imperials had replaced nearly all the Canadian-made equipment. True, some of the Canadian equipment was bad, but then some of the British equipment wasn't any better. One thing the captain was grateful for was that he was on this side of the Atlantic when Sam Hughes finally found out.

"We're only keeping them for the snipers," Llewellyn pointed out.

"Okay. I'm a sniper," he replied.

Llewellyn laughed. "Get out of here and get back to work."

"Sure, Captain," Duval said as he turned. Before he exited he paused to ask, "We're going over soon?"

"We're not, but the 1st Brigade will," he answered. "You saw them dragging three 18-pounders to Duck's Bill?"

When they were attached to the 4th Corps, they were assigned a thousand yards of trenches, which needed only one brigade to man. The line ran from Givenchy to Aubers Ridge. Duck's Bill jutted out toward the Huns' lines. There was only seventy-five yards of separation between them. Other areas were five hundred yards apart.

"Yeah, they had put rubber tires on the wheels. Makes them real quiet. They're to take out the machine guns."

"That's the plan," the captain replied. "I can't tell you much, but I can tell you we're going to try to hold their noses." The Imperial 7th and 51st divisions were going to attempt to pierce the German front line. The Canadian Division was to keep an eye on the Germans and protect the Imperial flanks if the Huns counterattacked. The decision was made that a good defence was an offence. So Brigadier-General Mercer's 1st Brigade would launch an attack. For a change they were given plenty of time to prepare. The 2nd Brigade would not be directly involved, since they were tunnelling under No Man's Land. They had filled the tunnel with three thousand pounds of ammonal. It was to be detonated to clear the trenches for the 1st Brigade's attack.

"How's the German wire?" asked Llewellyn. The Division's artillery had been using the 18-pounders' shrapnel shells to cut the wire.

"Waste of shells," replied Duval with a shake of his head. "When we stop firing, they push new coils of the stuff over top of their trench."

"Good to know. I'll past that bit along."

Both men knew what the wire meant.

CHAPTER 20

Paul was shaving when he spotted Captain Masterley in the small hand mirror he was using. The straight razor was cold as he scraped off the morning stubble. No surprise, since he didn't have any hot water or shaving cream to soften the previous night's growth. After he splashed his face to rinse, he was rather pleased that he hadn't nicked himself. It was very easy with a straight razor.

The captain nodded in approval when he saw Paul's jacket with the newly sewn sergeant stripes on it. He liked his men to look sharp. He ran his eyes over the morning shift that was checking the ammo stocks. Others were repairing some of the screens and nets they were using to blend in with the hedges they were parked beside. The captain also gave the guns a critical eye.

"How are things going?" he asked when Paul put on his forge cap.

"Everything is looking good," he replied. "We should be ready in time."

"Well, we are going to have to," the captain stated. "Orders have been changed."

"They have?" said Paul. "Why am I not surprised?" When the captain gave him a sharp look, Paul informed him, "We heard rumours that there were problems with the tunnel that the Imperials were digging."

"Where'd you hear that?" demanded the captain.

"It's common knowledge in the estaminets. Even the servers were talking about it."

"Shit," replied the captain in disgust. "I'll have to inform HQ."

"They just called with the all-clear," said Paul. For the last three days they had been bombarding the enemy trenches, starting at 8:00 a.m., after they had been given the word that the 1st Brigade was safely out of their front line, just in case an errant shell landed on top of them. They had estimated that they needed six shells for every yard of wire, and they had nine hundred yards to cut using shrapnel shells. High explosive was more effective, but they had a very limited supply.

"They decided to push back the attack for forty-eight hours," the captain answered. "It seems that the Germans are rebuilding their wire at night."

"Aren't the infantry supposed to stop them doing that?"

The captain shrugged. "Colonel MacLaren went out to take a look. He thinks that he can get an 18-pounder into the front line." Paul's eyes widened at the news, and he couldn't help look in a northeasterly direction, where the front lines were. Lieutenant-Colonel MacLaren was the OC of the 2nd Canadian Artillery Brigade. "He thinks that he can put one in at the Cow House to target the H.3 to I.2 trenches and another one in the wheat field that can hit H.2 and H.3."

"That's going to be tough. How's he going to get them through the trenches?"

"Not through. Over." When Paul gave him a puzzled look, he explained, "What he wants to do is build temporary bridges over the trenches. The wheat field has five trenches, but if we need to, it will be easy to get the gun out. The Cow House one will be a different matter."

Paul looked at the four 18-pounders that were placed near the hedges to make them less visible. "That's a hell of a lot of work. You'll need to dig a large enough space for the gun and dugouts to store the shells. The barrel can't be seen, so they'll need to build a parapet above it. This is all has to be done at night. We can't do it during the day."

"That's right. MacLaren thinks he can do it in forty-eight hours. He's also talking about cutting rubber tires and tying them to the gun wheels to keep them quiet. The guns will have to be dragged. There's no other way of doing it. They're planning to put guns at Corner House and Shaftesbury Road as well."

Paul tried to visualize what was left of Givenchy. Shaftesbury Road was essentially where the front trench was. "That's awfully close. Isn't it about a hundred yards that separate us from them?"

"That's right. They're bolting extra armour on the gun shields to protect the bombardiers. Once they dismantle the parapet, the shit will hit the fan."

"I guess we have to get started," Paul stated as he turned to give orders.

"What makes you think that it will be us?" questioned the captain.

"I thought the way that you were talking...." Paul said lamely.

"Nope. We're been assigned to counter-battery duty," he said.

"Oh," replied Paul. At least he'd get some sleep tonight, unless he got assigned to a work party.

"How are the new men doing?"

"The replacements are coming along. We have a couple of men who got badly burned by hot shells yesterday. I had to send them to the medics. They'll be out for the next few days."

"Okay," the captain acknowledged. "By the way, I just wanted to let you know that I put your name in for officer's training."

"You have?" Paul asked in surprise.

"Sure, you've come along quite fine. Also, you write well, if on occasion flowery. Your reports are usually written in a legible hand, and more importantly, clear and concise."

"Thank you, sir. I don't know what to say."

"Don't thank me just yet. We have need of subalterns. We're losing far too many of them."

JUNE 15, 1915
VENDIN-LÈS-BÉTHUNE

Brigadier-Generals Mercer, Currie, and Turner had been called to the principal's office, which Lieutenant-General Alderson thought was rather appropriate for his sometimes unruly subordinates. He had set up his headquarters in the primary school in Vendin-lès-Béthune. The village was two miles north of Béthune and nine miles west of Givenchy-lès-la-Bassée. The building his staff occupied was a one-storey red brick building discoloured by the dust from the nearby coal mine. It was normally home to one hundred and eighty students.

In fact, they were in one of the classrooms. A large map of Givenchy, with the Canadian and German current dispositions, covered the blackboard. Above the red line on the map was printed "134 Saxon Division." It was their opposite number manning the German trenches. He was listening to Brigadier-General Henry Burstall briefing the assembled officers on his artillery plans for the Canadian assault to take place late this afternoon. Burstall was forty-seven years old and from Quebec City. He had served in South Africa during the Boer War shortly after he graduated from the Royal Military College at Kingston. "I need to have confirmation that the H.2, H.3, and I.2 are cleared before we start our bombardment. All ranks in the trenches that cannot be cleared must be warned to keep their heads down as we continue to cut the German wire.

161

"Prior to General Mercer's assault, the howitzers and the field guns will bombard the German lines in three lifts. We will start at six o'clock and for five minutes will bombard the front trench. At 6:10 we will shift to their second line trenches to prevent the enemy reoccupying the front trenches. At 6:20 we will start attacking the German communications in the rear."

Lieutenant-General Alderson nodded in agreement then asked, "Were you able to get the four 18-pounders in position?"

"Yes, sir," replied Brigadier-General Burstall. "I have to give credit to the men for getting them there. They did one hell of a job." He pointed to a line that jutted out that resembled a duck's bill on the map. "We placed two 18-pounders here to neutralize the machine guns. They have orders to fire fifteen minutes before the assault."

"What about H.3?" Alderson asked Burstall. The H.3 was a twin redoubt that was barely within their objectives. The problem was that the machine guns could decimate Mercer's troops.

"Our intent was to place an 18-pounder directly across from H.3. Unfortunately, that was not feasible with the intervening ruined houses, shell holes, and trenches. We identified two other possible locations at three hundred and one at a thousand yards. The gunners would have a line of sight to find the range. The only problem is, as General Mercer pointed out, if we positioned them there, we will be firing over the heads of his men in the assembly area."

Brigadier-General Mercer nodded in agreement. "From those positions, there wouldn't be much clearance."

"So how will you deal with H.3 then?"

"We'll be using the 6-inch howitzers against H.3."

"Are you happy with the proposed solution?" Alderson asked Mercer.

"Yes," replied Mercer, who looked tense.

"Fine," said Lieutenant-General Alderson as he studied the map. He could think of several alternatives, but none were feasible at this late hour.

He glanced at Lieutenant-Colonel Gilbert Lafayette Foster, his ADMS, Assistant Director Medical Services for the Division. He was seated at one of the student tables to his right, listening intently to Burstall. The desk looked small, since the forty-year-old Nova Scotian was stocky and over six feet tall. He was born in Wolfville and had attended the New York Medical College before serving as a medical officer during the Boer War. "Medical Services?"

Foster turned his blue eyes to him and said, "I inspected all of the field ambulances, the advanced dressing stations, and regimental aid posts. Yesterday, I met with the DDMS to discuss arrangements for the removal of the wounded. I replaced the No. 1 ambulance with the No. 3 at Le Quesnoy and at the advanced dressing stations. I've assigned additional stretcher-bearers from the 2nd Field Ambulance to the regimental aid stations. As well, I've requisitioned an additional 150 stretchers from stores with additional supplies. I would like to get more of the wheeled stretchers, but they are in short supply."

Alderson nodded at the doctor, who he could tell was hoping that casualties would be light. They were going to lose some good people. The question was how many. "Thank you, Colonel."

He turned to Brigadier-General Mercer, who had been given the task of assaulting the German trenches. "Are your men ready?"

"We are. The 1st Company will lead the assault on the H.2 and the H.3 trenches. Once they have breached the line, they will proceed to the Germans' second line, I.14, and H.6. After the 7th Division has captured that line, they will attack the main communication trenches.

"Bombers will be on the flanks and 2nd company will help consolidate the enemy trench and build a communication trench between our lines and the captured German trench.

"As well, machine guns teams will be set up. One to direct their fire toward the south."

Alderson was watching Brigadier-General Mercer carefully, then asked, "You have a concern about the attack plan?"

"Yes, the mine that the engineers will detonate. I have been informed that they actually did not reach the H.2. They stopped short. They encountered water while they were digging the tunnel."

"Yes, we've been informed to that effect," replied Lieutenant-General Alderson as he glanced at Colonel Rohmer, his chief of staff. Since they had arrived at Givenchy, the 176th Tunnelling Company of the Royal Engineers had been digging under No Man's Land so they could place and detonate mines under the Germans.

"I still don't think that adding the additional three thousand pounds of ammonal will have the effect that we hope," argued Mercer. He had been complaining about that damn tunnel for several days now.

"The engineers from the 176th Tunnelling Company have assured me that it will do the job," Alderson replied. He had put an emphasis on the 176th.

He couldn't help the brief flash of annoyance when Currie joined in. "I'm in agreement with General Mercer. I have my doubts concerning the mines. I feel that we should delay until it has been properly sorted out."

"Are you an engineer now?" Alderson retorted. He was pleased by the look of consternation on Brigadier-General Currie's face.

He turned to back to Mercer and said firmly, "The attack has already been delayed. General Rawlinson is anxious that we proceed. The 7th and the 51st are attacking at six o'clock, and we will support them. Is that clear, gentlemen?"

When no one responded, he said, "Good. Divisional Headquarters will be at the Advance Reporting Centre at Le Quesnoy by noon. Now, let's get to work."

JUNE 15, 1915
LE QUESNOY

Samantha was standing with ten other nursing sisters with hoods over their heads. She could barely see out of the small rectangular glass eyepiece that had been sewn into the fabric. Breathing was difficult, since the hood covered her mouth, and the canvas cloth fell down past her collarbone. It was slightly damp, and she could taste the hypno it had been impregnated with.

It took a couple of loud shouts before she realized that the instructor for the weekly drill was ordering them to remove their gas masks. She held the canvas tube mask in her left hand while she ran her right through her blond hair to reset loose strands. The instructor, Lieutenant Erasmus Millis, impatient with the ladies' grooming, continued, "Once there is an indication of a gas attack, put on your masks immediately and don't remove them until the all-clear is given."

"What about the patients?" asked Charlene Sullivan, a redhead in her early thirties with a stocky build.

"Each patient will have one assigned to them," replied Lieutenant Millis. "The nurses will assist those who cannot pull a mask over their heads. Any further questions?"

"Who invented this form of torture?" asked Patty Bosley. She was the same age and had a similar build as Charlene, but her black hair had a touch of premature grey.

"One of your fellow Canadians, a Dr. Macpherson," replied the lieutenant. The instructor was from Middlesex, so he couldn't be faulted for not knowing of the friction between the Canadians and the Newfoundlanders. Not picking up on Patty's irritation, he continued, "He tested them himself in a gas chamber. They were much more efficient than the face masks."

Samantha had a touch of regret that the face masks that her French women had sewn were being replaced. But that was progress.

"Macpherson, you said?" asked Patty. "From St. John's?"

"I think so. Why?"

"He isn't a Canadian."

"Oh?"

"He's a Newfoundlander."

"There's a difference?" he asked.

Samantha could see that Patty was insulted. She was fiercely proud of being a Newfoundlander and didn't take kindly to being mistaken for a Canadian. Newfoundland was a separate country from Canada. The only reason that she had joined the CAMC was that they paid better than the Imperials.

"Okay, ladies. You are dismissed," he said as he marched hurriedly away.

Samantha joined Charlene and Patty when they stopped in front of the reception tent. She could tell from Patty's face that she would be venting for the next little while. What it made it worse was that she shared a tent with the two women. Patty was interrupted by a green-painted Austin three-ton truck that gave them a cheery beep from its horn as it rumbled by.

Charlene winced when the brakes squealed as the truck stopped beside the four parked ambulances. "My poor ears," she complained.

"You better get used to it," replied Patty with an evil smile. "Since you're the one who's going to ride the damn thing."

"Well, at least the driver's cute," she answered.

Samantha snorted as she watched the driver straighten his tunic and square his shoulders as he sauntered straight toward them. He really didn't have a chance.

"Good morning, sisters," the driver said as he saluted them.

"So the truck has been repaired?" Samantha asked.

"Yes, ma'am. We replaced the flexible clutch coupling and then we riveted the cracks that we found in the chassis under the driver's seat."

"So that's what we are calling it now," cooed Charlene as she winked at Samantha and Patty.

"Ma'am," the soldier replied, perplexed.

"Are you good at flexible clutch coupling and riveting?"

The man blinked then replied with a knowing smile, "When the occasion calls for it."

Samantha was relieved when Charlene and the driver's dance was interrupted by Dr. Moore, who had just exited the reception tent. He was wearing a grim face. "Glad I found you, Nurse Lonsdale. Orders just came in."

"About time," said Charlene with a hint of excitement. Samantha knew that Charlene had been eagerly expecting the new assignment. Patty, she knew, was simply glad to get a break from the regular nursing routine. The hospital has set up an experimental flying squad to be sent to a clearing or a casualty station that was being overwhelmed by patients. The unit was made of two officers, four NCOs, twenty stretcher-bearers, and three nurses.

"How bad is it?" asked Samantha.

"The 7th and the 51st Divisions got chewed up pretty bad," the doctor replied.

"What about our boys?" asked Charlene. She had a younger brother with the 1st Brigade.

"From the preliminary reports, the tunnel didn't go as planned," he answered.

"Oh God," she groaned.

The doctor turned to Samantha and ordered, "Get ready to travel; you're leaving in a half-hour."

"Yes, sir," replied Samantha.

The doctor turned and indicated the ambulances and the trucks with his hand. "Are they fuelled and ready to go?"

"Yes, sir," the driver answered, "the tanks have been topped up this morning, but we're short on petrol."

"Check with the Divisional Artillery. They may be able to spare us some," Dr. Moore ordered. The driver acknowledged him as he hurried away.

When the doctor returned his attention to Samantha, he asked, "You're still here?"

"We're ready to go," she replied, pointing to the small travel valises that were set beside the tent wall.

CHAPTER 21

JUNE 15, 1915
GIVENCHY

Paul was hot and sweaty, but he was too busy to notice. He, Private Lye Goodricke, and Lieutenant Alexis Meek were in the FOO post directing the 65th's fire on the H.2 trench.

"We're drifting again," the lieutenant remarked as he stared through his binoculars.

Paul peered through his and saw that they were landing slightly off the target grid that Brigadier-General Burstall had allocated to them. The plan the divisional staff had developed was a complex one, and they were quite emphatic that they stick with it unless HQ said otherwise.

He felt the vibrations in his feet and was a tad concerned with the stability of the walls. They had set up in a red-brick house. It was once two storeys, but now it was a crumbling frame without a roof. It was located about two hundred yards south of Duck's Bill. They were on a slight rise that gave them a clear view. That was a technicality, since the shell explosions kicked up clouds of dust.

"The 18-pounder in the front trench has opened up," stated the lieutenant with a hint of satisfaction. Paul glanced at the lieutenant, a grocer from Sarnia who was one of the reinforcements they had received from Shorncliffe. He was in his early thirties and a bit on the stiff side. Paul was surprised by the man's reaction, since it was his first time in combat. Paul shrugged then focused on the front trench of Duck's Bill. Part of the parapet that covered the trench was exposed, allowing the mouth of the 18-pounder to poke through just above the sandbags. The scuttlebutt confirmed what he had told the newly promoted Major Masterley a couple of days before. It had been a bitch to get the guns into the trenches. The men had been exhausted by the time they were done. The really tough part was lowering the damn things in. Somehow they managed without the Germans being the wiser.

He shifted his vision slightly to see the effect that the 18-pounder was having on the redoubt across from it. They were using high explosive rather than shrapnel. He saw the oddest site as machine guns and men being propelled skyward.

"Damn, the fucking Huns are good," muttered the lieutenant.

"How many did they get off?" asked Paul when he saw shells starting to bracket the 18-pounder.

"About twenty or so, I think?" Meek replied. "At least they took out the machine guns."

"When are they supposed to…" He was cut off when a massive explosion lifted No Man's Land, and smoke plumed into the evening sky. The earthquake knocked all three men down, and they were pelted with loose bricks from the walls. Paul covered his head but yelped in pain when several bricks punched him in the back. He had to cover his head again when dirt clods and stones from the mine explosion started raining down on them.

"Fuck," Paul exclaimed when he finally raised his head. "Everyone okay?"

"What the fuck," yelped Private Goodricke. The Calgarian was bleeding from various facial cuts and scrapes. The forge cap he had been wearing wasn't much for protection.

"Check the phone," Ryan ordered.

"Fuck," Goodricke said as he picked up a tan leather case that held the standard telephone type D MKIII that they had been equipped with. The case was open, revealing two compartments that held two batteries, a telegraph key, and vibrator, and a telephone handset. They used the telegraph when shell fire drowned them out or silence was imperative. Goodricke looked puzzled when he lifted the phone to his ear. He clicked twice on the handset then checked the wiring. Two black cables ran out of the building. Outside they used different paths in case one of the lines got cut. He checked the wires that attached to the case and retightened the screws. When he listened to the phone again, even Paul could hear the slight buzz of a crackling dial tone.

"Shit," Meek said as he looked over the bricks that covered the sandbags. He had similar scrapes and cuts.

"What?" asked Paul.

"You better take a look," he said.

After Ryan picked up the binoculars that he had fallen on, he blew the lens to clear them of dust. He then raised them to look at the battle-field. "Jesus!"

What he saw was a large crater where No Man's Land used to be. It was difficult to tell who had suffered the most damage, the Germans or the Canadians. He could see an 18-pounder had been toppled onto its side. Dirt and sandbags, many split, had spilled into the Canadian trench. Men were beginning to recover and were starting to dig to get those who had been buried when the trench had collapsed out.

Farther down, he could see a company of men assemble into two lines for their assault as the artillery suddenly went silent. The clock didn't tick long before the artillery rain started again on the German second line.

"Good, the second lift is starting," stated the lieutenant.

"Yeah," agreed Paul. He could hear the infantry's rally cry, "Lusitania! Lusitania!" over the din. "But the infantry is going to have a tough time crossing that crater."

Paul then made a mistake of rising slightly to get a better view. It was a small movement, but it was enough to catch someone's eye. The next he knew, something slammed into his right shoulder, spinning him around. When he landed, he hit his head hard against a pile of loose bricks, knocking him out.

JUNE 16, 1915
LE QUESNOY

Paul Ryan was lying in a cot just outside the casualty station as an ambulance was being loaded. Two bodysnatchers lifted a heavy stretcher and slid the injured man into the top shelf. The ambulance's capacity had been tripled by the addition of a steel frame above the two benches on top of the truck's wheel-wells. The frame added space to transport four more patients. Medical stores filled the empty spaces under the bottom stretchers.

A nurse was circulating among the soldiers lying on the ground, checking the medical tags that had been pinned to the men's left chests. She would indicate to the bodysnatchers which ones were next to be loaded. When she checked, she gave him a negative shake. It frustrated him. He still had to wait.

Earlier, a surgeon had looked at his shoulder wound. His face mask muffled his voice slightly when he said, "You're a lucky bugger."

"I am?" Paul gritted his teeth in pain when the surgeon probed the wound.

"Yeah," the doc said. "You got a dime-novel shoulder wound."

"What?" he had replied, perplexed, as the morphine started to kick in.

"The shoulder is a complex structure of muscle, bone, arteries, and nerve endings. If it had been an inch higher, it would have shattered the shoulder blade. That would have meant that I would have had to open you up, clean out the bone fragments, and reset the shoulder. You would be alive, but you would be out of commission for several months. You'd probably never regain full use of it. An inch to the left, it would have hit an artery and you would have bled to death. If it had torn some nerve endings, you wouldn't be moving that shoulder much.

"So what you've got will take a month to a month and a half to heal. If it doesn't get infected. So far the wound is pretty clean. You should be on the next truck out of here."

That had been five or six hours ago, and he still wasn't on his way. He wasn't sure for how long, since he had lost track of time.

"I need some water, sister," he demanded. His throat was parched, and he hadn't had anything to drink since the doctor saw him.

"Sure," replied the nurse. "I'll get one of the sisters to get you some."

"Thanks," he replied as he heard the ambulance engine roar to life as one of the stretcher bearers slammed the truck's gate shut. He clambered over and took his seat near the cab wall. The ambulance's exhaust gave a large spurt of grey haze.

"You asked for some water," said a new voice.

When he turned his head, he saw Samantha Lonsdale leaning toward him with a metal water jug and tin cup.

"Miss Lonsdale?" blurted Paul in surprise. She cocked an eyebrow above her tired and grim face. He had a fairly good idea why. "I don't think you would remember me, ma'am. We met about a month ago with Captain Llewellyn at Ypres." Behind her, he could see another ambulance being backed up to receive more patients.

"I'm sorry," she said. "I don't remember much from that night."

"That's alright. Thanks for the water," he said as he took a sip of lukewarm water.

"How's the captain?" she asked.

"I rightly don't know," he replied. "I haven't seen him since Ypres."

"Captain Llewellyn?" asked the soldier next to him.

"Yes," Samantha said as she turned her head toward him.

"He was alive the last time I saw him. He's the one who carried me out," said the 1st Brigade soldier. The man's chest was tightly wrapped with bandages.

"He did?" asked Samantha.

"Yes, ma'am. General Currie's orders. He wanted to get as many of the wounded out of No Man's Land as we can. I'm the fourth one he helped carry out."

Paul saw the flicker of concern in her face just before a nurse called out at her, "Sister Lonsdale, you're being ordered out on the next ambulance."

"Okay," she replied. She gave him a gentle tap on his good shoulder. "Don't worry, you'll get out of here soon."

Where did I hear that before? He sighed when he watched her clamber onto the back of the ambulance.

CHAPTER 22

"Strike twoooo!" shouted the umpire when the ball thudded into the catcher's mitt. Captain Llewellyn watched him settle behind the catcher. The ump ignored the boos and catcalls demanding that he get his eyes checked. He had a MP's brassard on his left cuff, which meant he had plenty of experience turning a deaf ear.

They were in the bottom of the second inning, and there were two men on first and third. The last man up had hit a grounder, putting the man on second out. The 65th Artillery was pitted against the Richmond Fusiliers. They were playing in a farmer's field about a thousand yards west of the 2nd Brigade Headquarters. The Fusiliers had the home team advantage, and the game was still 0-0.

The game had started around one, just after the men had been inspected by Lieutenant-General Alderson. The men who weren't in the line or on essential duty had been given a half-day's leave to celebrate Dominion Day. Naturally, headquarters didn't want the men to loaf, so interunit sporting events such as baseball, boxing, and football had been organized. The brass was of the opinion that these sports encouraged the fighting spirit. After all, didn't the victory at Waterloo begin on the playing fields of Eton?

"Wasn't Sergeant Henderson with the 5th Battalion?" asked Brigadier-General Currie, who was standing beside him. He watched the batter take a few practice swings.

Captain Llewellyn squinted as the batter tapped home plate and set into his stance. The bat had seen much use; its surface was full of dings and dents. The baseball wasn't much better. It was a difficult item to find in England and France. It hadn't come apart at the seams yet, but it would. All ballplayers had gloves, which they had scrounged from other men in the division.

"I believe that he is," he replied.

"When did he get transferred to the Fusiliers?"

"I'm not exactly sure, sir. But he seems to be a very good ball player," Llewellyn replied as he watched the pitcher spit on the ball. A curveball was coming. The players didn't like spitballs, but it was part of the game. The batter adjusted his stance to compensate. The ball came in a dropping curve, but Henderson managed to get a piece of it. The ball flew into left field, driving the man on third base home. "The 65th had some transfers as well," Llewellyn said as the man on first scrambled to get to second.

"Baseball players?"

"I don't know," replied Llewellyn, but he would be surprised if the COs didn't try to stack the deck. After all, unit honour was at stake. He knew Colonel Topham would.

"Did you get the latest list of men for the Colt machine gun course?" Captain Llewellyn had overheard Brigadier-General Currie ask Captain Lowell, who was standing on the other side of him.

The captain from Moosonee replied, "Got them this morning. I'm looking them over to see if they are suitable. The instructors at the last course were piqued that some of the men we had sent didn't meet the basic requirements."

"We're to get more machine guns, so I would like to have trained crews ready when they arrive," replied Currie.

"Understood, General," replied Lowell. "But we haven't been provided a date when they will arrive."

"Are we getting more Colts or Vickers?" Captain Lowell asked.

Currie shrugged. "We'll know when we get them.… Go! Go!" he yelled when he saw Henderson was trying to steal second base. He slid face-first into the sandbag.

Llewellyn suspected that Third Army HQ would probably have a fit for such frivolous use. They had been denied a recent request for more. HQ had been asking what the hell they were using them for, since the Third Army's 350,000 weekly sandbag allotment should have been sufficient to meet demand. It seemed that the Canadian Division would have to start economizing.

"I wish that I could stay for the rest of the game. Duty calls," stated Currie with a touch of regret.

"Of course, General," said Captain Llewellyn as he turned to accompany the general.

"No, you stay and enjoy yourself. Have a good Dominion Day. I expect you to be back in the office bright and early tomorrow morning," Currie ordered.

"Thank you, General," Llewellyn replied.

Currie paused when he spotted the markings on one of the nearby parked trucks. "You might want to tell the COs that non-regulation markings have to be removed," he said, indicating the trucks that had brought the men to the field with his chin. The canvas tops had been rolled back, and men were standing on the beds to get a better view of the game. A memo had come that only regulation markings were allowed.

"Yes, General. Right away," said Captain Lowell.

"Not right now. Tomorrow will be fine."

"Of course, General," Lowell stated as he saluted Currie.

Llewellyn turned his attention back to the game. The pitcher glanced to second base to pin Henderson to the bag. He hadn't seen the man spitting on the ball, but when he threw it, Llewellyn could tell that he had lost control. The batter dropped like a stone when the ball bounced off his head. The Fusiliers bench exploded and the 65th cleared theirs to protect their pitcher. The umpires and the MPs intervened when the men started shoving each other. It didn't take long before someone threw a punch.

"Come on guys, knock it off," yelled Captain Llewellyn.

There was fighting spirit, and there was fighting spirit.

FOLKESTONE CENTRAL TRAIN STATION, FOLKESTONE

"You know for once I would like to have Dominion Day as an actual holiday," complained Samantha as she stepped out of the truck stopped in front of the Folkestone Central Station. The station was nearly three miles east of Shorncliffe. It wasn't particularly pretty, since on one side the hills were bare and on the other side the slate-tiled houses didn't look particularly cheerful. It was a shame, really, because Folkestone had looked really pretty when she arrived the week before on the HMHS *Anglia* from Boulogne. The ship had carried about 450 patients. She wasn't assigned to the ship, but she had tried to help with the disembarkation as they moved the wounded to the waiting ambulances and trains.

"Is that a complaint I hear?" asked Matron Rita, who had followed her out of the truck's cab.

Samantha glanced at her friend as she slammed the door closed. "Yes."

Rita chuckled. "Patients don't get a day off."

"True," Samantha admitted. "But I do seem to have bad luck with Dominion Day. When I was a junior nurse, I had to work because the senior nurses wanted the day off. Now that I'm an assistant matron, I have to work to supervise the juniors."

"Poor you. That's what you get for being good at your job," replied Rita. She then cocked her head and asked, "Did you get up on the wrong side of the bed? You're not usually this whiny."

"Well, I didn't get much sleep," Samantha admitted. "I was worrying about the schedule. You know, we had thirteen nurses struck off strength yesterday."

"True, but we're getting nine replacements. That is why we're here rather than enjoying the music at the bandstand." Rita was referring to the Dominion Day concerts at the Lea grandstand that the 2nd Division's bands were offering to the residents of Folkestone.

"We're still four short."

"Well, we'll have to make do," replied the matron tartly.

"Yes, Matron," Samantha replied.

"Good," replied Rita. "That doesn't mean we can't give the new staff a walking tour of Folkestone before we head back to Shorncliffe. We might even visit the grandstand."

"Really?" said Samantha with a bright smile. "That would be nice. I heard that the 2nd Division band is quite good, and some of the locals are playing as well."

Rita rolled her eyes. Samantha knew that Rita was well aware how much she liked music. "Now, if I could attend one of these concerts without having my bottom pinched, I would enjoy them more."

Samantha shrugged. "Do what I do."

"What?"

"I wear an iron girdle."

Rita laughed. "That will teach them."

HMS *ADRIATIC*, NORTH ATLANTIC

"Tolstoy! You actually met Tolstoy!" exclaimed Borden.

He was sitting in the writing room of the HMS *Adriatic*. The room was large, spacious, and elegant with sunlight cascading through the gauze curtains covering the large picture window. The large, heavy black curtains had been pulled aside. He had come into the reading room hoping that by chance they might have some of the Canadian newspapers. There was some talk before he left Ottawa that the amateur and professional championships that were to be held at the Royal Ottawa and Rivermead golf courses would be cancelled. The simple fact was that most of the better golfers had volunteered.

When he entered, he had started chatting with the man with the Van Dyke beard across from him. Since they were the only occupants of the room, he had thought it would be rather rude not to introduce himself. Besides, you never knew whether the man was a fellow Canadian. To his pleasure, he discovered that the man was a Belgian and professor of French studies at Edinburgh University. He also learned that the good doctor was the Belgian consul-general. He spoke and read a variety of languages, one of them Russian. It seemed he had travelled extensively in that country and had learned the language.

"What was Tolstoy like?" Borden asked.

Before the good professor could answer, he was interrupted. "Sir Borden?"

Borden turned his head to find Captain Hayes, the ship's captain, standing beside him. "I'm glad that I found you, sir. I just wanted to wish you a happy Dominion Day."

"Thank you," replied Borden.

"And will you do me the honour of dining at my table this evening to celebrate the occasion?"

"Of course. It would be my pleasure."

"Also, I would like to extend the same invitation to you as well, Doctor Sarolea."

"*Merci*," the doctor replied with an acknowledging smile.

The captain turned his attention back to Borden. "I also wanted to inform you that we are now nearly 350 miles from New York, and we are making good time."

"That is good to hear," replied Borden. He had boarded the ship yesterday at noon. "Have you opened your sealed orders yet?"

"My orders are to open them when we are farther along," Hayes replied.

"I understand." Borden was well aware that the captains of large British passenger liners also held commissions in the Royal Naval Reserve. Hayes was a naval commander.

"And we'll be conducting ship's drills shortly."

"Very well," replied Borden. "I hope that my presence aboard hasn't inconvenienced you?"

"Not at all," replied the captain.

As the current captain, Borden was certain he had dealt with some demanding passengers, especially on a luxury vessel such as the *Adriatic* that carried nearly three thousand passengers. He was fairly certain that the 460 in first class were the most demanding.

One thing he knew was that some of the passengers had disembarked once they had discovered he was on board. They felt that they risk was too high to travel on the ship. The remaining passengers were divided on whether or not the prime minister of Canada had increased or decreased their danger. Several passengers had already sought him out and asked when British destroyers would arrive to escort them to England. All he could say was that he didn't know. What added to the passengers' tension was the fact that the ship carried a large cargo of ammunition in its hold, along with military equipment. This made the ship a legitimate target for German submarines.

British Ambassador Spring-Rice had been gravely concerned about Borden's safety. When he had dined with him and J.P. Morgan on Morgan's yacht two nights before, the man had been rather tiresome about the German Secret Service in New York City. It wasn't exactly a secret that Borden was aboard. The press was waiting for him on the gangplank.

Dangerous or not, he needed to have a face-to-face meetings with his counterparts in England. He also wanted to inspect the effort of the Canadian overseas force in England and France. One could get only so much from reading reports and telegrams. He hoped that Spring-Rice didn't relay his concerns to Laura. She had been quite worried when he left Ottawa.

"Is it possible to send a message to my wife?" he asked the captain.

Hayes shook his head. "I'm afraid not. We currently have a radio blackout."

Borden grimaced at the news that he couldn't inform his wife that he was safe. However, until they reached the rendezvous point, the ship was vulnerable.

EAST BLOCK, PARLIAMENT HILL, OTTAWA

"That was a waste of time," stated Major-General Sam Hughes as he exited the East Block. His aide, Captain Holly, had to quicken his pace to keep up with him.

Hughes had just come from a meeting with Eugene Foster, the minister of trade and commerce, who was now the acting prime minister since Sir Robert had left three days ago. Someone had to run the government, since Sir Borden would be out of the country for nearly two months. He also learned that Senator James Lougheed, the government leader in the Senate, was going to be his replacement when he joined Borden in England. He had argued that it was not necessary, since no one had been appointed when he joined the CEF in England last October. Both Borden and Foster had insisted. They pointed out that the CEF had suffered 9,600 men killed or wounded since April, and the opposition was hammering them on the various contract and shell committee scandals. Someone needed to be available to make decisions and defend the government from Liberal attack.

"Is everything in readiness for my trip?" he asked Holly as they headed toward the Hill's East Gate, made of sandstone and black steel. He acknowledged the Dominion Police constables as he and his aide walked through the gate. He noted that the usual complement had been doubled. He then recalled the memo that Commissioner Sherwood issued, indicating that he was doubling the security detail on the Hill. There was no specific threat, but a precaution.

Hughes glanced at the green lawn, which was practically empty since celebrations on the Hill tended to be infrequent. He could hear the faint music from the Fire Brigade Band that led the annual Dominion Day parade. The parade started at city hall on Queen Street and meandered down central Ottawa. The procession usually included the Governor General's Foot Guard. When it ended, the Foot Guard would be reviewed at the Cartier Drill Hall.

"Your luggage is already at the Central Station," the captain replied. "I have your train tickets for Valcartier. You'll be spending the night there. Colonel Hughes will have the men ready for your inspection tomorrow morning." The CO of the Valcartier Camp happened to be his brother John. "After your review, you will be taking the train from Quebec City to New York. Tickets have been purchased on the American liner *Philadelphia*."

Hughes grunted an acknowledgement. He would have preferred sailing on a British ship, but the Admiralty had indicated they could only spare destroyers for one ship, not two. His passage had been booked on an American liner, since it was unlikely that the Germans would anger the Americans any more than they had. The US authorities had been sending the sailing schedules of American flagged vessels and the estimated time that they would be arriving in the declared war zone. This was to prevent a recurrence of the *Lusitania* incident.

Hughes was happy going on the trip, because he wanted to inspect the 2nd Division. He knew Alderson wasn't pleased that Brigadier-General Turner would be assigned as the 2nd Division's GOC. He wanted to make it clear that it was his wish. With the 2nd Division in England, they were now able to activate the Canadian Corps. He had overridden the major-generals' and the War Office's advice that a Canadian Corps was not sustainable. He disagreed, and he had convinced Borden to increase the Canadian Army's authorized strength to 150,000 men.

That was one of the reasons he wanted to get to England. He needed to keep an eye on Borden. He was too soft-hearted for his own good.

CHAPTER 23

"Am I boring you, Sergeant Ryan?" asked Captain Leeds-Roberts. "No, sir," Paul replied. He was sitting in the rear of the barn that was being used for today's lecture. His arm was still in a sling, and he was rubbing his sore shoulder. The medical staff was telling him that he was healing nicely, and they had cleared him for light duty. He still was required to report to the hospital for massage therapy to regain full mobility. He had just come from a session with the masseur. He was convinced the man enjoyed making him groan as he manipulated his shoulder.

Since he was on light duty, he had been ordered to attend the quickie artillery officers' training course that was being run to replace losses. The army's attitude was that while your arms might not be of much use for the moment, it didn't mean your brain couldn't be. He had heard that in the future candidates would be sent to an artillery school being set up in Shorncliffe.

So there he was in the back of forty or so corporals and sergeants, listening rather attentively to the instructors and taking notes. For most of the men, it meant nearly a doubling of their pay to $2.00 a day plus a sixty cent field allowance. True that a fair number would spend it on beer and trollops. For the family men it was a practical consideration. It meant they could send more money home, and if they were killed, their pensions would be substantially better.

"Then can you explain the difference between an observer and a liaison officer?" the captain asked, putting him on the spot.

The captain was in his mid-thirties, with sandy brown hair and wire-framed spectacles. His loose uniform indicated that he had recently lost weight. He was a British officer who had been brought in to help with the training. There were several of them, and some of them were very good. This instructor had an attitude problem that rubbed the men the wrong way.

"Eyes and ears," Paul stated.

"What?" replied the captain as he peered at him over his lenses.

Paul was pleased that he had caught the captain by surprise. But he hid his smile. "The eyes are the observers and the liaison the ears," he said. "In my experience, the observers in the observation posts are usually the battery commander. He's the one who does most of the guns' registration and analyzes the fire during the barrages. The battery commander will send an FOO to observe the artillery fire from the trenches where he can directly observe the shell's landing.

"A liaison officer is usually organized when the CRA and the Division commander cannot be co-located their headquarters. They need to be in constant communication. Normally, a captain or above is attached to a brigade that is leading the attack. A forward liaison office is attached to battalion headquarters."

"And if the attack battalion reaches its objective?"

Paul knew that was a trick question. "Then the officer will transfer to the next battalion."

The captain had a sour look. He didn't like the fact that Paul had recited the field service manual back to him. And he didn't like being shown up by an NCO.

"Thank you, Acting Sergeant Ryan," he snapped with an emphasis on the "acting." "Part of liaison duty is to investigate reports of friendly fire. There are five essentials: time it takes for the shell to fall, the rate of fire, the calibre, the type of shell, and the direction that the shells are coming from," he stated. "These incidents are infrequent, but they do happen from time to time.

"Now," he said. "Let's discuss how to select and build observation posts."

Paul Ryan sighed as he rubbed his aching shoulder again. At least it would keep him awake until lunch.

JULY 12, 1915
WOODS BUILDING, SLATER STREET, OTTAWA

"The Army Council suggested a 3rd Division be formed, similar to the 2nd," Major-General Gwatkin informed Senator Lougheed.

"They don't want mounted troops?" Lougheed asked. He could feel the heat rise in the office. The forecast called for the temperature to be in the mid-eighties and with high humidity. That was one thing he had to get used to in Ottawa, since Calgary weather was rarely humid. The office window was open, and a floor fan was humming, trying to keep Hughes' office in the Woods Building cool.

"So far, the RCD, the LSH, and the FGH have been fighting in the trenches dismounted," added Major-General Fiset, who sat beside Gwatkin in the twin chairs in front of his desk. Lougheed didn't need the acronyms explained. The RCD was the Royal Canadian Dragoons based out of Toronto, the Lord Strathcona Horse based out of Edmonton, and the Fort Garry Horse out of Winnipeg. He had a keen interest in them, since he was one of the Alberta senators. He had been appointed to the Senate at age thirty-five to replace his uncle, who had died in office.

"General Fiset is correct, Minister," replied Gwatkin. The use of the title brought a smile to Lougheed's face. Prior to the prime minister and Sam Hughes' departure for England on Dominion Day, Borden had asked him to be the acting minister of militia and defence while they were out of the country. The prime minister wanted someone he could trust to run the place. Lougheed was the Conservative government leader in the Senate and a minister without portfolio in Borden's cabinet. "Until the war's character changes from a static defence to manoeuvre, the cavalry units will be fighting in the trenches dismounted. If you chose to recruit infantry instead of mounted units, it will represent a considerable savings to the government. We would not incur the expense of acquiring mounts for each recruit. Also, savings will be had with the horses' training, feeding, medical care, transport, and replacement resulting from battle loses."

Lougheed nodded in agreement. He had attended cabinet meetings where Finance Minister White had discussed the rising costs. "When do you think we can assemble a third division?"

Gwatkin shrugged. "In June we called up thirty-five thousand to create twenty-seven infantry regiments and six artillery batteries. We're currently recruiting an average of nearly thirty-five hundred men per week. We've been discussing calling up an additional fifteen thousand in late August once the current crop completes their primary training. We're hopeful, but at the current rate we don't see the 3rd Division being ready until December. We've started preliminary work for a fourth for the spring of 1916.

"Once the 2nd Division goes to France, the Military Council has agreed to create a Canadian Corps to command both divisions."

"General Alderson will command the Corps?"

"Yes," replied Gwatkin.

"Minister Hughes indicated Turner will command the 2nd Division. Who will take over from Alderson when he takes command of the Corps?"

"Current plans are to have General Currie take command. But that still has not been confirmed," replied Gwatkin.

"I see," Lougheed replied thoughtfully.

"Minister, you need to be aware that the War Office prefers we concentrate on supplying reinforcements for the current units in the field rather than creating new units."

"What were Minister Hughes' thoughts on the subject?" Lougheed had a good idea what they were.

"The minister prefers to create new units. He feels that since Canada has 1.5 million men between the ages of twenty and forty-four, we shouldn't have any problems recruiting volunteers," replied Fiset.

"Okay. The issue then is equipment. I'm sure you heard that last week seven prominent citizens of Vancouver subscribed $1,000 each to buy fifteen machine guns for the 47th Battalion. Then the Mountain Lumber Association donated $5,000 to the 54th Kootenay Battalion. From the latest reports, it seems to be spreading. Victoria announced they were buying sixteen, and Montreal is getting into the act."

"We currently allocate four machine guns per battalion. The problem is production delays, since the Colt and Vickers are in high demand," Major-General Gwatkin replied. "We're currently looking at the Lewis machine guns. They cost about $1,000 apiece compared with the Colt's $750.00."

Fiset added, "We're of the opinion that government funds should be used to acquire and equip our troops. If money is raised specifically for machine guns and the subscribers specify the units they wish them to be allocated to, there could be friction. Some of the rural battalions may not able to raise such funds."

"It also upsets our table of organization," interjected Major-General Gwatkin. "And since they specify machine guns, we can't use the funds to acquire other badly needed equipment and supplies. We are still suffering ammunition shortages."

"I know Lloyd George was appointed the minister of munitions several months ago to deal with shell shortages in England. Has the Shell Committee made progress?"

Both Gwatkin and Fiset gave each other glances, which raised his suspicions. Fiset finally spoke. "There has been some progress, but you might prefer having Colonel Bertram give a briefing on the situation." That didn't sound good, not good at all. He decided to pursue the subject at a later date.

"As you are aware on the 30th of June, I was made chairman of the War Hospital Commission. The commission has been tasked to look into the care of the wounded and disabled men who are being returned to Canada from the front," he stated.

Both men looked rather chagrined. Until now, the Department of Militia and Defence was responsible for the care of returning wounded and disabled veterans. Prior to the war, the numbers were quite low and were taken care of at the military hospitals at Halifax and Quebec City. No one had anticipated the vast number of wounded that the current battles were producing.

"I'll have lieutenant colonels Maunsell, Hallich, and Jacques meet with you to discuss what has been done to date," replied Fiset. They were the members of the current committee that had been struck to look into the issue. They represented the department's engineering, ordnance, and medical services. The department's focus to date had been on raising the overseas force and sending them to France. Not much attention had been devoted to the returning wounded.

"Good," Lougheed replied. "I'll be talking with the Red Cross and St. John Ambulance to get their opinion on what needs to be done."

"Yes, Minister," replied both men.

"Okay, now for my inspection visit to the Niagara-on-the-Lake camp next week."

JULY 20, 1915
MACHINE GUN SCHOOL, SAINT-OMER

Captain Llewellyn braced himself against the dashboard when the driver hit the brakes rather hard. He heard yelps and then a chorus of swearing from the back of the truck. There were, or had been nearly twenty men sitting behind him. Mostly there were privates, but there were a couple of lieutenants and NCOs in there as well.

He glared at the driver. "What the f..."

He was interrupted when a head appeared, poking out of the cab's canvas rear window, and a red-faced soldier shouted, "What the fuck are you doing? Are you trying to kill us?"

The captain had doubts about the driver when he got into the truck. It was a milk run for various units and officers in the Canadian Division's area of operations. When the eighteen-year-old had picked him up, he was rather blurry-eyed from what Llewellyn suspected was an overnight binge. He wasn't surprised that the driver managed to hit every single pothole.

"Sorry," the kid said. He didn't sound sorry. "I didn't see the sign until the last minute." He pointed to a black-and-white hand-painted sign that read *Machine Gun School*.

"Shit, thanks," the man in the rear said sarcastically. "Fucking rear pussy," could be heard from the back as the driver ground the gears, putting the truck in reverse, stopped, and then made a right turn. Again, he hit every pothole he could find until he came to a full stop a hundred yards inside the school's main entrance. The staccato of machine guns could be heard in the early morning. It looked as it might rain, but it seemed to be holding off. The captain heard the smacking sound of men jumping down on the wet mud. They were muttering veiled threats at the driver until the lieutenants ordered them to line up for a head count.

The driver turned to him and said, "God, I need to piss. I'll be right back."

The captain shook his head then glanced at another group of trainees who were waiting for a class to start. They had cigarettes out. He got out of the cab to stretch his legs and to remove the crick in his back.

"Hi, James," said a familiar voice.

When he turned, he grinned at Captain Grey. "What the hell are you doing here?"

"Same as you, it seems," he replied. The ordnance officer was in his early forties, with a stocky build and grey hair. The captain had dealt with him frequently when he was with the Fusiliers. A cigarette dangled from the corner of his mouth. "Cigarette?" he offered as his hand sneaked into his jacket.

"No thanks," the captain replied, waving it away. "I took the course last December. I'm on my way to a meeting, and I hitched a ride." He indicated the group of men lined up beside the truck.

"Ah yes," Grey said as he examined the men. "Some of the instructors will have a fit."

"Yeah, I know," replied Llewellyn. They had specifically asked that the men selected for the course be suitable and have an aptitude for the work. He had recognized some of the men. The only reason they were there was that the COs wanted to get rid of them for a couple of days. "Anything exciting happening?"

"Well, one of our guys, I don't know if you know him, Sergeant Northover?"

Llewellyn shook his head. "I haven't met him, but I've seen some of the work he's done on the Colts."

"He's still experimenting with that flash absorber. The school's commandant was impressed with it. Northover managed to cut the weight down to about five pounds. The CO wants to see if we can get one done for the Vickers."

"Really! That I would like to see, since we're getting rid of the Colts."

"Not a chance! My CO wrote up a report after we test fired 2,600 rounds. It only stopped when the extractor failed. It only took two minutes to replace the spring and to start up again. He feels that it's more efficient than the Vickers."

"Good luck convincing the War Office."

"Well, the home papers are saying they are raising money in Canada to buy more. Last I heard, we might be getting the Lewis machine gun."

"I never heard of it," the captain replied. Since the war started, there had been so many new models developed that he couldn't keep track.

"An American designed it. He tried to sell it to the US War Department, but they didn't want it. He licensed it to the British. It only weighs twenty-eight pounds and fires five to six hundred rounds a minute. You can use either a forty-seven or ninety-seven-pan magazine. It fits on top of the breech and drops the rounds into the receiver."

"No potato digger then. At least it sounds light. Does it have a tripod?"

"There is one on the air cooling shroud that surrounds the barrel. I've only seen pictures. I haven't gotten my hands on an actual copy. Like you said, it's light. But that Northover is a clever lad. He has designed a new tripod for the Colt that can carry a 250-round belt. A single man can carry the gun and the tripod."

Llewellyn grimaced. "If he tried to fire the potato digger from the hip, it will tear his guts out." That was one disadvantage with the Colt. It was the piston action that struck the ground when firing. "We need the machine guns for support on the attack, and we need more of them. If we can't get any Vickers, how are we going to get Lewises?"

"The Savage Gun Company are making a 30-06 model for the American market. They are modifying it for the .303 rounds."

"The Imperials will like that," Llewellyn said when the driver returned from the latrine.

"Won't they?" replied Grey with some concern.

Llewellyn had the same concern, whether or not the War Office would approve their version of the Lewis. "Well, good luck. We could sure use more of them," he said as he headed to the truck.

CHAPTER 24

JULY 21, 1915
NIEPPE

Prime Minister Borden stared in disbelief at the white crosses that covered the field. He couldn't help the frog that caught in his throat, and he was struggling to keep tears from swelling.

He had prepared himself intellectually, but he hadn't expected to be hit so hard. Partly, he knew he was dealing with remnants of his mother's passing. It had been expected, since she had been ailing for some time, but her death still hurt. She had been a woman of unusual strength and had a fierce love for her children. When he buried her on March 31, the four inches of snow that had fallen the previous day had turned to mud. That was not the only memorial he had attended. They had held a memorial service on Parliament Hill for those who had fallen. The Centre Block lawn had overflowed with those who came to offer their respect and condolences.

That poem "In Flanders Fields" that was making the rounds had it right. He hadn't really expected this when he had decided to travel to England to discuss the war effort. Sometimes it was the best method to get to the heart of the matter and to clear misunderstandings.

He knew that Laura had been concerned when he took the train for New York. His last view of her was on the platform at the Ottawa train station with fearful tears in her eyes. He had been upset when he found out the *Citizen* had published an article that stated his ship had been targeted by German submarines.

The weather during the voyage had been fine for most of the trip, with only a couple of days of rough seas. When the *Adriatic*'s captain finally opened his sealed orders, they contained the rendezvous point where she would meet her Royal Navy escort. Three days later, on the 8th of July, three British destroyers appeared out of the morning mist and took their stations for the final leg of her journey to England.

Most of the passengers had become quite friendly, even giddy, as they eyed the three destroyers. They were now safe, although they knew that the armed vessels were not there for them but for the Canadian prime minister.

When he had arrived in port, he was greeted by George Perley and Brigadier-General Carson, with whom he had a long talk on the train to London. He had been impressed by the man's tactfulness and competence, but it was clear from the hints that Carson made he didn't think highly of Lieutenant-General Alderson. Later, after Carson had left, George had a long list of complaints, to which Borden had listened dutifully. The man could be tedious at times, but he was a very good golf companion. He had a busy schedule planned, and he was not as young as he used to be. He was hoping to free up some time to play a round of golf to help recharge.

The last few weeks had been busy with meeting with British and Canadian senior military officials. He had lunch with Prime Minister Asquith and attended a British cabinet meeting. A rather rare event, so he was informed, although Borden had been pushing for such an invitation ever since he was elected. He had visited wounded Canadian soldiers and reviewed the 2nd Contingent at Shorncliffe. He had discussions with Alderson and had an audience with the king.

All this before he crossed the channel to visit the troops at the front in France. That would be tomorrow, where he could view the front lines from a safe distance.

But today he was here to acknowledge the men who had died during the battle of Ypres.

"The sack, please," he said as he put out his hand.

"Yes, prime minister," said the colonel standing beside him as he handed Borden a tan-coloured sack that the prime minister had brought with him from Canada.

It seemed a rather appropriate tribute as the gold-coloured maple seeds helicoptered onto the nearest earth mounds. As he walked down the rows of white crosses, scattering more, he realized that he hadn't brought nearly enough.

JULY 22, 1915
NIEPPE

Captain Llewellyn nearly started laughing when a mixture of surprise and bewilderment appeared on the faces of the men of the 1st Brigade. They were marching to relieve the 3rd Brigade battalion currently in the trenches nearly a mile away. The captain was behind the small knot of men standing at the road junction. It didn't have a name, only a map coordinate, T.28.c2.5.

The men in the last four months of fighting had seen strange and inexplicable things. But the last thing they expected as they marched to a week's duty in the mud was to see the Canadian prime minister standing at the side of the road, doffing his hat at them and thanking them for making Canada proud.

Llewellyn was pleased that the tight security surrounding the flying visit by Sir Robert Borden had held. The men had no clue who the visiting dignitary was until the last minute. The captain was tense as he scanned the men and the tree lines. He had scouts and snipers out to make sure that they didn't have any gate crashers. He was responsible for Borden's safety. They were less than a mile from the front. There was always a possibility of a stray bullet, an aircraft flying overhead, or an artillery shell landing near.

The captain glanced at his wristwatch and saw that it was nearly five thirty. In an hour's time the prime minister would be on a train back to Saint-Omer, and his job would be over.

The schedule had been tight. Borden had arrived at the Nieppe train station at twelve thirty, when he had been greeted by Lieutenant-General Alderson, the three brigade commanders, the divisional staff, and the mayor with his town council. After lunch he had inspected the 1st Field Ambulance at Le Romarin, followed by a review of the reserve and support battalions, the engineers, and the 3rd Brigade headquarters staff. After that he had been whisked to Le Petit Munque Farm, where he spent a scant fifteen minutes with the 2nd Infantry Brigade.

Borden had been impressed by Hill 63, an important feature of the four thousand yards of trenches that ran from the northeast corner of Ploegsteert Woods to the southeast corner of Armentières-Messines Road. The hill had a good view of the cultivated ridge of hills that ran along the French-Belgian border. To the south one could see the Lys Plain and to the north Douve Valley, through which the trenches they had taken over from the French ran.

Borden had peered at the trenches through powerful binoculars that had been set up to observe the German lines. The trenches were clearly visible. A stark contrast to the green hills and valleys through which Borden was currently being escorted.

"So those are the German lines?" he had inquired.

"Yes, prime minister," the OC of the 118th Field Artillery replied. "This is an excellent position to support our men, as we have a very good observation post. We're only two thousand yards away from the first line of trenches."

Borden looked startled. "Are we in range of the German guns?"

"Yes. Some of the naval guns and 45-mm guns are within reach of us."

"I see." Borden had looked up at the sky above the bulwark that had been constructed to protect to artillery position. The binoculars that the prime minister had been using had been set up so they could look over top the bulwark without putting the observers in danger.

Borden glanced at the 18-pounders that were pointing at the trenches. "No firing today?"

"Not until you leave, sir. We don't want them to retaliate while you are present," he replied.

"I see," replied Borden gravely. He glanced at the stockpile of artillery shells. He had been somewhat surprise, since he had been informed that there was a shortage.

Once they had passed by, Llewellyn saw a shadow behind Borden's eyes. He knew that some of the men he saw would not come back.

"Prime Minister, you have the divisional train and the Princess Patricia's to visit, and there isn't much time," said Lieutenant-General Alderson as he led the prime minister to the nearby staff cars.

"Of course," replied Borden.

JULY 26, 1915
MOORE BARRACKS MILITARY HOSPITAL, SHORNCLIFFE

"Welcome, Prime Minister, to the 3rd Stationary Hospital," greeted Lieutenant-Colonel Henry Casgrain as he and his accompanying entourage stepped into the main lobby of the Moore Military Barracks Hospital.

Borden glanced at the row of senior officers, nurses, and orderlies lined up for his inspection. It was a familiar routine, and this was the second hospital he was inspecting today. This one was of special interest to him. The 3rd Stationary Hospital had been activated in February. Most of the officers and staff were from London, Ontario. The rest of the men had been recruited from Windsor and Sarnia just before they arrived in England last April. They had been transferred to Shorncliffe a month later.

"Let me introduce you to my senior staff," said Casgrain. The unit's CO was in his late fifties, with grey hair and blue eyes. Borden had been informed that Casgrain's wife was a nurse and had volunteered to serve with the CEF. She had been assigned to a different unit to avoid complications. "This is Major Davis, from London, Ontario, and Major Guest from St. Thomas. Of course you are familiar with Matron Jaggard."

Borden beamed at his cousin, who was the main reason for his visit. "Of course. I'm glad to see you, Mrs. Jaggard," he stated. He felt awkward greeting her this way, but protocol demanded it. "You're looking well."

A smile lighted her face, and her blue eyes twinkled. She was dressed in the standard nurse's working uniform, a blue dress with a starched white apron on top. On her shoulders she wore captain's stars. Ever since she had married an American, a senior executive at the Pennsylvania Railroad Company, he hadn't seen much of her or her seventeen-year-old son. But they stayed in touch by mail.

"Yes, Prime Minister," she replied. "You're looking well."

"They're keeping you busy?"

"Of course."

Borden chuckled.

"Is Lady Borden with you?"

Borden shook his head. "I'm afraid that she couldn't accompany me on this trip."

"Pity, I would have liked to have seen her."

"I'm sure she is disappointed that she couldn't come. She would have liked to see you too."

"Very well. I'm looking forward to that. So you getting a game in now and then?" she said with a teasing smile.

A small smile twitched briefly under his white moustache. She knew him too well.

"I heard that you will be leaving soon?"

"Yes, Prime Minister. We're being deployed to the Dardanelles," she answered.

Casgrain added, "We received orders that we are to move to Southampton on the 1st."

Borden nodded. "If your duties allow, I'll sent a car for you this evening. I can't promise that the food will better than army cooking, but we have a lot of catching up to do."

Matron Jaggard glanced at Casgrain, who said, "I'm sure that something could be arranged."

"Good. At five o'clock then."

"I'll be ready, Prime Minister."

CHAPTER 25

"What's with Hughes and the fucking rain? Doesn't he believe in sunshine?" demanded Captain Sommerfield of the 4th Canadian Infantry Brigade.

"He does seem to have bad luck with the weather," conceded Captain Llewellyn as the droplets fell off his visor. "It's not as if he picked August 4th to start a war."

"You never know," replied Sommerfield. He shrugged to adjust the collar of his greatcoat and prevent water dripping down the back of his neck.

Captain Llewellyn chuckled as he looked away from him to glance at the saluting post located between the Napier Barracks and the R.E. Barracks. The staff near the post were waiting for the arrival of Major-General Sam Hughes and the Honourable Bonar Law, the Secretary of State for the Colonies.

"Do you remember that downpour he had us stand in last year?"

"You had to remind me!" winced Llewellyn.

Sommerfield gave him a grin before he turned his gaze on the men who were neatly arranged on the Sir John Moore Field. The field was surrounded on three sides by rows of one-storey red-brick barracks. They were standing in front of buildings that hid Somerset Barracks, now the home of the Canadian cavalry. The horse troops were neatly arranged on the three hundred by eight hundred yards of grass, now mud plain in front of them. Besides the cavalry, frontage had been allocated for the artillery and the infantry battalions.

To the east, a martello tower was visible. There was a series of them strung along the coast, armed with naval guns, to protect southern England. On a clear day one could see across the English Channel to the French coast. Past the tower, parts of Folkestone were visible.

"I hope they arrive on time."

Llewellyn glanced at the officer. Hughes and Bonar Law were scheduled to review the 2nd Division at Bargrove Farm on the Beachborough Estate at 2:30 p.m. Afterward, they were to drive the four miles or so to review the rest of the Canadians stationed at the Shorncliffe training base.

"Why? You have a date?"

"Sure do, tonight at the Dawn Rooster pub."

"You're not attending the honourable Bonar's speech this evening?" Llewellyn asked. All the officers were ordered to attend.

"I wish I could get out of it, but I'm seeing her after."

"Have you tumbled her yet?"

Sommerfield grinned. "I hope to. I have orders for France. I'm leaving on Friday." There was a hint of excitement in his voice. Llewellyn understood. The 4th Brigade officer had never crossed into France since he had arrived with the 1st Contingent last October. "You can have my billet when I leave. It's near the hospital."

"Thanks. I appreciate that," replied Llewellyn. The Moore Barracks Military Hospital was the two-storey, eight hundred-bed facility that the Canadian Medical Corps had been assigned to. He had received orders shortly after Prime Minister Borden inspected them last week to report to Shorncliffe. He would be spending the next several months passing on his experience to the green 2nd Division. "I have a friend there that I want to visit before the afternoon meeting."

"Here they come," Sommerfield said as a motorcade appeared near the Napier Barracks. As the Highland pipe band announced their arrival, the rain stopped. He had a fairly good idea what Bonar was going to say. That it had been a year since the war started, and that it was a fight that all free men had a duty to contribute to. What else was he going to say?

MOORE BARRACKS MILITARY HOSPITAL, SHORNCLIFFE

"What the hell are you doing here?" Samantha demanded when she spotted the familiar gait in the corridor. She could see the shocked look on Emily's face. She had dared to use the H word.

"I was going to ask you the same thing," a grinning Captain Llewellyn said when he turned to face her. "A bit more diplomatically, of course. It's been my experience that women tend to be sensitive to such things."

"Really! You have a lot of experience with women?" Samantha could see that Emily was trying not to grin. The patient in the wheelchair Emily was pushing didn't make any such effort.

The captain snapped to attention then barked, "Llewellyn, James. Captain. Serial number 015678…"

Emily and patient broke out laughing. Samantha glared at them, which caused them to laugh harder. She turned her blonde head back to the captain. "At ease, Captain. At ease."

"Yes, ma'am," he replied as he relaxed.

Samantha shook her head. "So what are you doing here?"

"I came to visit a friend of mine. A Colonel Tennison."

"But the last I saw you, you were with the 2nd Brigade in Flanders," she stated. "Are you on leave?"

"No," he said as he removed his khaki overcoat and draped it over his arm. "I've been assigned to Shorncliffe to help train the 2nd Division. What are you doing here?"

"We've been ordered here by Matron Macdonald. The No. 2 Casualty Clearing Station has recently taken over this building."

"And they are green," he said. He turned his gaze to Emily. "Good to see you again, Mrs. Creighton. How's your husband faring?"

"He's doing well. He's at the Hotel du Golf. How did you know?"

"Father Stoats told me all about the wedding. He was pleased to marry such a suitable couple."

Emily blushed at the compliment. "Well, I better take care of my patient here."

"I'm in no rush," the patient said.

"You're scheduled for physio."

"Oh God! Save me," he entreated as Emily rolled him down the hall.

"I'll take you to the colonel," Samantha said. She led him up the stairs to the second floor. When he stepped onto the floor, the captain had to make room for two orderlies who were carrying a patient on a stretcher. At the entrance to one of the wards, they had to tilt the stretcher in order to pass through.

Samantha frowned when she saw what they did. "We're going to have to fix that."

"I saw all the construction when I came in," stated the captain. "You'll have to add it to the list."

"I'll make the suggestion. We currently have 540 beds, and the plans are for 260 more. We've been authorized for eight hundred beds. We're converting the Drill Shed out back into a dining room and recreation centre for the patients. The kitchen's being expanded, and they are looking at connecting it to the dining hall. We have to find more stoves to provide heat for the men. It gets kind of cold here in winter."

"Are you billeted in the tents outside?"

"Nope," she said cheerfully. "I'm staying at a hotel in Folkestone."

"So you're the matron here now?" He glanced at her stars to see if she had been promoted.

"I'm afraid not," she answered curtly. "A matron and thirty nurses are scheduled to arrive in a couple of days."

"No more gas masks then?"

"I certainly hope not," she replied as they entered the officers' ward. The ward was a typical one with about a dozen white enamel beds. The ward had whitewashed walls, but the floor that shined with wax had the aged look from the pounding of thousands of boots. The beds were filled with senior ranked officers. The captain was struck by how many of the officers' heads were wrapped in bandages.

"Well, look at what the cat dragged in," said Lieutenant-Colonel Tennison with a slight slur. He was seated on a bed with a familiar pipe clenched in his teeth. The left side of his face was lightly bandaged, covering his shrapnel wounds. He had barely recovered from Ypres when he got peppered at Givenchy by an unlucky shell. He looked tired, but he seemed to be on the mend.

"So how are you doing?" said the captain.

"Eh! I see that you brought Bermuda weather with you," he said as he pointed to the nearby single hung window covered with raindrops. The bottom glass had been raised slightly to allow for air circulation.

The captain rolled his eyes.

"Bermuda weather?" Samantha asked in confusion.

"A private joke," replied Tennison. "So Hughes and Bonar Law came to visit?"

"This morning for the review. Aikens was with them."

"The newspaper magnate?"

"Yep. He's writing a glowing account how we saved the day at Ypres."

"Oh God! The Imperials are going to like that," Tennison exclaimed.

"I'm afraid that I have to go. Duty calls," Samantha said after glancing at the small timepiece pinned to her apron. "Try not to tire him."

"Of course, Samantha. It was nice seeing you again," he said. She touched his arm as she turned to leave.

"Nice ass," the lieutenant-colonel said when he was sure that she was out of earshot. When Llewellyn frowned at him, he added, "I might be married, but I'm not dead. You should ask her out. She likes you."

"Why does everyone keep saying that?" griped Llewellyn.

"Look around, lad! Look around!"

ESTAMINET, NIEPPE

"God, this is awful," Sergeant Ryan said as he took a sip of the muddy red wine the estaminet owner had sloshed into his tin cup after she had taken his francs. Josette was a middle-aged woman, pleasantly plump, with a hawk nose. She had seen a lot of mileage, and the war was adding more. Her husband, twenty years older, was seated on a stool playing a soulful song on a concertina. Josette wasn't adverse to a quick tumble if the price was right. Her daughters, however, were off limits. She was pretty handy with the meat cleaver. She proved that quite effectively whenever that delicacy came in.

"Well, that's all she's got. She ran out of beer, and she can't sell any of the hard stuff," Reggie answered as he emptied his mug. "Tough to get drunk on this stuff. I want to get drunk. I want to get fucking falling down pissing drunk."

Ryan could see that his friend was already well on his way. If he had been drinking hard liquor, he would be falling down by now. But the estaminets were not allowed to. If they were caught, the bar would be summarily closed.

"Damn inspections. We didn't get our rum today," Reggie slurred as his mood swung from cheerful to morose. "Damn fucking inspections."

Ryan was actually happy not to have received his today. The 186-proof dark Jamaican rum was actually undrinkable, but Major Masterley made sure that everyone got their daily ration when they were on the line and twice weekly when they were in their billets or on work parties.

Ryan would wait in the line with the men. When he finally reached the quartermaster corporal, he would be holding a one-gallon grey clay rum jar. The jar usually had a brown-painted mouth with "SRD" printed over top in black letters. He would pour out exactly 2.5 ounces into a measuring cup before transferring it into Paul's mess tin.

"Drink it," the major would order. Paul would try to pour it down his throat without it touching his taste buds. Even then the aftertaste clung for an hour or so. Once he finished drinking his ration, he had to show the cup to Masterley to verify that it was empty. It was his way to ensure that none of his men were hoarding rum. Ryan only drank to be sociable, but a lot wanted to get pissed drunk.

"Damn inspections. Mean buggers, today of all days," Reggie muttered as he waved Josette over. "They deliberately did it to wear us out. We spent most of the morning grooming the horses and cleaning tack. What did we get out of it?" Reggie demanded, pounding the table with his fist. "Besides the general telling us we had the best damned groomed horses in the division."

"I know! I know! I was there," Paul replied. Lieutenant-General Alderson had inspected the division's artillery and horse lines in late afternoon.

"Yep, this would be a perfect day to celebrate the war. A great day to get drunk," he rambled as Josette filled both their mugs and then snatched more centimes from their table. Ryan knew that Reggie was really down, since he didn't pinch Josette's bottom when she presented it to them as she served the table beside them.

"To old friends," Reggie said as he raised his cup.

Damn it, you had to say that, as memories flooded Ryan. "To old friends," he answered as they clinked their mugs together. Now he too really wanted to get drunk.

LONDON OPERA HOUSE, LONDON

"An excellent speech, Prime Minister," said Sir Arthur Balfour when Sir Robert Borden took his seat beside him on the stage as the standing ovation died down.

"Thank you," said Borden. He hadn't been particularly happy with his speech. Balfour, the First Lord of the Admiralty, was a tough act to follow. Balfour earlier had ended his speech with, "We are determined to see the war through to a good end, and that determination is shared in every part of the British Empire."

Borden had echoed some of that in his own, but some his phrasing had been awkward and didn't flow naturally. He had spent part of his morning working with Percy trying to fix it for this evening's Imperial patriotic gathering held at the London Opera House in Covent Garden, but they had run out of time. They had to attend the prayer and intercession mass, along with the Imperial Cabinet and the royals, at St. Paul's

Cathedral. Thoughts of Laura drifted into his mind. He knew that she was attending a similar mass in Ottawa. Then he had luncheon at Mansion House, the home of the lord mayor of London. The queen had been in attendance, and he had watched as she touched the Pearl Sword. After that he was glad to get out of his court dress, a blue single-breasted tail coat embroidered with gold thread cuffs and collar, which he hated wearing, to visit a local hospital.

He had been nervous when he finally arrived at the Opera House. The management was quite pleased that the main hall was filled to capacity and that they had to turn away thousands who wanted to attend. Madame Clara Butt had opened the meeting with a rousing rendition of "God Save the King." He had been impressed by the contralto's voice. He sang, somewhat, and he recognized a superb singer when he heard one. There weren't that many people that he had to look up to. Literally, he had to since she was well over six feet tall. When he rose to speak, the audience had risen to their feet to cheer him and to wave white handkerchiefs.

From the table in front of him, he took a sip of water to parch his thirst. He had been speaking for well over an hour, and the heat was beginning to rise. He glanced over at Balfour and was trying to determine when would be a good time to address the submarine issue. Borden was hoping that he might reverse Winston Churchill's decision not to hand over a couple of the submarines that the British government had ordered built in Montreal. Borden wanted to use them to help protect Canada's coasts.

When the Marquis de Crewe rose to close the evening, Borden hoped that he would be brief. It soon became clear that Crewe would be babbling for a while.

Borden glanced at Balfour again. It reminded him of the discussions he had been having with the members of the imperial cabinet. One of them was how Canada could gain a voice in imperial affairs. The other, the one that concerned him most, was their pessimism about when the war would end. Three or four years was their best guess. Three or four more years!

CHAPTER 26

"What a despicable old man," declared Emily when the British colonel was out of hearing range.

"I know. I'm afraid he's going to lodge a complaint," Samantha said as she patted the black-brown rider she was sitting on. "Matron Macdonald won't be happy when she hears about it."

"You don't say," Emily replied sarcastically. "What a way to ruin a perfectly good day! What business is it of his whether or not we ride side-saddle."

The colonel hadn't been too happy to see the small group of nurses out for an afternoon picnic riding astride. There were still people who thought that those women who did not ride side-saddle were wanton harlots. She had seen some of the upper-class women on their morning rides with their skirts hiding their ankles. If they had ridden in the Sudbury bush, they would have learned rather quickly how impractical a side-saddle was; especially when a black bear was chasing you.

"Some people are rather set in their ways," Samantha sighed. She wondered how many complaints the matron had to deal with concerning the nurses' riding attire. Since they were only a few miles away from the hospital, they were still in their uniforms.

"Why don't we have our picnic here?" asked Mabel Tatlock, a doughty woman in her early thirties, hunched on her horse with both hands on the pommel. The other two nurses, Fae and Sadie, looked comfortable on theirs. Fae Timson was a wiry New Brunswicker in her mid-thirties with thin brown hair, while Sadie Rann was a Torontonian in her early twenties, a redhead with a pale complexion and green eyes. Both nurses had arrived in England in early July with the 2nd Canadian Division.

They had requested docile and placid animals from the remount depot, and the grooms had been quite happy to provide them with the better ones. The horses seemed happy with the change of pace.

Emily shrugged as Samantha said, "At least it's still a nice day."

It was. There were a few wisps of cloud in the blue sky. A bit of wind was pushing the whitecaps to slap against the squawking seagulls that flocked the beach looking for food. Across the English Channel they could see the thin brown line of the French coast.

Samantha swung out of the saddle and dropped the reins so they touched the ground. The horses had been trained not to wonder off with the reins trailing. "I'll help with the basket," she said. Tied to Mabel's horse were two wicker baskets that contained their picnic lunch.

"It's good to get away from the hospital for a couple of hours," Mabel said. She sighed with relief when her feet touched the ground.

"A bad night?" asked Emily. Samantha noticed that Emily had lost some of her airiness since she first met her on the train to Valcartier nearly a year ago. She didn't know if it was her marriage to Major Creighton or simply the toll of her day-to-day duties.

"You can say that," Mabel replied. "I caught a bleeder last night. It was just by chance. I was doing a spot-check when I noticed some blood on the blanket. It was a close call. A few minutes later, he would have been gone."

Samantha grimaced as she set a blue-checked tablecloth on the ground. "What were his wounds?" she asked as she anchored the cloth with stones on the corners.

"Both legs were amputated," Mabel replied. "At least it was a bit of excitement. Things have been pretty quiet of late."

"Oh yes," said Fae as she handed Samantha mess tins from the basket. "Only five hundred or so of the eight hundred of the beds are filled at the moment."

"That is not going to last, unfortunately," said Sadie as she took out two roasted chickens that had been wrapped in wax paper.

"Sadly, true," Mabel sighed.

"They've been keeping us busy with the training courses," Emily said as she tried to shoo away seagulls that had taken an interest in them. "I must admit the one Major Tennet gave on diseases of the mind was quite interesting."

"He was cute," Sadie stated. When they looked at her, she shrugged. "He is. Is he married?"

"I'm afraid so," replied Emily.

Sadie's face dropped in disappointment. "Well, they're creating a separate ward with straitjackets and restraints for the mental patients."

"When are they planning to have it ready?" asked Emily.

"When the engineers can get to it," replied Sadie.

Samantha chuckled. "That means that it won't get done until October. They've been pretty slow on some of the ward work. They're already a couple of weeks behind."

"That's right," replied Mabel. "Also, they haven't completed the installation of the X-ray equipment yet."

"I thought it was working," Samantha said.

"It is. Just don't get too close to it."

"Great," replied Sadie. "Where is the tea?"

"It should be in there. I packed it myself," Samantha told her as she used a knife to cut up the chicken.

"Got it," said Sadie said as she handed her the flask. "Did anyone hear from Jane?"

"Not since she left for the St. Helena hospital last week," replied Mabel. The St. Helena Military hospital had been designated to treat officers and nurses only. The authorities wanted to keep the convalescent officers and nurses separated from the other ranks.

"Hope that she's getting better. She was pretty sick with some kind of stomach ailment," Emily said before biting into a chicken leg.

"We should visit her tomorrow and bring her some flowers," said Samantha.

"Anything but poppies," said Mabel. "She doesn't like those."

"Okay. It's too bad that Matron Jaggard didn't come," said Emily. The nurses frowned at her. "What?"

"Matrons don't socialize with us lower folks," stated Mabel.

Samantha agreed. It was a common practice to keep their distance from their staff. They didn't want to compromise their authority by being too familiar.

"Well, I still think that she's nice," she replied as she took another bite of her chicken leg.

"So have you finally got a date yet?" Samantha asked Sadie.

"No, not yet. But it's going to be soon," she said, wrinkling her nose in disgust. "They're waiting to ensure they can fill the *Metagama* before it sails." Sadie had received unofficial orders that she was to accompany patients being shipped back to Canada for convalescence and release. "I'm not happy about it. It's a two-week voyage home. Then I have to wait for the next ship back. I'd rather stay here. What can I do? Orders are orders."

"You might get lucky and come back with a new batch of nurses," said Fae. "Have you met the new ones who just have come in?"

"We're going to be introduced when we get back to the hospital," replied Samantha. "Speaking of which, did anyone hear rumours that some of us are being sent to Malta?"

"Didn't Nurse Commings just get transferred there?" asked Mabel.

"Why?" asked Emily.

"Last I heard there is some fighting in the Dardanelles, and they are sending the casualties to the hospitals on Malta."

"Who would have thought? Us going to the Mediterranean?" Emily said in wonder.

"What will your husband say?" asked Samantha.

"What can he say? Orders are orders," replied Emily.

CHAPTER 27

Matron Jaggard was feeling moisture starting to bead on her forehead. The blue linen nursing uniform that she was wearing was beginning to feel clammy, and it was early morning. The awning above her head did provide some protection from the intense sun. She was standing at the rail, staring at the two-mile breakwater that protected the port of Alexandria. She wanted to take off her Panama hat to create a breeze, but it would have set a bad example for her charges. At least the waxed wooden deck of the HMHS *Asturias* provided some protection from the ship's steel plates. She wondered if it would be as hot when they finally arrived at the Greek island of Lemnos in the Aegean Sea.

Emily, the twenty-five-year-old Calgarian with chestnut hair and emerald eyes, emerged from the stairs that led to the first-class cabins on the upper deck assigned to the senior medical officers and the matrons. Before the war, the *Asturias* had been a Royal Mail Steam Packet liner on the Southampton–Buenos Aires run. While she had been retrofitted as a hospital ship, one could still see that she had carried the 1,430 passengers in style. Once upon a time she carried 422 in 1st class, 233 in 2nd, and 775 in 3rd. The retrofit had reduced her capacity to 896 patients.

"Any word yet?" she asked. She was puffing slightly, as the intense heat was draining.

"I'm afraid not," the matron replied.

A frown appeared at the corner of Emily's mouth. "Any chance that we can go ashore? It would be a shame to be close to so much history and unable to see it." The frown deepened when Jaggard shook her head. "Pity. That's the army for you. Hurry up and wait. You would have thought Malta would have informed them that we were coming."

"They probably thought London would have sent a message. I don't know why they would have. They didn't bother sending one to Malta." When they had arrived on the 8th of August after sailing for seven days from Folkestone, the port officials had come on board demanding to know who they were and what they were doing there. The matron had agreed with her nurses that the reason they were there was fairly obvious, since the ship was painted as per the Geneva Convention. The

Asturias had been repainted bright white. A green band, broken up by red crosses on her bow, stern, and amidship, ran the length of the 660-foot vessel. The authorities at Malta were perplexed by the fact that everyone on board was Canadian. Technically, Jaggard wasn't; she had lost her citizenship since she married an American.

Once the Maltese had telegraphed London, they got a reply informing them that they were indeed there on instructions from the War Office and that their next port of call was Alexandria. When they finally arrived three days later at five o'clock in the morning, the British officials didn't know what to do with them either, especially after they discovered that there were three Canadian stationary hospitals on board: the 1st Canadian Division's 1st, which had seen service at Ypres and Festubert, and the 2nd Canadian Division's 3rd and 5th that had been based at Shorncliffe.

"I wonder what's taking so long? It's been two days," Emily complained as she eyed the harbour traffic. It was a busy port; it handled nearly three thousand ships a year. Most of the vessels anchored were British and French war and cargo ships supporting the Gallipoli campaign. Also, local fishing boats and lighters were bobbing in the water as they made their daily runs. A couple had pulled alongside to sell their daily catch. The ship's cooks had been happy for fresh fish to supplement their menus.

"They've probably been using carrier pigeons," replied Jaggard, which caused Emily to chuckle. "In the meantime, let's keep the regular training schedule."

While the basics were similar between land and sea, there were differences they needed to adjust to. Simple little things such as caring for patients in bunk beds. How to treat the upper patient without disturbing the lower one? Handling patients in the swinging cots. They had been warned that in rough seas patients had been known to be tossed out onto the floor, or the deck, as the sailors called it.

"Yes, ma'am," Emily replied as she watched a lighter that had seen better days pull alongside the *Asturias*. Officers jumped onto the stairs and climbed up to the upper decks.

"Now be off with you," ordered the matron.

Emily was reluctant to leave, and Jaggard understood why. She was hoping that they would be bringing their sailing orders from the Mediterranean Expeditionary Force command.

A few minutes later, a sergeant approached her. "Ma'am, Colonel Casgrain requested your presence in the officers' mess."

"I see. Have Matrons Charleson and Willoughby been notified?" Eleanor Charleson from Gananoque, Ontario, was the matron for the nursing sisters assigned to the 1st. Jaggard had learned a lot from her experience. Bertha Willoughby from Quebec City was the matron for the Queen's University Stationary Hospital, the 5th.

"Yes, ma'am," he replied.

"Very well," she replied with a sense of relief that the waiting was finally over and they could get on with the job of saving lives.

AUGUST 15, 1915
QUEEN'S CANADIAN MILITARY HOSPITAL, BEACHBOROUGH,
ENGLAND

"Miss Lonsdale," Captain Llewellyn asked, "are you all right?"

He had been somewhat surprised to find her on the side of the road, shaking an angry finger in the face of a chestnut horse. When he recognized the horse, he understood why she had been threatening him with the glue factory several times.

She turned her head rapidly to him. Several twigs and blades of grass tumbled from her hair and her shoulders. From his angle, he could see that the back of her nurse's uniform was stained. He admired her curves for a brief moment before returning his gaze to her blue eyes.

"Yes, I'm fine," she snapped. She added indignantly, "This brute threw me!"

"Well, Old Sam has that reputation," replied Llewellyn.

"Old Sam?"

"I'm afraid so. Someone's perverse sense of humour, naming him after the minister."

"That explains the funny looks I got when I asked for him," Samantha replied in a sour tone.

"You asked for him?" he said incredulously.

Samantha shook her head. "One of the nurses said that he was one of the gentlest horses in the entire stable."

"I see."

When the light finally came on, she declared, "Oh she'll pay once I get my hands on her. Oh she'll pay!"

Llewellyn laughed. "I'm sure that she will."

When she finally turned her attention to the captain, she demanded, "What are you doing here..." The rest of the question was unanswered when she saw behind Llewellyn a company of a hundred men marching on the macadam road. Llewellyn had decided to join the 5th Company of the 2nd Canadian Division on one of its regular forced marches. The hobnail boots grew louder as they caught up with the captain. Most of the men gave Samantha a grin, and even a few gave her some wolf whistles as they passed.

"Lucky bastard," the captain heard from someone as the men headed west. He didn't bother trying to identify the man. What was the point?

"Sorry," he said lamely.

"Boys will be boys," Samantha stated. Llewellyn sensed that it had bothered her.

"I'll walk with you to the Queen's hospital. We're only a half-mile away."

"I know, that's where I was heading. I had decided to get a rider from the remount depot. I needed to get some fresh air and exercise," she replied.

"Well, it's a nice day for it." It was early morning, and the breeze was pushing some of the cumulus clouds inland. It was comfortable for marching. A flock of seagulls squawked above them.

"You've been to the hospital before?"

"We pass it several times during our route marches," he replied. The Beachborough manor was two and a half miles west from Shorncliffe. The Canadians had taken over the mansion from the current owner last October and had transformed it into a hospital. "I've been trying to stay out of hospitals, as you well know. Are you being transferred there?"

"No, I'm being sent to brief the nurses on the new procedures that they are to follow for jaundice cases. We've been getting quite a few of them lately. All of them are being transferred to a new hospital, where doctors are investigating how to treat them."

"Is it infectious?"

"Yes," replied Samantha. "Why?"

"I've seen several men with yellow skin complaining of itching. I guess that they'll have to be put on the sick roll."

"Best that you do that."

"We're almost there," said Captain Llewellyn when they came over the rise. His company was about a hundred yards from the hospital. The manor house was sitting in a field of green and brown. Several stands of trees obscured one of the wings. The white building was three storeys high, with nine columns of windows. A drive curved off the road to the main entrance, where an ambulance was unloading patients. Behind the building, they could see the top of the greenhouses' glass roofs where they were growing vegetables for the patients.

"Thank you, Captain, for escorting me. I greatly appreciate it," she stated. The horse behind them snorted in agreement.

"It's my pleasure," replied the captain. "But I insist that I escort you to the front door and that you get examined by a doctor. You might have suffered an injury."

"I feel fine," Samantha replied.

Oh, what the hell, thought the captain, *might as well ask.* He was about to pose his personal question when he heard the drone of aircraft engines. Aircraft around Shorncliffe wasn't unusual, but when he turned his head to locate them, he swore when he spotted them. "Shit."

A sand-coloured airship emerged from the clouds with two gondolas below its sausage shape. The blades of its four engines hummed in the morning sky. He could see LZ 45 painted on its nose. It was over five hundred feet long and forty-six feet around. Llewellyn recognized it, since it matched the Zeppelin in the drawings and intelligence reports on the German airship raids along the English coast. It was estimated that it was capable of carrying a couple of thousand pounds of bombs on board.

Llewellyn watched grimly as the Zeppelin lined up for a bombing run on his company. He watched the men scatter off the road, but it was too late as the bombs started dropping. Bursts of dirt flew in the sky, taking body parts with them.

Samantha started running to the men. Captain Llewellyn was keeping pace with her. They knew that they couldn't stop the bombing, but at least they could help the wounded.

AUGUST 17, 1915
MUDROS HARBOUR, ISLAND OF LEMNOS, GREECE

Matron Jaggard was watching a black-painted ship run aground about eight hundred yards or so south of the hospital pier. The sound of metal hitting sand reached the small hill named Turk's Head on West Mudros. The sound and look on her face caused Lieutenant-Colonel Casgrain to look behind him. Her main concern was how they were going to treat the wounded. Most of their equipment and supplies were still in crates and boxes that were being unloaded from the SS *Nordic* that was anchored in the harbour. The No. 1 and No. 3 hospitals had been transferred here for the final three-day leg of the voyage to Lemnos, the Mediterranean Expeditionary Force's main support base for Gallipoli campaign. Gallipoli was only about forty miles away.

She and her nurses had embarked aboard the MMHS *Delta* for the voyage to the island. The colonel had informed her it had been a wise choice. He had been aboard the *Nordic*, a refrigerated cattle transport that had been used to carry 100,000 carcasses in her holds. She had 320 passenger cabins added as an afterthought. The ship belonged to the White Star company and had plied the Liverpool–Cape Town–Sydney route. She hadn't been painted with the standard hospital ship colours and therefore was considered a "black ship" when transporting medical staff and patients from Lemnos to Alexandria. This meant that the ship was a legitimate target for German submarines that hunted in the Mediterranean.

The matron's ship, the *Delta*, was a "white ship" and was a Peninsular and Orient Steam Navigation Company vessel that had been reconfigured to carry 597 patients, 287 in cots and 210 in berths. She had been on her deck enjoying the cool early morning air about a day out from Lemnos when a French destroyer slid alongside. After the *Nordic* and the *Delta* changed course and picked up steam to keep pace with the destroyer, extra lookouts were stationed fore and aft, scanning the sea with binoculars.

When she had asked what was happening, one of the sailors informed her that the RMT *King Edward*, a Canadian Northern Steamship Company vessel, had been sunk by a German sub three days earlier. Of the 1,367 men aboard, nine hundred of them had lost their lives. They had been reinforcements for the Imperial 29th Division at Gallipoli.

Everyone on board was tense, and she hadn't gotten any rest until they arrived at Lemnos. Security at the Mudros harbour was tight. They had to comply with Admiral Wemyss's orders, the same admiral who had commanded the 1st Contingent's fleet last October, that all ships be inspected prior to being allowed to take anchorage.

"They're Aussies," Colonel Fiaschi said with great pride. The CO of the 3rd Australian General Hospital was tall, with the typical bearing of a man who had spent most of his life in the army. He was an Italian who had immigrated to Australia in his youth. "They are training with the X lighter, a new landing craft for the infantry. She's slightly over a hundred feet long, bulletproof, and can carry five hundred men. When they lower the front ramp, the men will disembark rather sharply."

The matron watched as the thin ramp on the bow slapped the beach, and then two lines of men ran down it onto the sand. It didn't take long for the ship to empty. "I was wondering there for a moment. I thought I was watching an accident happen."

"Quite," the Australian colonel said as he glanced at the captain's stars on her uniform. He turned his attention back to Lieutenant-Colonel Casgrain. Jaggard didn't display any emotion. As a hospital nursing superintendent, she had dealt with doctors of all stripes.

"We're glad to have you here. The current projections are we're about to receive eight hundred patients per day. We've been notified that there will be an August push."

Casgrain's face was grim. "What percentage will be due to battle wounds?"

"We're currently seeing about 70 percent. They'll be transported here by ship from Gallipoli, where we'll stabilize them. Once they are fit to travel they will be sent to Alexandria or Malta."

The fifty-seven-year-old Casgrain acknowledged that with a nod. She had gotten to know the London, Ontario, doctor well on the voyage. Most of the men of the 3rd had been recruited from the London and Sarnia area. "It will take a couple of days for us to get set up," he replied as he waved away some pesky flies that were starting to make their presence felt.

Jaggard had a fairly good idea where they were coming from. Their hospital site was located on a rocky hill on an isthmus that jutted out into the bay. The island's hills were treeless, and the tall grass was turning a green brown. It was obvious that it had been a previous campsite. Whoever was there before hadn't bothered with proper sanitation, since she could see open ditches filled with sewage. This was the site that they had been assigned, and they would have to make do. The engineers were to prepare the ground for their arrival, but they hadn't started the work yet.

"What about food and water?" asked Casgrain.

"We have to make do with army rations," replied Fiaschi. "The locals produce mostly grapes, grain, and sheep. There are some Greek traders for fruits and vegetables, but the prices are high."

"And water?" asked Jaggard. This was a major concern. They needed fresh water for the incoming patients to prepare meals, to clean clothes and bandages, and to sterilize medical equipment.

"We're currently rationing water," Fiaschi said, directing his comments to Casgrain. "Until the engineers can get pipes in or build storage tanks, you will need to haul water. The wells here are sufficient for the local population, and we're having water shipped in from Alexandria."

Jaggard saw Casgrain grimace at the news. "Can you spare a water cart? We're missing that piece of kit."

Fiaschi shook his head. "I'm in the same situation. Most of my hospital's equipment has not arrived. We'll have to put in a request with GHQ to see if they can spare any."

"Understood," replied Casgrain as he gave Matron Jaggard a glance. She understood the look. Without clean, fresh water, they were going to lose patients.

CHAPTER 28

Major-General Hughes rested his hand on the hilt of the sword strapped to his left hip. From time to time the scabbard would gently tap against his thigh as he waited to be called before the king. It was his only sign of nervousness. His right arm clasped his cock hat with the white ostrich feathers tightly against his scarlet tunic. His mandarin collar felt stiffer than usual.

He glanced over at Bonar Law, who gave him a brief smile. The secretary of state for the colonies appeared more relaxed in his blue court dress uniform with a single row of gleaming buttons. The jacket's lapel and cuffs were black velvet, with gold embroidery. Gold oak-leaf lace ran down the seams of his pants.

He was disappointed that only Bonar Law was here for his investiture. He had hoped other members of the Imperial British cabinet, especially Lord Kitchener, would be in attendance. Borden's absence irritated him as well, but the prime minister had a good excuse. He was aboard ship returning to Canada. As for the rest of the imperial cabinet, they had been invited to private morning audiences with King George V after the king's arrival from Windsor Castle.

It was at the morning session that the king had presented various medals and awards. Several DSOs and Military Crosses had been given. One DSO had been given to Major Godson, who was with the Canadian Scottish. A Victoria Cross was awarded to a Captain Butler for conspicuous bravery in West Africa's Cameroon. Hughes had been disappointed that his investiture had been scheduled for the afternoon after the king had lunch with Queen Alexandria at Marlborough House. He would have preferred attending the morning ceremony, where several officers had been granted knighthoods and had been invested in the Most Honourable Order of the Bath.

He had to settle for Bonar Law, which in a way made sense, since he was after all secretary of state for the colonies. In fact, Law had been born in New Brunswick in 1858 before his family had returned to Scotland. He had made his fortune in the steel trade before he entered politics.

Hughes was being awarded a knighthood in the civil division rather than the military division, which also rankled him a bit. His rank as a major-general allowed him to wear his military dress uniform with his medals on his left breast. He could feel them on his chest under the gold cord and tassels that ran from his shoulder board to the button-hole on his jacket. If Borden hadn't promoted him, he would have been required to wear a similar uniform to Bonar Law's. Protocol would have demanded that he wear a class 2 court dress. The difference between classes 1 and 2 was the width of the gold embroidery and edging.

But still, a knighthood was a knighthood. What higher honour could one ask for? Even Borden thought so. He had heard Borden had been pushing hard that one be granted to him.

When the trumpets sounded and the doors opened, he entered the ballroom and marched across the carpeted floor to the two red upholstered thrones at the far end of the room. The taller one was for the king, the other for the queen consort. He was so focused on King George that he didn't notice the brilliant white walls with gold leaf trim and the pipe organ behind him.

When he reached the dais on which the throne chairs rested, he knelt on the small red upholstered stool waiting for him. King George rose from his chair and stepped up to Hughes. Two footmen appeared at his side, holding cushions. One balanced a sword, while on the other rested the insignia that Hughes would be entitled to wear as a Knight Commander of the Order of the Bath.

King George took the sword and tapped Sam Hughes with the flat of the blade on his right and left shoulder. Hughes was disappointed that the king did not say, "Rise, sir knight."

Still, he was beaming broadly when he rose and bowed his head for the king to drape his knight's insignia around his neck.

SEPTEMBER 7, 1915
PRIVY COUNCIL CHAMBER, EAST BLOCK, PARLIAMENT HILL,
OTTAWA

"Glad to see you back," said Senator James Lougheed as he greeted Borden with a handshake.

"If I got such a warm welcome every time, I would travel to England more often," Borden replied. He indicated to the Alberta senator to take the seat next to him in the Privy Council Chamber.

"I read in the paper that you got quite a reception in Montreal last Friday."

"I was frankly surprised by the crowd at Fletcher Field. It was the largest that I have ever seen. My speech that I gave in English and French seemed to be well received."

"How was the sea voyage back? Did you make good time?"

"It was quite pleasant, actually. I got plenty of rest, and some of my travel companions were interesting. We had three destroyers escort us until we were three days out. After that it was rather uneventful." Borden paused then asked, "How was your time with the Militia Department?"

Lougheed shrugged. "Sam's a lot of things, but an administrator he is not. He hasn't been running it in a businesslike manner," he replied.

Borden gave him a sour look. Lougheed had plenty of business experience. He was, like Borden, a lawyer with a lucrative practice in Calgary, he owned a brokerage firm, and he had invested heavily in real estate. "You're not the first person who has told me that. Did you straighten things out?"

Lougheed gave Borden a so-so wave. "There is only so much I could do. I was only there keeping the seat warm while you and Sam were gone. By the way, how did Sam behave?"

"For him he was actually quite good. Especially after he found out about the knighthood," Borden replied. He knew what Lougheed was really asking. How long would he put up with Hughes' behaviour? Borden wasn't willing to answer that — at least not now. But he was also well aware that Hughes' current good behaviour wouldn't last long.

"What's this I hear about machine gun subscription?" Borden asked, changing the subject.

"In July, the newspapers reported that the Germans had over fifty thousand machine guns when the war started," he explained. "About a half dozen or so Vancouverites started donating a thousand dollars each to help buy machine guns for their local units. Then some of my patriotic Calgarians raised five thousand dollars for their regiments. From there it spread. When I was asked about subscriptions, I said that we were fully aware of the need for machine guns and have placed contracts. When we received them, our men will be better equipped than the regular British units."

"How much has been raised so far?"

"Nearly a million dollars," replied Lougheed. "The Ontario government just indicated they would donate a half million dollars. More is being raised as we speak."

Borden grimaced at the news. "It's been my policy that the cost of equipping and maintaining our men in the field would be borne by the treasury."

"I know," replied Lougheed. "What could I do? The people wanted to give, and I couldn't well refuse. If we had done, the Liberals would have been quick to attack us for not supporting our men. And I didn't want to discourage public's support for the war effort."

"No, of course not," Borden assured him. "We now have a delicate problem of what to do with the money that was raised. I'll have to talk with Sam about that. We have to be careful how we discourage further raising of funds for such purposes. Ideally, I would prefer that future subscriptions be focused on the Patriotic Fund, Belgian Relief, or the Red Cross."

"Understood."

"Speaking of the Red Cross, I've seen some of their work supplying comforts to our men in England and in France. They've been doing a splendid job. My concern is for those who will need convalescence when they return home. Have you made much progress?" Borden asked. "The horrendous casualties that I saw in the hospitals have driven home how ill prepared we are."

"We've established seventy-five homes across the country so far. We recently opened a hospital in Quebec City. There are about 350 beds currently available. If the War Office is right that the war will last at least another year or so, we'll have to start looking at increasing the number of beds.

"The other problem we have is, constitutionally, medical care is a provincial responsibility, so they need to be involved," Lougheed pointed out.

Borden nodded in agreement. That was a delicate issue. "What do you suggest?"

"I'm calling a meeting and inviting the premiers and their health ministers to Ottawa in October to discuss it with them and to see what we can do to coordinate our efforts."

"When I visited the hospitals in England and France," Borden said soberly, "many of the wounded men were worried about how they will be able to support themselves and their families. We'll need to provide them with appropriate pensions, but we'll need to look at their retraining. We'll also have to provide jobs for those who have lost their limbs."

"We've starting looking at that. I'll have to talk with Thomas concerning the budget. Subscriptions for the hospitals and convalescent homes would be a benefit."

"Okay," replied Borden. "One of the reasons that I called today's meeting with Sam and Colonel Bertram is the Shell Committee."

Lougheed shook his head. "I have several concerns about the committee as well."

"Oh?" replied Borden. "In my discussions with British officials, they revealed that there is a severe shortage of artillery shells. They have been increasing their capacity, but they won't have adequate supply for another five to six months. Lloyd George is asking to increase our own production."

"Unfortunately, the Shell Committee has run into production problems."

"I'm aware of that," replied Borden. He had seen the reports on the ammunition supply.

"Were you aware that they pay a fixed price for the shells?" said Lougheed.

"That I wasn't aware of. Why haven't they gone to the lowest bidder?" asked Borden.

"They are still of the opinion that the Canadian manufacturers are not willing to invest the capital. Everyone thought it was supposed to be a short war. Having a fixed price would encourage Canadian firms to build up capacity."

"I would think by now that obviously it's going to be a long one."

"Well, yes," Lougheed replied. "There is another concern. It seems some members of the Shell Committee have been awarding themselves contracts."

"What the hell for?" exploded Borden. He was getting tired of middlemen. "Is Allison involved?"

"That I can't rightly say," replied Lougheed.

"In New York I saw that Sam, Allison, and Yochum are thick as thieves," Borden said hotly.

"Maybe I should have waited until after the meeting...."

Borden waved Lougheed down. "No, it's good you have told me.

They'll be here in a few minutes. It's imperative that we strengthen the Shell Committee. Our men need the shells."

CHAPTER 29

SEPTEMBER 13, 1915
CANADIAN CORPS HEADQUARTERS, BAILLEUL

Lieutenant-General Alderson glanced at Bailleul's Hôtel de Ville when his staff car entered Grand Place Square. His car rattled on the cobblestones as it drove to the two-storey tan brick building. The belfry on the left side that dominated the skyline was unusually large for a town this size. A year ago it had only thirteen thousand inhabitants, but now it housed nearly forty thousand British, French, and Belgian headquarters staff, administrative, and support troops. He was pleased with the square, since it was quite adequate for troop reviews.

"When will the 2nd Division start arriving?" he asked Brigadier-General Charles Harington, who was seated beside him. The forty-five-year-old officer had just been transferred to his command as his new senior staff officer. Alderson was glad to have him, although he was fairly certain Harington would have preferred to command a brigade in the 14th Division. Lieutenant-General Plumer had promised it to him before he had taken a five-day leave. Harington had been a staff officer with the 3rd Corps and with the 49th Division.

"They are on schedule for embarking at Folkestone tomorrow. General Turner should be setting up his headquarters at the Hôtel du Commerce at Saint-Omer by the 15th."

Alderson frowned at the mention of Major-General Turner. He was tempted to brief Harington on the situation, but he decided to wait and let him make his own judgement. He hadn't been pleased that Turner had been given command of the 2nd. There was very little he could do, since the Canadian government had made the public announcement several months earlier, tying his hands. There was no point in fighting it. At least he had left command of the 1st Division in Currie's capable hands. Currie's promotion to major-general was well deserved. "Once he's opened his divisional headquarters, let him know that I would like to see him."

"Yes, sir," replied Harington.

"How are we coming with staff?" he asked. That was his priority ever since Field Marshal French had given him the newly formed Canadian Corps. He had left the bulk of his divisional staff behind, bringing only a few officers who would be the backbone of his new command. The creation of the Canadian Corps had been in the works since April, and the imminent arrival of the 2nd Division had triggered its activation. This meant that a new headquarters had to be created to command and administer the Canadian divisions.

Hughes and Borden disliked the British practice of transferring divisions from one corps to another based on operational requirements. They had been quite insistent that the Canadians fight together as a unit. No decision had been rendered yet as to whether or not the Princess Patricia's Canadian Light Infantry, currently assigned to the 80th Brigade, would be added to the Canadian Corps.

"It's coming along. We finally got a paymaster assigned."

"That's good news. The field cashiers are having problems drawing cash from the Banque de France here at Bailleul and at Hazebrouck."

"He should try their branch at Boulogne and see whether he can sort it out."

"We found him an office on rue Saint-Jacques, and the ammunition column will be located on rue D'Occident. Brigadier-General Mercer will be arriving shortly to take command for the Corps troops."

"Good. We need someone to get a handle on the ad hoc units that have been created to date and those that do not fall under anyone's divisional command. We'll be giving General Seely's dismounted cavalry to him."

"Billets have been found for them at Place Plichon."

"I would prefer having everyone in the same building," Alderson stated.

"I agree. It would be more efficient. We're looking for space, but it's difficult with all of the troop movements," Harington replied. "Signals will be in the next few days to lay the cables and circuits so we can communicate with the divisional and 2nd Army HQs."

"Things are progressing well. Let's hope that it will be quiet for the next couple of weeks as we get ourselves sorted out. Most of our key personnel will be in place soon."

It was a delicate balancing act. The table of organization for the Corps HQ called for 230 staff, with about 220 being signal and clerical personnel ranging from quarter-masters, medical, engineers, signals ammunition, artillery, and troop branches. Part of the org chart called for 1,500 Corps troops to be under Brigadier-General Mercer's command. Most of the men were being drawn from the 1st and the 2nd Division. Others he had to draw in from other British units to fill in for lack of experience, which put some of his prickly Canadian officers noses out of joint. He needed good people, but he couldn't get them all from the Canadians without impacting unit efficiency.

"The Big Push is scheduled in two weeks," Harington pointed out.

"I'm aware. Field Marshal French has been planning the attack on Loos since June. We may have a small part to play in it."

"We're to provide a diversion?"

"Yes, the 1st Division has been gathering six thousand oat sacks and sandbags. They have orders to stuff them with straw and sulphur and light them. It should fool the Germans into thinking we are launching a gas attack from our trenches. We will need to draw as much German attention and their reserves as we can so that General Haig can penetrate their lines."

"It's worth a try," Harington stated. "Haig doesn't like the ground there, but we have orders to support Joffre's plans for Artois and Champagne." Alderson nodded in agreement.

From the rumours, he had heard that Sir John French had not been too keen on the attack, since he had only twenty-eight divisions, and most of them were inexperienced. He was also still short of ammunition and heavy artillery, but the French were quite insistent. They were committing nearly a hundred divisions to the operation.

"We'll need some planning, as we could be called upon to provide more support," replied Alderson.

"Yes, General. By the way, you have a meeting scheduled with the mayor this afternoon."

"How could I forget," he said with a wry smile. The Canadians could still be unruly at times. It was best to have good relations with the local authorities to reduce any friction. "I'm looking forward to it."

SEPTEMBER 25, 1915
MUDROS HARBOUR, ISLAND OF LEMNOS, GREECE

Dear Sam,

I mailed a letter to my husband several days ago to let him know that I was alright and that I miss him dearly. Can you mention it to him in case he never received it? The Huns sank another ship the other day. With my luck, my letter was on it. If you do see him, let him know that I'm doing fine.

First, the bad news. You know Matron Jaggard, the prime minister's cousin? We buried her today. She died last night. Dysentery. I think you might have met her at Shorncliffe when you worked at the Moore's Barracks hospital.

She was quite nice. She would check on us at night. When we woke up and caught her she would say she was checking to make sure we were following the lights out regulations. We didn't believe her. We knew that she was worried about us and wanted to make sure that we were okay. Conditions here are pretty bad. Do you remember the food last November when we first arrived at Salisbury Plain? The food here is worse. Much, much worse!!! Then we have to contend with the flies. There are swarms of them everywhere. It's difficult to eat anything without having them crawling all over the food.

We try to keep everything clean, but getting supplies and disinfectants has been very difficult. Water is being rationed here. What we do get needs to be hauled in by cart. We managed to borrow one from the nearby Aussie regiment, which meant that they had to do without. It's very hard doing laundry with so little water. We tried washing our clothes and the men's uniforms with salt water from the nearby bay. Big mistake. The clothes took forever to dry. They were extremely stiff, and I itched for days. It was awful. We finally had to wash them in buckets, hand wring them dry, and hang them. You should have seen the men's faces when they saw our knickers flapping in the wind.

Because of the lack of supplies and rations, we've been having an epidemic of dysentery. God bless these Aussies and New Zealanders. They are great fellows. We don't get a nigh a complaint from them. They're having a rough go. First getting shot up on a beach, then transported on a dirty scowl to land on our doorstep, where we try to patch them up and feed them properly. Not only are they suffering from it, so are a lot of the

223

medical staff. We lost Mary Munro two weeks ago on the 7th because of it, and our CO, Casgrain, got it as well. He doesn't look good. We don't think that he's going to make it.

I don't know who is going to tell the prime minister about his cousin. The matron had a husband and a seventeen-year-old son in the States. I guess they will be informed by gram.

I'm doing fine so far. Knock on wood. I'm sharing a tent with Victoria Bearman, who's from Cold Lake. She doesn't snore, thank God. We're pretty exhausted by the time that we put on our nightgowns. If you think we have it bad, the Aussie nurses have it worse than we do. It took forever for them to get their equipment. No one bothered to try to find it. They aren't treated well by the doctors, but the Aussie Tommies adore them. Did you know that they earn half the pay that we do?

We have some extra money to buy local fruits from the Greek traders, mainly figs and grapes and vegetables to supplement our diet. Some of them are liars and cheaters, as they charge us a pretty penny. What can we do? We share what we can, but it isn't much.

On our half days, we travel the island. There isn't much to see. There isn't a single tree on the whole island. And it's quite rocky and hilly. The people are very poor and don't have much. Most of their clothes are made from sheepskin. The little ones are darlings but quite shy.

We have our usual entertainments. Books are being passed around. If you can send me some new ones, I would be grateful. We play bridge, a lot. The Aussies put on a concert the other evening. I couldn't go because I was on duty. The ones who went were very impressed by the Maori who did their war chant.

Well, I have to close my letter, since it's lights out. You take care, and I hope that I will be seeing you soon.

Your friend
Emily

SEPTEMBER 26, 1915
ST. CATHARINES, ONTARIO

"It rained last night," said Laura as she glanced out of the window beaded with water drops. It was nearly seven o'clock, and the sunlight was beginning to stream through the glass. There wasn't very much to see, since their passenger car had been placed on a siding.

Borden nodded as he took a sip of his coffee. "I heard it pounding on the roof last night." Both he and his wife had elected to spend the night in the train car rather than take the expense of booking a hotel room. The sleeping quarters actually rivalled any that could be found in a five-star hotel. It also made it easy to arrive on schedule, eleven o'clock, to be precise, in Toronto.

"I feel sorry for the poor men who are guarding us," she stated as she took a bite of buttered toast.

Borden glanced out and saw his protection detail. "Colonel Campbell insisted!" he replied grumpily.

St. Catharines was only thirteen miles from the Canada-US border. The previous day he and Laura had been at the Niagara-on-the-Lake camp to review the fourteen thousand troops that were training there. He had been very pleased with the conditions of the camp and the men. The colonel had been concerned that German sympathizers on the American side might get some ideas. Laura paused then glanced out at the soldiers again.

"What did you think of the hospital?"

"I was impressed. It was first-class," she replied. Laura and Lady Egan had visited the new hospital in Niagara Falls while he had lunch at the officers' mess, attended a civic reception, and gave a speech at the Opera House.

While he regretted not attending Sunday mass at All Saints, he was rather glad that he had gotten out of Ottawa. He had spent most of the week dealing with the Shell Committee mess. Thomas White wanted to bring in someone from England to replace Colonel Bertram. He was adamantly opposed to the idea. If he had to replace the chairman, he wanted a Canadian in the job. It seemed that Hughes was leaving messes wherever he went.

It wasn't much of a holiday; he was to arrive in Toronto at eleven then meet with Ontario's lieutenant governor. Tomorrow, he was to give a speech at the Board of Trade and in the evening give another at the arena. He had been informed that twelve thousand would be in attendance.

The steward came in and announced, "Prime Minister, we'll be attaching the car to the engine shortly."

"Very well. Thank you," Borden replied.

"The morning newspaper and mail has arrived," the steward said as he handed Borden a bundle of messages.

The prime minister read the newspaper headlines with interest. It announced that Russia had recaptured the town of Lutsk. There were several articles on the British and French offensive that Perley had informed him earlier in the week was to be launched over the weekend. He was glad that the early reports indicated it was going well.

"Any news concerning Jessie?" Laura asked.

Borden grimaced when he saw the telegram with Surgeon-General Jones's name on it. "I'm afraid there is." Earlier in the week the general had sent him a gram informing him that Mrs. Jaggard was in critical condition.

He unfolded the message and read it. When he looked up he shook his head.

Laura sucked in her breath for a moment then said, "We'll have to send a message of condolence to her husband and son."

"Yes, we will," replied Borden dully.

CHAPTER 30

OCTOBER 11, 1915
CECIL HOTEL, LONDON

"Your pass?" demanded the military police corporal. The man was of medium height, with a slight paunch. The lance-corporal beside him was almost his twin. Both of them were in standard military policeman's uniform with red forge caps. On their right arms they had black armbands with "MP" embroidered in red. Wooden batons dangled from wrist cords.

Captain Llewellyn was cursing silently. He had been so engrossed in talking with Samantha that he hadn't spotted the red caps on the busy street until it was too late. He had been told to avoid them if he could, but that was difficult in central London. Some of them had a nasty habit of baiting unsuspecting men on leave.

When the corporal examined him, he suspected it was his Canadian uniform that attracted their attention, since it was a slightly different pattern from the standard Imperial. He had also removed the wire stiffener from his cap to give him a jauntier look to impress Samantha. He wondered if it was going to cost him.

"Of course, Corporal," he replied as he unbuttoned his overcoat and removed his pass from his breast pocket.

The corporal looked up at him asked, "Name, rank, and unit?"

"Llewellyn, James, Captain, 1st Canadian Division," he replied.

He had made sure that the pass was correctly filled in before he left France for a week's leave in London. His pass had to be signed by the Corps commander, Lieutenant-General Alderson. In fact, it had the signature of one of the general's staff officers, who had been given the signing authority. As a general rule, you need didn't need a pass if you were within a half mile of your billet. The farther away from your billet, the higher up the chain of command it had to be signed. Since they tried to keep divisional leaves about 5 percent of the ranks, nearly two thousand passes needed to be signed. An awful number for one man to do.

"And you, miss?" the corporal asked Samantha. She had been clutching Llewellyn's arm a few moments before. The man's tone irritated the captain. The corporal thought that Samantha was a trollop, although she was dressed in a respectful mufti outfit. She was wearing a serge wool

227

suit, flared jacket, and a skirt that fell to her ankles, with a single row of large buttons. Her blouse was buttoned to her neck. Her blonde hair was covered by a drooping brim hat with a button flower in the centre.

He was startled when she reached into her purse and extracted a military pass similar to the captain's. It took the corporal a moment to finally croak, "Name, rank, and unit?"

Samantha replied, "Samantha Lonsdale, Captain, Canadian Nursing Service."

"You're not in uniform," he stated. He then added, "Ma'am."

"Our regulations allow us to be in mufti while on leave outside our designated units," she replied.

When the corporal glanced at Llewellyn, he answered, "She is indeed a captain in the Canadian Medical Services."

"Well, I never," muttered the lance corporal as he made a note of their passes for verification later.

"My fiancé," Llewellyn said hoping he would score points with the officers, "and I wanted to celebrate Thanksgiving together. I thought it might be nice that I dress up a bit."

"But you look lovely in uniform," Llewellyn protested.

"Why, thank you, dear," she replied with a slight blush.

The MPs looked rather flummoxed as they glanced at each other. It was obvious they didn't know quite what to do with them.

Then Samantha asked, "Do you know of a good restaurant that serves turkey?"

"Turkey?" blurted the lance corporal.

"Why, yes, that is the traditional Thanksgiving dinner in Canada. Turkey with dressing, mashed potatoes, and corn on the cob."

"Don't forget the cranberry sauce," he added.

"Of course, dear," Samantha agreed.

By the now the two men thought both of them were definitely off their rockers. "I don't know, ma'am," said the corporal. "Carry on."

Llewellyn returned the men's salute. Samantha didn't, since she wasn't in uniform. She started chuckling when they were out of earshot. "I don't think they believed me."

"I really don't care," he replied. "I was worried that they would disrupt my leave."

"Oh?"

"Well, I had plans."

"What kind of plans?"

"Well, turkey wasn't what I had in mind," he replied as he offered her his arm. When she took it, he started leading her to the Cecil Hotel. "I have a room booked."

"What will we be doing?" she asked with a blush.

"I'm sure we can think of something."

OCTOBER 15, 1915
ARTILLERY RANGE, SAINT-OMER

"Pull man! Pull!" shouted Major Linseed. Subaltern Ryan struggled as he and three other men dragged the German heavy mortar into position on the artillery range.

"This is a fucking heavy pig," grunted the lieutenant with the RCA badge on his cap.

"Yeah," replied Paul as his foot slipped on the thin layer of mud. It had rained lightly in the morning, but it was enough to make the churned-up turf rather slick. At least the mortar, rather *schwerer Minenwerfer's* steel wheels hadn't sunk in too deep. He just had to make sure that he got out of its way when they finally needed it to stop. Thank God they were on level ground.

He glanced behind him at the grey barrel that had scar marks from shrapnel and bullets. The barrel was only two and a half feet long, with a recoil spring set on top of the barrel. It was capable of firing a 9.8-inch shell that weighed two hundred pounds nearly six hundred yards. He had seen the effect of the shell on some of the Canadian Division's, rather Corps', fortifications. It had not been pretty.

When they finally wheeled the mortar into position, everyone released the drag ropes with relief. Major Masterley had sent him to the lecture as a reward for the excellent work he had been doing recently. Some reward!

One of the men in the pull team asked, "Are we going to fire the damn thing?"

The captain gave them a look of surprise. "Good God, man, no! We don't really have any ammunition for it. Only a few rounds for instructional purposes. If we had any we would have used them on the Boche."

"What the hell did we drag it here for?" the lieutenant demanded.

"We needed them out of the storage shed for the instructions, my good man," the captain said in a cross tone.

Paul winced when the captain said that. He hoped that the lieutenant would hold his tongue. He got the impression that the captain was one of the touchy types.

"Very good," the captain said as the other captured mortars were rolled into place. The other two were considered medium and light mortars. The medium one could launch a 6.7-inch shell, but it weighed nearly a thousand pounds, while the light one weight in at three hundred pounds and fired a 3-inch shell.

When Major Masterley had sent him out here to gain experience, neither they nor the French considered using mortars when the war started; therefore, they had very few their arsenals. It had been surprising how effective the German mortars had been when the Boche had turned theirs, designed to take out French forts along the frontier, against the trenches. It had been a painful lesson.

In the meantime, Lieutenant-General Alderson was desirous of organizing mortar brigades, and the Ryan had been selected to attend to see if he could learn anything.

"We will begin with the Russo-Japanese war, where the Japanese used mortars with great effect against Russian bunkers and fortifications...." The captain started his lecture.

Paul nearly groaned. It was going to be a rather long day. For a moment he thought dragging the mortars would have been preferable. He sighed. He knew he couldn't let Major Masterley down.

OCTOBER 29, 1915
PRIME MINISTER'S OFFICE, EAST BLOCK, PARLIAMENT HILL,
OTTAWA

Blount entered his office and announced, "They are waiting for you in the conference room."

Prime Minister Borden sighed. He wasn't looking forward to his eleven thirty meeting. He was not looking forward to it at all. He had known that the crisis was coming for some time. It was now time to face it.

At least he had managed to delay the meeting by a week or so, since he was away in Nova Scotia. He had gone to visit his sister to see how she was coping with Mother's passing. While he was there he had laid a cornerstone at the Halifax harbour and reviewed some of the new recruits. Quite a few of them looked rather seedy. He also did some glad-handing to shore up political support in case Laurier decided to score points by not supporting extending the current parliamentary session. In Moncton, there had been some excitement when he had to save a poor young girl from being killed. She had fallen onto the tracks after she tripped stepping off the train.

During the trip, the same question was put to him. What the hell is going on with the Shell Committee?

"Thank you," replied Borden as he rose from his desk and walked down the corridor.

When he entered the meeting room, three men rose to their feet. "It is kind of you to take the time from your busy schedule to meet with us," said David Alfred Thomas as he shook Sir Robert's hand.

"My pleasure," Borden said as he examined the man after he had taken a seat across from him. Thomas was nearly sixty years old, clean-shaven, with thin hair and horn-rimmed glasses. He had been sent by the British government to review the various Canadian and US manu-facturers that had submitted bids to supply England with artillery shells. Thomas was an industrialist who had expanded the coal conglomerate in Wales that his father had left him by buying coal interests in North America. The man was also famous for surviving, with his daughter, the sinking of the *Lusitania* last May.

The other two men were Lionel Hichens, the chairman of Camnel, Laird, and Co., and the Honourable R.H. Brand. Brand was a former civil servant in South Africa and now was a managing director of the Lazard Brothers and Company investment firm.

"As you are aware, I was sent by the minister of munitions to see how far you can make good in Canada on the present contracts that have been issued by our government. Prior to my arrival, $160 million worth of shell contracts had been signed. I was amazed at the progress you have made. What I understand is you went from one small arsenal in Quebec that employed about four hundred workers to nearly 150 plants in a hundred cities employing thousands," stated Thomas as he adjusted his glasses.

"Now, the only criticism that I have to date is that some of your factories are rather outdated. There have been complaints from firms with engineering experience that have not seen any contracts, but they claim firms with little or no experience have won bids. As well, orders have been slow to fill. Only ten million worth has been shipped to England," he continued.

Borden grimaced. "It has been a new endeavour, and it has taken time for the various manufacturers to produce shells that are acceptable to the War Office. It's my understanding that for the first months many of the shells had to be scrapped because they didn't meet the specifications. I have been informed that it has since been addressed."

Thomas glanced at Hichens and Brand. "Those are technical issues that can be addressed. We're looking to having fixed ammunition being produced instead of shrapnel. We're contracting for 4.5-, 5-, and 6-inch shells as well as the 18-pounders. It is our information that a firm has been organized to manufacture fuses for the shells. It will take some time for them, since they require a considerable amount of engineering and experience to create reliable fuses."

"I'm quite confident that our people are up to the task," Borden replied.

"I tend to agree. However, I have a concern, since the cost of shells being produced have been higher than in other competitive centres," Thomas stated.

Borden reluctantly admitted, "That has been the case since the Shell Committee was first formed. Minister Hughes' view was that fixed prices were needed to ensure that the manufacturers invested in production. He has indicated that the costs have been significantly reduced, up to two dollars per shell."

"That may be, but in discussions with Minister Hughes, he indicated that there were currently three hundred firms employing 175,000 workers involved in a variety of war production activity. We feel that if they were properly organized, the output could easily be doubled and the costs could be lowered considerably," said Thomas. "Also, we would prefer a competitive system similar to what you have instituted for your War Purchasing Commission."

Brand then interrupted, "It's my understanding that you were briefed on the state of the shell shortages that our forces in France are currently experiencing."

"What are you proposing?" Borden demanded.

"The Shell Committee is now an enormous enterprise that needs to be properly managed. The minister of munitions has informed me that an additional $250 million of shell contracts are going to be placed in Canada. That would mean we would be spending $500 million on shells alone," Thomas said.

Borden's eyes narrowed. He knew full well what Thomas was dangling the impact those orders would have on the Canadian economy.

"Of course, we would need to remove some of the middlemen such as Colonel Allison," Brand said.

Borden gave him a sharp glance before asking, "What are you proposing?"

He knew that he really didn't have a leg to stand on, since his erratic minister of militia and defence and Hughes' good friend had put him in this position.

"What we suggest is that the Shell Committee is reorganized and that it comes under the Imperial Munitions Committee. It will be under the control of the minister of munitions in London," stated Thomas.

"Also, since they are under Imperial control," Brand stated. "It would be immune to inquiries and investigations by the Canadian parliament."

Borden wasn't pleased by that. But there was very little that he could do. He was at the mercy of the golden rule.

"Of course," Thomas added, "we will present this as your idea."

CHAPTER 31

OCTOBER 31, 1915
1ST DIVISION HEADQUARTERS, NIEPPE

Major-General Currie finally gave up trying to sleep. He had been tossing and turning most of the night. He knew what was keeping him up. It was usually a rather easy decision to make, but he couldn't make it just yet.

After he turned on the light, he checked the time. It was four thirty. He knew that once he started his morning ablutions, his batman would awaken. That man was a light sleeper. He was tempted to simply put on his uniform and try to slip quietly out, but he knew that he would never hear the end of it. Sergeant Cracknell would berate him in a hurt tone that the GOC of the 1st Canadian Division needed to set an example. When hot water pipes rattled, he knew he had sealed his fate.

When he finished, he exited the bathroom and found that a freshly laundered and pressed uniform had been laid out for him on the bed. The bedroom was a small one set aside for his use at the 1st Canadian Division's headquarters in Nieppe. It was on the ground floor and in the cellar that the working offices had been set up.

"You're spoiling me," said Currie to Sergeant Cracknell. The sergeant was a grizzled veteran from Victoria, BC.

"Yes, sir," he replied as he put a freshly laundered uniform into an ornate wood armoire situated at the far wall near the window. The closed shades prevented light escaping into the building's backyard.

"I'll be in my office. If you can have breakfast brought to me, I would appreciate it," Major-General Currie asked as the sergeant handed Currie his forge cap.

Currie carried it in his hands as he made his way to his work office on the ground floor. Even at this hour he could hear the phones ringing and the clacking of typewriters. Most of the men had the haggard look of those near the end of a long shift. Relief was in about a half-hour's time. As he moved papers on his desk, looking for the latest intelligence summaries, Lieutenant Howley entered his office through the open door with a clutch of papers in his hands.

"Good morning, General, I just completed the intelligence summaries," he said earnestly. "I'm sorry that they are late."

Currie waved away his apology with a tired wrist. "I'm early this morning," he said as he took the papers that the captain held. Howley was a tall, thin former farmhand from Regina. Captain Llewellyn spoke highly of the junior intelligence officer. He was bright and eager to learn but needed some seasoning. He sighed at the thought of the captain. While he was doing a good job as his senior intelligence officer, Currie knew he might make better use of him as a brigade-major.

"Sir?" said the lieutenant with a touch of concern, misinterpreting the general's sigh.

"Nothing," said Currie as he read his division's two-page intelligence summary that was to be forwarded to Corps HQ. At the top there was the standard warning headers stating that the information was confidential and was not to be shared outside the service. The *Artillery* section detailed the observation and activities of the 1st, 2nd, and 3rd artillery brigades. It seemed that the German work parties had been active and the Hun artillery had fired a number of shells, which had damaged the forward trenches. The *General Trench* section summarized what had happened on his left, centre, and right sectors. He grunted with approval when he read how his men responded to a German rifle grenade attack on his left section. They had replied with two jam tins for every German grenade. His orders had been quite clear. He wanted to own No Man's Land.

He read the section that reported on the activities in the German trenches. He frowned with concern when they indicated that the Huns were working hard on repairs and putting up wire. It deepened when he read the previous afternoon's 5th Battalion's reconnaissance report on the Douve River. The water was three feet deep and on top of a muddy bed. *We're going to have to figure out a way to cross that damn river when the time comes* was his thought.

When he read that the Germans had fired flares across No Man's Land, he shook his head. His men had experimented with coloured rockets as a simple signalling method. They found they had been difficult for the artillery observer to spot. Also, there was no way to prevent the Germans duplicating them and using similar ones to disrupt his operations. What was interesting was that they had fired the flares horizontally rather than vertically. It seemed they were using them to help spot the patrols that had been sent out. He was happy that there was no report of any of his men of being spotted.

"It looks fine," Currie said. "You can tell Colonel Tennison to forward them to Corps HQ. Have you received the Second Army's intelligence summary?"

"Yes, General. It's on my desk."

"Well, go get it," ordered Major-General Currie. "It's not doing much good there."

A chagrined Howley hurried away. The intelligence summary was essentially a printed newsletter. It gave him a brief summary of the current distribution of enemy forces in Second Army's sector, as well as any political events that might affect his current dispositions. It also contained weather forecasts and air reconnaissance reports. What Currie found useful was the reported lessons learned from various other operations that the British and French had conducted. In a number of cases he had sent officers to his allies to observe and report back to him.

He was interrupted when the candlestick phone rang on his desk. He picked up the receiver and spoke. "General Currie here!"

"One moment, please. General Alderson is on the line," said a voice.

"Allo! Allo!" said Lieutenant-General Alderson. "General Currie. Good that I was able to talk to you. I'm calling a meeting at ten o'clock."

Currie's mouth thinned a bit. He already had a meeting schedule with his brigade commanders at ten o'clock. "Yes, General. What is the topic for the meeting?"

"The discussion will be what we can do for small enterprises that Field Marshal French wants us to consider."

"I'll be there," replied Currie. He had some ideas he wanted run pass Alderson.

"Good. Also, I just received word that the king was impressed by us yesterday. He said we were a fine body of men."

"That's good to hear," Currie replied. Nearly eight hundred officers and men had been arrayed at Loche to be reviewed by King George V, who was in France visiting his armies. Loche was close enough to assemble the men easily and far enough to keep the king safe.

"Ten o'clock then," said Currie as he hung up.

When he looked up he saw that Lieutenant Howley had arrived with the latest intelligence summary. "Can you inform the brigade commanders that our ten o'clock meeting is postponed?"

"Yes, General. When do you want to postpone it to?"

"I don't think I have anything at seven tonight," Currie said as he rose to his feet. "If there is anything urgent, I'll be at the rest station for the next few hours." As Currie marched past him, the lieutenant gave him an acknowledgement. Currie knew that once he was gone, Howley would be on the phone to the ambulance people to warn them he was on his way.

NO. 8 CASUALTY CLEARING STATION, ASYLUM FIELD, BAILLEUL

When Currie arrived at the Asylum Field, he saw a flight of F.E. 2D planes lift off into the morning sky. The F.E. 2D fighter was a pusher type; the propeller was in the back. This allowed the observer to fire forward the Lewis machine guns, attached to rails that surrounded the cockpit. He also noticed that the plane was on a photo reconnaissance mission, since it wasn't carrying bombs.

The clearing hospital tents were set up near the back wall of the asylum, a large, grey stone, three-floor edifice. A large brick wall surrounded the hospital to keep in the mental patients. Currently it was being shared between the French and the Imperial medical units.

He found the recently promoted Major Moore helping load a patient into the back of the ambulance. He raised an eyebrow when he saw the markings on the bonnet. There were three other patients waiting to be placed in the truck. He recognized them, since they were members of the 2nd Brigade.

It took a moment to dredge up the man's name. "Corporal Dingle, how are you feeling?"

"I'm fine, General," replied the corporal. "I'm peachy keen."

Currie couldn't help his smile. "You're in good hands. Is there anything I can do for you?"

"Yeah, General. Get the fucking bastard that shot me," he muttered as they raised him and slid him into the second bench of the truck.

"We'll get him," replied Currie.

When the ambulance was loaded, the doctor signalled it to move off. He then turned to Currie and asked, "How can I help, General?"

"I noticed the nonstandard markings on the lorry," Currie stated. "You didn't get the memo?"

The doctor shrugged. "The ambulance was a gift from the Ottawa Canadian Women's Club. They have been a godsend. And they're paying for the maintenance and upkeep. It would be rather churlish not to recognize their support."

"You have a point," Currie conceded. "I just wanted to visit the men injured last night to see how they were coming along."

Major Moore's face soured. "Two of them are doing well, but we lost Sergeant Tellis."

Currie looked away and watched another flight of aircraft lift off. This time they were Sopwith Pups. That was one thing his job demanded, finding the balance between treating the men as ciphers on a return and real-life human beings. He felt that he never could balance them correctly. All he could do was keep trying.

When he returned his gaze back to Dr. Moore, he said, "I was reading your report. What is this about the men's shins?"

"We got about six cases of men complaining of painful shins just this week. For some of these men, the pain was so bad that we had to give them morphine. What we've seen from previous patients it takes about three or four weeks of rest before they are pain-free again."

"What's causing it?"

"We're not exactly sure," admitted Moore, "but we are investigating to find the causes and a solution."

"That's the same thing for trench foot," Currie stated flatly. He wasn't happy with that particular bit of news.

"We've been getting a surprising number of cases already. The men are coming in with swollen feet that are hot, a bluish-red colour, and with open sores. Also, they have been complaining of severe itching and that walking was painful."

"If a man can't walk, he isn't much use to me," Currie pointed out.

"Quite," the doctor replied. It was obvious that he didn't like it. He glanced at the asylum building then back to Currie. Moore shook his head. "Prevention is the key. The instructions are in my report. Hot foot baths and rubbing salts have helped in some cases once they develop."

"I recall," stated Currie. "I'll reissue them as a general order. Let's see if we can reduce the trench foot rates. As for now, I want to visit the rest of your patients before I head over to Corps HQ for a meeting."

"Of course, General. Follow me," Moore said as he led the general to the nearest tent.

"How are we coming along?" General Currie asked as he eyed the trench with a critical eye.

He was embarrassed when his stomach rumbled. He hadn't eaten lunch yet. The two-hour meeting Lieutenant-General Alderson had called had been a waste of time. Most of the meeting had been about troop status reports, ammunition requisitions, and food rations. They had spent a considerable amount of it arguing about changing bully beef to beef stew. They also rehashed what could be done to break the current stalemate.

Lieutenant-General Alderson hadn't been too pleased at how Turner and Mercer were handling their troops. He had been giving them dark looks and getting on their cases. The steward had offered snacks, but Currie had to beg off, since he needed to leave to review the work that was being done on his secondary trenches.

A couple of workhorses were pulling a steel plow to break up the ground. Men with shovels and picks followed up to pile the dirt on the sides. Others came behind with sandbags. The horses would make a couple of passes until the ditch reached the appropriate depth. It was actually a Massey-Harris walking plow that had been brought from Canada. The thick steel blade turned over a furrow of dirt nine inches wide and eight inches deep. Since they were outside the enemy's direct line of observation, they could use the workhorses to lighten the load on the men.

"It's coming along quite well," said Captain Parker. The officer was in his late twenties and had a footballer's physique. "We're connecting trench 132 to Winnipeg Ave. in front of Fort Steward."

Currie turned his gaze toward the trenches and grunted an acknowledgement. The trench was being situated to bring flanking fire on Douve in case they needed to evacuate the front-line trenches B3 and B4. The engineers were telling him that with winter coming, this lowland area tended to flood. Since they could only use hand pumps, they didn't think that they could keep them dry. This meant the men would be sitting in wet trenches getting trench foot.

"How are the work parties coming along?" he asked. The men in front of him were working, but they knew who he was. If the officers were competent, the men would continue working after he had left.

FRANK ROCKLAND

"It's going okay," the engineer said.

Currie caught a slight frustration in the man's tone, and he stared at the captain. After a minute or two of silence, the captain finally broke down. "I had to kick some arses last night."

"Oh?"

"Yeah. The lieutenant in charge had left the men with instructions and left. I found them sitting around having a grand old time. The lazy bastards."

Currie exploded. "Who the fuck was the lieutenant and the unit?"

The captain began to backtrack. "It's been taken care of, General."

"I still want their names and the unit," Currie demanded.

"It was Lieutenant Fowles and the 1st Company of the Richmond Fusiliers," he gulped.

"Fuck," said Major-General Currie. That unit was giving him nothing but trouble. It was also telling that the captain didn't bother to cover for them. The order was sitting on his desk waiting for his signature. He still hated doing it.

"Well, at least you're making progress. I see that you started work on the communication trenches as well."

"Yes, General. So far we're maintaining the work schedule."

"Good! I'm pleased," Currie replied as he turned to his waiting car. "If anyone is looking for me, I'll be with Major Culkin."

"Yes, General," the captain replied as he saluted the departing GOC.

1ST CANADIAN ENGINEERING TENTS, NIEPPE

"So this is it?" asked Major-General Currie with a raised eyebrow as he watched a sapper roll black tar paper while a second sapper followed, tacking it to the wood frame.

"Yes, General," said Major Culkin. Currie knew that the engineer was gauging his reaction.

"They are easy to make. They're fast and cheap," Culkin added, hoping to forestall any objections that the general would have.

"I can see that," replied Currie. He had been a real estate promoter in BC, so he knew a thing or two about housing. He had a fairly good idea what the men's reaction would be when they moved into the new shelters. He didn't have many options, since winter was coming and the men badly needed shelter from the elements.

240

"We couldn't use wood for the exterior?"

Culkin shook his head. "There is a great demand for wood. We need it for duckboard, shoring timber for the dugouts, and the mining tunnels we're digging."

"How are we going to keep the men warm?"

The engineer indicated a bell tent across the field, where empty metal drums were stacked. "We're converting those into stoves. We're cutting an opening into the side and putting a pipe on top to vent the smoke."

Currie winced. "How safe will they be for the men?"

"Safe enough," the engineer assured him.

"I would like to see one in operation before I provide an approval," said Currie.

"Of course, General," Culkin said as he led Currie toward the steel barrels.

"Have you given much thought on how we can cross the Douve River?"

"The COs of the 2nd and the 5th Battalions have asked me the same thing. The only thing we can use is the ladders."

"We need them as soon as we can so the assault teams can start training on them."

"You'll have them in a few days."

They were a few steps away when a messenger drove up to them on an Indian motorbike. The corporal lifted his goggles and saluted the two officers. "General Currie, I'm glad I found you."

"So you've found me. What's the urgency?"

"The king has been injured," the man blurted.

"What? How?" demanded Currie.

"He was thrown by his horse," replied the corporal. "When the king was inspecting the troops, the men's cheering spooked his animal."

Currie winced. The men had been ordered to cheer when the king passed the Canadian troops that had lined the road. But then the king had reviewed them in a staff car. The only thing that had been dangerous were the out-of-joint noses. The senior officers had argued as to which units were to stand for review and in which order.

"Well, I better return to my headquarters just in case I'm needed," Currie said with a sigh. There was probably nothing he would be able to do, but it would be wise to be available if needed.

"Yes, General," the major said as he saluted.

1ST DIVISION HEADQUARTERS, NIEPPE

Major-General Currie ran into Captain Llewellyn when he came from the officers' mess. The beef had been a bit on the tough side, but then he was eating essentially what the men were eating. The main difference was not the raw ingredients but the personal touch of the cook preparing the meal. Cooking food for thirty versus for a thousand men made a huge difference.

But the main reason he ate in the officers' mess was to gauge the mood of his senior officers. Who was getting along with whom? Who was on the outs? He was also looking for signs of stress. For some officers, being in headquarters was a strain, especially when they were not performing well at their jobs. They would give thin smiles and drop their heads in their plates. Others were the cheerful and seemed to tell him what he wanted to hear. That could be just as trying. That was one thing that he appreciated about the captain. He usually gave it to you between the eyes.

"Captain, anything of interest today?"

The captain looked up from the sheet of messages and signal notes he was reading. "I'm not sure. Some of the men's handwriting is atrocious."

"Look on the bright side," replied Currie. "If they fall into German hands, it will keep them busy."

"Oh?"

"Oh yes. They'll think we developed a new cipher."

The captain chuckled. "I'm starting to complete the intelligence summary for tomorrow." Currie acknowledged with a nod. The *Summary of Intelligence* reports were compiled daily and had to be distributed by noon every day.

"It seems that the machine gun emplacement at U.2.C.75.79 we damaged several days ago has been completely repaired." Currie scowled at the news. The German machine guns had proven to be a real nuisance. "Also, it seems that one of our artillery retaliatory salvos hit one of their ammo depots. There were a considerable number of explosions and damage to their communication trenches."

"Good," Currie replied. "That's what I want to hear."

"Otherwise, it seems that it's been relatively quiet, with the usual amount of artillery and sniper rifle fire. The German work parties have been seen, and some of our 18-pounders fired to disperse them.

"Other than that, they're bailing water like we are, and there isn't much else........ Oh wait," the captain said as he flipped through the messages. "There seemed to be some temporary blockage of the Douve River. The men noticed the river had been rising for most of the afternoon."

"Damn," cursed Currie. "By how much?" The Douve divided his trenches from the Germans.

"A couple of feet before it stopped rising. There's a second report stating that whatever the blockage was, it has been cleared and the river is starting to fall. It could be back to normal by morning."

"Keep me updated on the river," ordered the general. "There's a ton of paperwork on my desk that needs my attention. I'll see you in the morning."

"Yes, General."

Currie finally made a decision. He hated to lose Llewellyn, but he would be of more value to him as the Fusiliers brigade-major. He also hoped promoting Llewellyn to major would take the sting out of returning him back to the Fusiliers, but he needed that outfit straightened out.

MAJOR-GENERAL CURRIE'S BEDROOM, 1ST DIVISION HEAD-
QUARTERS, NIEPPE

Currie was lying in bed scowling at the *Victoria Daily Colonial* newspaper. He was reading the business section, and the news was not good. The paper was nearly four weeks old, but the real estate market hadn't changed much.

He folded the paper and tossed it onto the floor. He then picked up the five letters that had arrived in a batch from his wife, Lily. This was a pleasant diversion from the paperwork that he had to review and sign off. It was rather surprising how much needed his approval and signature. On a regular basis, he had to look at reports to Corps HQ, weekly and monthly reports, casualty reports, men struck off strength due to transfers or court martial, request to have court martial sentences set aside, leave passes, and promotions and demotions.

He smiled warmly when he started reading Lily's first letter. He was rather surprised that the post office had delivered them in sequence.

He would often receive a letter complaining why he hadn't replied back, then the offending original letter would arrive.

He shifted to make himself more comfortable as the letters lay on his round stomach. He had been taken aback two weeks ago when she sent him a telegram informing him she and the children were sailing for England. They should be aboard ship now, and they would be in England in a few weeks. He was eagerly looking forward to it, since he hadn't seen Lily, his daughter Marjorie, and his son Garner since he left Canada last year.

He sighed. He needed to put in a request with Lieutenant-General Alderson for leave. He wondered briefly if he would get approval.

"So what did the scouts report?" asked Major Llewellyn as he sat in the Fusiliers 1st Battalion headquarters dugout near Petit Douve Farm. Sitting in the cramped space with him was Captain Larry McGlynn, the battalion CO, and Lieutenant Garrett Ringham of the 1st Platoon.

Standing in front of them was Sergeant Duval. Behind him they could see the grey sky starting to appear. The sergeant's uniform was encrusted with wet mud that was starting to dry. Llewellyn could see a thin layer of grey on back of his hands that a quick washing had missed. A smear of dirt could be seen on the man's neck.

"Two of my scouts reported back," the sergeant informed them. "They got within ten yards of the German wire south of Ash Road. They said it was solidly built with fresh wood posts. There's cans on the wire to alert them if we try to cut them. They got out without being spotted."

"What did they have to say about the trenches?" McGlynn asked.

"They said that they are in pretty bad shape. Like the one I scouted this evening. The sides have caved in. It was so bad that it actually dragged the wire down. I had to leave right quick. A work party showed up to repair it, and they were putting sentries out. If I hadn't skedaddled they would have flanked me."

"How many men?" asked Ringham.

"Four, and they were wearing red caps," Duval replied. "That trench is flooded. I heard them bailing water."

"With the rain we're getting, it's not surprising," replied Lieutenant Ringham.

"The Douve River?" asked Major Llewellyn.

The three men didn't say anything, but he had the distinct impression they had a good idea why he was asking. "We checked it about two hundred yards below Messines Road. It has five to six feet of water and in places it's fifteen yards wide."

"Hmm," replied Major Llewellyn as he digested the news.

"What is worrisome is the heavy transport trucks that we've been hearing heading toward Messines," stated McGlynn.

Llewellyn turned to Major McGlynn. "Any idea what they might be carrying?" He was concerned that they were reinforcing their front lines.

"The listening posts heard metallic sounds being unloaded. We think they could be shells," stated Duval.

"Or gas cylinders," said the lieutenant as he stroked his gas mask. "Any signs of tubing or gas men?"

"Not yet," replied the McGlynn. "We had the artillery fire a couple of shells in their direction."

"Any effect?" asked Llewellyn.

"They were on the other side of the rise. We can't confirm anything," replied McGlynn.

Duval added, "We've seen lamps signalling back and forth. We recorded what we could and sent it to HQ for them to decipher and translate."

"I haven't seen that yet. I'll check with them when I get back," said Llewellyn. "Did they retaliate?"

"Yes, but it was light. They lobbed a few shells. One of them hit a communication trench. I lost a couple of good men," McGlynn said tersely.

Major Llewellyn nodded acknowledgment. "Anything else significant?"

"The usual. They put new wire at trenches .03 to .06. New timber was seen being carried. It looks like they're building a new dugout or a machine gun post," answered Sergeant Duval.

"Okay," replied Llewellyn. He was interrupted when a private dragged a wooden crate into the dugout and dropped it on the dirt floor. When he read the stencilling, he knew what it was.

"What the hell is this?" demanded McGlynn.

"New accoutrements," replied the private.

"What new accoutrements? I didn't order anything," McGlynn said.

"I don't know, sir. I have nine more boxes of them," the private replied. "They're heavy and they rattled."

"Take off the lid, and let's take a look," ordered McGlynn.

The private used his bayonet to pry off the lid. The factory had done a good job, since it took several tries before the nails popped out. When they finally looked in, they saw five grey-painted metal domes visible.

"What did the hell did the quartermaster send us?" asked Ringham.

Duval looked at them then said, "They finally sent us a pot to piss in."

"Hand me one of those things. For Pete's sake, it's head gear," McGlynn exclaimed as he put on the helmet and it promptly fell below his ears.

"I'm glad to see that you don't have a swell head." Llewellyn chuckled. "You can adjust the liner for a better fit."

"I ain't wearing no piss pot on my head," proclaimed the private.

"You knew about this?" the lieutenant asked Llewellyn.

Llewellyn shrugged. "The French have been issuing steel helmets to their troops since July or August. They're claiming it significantly reduces head wounds from shrapnel and flying debris by about 70 percent. This is our version of it. It weighs nearly two pounds and is made of one piece of pressed steel. Until the Imperials ramp up production, they will be kept in the trenches, and only the troops on trench duty will have them."

"Well, I still ain't wearing no piss pot on my head," the private said stubbornly.

"You may go," ordered Captain McGlynn.

When the private was gone, the captain said to Llewellyn, "I'm afraid that some of the men will have the same attitude."

"I wouldn't worry about the empty-headers too much. Nothing much rattles in their heads." Llewellyn shrugged. "Well, you can always use them to test the damn things."

"How?"

"Put it on the head on of them empty-headers and have the Germans take a shot at it."

"Is it bulletproof?" said Captain McGlynn asked with a grin.

"Not really. But once they see how much it protects them from shrapnel, they'll come around."

"I certainly hope so," replied McGlynn. "I hate writing condolence letters."

NOVEMBER 11, 1915
ALDERSHOT CAMP

Major Llewellyn slid off his horse when he arrived at the estaminet on Waterloo Road. He tied up his horse beside a couple of others with maple leaves brushed on their hindquarters. He admired the olive-grey Rolls-Royce parked nearby. He would have liked to have taken a staff car, but they were in high demand. They weren't supposed to be used for personal errands, but rank had its privileges.

He glanced across the busy road to the Aldershot Camp. He guessed that someone had a sense of humour, since the wooden huts were quite similar to the ones found at the Aldershot military base in England. There were four huts that surrounded a parade square, with an additional eight long huts behind them. The thousand-strong Royal Canadian Regiment was currently occupying the camp.

A guard lifted a gate to let out two companies. One was heading for the front lines, since they carried Rosses and their webbing with full ammo loads weighing down their trench coats. All them wore the new Brodie steel helmets. They still looked odd, but he was getting used to the men wearing them. The second company was a work party, since they were wearing forge caps. They were armed with shovels, picks, axes, and sandbags slung over their shoulders. Most of the men wore maple leaves, but there were a few imperials mixed in. He couldn't readily tell which division the men belonged to, since none wore divisional markings. He would have to suggest to Corps HQ that they develop a system so officers could easily tell to which division a man belonged. Something simple like a 1 or 2 stitched on the shoulder patch. He'd have to write it and send it up the line. *It wouldn't probably go anywhere, but what the hell,* he thought. *It wouldn't hurt.*

When he entered the estaminet, the low-slung room was full, and a couple of middle-aged waitresses manoeuvred among the tables, loaded with beer. A scratchy gramophone was playing a ballad. It was obvious who in the bar were the newbies and the veterans. The newbies were clustered together, looking nervously at the veterans. He spotted his friend where he expected, among the newbies.

Simon Rawlings put down his pint when he spotted him. He smiled and rose to shake Llewellyn's hand.

"You're looking good, Simon. Bermuda must have agreed with you," the major said as he took the seat across from him.

Last September at the Valcartier Camp, Simon Rawlings had joined the Royal Canadian Regiment when they requested volunteers. The Halifax-based regiment had been sent to Bermuda to replace the 2nd Battalion of the Lincolnshire Regiment. It had been felt at the time that the RCR was being sent to the Caribbean island because Sam Hughes didn't want them anywhere near the front. This suited Simon fine, since he despised Hughes and he firmly believed that Hughes was going to appoint himself the GOC of the Canadian Contingent.

"How was it?" asked the major.

"Hot and sunny."

"And the women?"

"Hot and sunny."

The major chuckled. He ordered a beer when the waitress came by. "I see that you got your lieutenant stars back." Simon had held the rank of lieutenant in the militia but had been reduced to sergeant when he joined the first contingent in August of last year.

"They recognize talent when they see it."

"Yeah, right."

"You've come up in the world yourself," he stated as he pointed to the major's stars on Llewellyn's shoulders.

Llewellyn brushed them with his hand. "They come with the job. I've been asked to be the brigade-major for the Richmond Fusiliers."

"You're kidding?" Rawlings said. "The last you wrote Colonel Topham had fired you, but you managed to get a spot on General Currie's staff."

"Well, things have changed."

"Really?"

They were interrupted when a fight broke out. A large bouncer from the back came out and tossed the two brawlers outside. Half the crowd followed them, since they were sure that the fight would be entertaining.

When the bar quieted, Llewellyn asked, "What have they been training you on?"

"They're putting us through the hand grenade training course that General Mercer has set up for the Corps troops. That plus trench instructions and the work parties are keeping us busy. Thank God. The Aldershot Camp is a mud hole."

"Welcome to France."

"Shit," Rawlings said. "Join the army and dig trenches. Most of the men are complaining about the work parties. They'd rather be training."

"I'm afraid it's necessary. With the rain, some of the trenches have collapsed, and believe me, we need those secondary trenches just in case."

"Ypres was that bad?"

"Worse than you can imagine."

"Any of the old gang still around?"

Llewellyn shook his head. "A few, but most of them have been killed or wounded."

Rawlings's face turned sober as he stared at his beer. He picked it up and said, "To old friends."

"To old friends," Llewellyn said as they touched glasses.

Once they finished their beers, Rawlings asked, "I heard that you might be going to the Fusiliers? Why? Colonel Topham doesn't like you."

"It's not official yet, but they are sending Colonel Topham home," Llewellyn murmured as he leaned forward. "Colonel Tennison will be taking over the Fusiliers."

"Topham screwed up that badly?"

"I'm afraid so. He put himself in for a DSO." The Distinguished Service Order was a medal given to officers who had distinguished themselves in combat.

"He did?"

"Yes."

"Whatever for?"

"Saving a woman from an exploding shrapnel shell."

"He did?" Rawlings said, surprised. "Who would have thought?" When Llewellyn snorted, Rawlings asked, "What?"

"Well, he was naked at the time and in the saddle."

"No! He got his arse blown off?"

"Peppered, actually. The woman was put out because she didn't get paid."

"And they still gave him the DSO? Fuck, why?"

"They wanted to get rid of him ever since Givenchy. He had never left his dugout during the battle. But the bastard has a lot of connections back home. This way he gets a medal and a one-way ticket home as a war hero."

Rawlings rolled his eyes. "Wouldn't it be easier for the Germans to get another shot at him?"

"They thought of it, but they couldn't get him near the front."

"What a way to fight a war!" muttered Rawlings.

CHAPTER 33

"Empty your pockets!" ordered Captain Thomas.

Major Llewellyn watched as the soldier standing before a plank table reluctantly pulled out his pay book from his breast pocket.

"Money, too?" he asked as he displayed the francs that he had folded inside the book to the officer who had given him the order and the sergeant standing beside him.

"You're not likely to spend it where you are going this evening," answered Captain Thomas in a thick English accent. The captain was a tall, thin man with brown hair and blue eyes.

"You never know, Captain. There could be a couple of pretty girls over there," the private replied. After the captain snorted derisively, the private turned to the sergeant. "I got ten francs in there. They better be there when I get back," he admonished the sergeant as he slid the pay book into the trench coat that he had placed moments before on the table. The private ignored the sergeant's offended scowl.

"Identity disk!" Captain Thomas said as he pointed to his neck. The captain's insignia was missing from his tunic collar. Also, his shoulder boards were gone, and the locations on his sleeves where the unit flashes normally were sewn were bare. Even in the dim light he could see brighter patches of cloth that had been protected from the elements. The private was similarly attired.

"Yeah, sure," the private replied as he reached under his collar and pulled it over his head. He slipped that too into the overcoat pocket. The sergeant pulled the overcoat into a sandbag and pulled on the drawstring to close it. He wrote on the tag the man's name and the contents then attached it to the bag. He then placed it with the others that were neatly stacked in the shed.

"It will be here you get back," Captain Thomas said to the private.

"Of course, sir."

"Get in line with the others," he ordered after returning the man's salute.

"Any last-minute changes?" Thomas asked Llewellyn.

Llewellyn shook his head. "All reports indicate they remain the same." That was the main reason why he was at French Farm this evening — to pass along any new intelligence.

Both men walked out of the storage shed to the assembled attack force. The seven-man scout team had already left, and eighty men remained clustered in sections. The key men were the seventeen bombers armed with Mills grenades. Beside them were two squads of bayonet men armed with Lee-Enfields. Below the rifle barrels they had attached torches with wire and twine so they could blind any defenders they might encounter.

Next to them were a dozen wire and shovel men. They were lightly armed with bayonets, pistols, and shovels. They were tasked to erect barricades once the bombers accomplished their tasks. Also, they carried the reserve supply of Mills bombs in vests and satchels. Beside them were two squads of riflemen to provide cover for the assault party, and behind them were an additional twenty men for a reserve. Separated from the rest were four men leaning on upright stretchers.

Their amiable chatting died down when Captain Thomas stood in front of them and asked, "Anybody have any questions?"

When no arm was raised, he nodded. "Good, everyone knows what to do. Get the mats and the ladders and let's get to it."

The mats were to be used to cross any uncut wire and the ladders to bridge the Douve River. They had actually intended the raid to take place the previous evening, but the weather hadn't cooperated. The river had swollen to twice its normal size, but the water had diminished sufficiently for the night attack to proceed.

"You want to come?" asked Captain Thomas as he headed to the front of the column.

"General Currie would have me shot when I get back," the major replied. "He went to a lot of trouble getting me the promotion."

The captain chuckled. Llewellyn actually did want to join the team, but at this late stage he would be more of a hindrance. He had come over to watch the balaclava-clad assault teams rehearse for the past weeks in the trenches they had replicated to match the ones that the 7th Battalion was going to assault. The men were comfortable with each other and knew each other's moves.

"Good luck," said the major as the captain took his place at the head of the column and motioned the men forward.

"Any news?" Major Llewellyn asked when he entered the 1st Canadian Division's reporting centre in Nieppe. The reporting centre was in a two-storey white stone building on the village's main street.

"The reports are starting to come in," replied Colonel Romer, Currie's chief of staff.

"It's too bad that the general couldn't be here for this," stated Llewellyn. Major-General Currie was on leave and had left a few days earlier for England.

The colonel shrugged. "His wife and family have just arrived in London from Canada."

"Well, there's that," replied the major. He wondered if he and Samantha would have a family when the war was over, if they were still together. He didn't blame Currie. The general hadn't seen his family since August. He wondered briefly how the general could support his family with the rising prices in England. Even a major-general's pay could only go so far.

"Damn," said the colonel when an orderly handed him a note. "The 5th had to call off their attack."

"What the hell happened?" asked Llewellyn. The 5th Battalion had been assigned to attack a trench at map coordinates U.8.2.7.10. Both the 5th and 7th were to assault simultaneously.

The orderly who had taken the message replied, "The ditch in front of the trench was still filled with water, and they couldn't get across. The CO sounded pretty pissed over the phone."

Llewellyn winced. He was going to get a reaming in the morning. He was the intelligence officer, after all.

"The 7th?" Llewellyn asked. Both battalions had telephone and cable teams with them for communications.

"Nothing now," the orderly replied.

Llewellyn glanced at the map on the table, trying to decide if no news was good news. The Petit Douve Farm's house and barns were clearly represented by four red rectangles. He had viewed the buildings often from the trenches. Shells had reduced them considerably. The Germans were using the cellars as dugouts, and they had a covered trench to move between the buildings.

The time he saw on his wristwatch was nearly 12:10. If everything were going to plan, the 7th should be penetrating the German trenches, smashing what they could, taking prisoners, and gathering what documents they could get their hands on. In ten minutes, they would be firing red flares to indicate to the artillery observers that they were leaving via the designated escape routes.

"How did the preliminary barrages go?" he asked.

"The scouts reported that they did a pretty good job of cutting the wire. But in places they'll need to cut them by hand." Llewellyn grimaced. Cutting wire by hand added time. That was what the traverse mats were for.

"Did they report that the Huns pulled out of the trenches?" For the last several months they had been sending out aggressive scouts and patrols. It had gotten to the point that the Germans in this sector were abandoning their listening posts in No Man's Land.

"Yes, it seems that they are falling for it," replied the colonel.

The entire raid was predicated on the Germans' standard response to a frontal assault. Llewellyn had read the captured translations of German reports and documents that the 1st Canadian Division had received from the Imperials and the French. The Division had also continually observed and analyzed how the Huns reacted under fire.

The Germans generally knew when an attack was coming. A heavy preliminary barrage usually announced that one was heading their way. The Germans' front-line trenches were lightly defended, so they would pull out to ride out the barrage. Just prior to the actual assault, the rain of shells would stop, telling them that they needed to reoccupy their trenches fast and to call up their reserves and artillery support. That was what the 7th was counting on. They weren't planning to stay for morning tea.

"They should be pulling out," said the colonel as he glanced at the wall clock that read twenty after midnight.

The major nodded in agreement. The men should be withdrawing, since the plan was very specific that they had only twenty minutes before their covering barrage would start. He couldn't help stare at the orderly, who had his hand hovering over the telephone waiting for the news.

When it rang, the corporal snatched it up. "Reporting Centre!"

In the message pad he scribbled rapidly. He left hand rattled the hook to disengage and re-engage the line. "Artillery, it's a go."

The box barrage was on its way. The Germans were going to be hurt.

The orderly looked up at them with a hint of satisfied excitement.

"They did it!"

"Casualties?" asked the colonel.

"One dead and one wounded."

"I'll be damned!" said the colonel. The casualties were amazingly light.

"The general will be tickled pink," said Llewellyn.

CHAPTER 34

Sir Robert was saddened as he looked into the face of his friend and mentor who lay peacefully in his casket. He had been attending too many funerals lately, partly due to his current stage in life. His mother passing in April and now Sir Charles Tupper, who had died nearly two weeks ago.

Last August he had visited Tupper at his daughter's home in Bexleyheath when he was in England. Tupper had retired there after passing the torch of the Conservative Party to him. He had gone to see Charles to bounce several ideas off him about how his government should be represented in London. At ninety-five, Charles had been still quite sharp and had given him some useful advice.

It had been a blow when Borden was given the news. There was no question that the former Canadian prime minister would lie in state in his beloved Nova Scotia. Normally, a warship would have been tasked to transport the body back to Canada. Since none could be freed for such duty, Sir Charles Tupper made the voyage back home on the RMS *Metagama*. The ship was a CPR passenger liner that had been pressed into service to transport Canadian troops and supplies to England. Once the casket had arrived at Quebec City, it was transferred to the CGS *Lady Evelyn* for the trip to Halifax. The Royal Canadian Garrison Artillery had met the ship at eight the previous day and escorted the casket on a gun carriage to the General Assembly's council chamber, where he was laid for public viewing.

The council room was draped in black and purple, and the smell of flower wreaths that overflowed the space was nearly overpowering. Four khaki-uniformed members of the Royal Canadian Regiment stood guard beside the casket. Opposite them was the desk where Sir Tupper had frequently sat when he was premier of the province. On the desk was a simple wreath with *Nova Scotia* emblazoned on it.

Borden and most of his cabinet had arrived the previous day on a special nine-car train that the Grand Trunk had put on for them. The trip had been unduly long due to sleet and snowstorms they encountered.

He stepped away from the dais and followed the potted fern-lined path to the chamber's main doors. Near the entrance he spotted the House of Commons' sergeant-at-arms and the Senate's gentlemen of the Black Usher who had accompanied him. He watched as they placed their ceremonial maces on their shoulders, preparing for the procession to St. Paul's Church, where the funeral service was to be held. It was rare that the maces left the Centre Block, but an exception had been made in this case. Lord Richard Nelville, representing the governor general, stood beside the recently appointed lieutenant governor of Nova Scotia, David McKeen.

Borden frowned slightly when he saw some of the local Conservatives were hanging back. He had a meeting schedule with them after Sir Tupper's body was laid to rest beside his wife at the St. John Cemetery to listen to their gripes and complaints before he headed back to Ottawa.

He could hear some of the crowds buzzing outside. The weather was dull and grey, but he expected large crowds would line the route to St. Paul Hill and to the cemetery. Halifax had declared the day as a public holiday. Many would be there simply to view the show, since the procession would be a long one with all the visiting dignitaries and military units in attendance.

It was fitting, since Sir Charles Tupper had been the last living father of the Canadian Confederation.

Sir Robert felt it was an end of an era. What the future portended for the country, no one knew.

CHAPTER 35

"This is not acceptable," Major Llewellyn said as he glared at two captains.

"But Major," Captain Winslow replied quickly, "those are the instructions that we've received." He then looked at Captain Tremblay, who stood beside him for support. Llewellyn wasn't familiar with the two, since they were replacements, but he had hoped the old-timers would have informed them about him. It looked as if they hadn't.

Llewellyn snorted. "Really!"

When he arrived at the Fusiliers' headquarters, one of the first things he did was take a look at stores. One could tell a lot about how a unit was managed by the state of its stores. Llewellyn had expected them to be in pretty good shape, since Lieutenant-Colonel Topham was the owner of a five-and-dime chain. He at least should have known the value of good logistics.

That was not what he saw when he inspected the first couple of sheds. They were currently in a cellar of an old farmhouse with the usual missing roof. Actually, he had concerns about the building, since the beams seemed to be sagging. He'd have to call the engineers to take a look at it.

He glanced back at the two officers. He hated lowering the boom on them. Normally, he would have liked to have worked with the previous brigade-major during the transition to see how he did his job. Not everyone approached the work in the same manner. Some were sticklers on how the job needed to be done. Llewellyn didn't put much stock in that. He was willing to allow the man to use his initiative as long as he produced results in an efficient manner.

However, the stores were a mess. Sure, he'd expected some chaos. Supplies were constantly moving in and out. That was why they tried to locate stores as near as possible to the communication trenches. When it started to go to crap, as it had at Ypres, lack of stores had been a major problem, and he didn't want to go through that again.

"I want a complete inventory on my desk by Friday morning," Major Llewellyn ordered.

Both men's eyes bulged at his order. This was Wednesday afternoon. There were thousands of items in the inventory that they needed to account for.

"Sir, by Friday?" Captain Winslow asked with a touch of hesitation.

"Problem?" asked Llewellyn with a raised eyebrow. He pretended not to notice the glance that Captain Tremblay gave Winslow.

"No sir, not a problem," Winslow replied hurriedly.

Llewellyn acknowledged with a nod as he took the communication trench that would lead him back to the Fusiliers' HQ. He knew that he had given them an impossible task, but he was testing to see how well they would perform and what excuses they would have. The duckboards under his feet bent slightly as he moved to the side to let a squad pass him. He glanced at the communication cables branching out from a junction. He assumed they were going to the various observation posts that dotted the trenches.

When he first arrived at the Fusiliers' HQ, he had been rather nervous. It was mainly due to Lieutenant-Colonel Topham firing him last October. Now he was back and Topham was gone. Also, the previous brigade-major had been transferred back to Shorncliffe to the training division. Lieutenant-Colonel Tennison had been made CO. He was taking a wait-and-see attitude with the remaining staff and line officers. In the next few days Tennison would be visiting all the units to gauge the quality of the officers and men to determine how far the rot went. Depending on what he found, there could be some serious pruning.

What worried Llewellyn was how much the current men would resent him. Some, he knew, would welcome him back while others would not be pleased to see him. Well, that was too bad. Either they shaped up or he would ship them out to join the former brigade-major at Shorncliffe.

DECEMBER 4, 1915
PRIME MINISTER'S HOME, GLENSMERE, OTTAWA

Sir Robert's cheeks still had a slight tinge of pink when the Dominion Police constable opened the door and escorted him into the meeting room. He had just come from a brief walk in the crisp afternoon air on Parliament Hill. He had taken the long route along the Lover's Lane path behind the East Block that faced the Château Laurier and that ran to the back of the rear entrance of the new wing of the Centre Block. Before taking the stairs to the second floor to the meeting room, he had dropped off his jacket and hat in his office.

Seated at the table, wearing a full beard, was Joseph Wesley Flavelle, the man he had appointed as chairman of the Imperial Munitions Board. Beside him was a male secretary with the standard steno pad for shorthand notes. The rows of chairs facing the tables were filled with stern-faced labour men with crossed arms. They all had risen to their feet until he took his seat beside Flavelle.

He needed all of the energy he could gather. Borden knew that this meeting would be a rather fractious one. He thought wistfully of the teenage boys he had seen with skates hanging around their shoulders as they headed to the canal. It wasn't unusual for some to be impatient, waiting for the ice to thicken to the right depth. It usually resulted in unfortunate accidents. In fact, one of the statues on the Hill had been commissioned by William Lyon Mackenzie King to commemorate a friend who had died trying to save a man who had fallen through thin ice on the Ottawa River.

As Borden settled in his chair as the meeting was being brought to order, he couldn't help think that this week had been a mixed bag of good and bad news. He had to deal with the uproar that Foster had created when he ordered the commandeering of nearly fifteen million bushels of western wheat at the imperial government's insistence. Rogers hadn't been pleased with Foster, since Rogers believed the commandeering would hurt the party in an election. At least Laurier had agreed to an extension, so they were safe for now.

Next week wasn't going to be any better, since he was planning to go on vacation to Atlantic City with Laura over the Christmas holidays.

At least he had received some good news earlier in the day. The papers were reporting that the US government was declaring German military attachés captains von Papen and Boy-ed as persona non grata. He was going to see Commissioner Sherwood and Inspector MacNutt on the implications following this meeting with the labour people. They would also give him a preliminary report on the explosion at the munitions plant near Parry Sound that atomized five buildings. Initial reports were that it had been German sabotage. He had hoped with the expulsions of the attachés, he wouldn't have to deal with the constant barrage of telegrams from British ambassador Spring-Rice in New York complaining about the German Secret Service. Once the ambassador found out about Parry Sound, he wouldn't hear the end of it.

The other piece of good news was that the subscriptions to the war loans that White had floated had exceeded all expectations. They had hoped for $50 million, but the returns showed double that amount. They decided to take the money and to assign half to the Imperial Munitions Board as working capital. Flavelle had been pleased when he was informed, but he wasn't happy that it had been announced in the papers. It had put them in an awkward bargaining position to meet the demands of the labour people.

Well, at least they had money to buy new machine guns that the overseas force needed. It looked like that the Ross rifle issue had been resolved. Major-General Gwatkin had assured him that the rifle was perfectly fine.

"Shall we begin?" he announced to start the beginning of the discussion.

One of the men rose to his feet and demanded, "What's this about how there isn't a fair wage clause in the Imperial munitions contracts?"

DECEMBER 5, 1915
PLOEGSTEERT WOODS

Major Llewellyn's boots sloshed as he approached the Fusiliers HQ. He was rather pleased that his feet were still dry, especially since he had spent most of the early morning waterproofing the leather with grease. Even though he was starting to lose some feeling in his right toe, his wool socks were still comfortable. It was cold enough that he could see his breath.

When the entrance came into view, he was satisfied that the two sentries were alert. Llewellyn ducked under the low beam holding up the corrugated iron roof and had to take a moment for his eyes to adjust to the dim light. He spotted the Fusiliers' CO at the back with a field phone stuck to his ear. To the man's left was a map of the trenches they were responsible for. Llewellyn was quite familiar with it, since he updated it regularly with the latest intel on the German regiments they were facing. With Christmas fast approaching, both armies were hoping for a lull so they could give some of the soldiers leave.

"That sounds great. Thanks for the update. I would like to see it some time," he said as he finally placed the phone on the hook.

"What was that all about?" asked Llewellyn when he took his seat next to Lieutenant-Colonel Tennison. He hung his steel helmet on the nail on the wall beside him. Sufficient supply had arrived so that everyone in the regiment had been issued a Brodie helmet.

"Oh, yes. The French asked for copies of the orders for last month's raid on Petit Douve Farm." Tennison motioned to the phone. "The adjutant said our Canadian toughs impressed the hell out of the French high command. HQ is printing four to five thousand copies of General Currie's orders for the raid. The Frenchies are sending officers to the 7th Battalion as observers."

"I'm sure the 7th will be happy."

"Not as happy as the adjutant about the new bathhouse over at Neuve-Église Road. It is supposed to have a disinfector the sanitation officers installed to clean the men's uniforms after they are relieved from the trenches. It also has a gasoline engine to turn the fans in the drying area. They say it helps dry the clothes quicker."

"We'll have to give it a try when we get relieved," Llewellyn replied.

Tennison snorted. "Anything I should know from last night's scouting reports?"

Llewellyn shook his head. "Everything was pretty quiet last night."

"Well, we can't have that, can we?"

"No sir, we can't," Llewellyn replied. He got the message. He would be sending it along to the company commanders. "I was going to through the daily orders from Corps HQ. There are a few things that need your attention."

"The one about the new machine gun company they want to form?"

"Yes, they asked for volunteers."

"I know. We're going to lose some of our best people to them."

"Yes, that we will. They're looking at about eight officers, 140 other ranks, and sixteen machine guns."

"It's easier replacing men than machine guns. I hate to lose them," stated Tennison as he rubbed the shrapnel scar on his left cheek.

"We have to give up some of our Colts, unless we suddenly get some Vickers or some of the Lewis guns we were promised."

"The last I heard, the Lewises are in the pipeline, but we won't get them for a while."

"Why the hell not?"

"The War Office won't approve them until they pass the .303 Mark VI testing."

"What the hell for?" Llewellyn said in disgust. "We don't use the Mark VI, only the VII."

"What can I tell you? It's the War Office. They must have a stockpile they have to use up."

Llewellyn rolled his eyes. "That explains the latest orders that we should only use the No. 5 Mills grenade from now on. I would love to comply, if we had them."

"The supply people haven't been able to get them yet?"

The major shrugged. "One of our supply people is quite enterprising. He told me we should be getting a couple of hundred by the end of the week."

"Do I want to know how?" asked Tennison.

"I don't think so," replied Llewellyn with as innocent face as he could manage.

"We'll need to give some thought as what we're going to do with our jam tins when we start getting a regular supply." Llewellyn nodded in agreement. He had used the No. 5 Mills Grenade a couple of times, but they had been in short supply since their introduction last May. It looks like production was finally catching up to the demand. The grenade weighed slightly less than two pounds and could throw shrapnel nearly a hundred yards. The Mills would make life easier and less dangerous for the men than the jam tin bombs, since they already came pre-assembled with safety features to prevent premature explosions.

"We'll have to talk to the supply people and the cooks about food for Christmas and New Year."

Llewellyn grimaced. "Getting turkeys is going to be tough."

"I'm sure your enterprising supply officer is up to the task," Tennison replied.

"I'll mention it to him and see what he can do," answered Llewellyn. "We'll have to put some extra people on the mail. We're expecting double the volume with the outgoing and incoming. The communications people are not going to be happy."

"I know."

"I also saw that HQ is setting a sniper school and is looking for instructors."

"Do you have anyone in mind?"

"Actually, I do. I was considering Sergeant Duval."

"He's going to love that." Tennison chuckled.

"I know."

CHAPTER 36

"What are you doing here?" asked Samantha when she spotted Dr. Moore standing in front of the dental office at the Moore Barracks Military Hospital. He was dressed in a freshly pressed khaki uniform with his brass buttons, major's insignia, and cap badge sparkling in the morning light streaming through the waiting room's window. The room was full of young men waiting for dental exam clearances and patients who needed dental care. There was a duffle bag at his feet.

"I was going to ask the same thing," he replied with a warm smile.

"Are you assigned to Shorncliffe?" She couldn't help the hopeful tone in her voice.

"I'm afraid not. I'm on a ten-day leave to London."

"And you're spending it here!"

"What can I say, I'm a glutton for punishment," he replied with a wider smile. "Where are you taking the young man?"

Samantha had been wheeling a young man in a wheelchair. The private's left leg was in a white plaster cast, and his left arm was heavily bandaged. There were yellow-blue splotches on his cheek. "I'm taking him to see the dental surgeon."

Dr. Moore's eyes sharpened when he focused on her patient's mouth. He must have seen the red swollen and bleeding gums.

"Well, the dentist's a good man. He'll take care of you," the doctor said to the patient.

"You know him?" Samantha asked.

"Oh yes, for twenty years. He's also my dentist in Richmond."

Samantha rolled her eyes. The medical profession in Canada was a small one. Everyone knew everyone. She parked the patient near the entrance and leaned over to adjust the blanket that covered the man's knees. "Wait here, I'll get the doctor."

She glanced at Dr. Moore. He must have seen the question on her face that she was hesitant to ask. "He's fine," he answered. "At least he was when I saw him a few days ago."

"He wasn't injured?"

"No, I saw him at the Fusiliers' HQ."

Samantha sighed in relief and then said with consternation, "Does everyone know?"

The doctor shook his head. "Your young man is a very private person."

Samantha felt her cheeks flush. "Thank you."

"Ah, I thought I recognized that voice. What the hell are you doing here, Dr. Moore?" said a white-coated major that looked a lot like Dr. Moore himself. Samantha judged that he was in his mid-forties and rotund. Based on the lack of hair peering from under his white surgeon's cap, he was bald. "Here for a checkup, are you? And who is this young lady?"

"My teeth are fine," Moore said. He then grinned, pulling his lips and showing his teeth. "See, I brush them twice a day, whether I need to or not. Miss Lonsdale, I would like to introduce you to Dr. Lawrence. Nurse Lonsdale was with me at Ypres."

Dr. Lawrence examined Samantha with interest. "Was she? So you're here for a checkup too. Please say yes. I've been staring down men's throats all day."

"I'm afraid I brought you another patient," she said, pointing to her patient in the wheelchair.

Lawrence sighed. "Let's take a look, shall we."

The moment that the soldier opened his mouth, Lawrence glanced sharply at Samantha. "When did he arrive at the hospital?"

"Only a few days ago."

"No one noticed until now?"

"Not really. I took a look at him when he complained that he couldn't eat solid food and chewing was painful. When I saw how bad his gums were, I got permission to bring him here right away."

"Good thing you did," he said. His face turned into a scowl when he saw the young man's unit badges. "This is the third man from this outfit with trench mouth that I've seen this week."

"The third one?" asked Dr. Moore sharply.

"Yes," said Lawrence with disgust. "Begs the question how bad are the rest of the men in his unit?"

Samantha knew that trench mouth was the result of poor dental hygiene mainly resulting from the lack of potable water in the trenches and diet. Also, food on dirty tin plates and eating utensils didn't help much.

"That pissed me off," Dr. Lawrence said to Dr. Moore as they stepped out into the corridor for privacy. "Some of the brigade commanders are refusing the dental surgeons we sent for preventive care and to repair the soldiers' teeth. The usual principle. Get them fast and early. Relieves a lot of suffering later on. We've assigned two officers to each brigade. That boy's idiot commander is one of them. He claims the army managed to survive this long without dentists, so what the hell did they need us for. When they offered to conduct a clinic in the billets, he cursed them, sent them back to Le Havre, then ordered his men not to attend any dental surgeries."

"Isn't that against regulations?" blurted Samantha. Regulations required that all the volunteers obtain medical and dental clearances before they were accepted. Some of the men had been rejected because of the state of their teeth. Once they had volunteered, the Canadian Army's Dental Corps was responsible for the men's dental health. The CADC was separate from the CAMC. What Samantha didn't know was that the Canadian army was unique from other Allied armies with an official dental corps as part of the overseas force.

Dr. Lawrence smiled and said patiently, "Of course it is. Our director will be having a word with General Alderson." Samantha blushed at how naive she had sounded. She knew better how the army worked.

"In the meantime, we'll take care of that young man." Then the dentist grinned widely at Moore and Samantha. "But first, I should take a look at your teeth."

"Ah," Samantha replied as she took a step back.

"Now, now, you'll have to wait until you're in the chair before you say 'Ah,'" he said as he directed her into his office. The door was open, and she could see the empty dentist's chair waiting for her.

DECEMBER 15, 1915
PLOEGSTEERT WOODS

Ryan was sitting on his cot reading his mail. He was trying to blot out the sounds of his men putting away their kit before marching over to the nearby estaminet for a meal and a glass of warm beer. He absentmindedly rubbed his shoulder that had been hit. It felt weary, since he and his men had been on fatigue duty making improvements on a communication trench that morning. Major Masterley had been pleased enough to grant his squad a half-day's leave. It was Sunday, and they had missed the morning's church parade.

"You coming?" asked Corporal Keats.

Ryan shook his head. "No, I have some paperwork."

When the corporal saw a box of pencils and a pad of paper on the cot, he nodded sagely. "The captain asked you to write next week's newsletter?"

"He did after he found out I wanted to be a writer. He wants to maintain the men's morale, and he thinks a newsletter helps. I have to come up with ideas for next week's addition."

"Better you than me. Be seeing you."

"You have a good time and stay out of trouble."

"What's the fun in that?"

Paul sighed. Most of the men were looking forward to the evening's entertainment. A regimental band was giving a Christmas concert. They needed all the distractions they could get. It looked like they would be enduring another miserable, wet Christmas.

He reread his dad's letter. He didn't say much, only that his mother, brother, and sister were doing well. Trade was good. They had gotten a lot of government orders. His sister's letter was full of gossip. Marie, his ex-girlfriend, had announced her engagement, and the wedding was to take place in the spring. He felt a pang of jealousy. There wasn't much he could do about it. Emile mentioned that they sent him a Christmas package that they hoped he would get before the 25th. He hoped so too.

He had left the letter from Maggie for last. When he opened it, he sniffed the sheet of paper to get a whiff of her perfume. There was barely a hint. As he read the letter, he could hear her voice. He was trying to get a sense of her true feelings about him. He felt guilty that he had not been able to get a pass for England. Major Masterley had put in a word for him, but the pass always seemed to have fallen through.

He put the letters in a small wooden locker he pulled from under his cot. He then took out a thick 5 by 8 tan leather-bound notebook. When he opened it, he glanced at the John McCrae's poem "In Flanders Fields" that he had clipped from a newspaper and pasted to the inside cover. He flipped the pages until he found the last entry. He then wrote his observations and dated it.

Technically, he shouldn't be keeping a journal. If it fell into German hands, it could provide them with valuable intelligence. But he couldn't help it. If he wanted to be a writer, he needed to jot down his impressions on a regular basis. After the war, if he survived, he was planning to write a book. He hadn't decided whether it would be fiction or an actual account of his experiences.

He would have loved to find the time, but the captain was keeping him busy. Masterley had assigned him to the new mortar unit the Division was experimenting with. If he did well, the captain had promised him a ten-day pass to England. He knew he had to wait and see.

DECEMBER 20, 1915
TRENCHES, NIEPPE

"Hey, take your fucking finger out of the fucking cup," demanded Sergeant Ellis as he presented his fist under the Sergeant Ferguson's chin.

"Fuck you," replied the quartermaster sergeant, who didn't appear to be intimidated. The man wouldn't be, since he held a one-gallon rum jar under his arm. The clay jar's body was grey, with "SRD" printed in black letters on top of the brown glaze that covered the top third of the container.

When Sergeant Ellis pulled back his arm, Major Llewellyn stepped in. "What the hell do you think you are doing?"

"I'm going to beat the lights out of this fucker!" The sergeant indicated with his fist. Ellis was wearing light battle dress, and his rifle was slung over his right shoulder. Behind him his squad stood lined up in the trench, watching the entertainment.

Llewellyn glanced back at Sergeant Ferguson. He didn't particularly like man. The man's uniform was too neat and well taken care of. It also stretched across his stomach, rather than across his chest, like Sergeant Ellis's. The man was relatively new to the regiment, and the officer who had recommended him said he was competent. And that was what the captain cared most about. When he first arrived, Ferguson had cleaned up the weekly supply reports quite nicely.

That this is all I need, Llewellyn thought. A good supply sergeant was hard to come by. "What seems to be the problem?"

"He shorting the rum ration," Ellis stated flatly as his fist dropped.

"No I'm not!" declared the quartermaster indignantly.

Shit, thought the major as he scanned the men in the line he had come to inspect. He would have preferred to have the accusation made to him privately so that he could investigate it quietly. If there had been any truth to it, he would have transferred him to another unit. In the man's docket, he would have indicated the man's unreliability concerning the rum ration. Something to about his ability to ensure that essential stores were not properly documented and accounted for. Not something a quartermaster wanted on his record.

The sergeant turned to Major Llewellyn, presenting him the cup. "Look, I'm using the same one that you marked for the rum ration."

Llewellyn glanced at the interior. There it was, his thin scratch line. Also at the bottom there were a couple of drops of dark rum.

"I measured the cup myself. It's two and a half ounces," the major stated. "That's what regulations require, and that is what you are getting."

"No sir, that is not what we are getting," Sergeant Ellis insisted.

Now the major was getting irritated. "If you don't have any proof, move along so that the rest of the men can get theirs."

"I'm telling you, sir, that he is giving us a short pour! I should know. I was a bartender in Halifax working the sailor bars. I learned every trick of the trade, from watering down booze to shorting drinks."

"Oh?" When he saw the quartermaster's face pale slightly, Major Llewellyn asked, "What tricks?"

"Why do you think he was holding the cup with one of his fingers inside it?" The major glanced at the cup and saw that it didn't have a handle. You either had to cup it in the palm of your hand or hold it steady by pinching it with your thumb and forefinger. That method wasn't particularly hygienic, but then 186-proof rum would pretty well kill anything.

"Now, if you hold it like that, see where your fingers land?" The sergeant pointed out to him. His forefinger landed on top of the mark.

When Llewellyn realized what the sergeant had been doing, he gave him a glare. In placing the thumb beside the mark, he would naturally ensure that he would fill it so it would never touch his thumb. The rum jar he was holding was 160 ounces per imperial gallon. At two and a half ounces per man, a one-gallon rum jar was sufficient for sixty-four men. Then there was one or two for spillage plus the devil's due. A quarter ounce less didn't seem like much, but it meant that Ferguson would have seven ounces left over when he was done serving the men. In the trenches, the rum service was before the morning hate and in the evening before the night tour. That meant he would have nearly fourteen ounces per day of rum that was not accounted for on the books that he could do with as he saw fit. He was probably making a pretty penny on the side selling it back on the sly to the men.

The quartermaster gave him a sheepish look, which infuriated Llewellyn. His expression was such that even Sergeant Ellis stepped back.

The major then stared at the sandbags and at the fire steps for a moment. The quartermaster's lips were quivering when Llewellyn looked back at him. The smiles that appeared on the men waiting in the line were definitely not comforting.

CHAPTER 37

As Samantha entered the ward, she skirted the mistletoe hanging near the entrance. The two men in the nearest bed noticed and grinned at her. The one in the bed was working on a picture puzzle placed on a tray on his lap. Another man who had a leg missing was leaning on crutches as he tried to help complete the puzzle. The bed patient was having none of that. He kept swatting the other man's hand away.

The puzzles were popular items in the Christmas stockings that all the men had received that morning. Sent by the Red Cross, they were considered wholesome entertainment for the wounded, and these were the latest arrivals. Most of them were pastoral scenes, historic places, and events. They were a blessing and a curse. The puzzles kept the men's minds occupied, especially those who couldn't read. However, if dropped, as they were prone to do, pieces would scatter all over the floor.

"I hope I don't have to separate you to again," Samantha said with a grin. She'd had to mediate between the two the prior week. They had spent most the day bickering about who was responsible as they sorted out the pieces from two different but similar puzzles that had scattered to the far corners of the ward.

"No, ma'am," Floyd replied. He was a spindly nineteen-year-old from Parry Sound. His brown eyes flickered behind her for a moment as he shifted his weight on his crutches before returning them back to her. "Merry Christmas!"

"Yeah, Merry Christmas," added Ernest, a twenty-four-year-old bombardier from Uxbridge from his bed.

"The same," Samantha replied as she headed to Sadie, who was at the far end of the ward. There was a Christmas tree set up beside her near the window. There was an angel on top, and multicoloured paper ornaments hung from the branches.

Sadie looked up at her when she completed a note in the chart. The patient she was observing asked, "So can I go?" He had five o'clock shadow, and his left shoulder was heavily bandaged where shrapnel had struck him.

"Yes," Sadie replied. "Just make sure you don't overdo it."

"Yes, sister," Private Robins replied with a wide grin. The thirty-year-old from Comox, BC, was anxious to get off the ward. All the ambulatory patients were attending an afternoon Christmas concert at the Papillon Hall in Shorncliffe, after which they would be treated to tea by the local townsfolk.

"Where's Linda?" Samantha asked.

"She reported sick this morning."

"Again!"

"I'm afraid so."

"When did you find out?" Samantha asked as she grimaced at the news. Linda didn't appear to have a robust constitution, as she seemed to catch every disease that the men caught, except the sexual ones, and there was very little chance of that happening. She flashed back for a moment to Claire's death at La Touquet. She took some comfort at least that they hadn't lost any nurses this month. As the assistant matron, it was her responsibility to help in her matron's evaluation of the nurses' performance. Linda was on the cut-line for being sent home.

"Did everyone get a stocking?" Samantha asked. The nurses had spent the last few weeks preparing them for the men. They had made sure the latest puzzles, cigarettes, and sweets were found in the socks.

"Yes, they all liked the box of maple sugar that the governor general sent." Actually, they were from the Duchess of Connaught, the governor general's spouse, but Samantha didn't bother to correct her.

"It was mighty tasty," said Robins, who had overheard them. "Is there any left?"

"I'm afraid not," replied Sadie.

"Too bad," said a disappointed Robins.

"Maybe the townsfolk will have some sweets after the concert at the tea," Samantha suggested.

"What about the rest of the guys who can't make it?" he asked.

"I wouldn't worry," Samantha assured him. "The townsfolk are putting on a concert for them at the recreation hall. We'll have some eggnog for them."

"Eggnog is not eggnog without rum," Robins muttered.

Samantha chuckled. "Are you trying to get us into trouble?"

"Me?" the man said with an innocent face.

Samantha shook her head. "Okay, Sadie. I'll see if Ethel is available to help you get them ready."

"That would be great," Sadie replied. "Did you get a card from your secret admirer yet?"

"You get back to work," Samantha ordered as Sadie gave her a teasing grin.

When she turned to leave, she saw Floyd was standing at the entrance under the mistletoe. He was not the only one. Samantha gave them a stern look that didn't seem to faze them at all.

She shook her head as she gave them each a peck on the cheek as she kept an appropriate distance from them. What she really wanted to do was give the man who wrote the card that she had in her pocket a kiss.

DECEMBER 25, 1915
PLOEGSTEERT WOODS

When Major Llewellyn looked in on the men of the 1st Platoon in the reserve dugout, they gave him a baleful glare. With good reason, since he had cancelled their leave. This meant that they had to spend Christmas in a wet trench. He had just come from the 2nd Platoon's dugout, and they had given him the same look.

He indicated to Sergeant Duval, who was the platoon's acting CO, to give the order. "Okay, men. Off with your boots!"

The few who groaned in protest got a quick elbow to silence them. When the twenty or so men had their boots off, Llewellyn walked down the line, inspecting the men's feet. They had spent the last twelve hours in a wet trench and were to be rotated out soon. What he was looking for was signs of swelling and grey discolouration, which indicated trench foot.

That was why they were pissed at him. Their lieutenant, whose name was not to be spoken, had come down with the disease. He didn't know how Major-General Currie found out, but he got a rather angry phone call wanting to know what the hell was going on. After the tongue-lashing, he had to give Currie assurances that the appropriate punishment would be meted out. Then he had to explain what had happened to his own CO.

He could have covered the lieutenant's lapse, since the man was a relatively new transfer and was still learning. The major himself had suffered a mild case last March. But that changed when he spoke with the NCOs.

He had passed on the routine orders concerning trench foot prevention, since the trenches they were occupying were extremely wet, and all efforts to drain them had been futile. The orders were specific. The regiment's time in the trenches was reduced to forty-eight hours. The first trench was lightly defended, with half the men in the dry reserve dugout. After their shift, the men would be marched to a heated rest station, where they would be given their rum ration, stripped of their wet clothing, given a warm blanket, and gotten a rubdown.

During their time on duty, the lieutenant was to inspect his men's feet to ensure their boots had been oiled, their socks relatively dry, and their puttees had not been pulled so tight that they had cut off circulation. The lieutenant hadn't done any of that because he thought it was distasteful. When Llewellyn discovered that he had lied about it, he had relieved the man on the spot. He was also pissed at himself that he had trusted the man to do his job. There was that old adage about trust but verify.

He noticed one of the men was rubbing his feet. "Problem?" Llewellyn asked.

"No, sir," replied Private Rees.

Llewellyn was familiar with the twenty-eight-year-old from Kingston. Like many of the others, he hated admitting any weakness. "Did you rub your feet with warm oil to get circulation going?"

The man pursed his lips. "Yes, sir, I did."

"Well, you better do it again," replied the major. "I don't want to see your name on the sick roll. Do you understand me?"

"Yes, sir," Rees replied tersely.

As he walked past he caught him out of the corner of his eye mouth a silent *Merry Christmas, you bastard*. He wasn't surprised. He hadn't offered any Christmas greetings, since he knew it would add salt to the wound. They weren't happy that they were foregoing the Christmas dinner they had been eagerly awaiting and the other units were currently enjoying.

Sometimes you just have to punch a man in the nose to get his attention.

Also, what added to their misery was that he had to enforce the orders that had come down from the First Army. Last year's unofficial Christmas truce, where both sides had climbed out of the trenches to shake hands and sing Christmas carols together, had pissed off the British high command.

How dare the men be friendly with the enemy at Christmas! The men's fighting spirit had to be maintained. For God's sake, they're the enemy!

DECEMBER 26, 1915
CHÂTEAU FLÊTRE

Lieutenant-General Alderson walked up the path that was still wet from the previous night's rain to the Château Flêtre's stone porch. The chateau was a small one, more like a cottage. It had been built in the thirteenth century to protect the nearby village from bandits. Over the centuries it had been renovated, changed hands and names, and the locals called it the Château de Wignacourt. Now, it was a pretty two-storey red-brick building with contrasting grey stone corners and window frames. There was a circular tower to his left that he assumed contained a staircase.

The sentry saluted Alderson as he opened one of the double half stained glass wooden doors for him. A couple of signalmen who were leaving snapped to attention and didn't move until he released them. They hurried out to complete their assignments. Their truck was parked out front, and he had seen a squad of men digging a shallow trench for communication cables.

"Where can I find General Mercer?" he asked the sergeant seated at the front desk.

"Follow me, sir," the sergeant replied as he led Alderson into the main hall. He noticed that there were places where paintings were missing. He assumed that the owners had removed and stored them for safekeeping. Probably didn't want ham-fisted soldiers damaging them. The hall was filled with the familiar pattern of desks and tables with officers answering phone calls. A couple of signallers with telegraph headsets on were listening intently to the incoming messages.

At the far end of the hall, he spotted Major-General Mercer talking with his two brigade commanders. Brigadier-General A.C. MacDonell, the GOC of the 7th Brigade, was listening intently while Brigadier-General A.S. Williams, the GOC of the 8th, was staring at a paper in his hand.

They turned when silence enveloped the room.

"As you were," Alderson said as he made his way to Mercer. He glanced at the insignia on Mercer's shoulder boards. With the activation of the Canadian 3rd Division, Mercer had been temporarily promoted to major-general. He knew the man had been chafing, and he could see Mercer's satisfaction that it finally had arrived. He was the last of the three original brigade commanders to get one. The other two men had received temporary promotions as well.

"General Alderson, I wasn't expecting you today," Mercer stated as he saluted him.

"Getting everything organized?" Alderson asked.

"We're getting there," replied Mercer.

Through the window Alderson could see men pitching tents. While they had been planning this for a while, there was still much administration work to be done. Until today Mercer had been the GOC of the troops attached to the Canadian Corps HQ. Initially, the Canadian government's thoughts were that with the current levels of recruitment a 3rd Division wouldn't be ready until March of 1916. However, the Corps had been oversized for at the last month or two, especially with the recent arrival of the Royal Canadian Regiment from Bermuda and the Princess Patricia's that had been transferred to them from the 80th Brigade. He was well aware that both units were not Hughes' favourites, but the minister was insisting that the Canadians remain together. Along with that insistence was Hughes' position that Canadians were promoted, as many as possible, to the command slots. When he glanced at Brigadiers MacDonell and Williams, he was rather amused that he had actual Mounties as the 3rd Division's brigade commanders. Both men had been with the North-West Mounted Police before they served in the Boer War with the Canadian Mounted Rifles. That Williams had commanded the Valcartier Camp a year ago was a bonus.

"How the Patricia's coming along. Have they settled in?" he asked MacDonnell.

The Princess Patricia's Canadian Light Infantry had finally come into the fold. He had welcomed them at the train station with the 1st Canadian Division's band when they arrived at Flêtre.

He knew that MacDonnell had some work to do. Some of the Patricia's were not pleased leaving the 80th Brigade, since they had bonded tightly with them after spending ten months in the trenches together.

Only time would tell how well they would fit in with the rest of the Corps, since there still was a lingering resentment. The Patricia's senior officers had made a point of keeping themselves separate from the rest of the Canadians. But one thing everyone had to accept, the Patricia's had won a well-earned reputation as a fighting unit, and he hoped that it would continue. There was a bonus in that the Patricia's didn't need the basic training that Mercer was putting the RCR and the Mounted Rifles through.

"I've been assigning them to work parties. The engineers are keeping them busy. They took over the RCR tents at La Clytte. With the recent rain..."

"Yes, I know it turned into a field of mud," Alderson said with a sigh. "Have you finished the training syllabus for the Mounted Rifles?" he asked Colonel Williams. Before he ran the Valcartier camp last year, Williams had been a cavalryman.

"I will be forwarding it to you shortly," replied Williams. "We're cutting as much of the cavalry training and replacing it with infantry instruction. We may have to look at reorganizing them. They aren't structured for trench warfare."

Alderson nodded in agreement. "Based on what happened a few weeks ago, I tend to agree. General Currie wasn't pleased with their performance."

Alderson was referring to the incident several weeks prior where the Canadian Mounted Rifles had allowed the Germans to erect a barrier under their watch and then couldn't destroy it when ordered. Currie wasn't happy when he had to use his 2nd Brigade to do the job. Williams was well aware of the problems respecting the Mounted Rifles. The unit's training had been based on the Canadian experience during the Boer War. They had been trained to be mobile and to fight on and off their mounts in limited engagements. They had to be retrained for the trenches.

"What was the reaction to the proposed training?" Alderson asked.

"They're not happy about it. Some of the officers don't want to be infantrymen," replied Williams. "I'll have to start weeding some of them out."

"Do what you can. We need trained men. Maybe the machine guns and the artillery will change their attitude," stated Alderson. Changing the opinions of cavalrymen who believed that it was superior to the infantry would be a tough challenge.

"We can only hope," replied Mercer. "I'm meeting with Brigadier Naire later this afternoon to discuss how we can incorporate his artillery into the division."

"Good," replied Alderson. Brigadier-General Naire commanded the 3rd Lahore Division's Divisional Artillery. The Indian division was a mixture of British and Indian units from the Indian Army. It had suffered heavy casualties since Ypres and was being rebuilt. There was talk that they were being sent to the Middle East theatre. Meanwhile, their artillery would provide the 3rd with much needed fire support until Mercer received his complement of guns and personnel.

"With the arrival of the 9th Brigade in January, we will be up to strength," Mercer stated. "The 9th will be comprised of the 43, 52, 53, 60, and 111 battalions that are still in England."

"Anything else?" Alderson asked.

"The Patricia's were a bit concerned whether they would have to give up their Lee-Enfields," Mercer said with a smile. When he saw the look on Alderson's face, he quickly said, "I've also seen the reports from the 2nd Canadian Division's testing of the Ross."

Alderson snorted. Everyone was testing that damn rifle. "I've sent a copy of the report to General Gwatkin. I thought he might find it interesting."

Little did he know that his letter would be released to the Canadian public and would cause a political firestorm.

DECEMBER 27, 1915
PLOEGSTEERT WOODS

"Fuck," said Subaltern Ryan when he saw that the mortar had shifted after the last round was fired. He glanced over at Lieutenant MacKenny, who was thirty yards away with a telephone attached to his left ear. He had a finger stuck in his right one so that he could hear the incoming reports from the red kit observation balloons that were floating in the late afternoon sky about a thousand yards overhead. So far, German aircraft hadn't appeared to poke holes in them. How long that would last was anyone's guess.

The lieutenant had initially been pleased by the accuracy of the first dozen or so shells that they had launched at the German positions that they called "Birdcage" just east of Ploegsteert Woods. Ryan didn't know why it was called Birdcage, and frankly he didn't care. The lieutenant was probably getting reports that the rounds were now landing short of the target. He wasn't really surprised. He had told the lieutenant that it was going to happen.

"What the fuck are you doing?" he demanded when he ran over after he had dropped the phone onto the map board. Ryan didn't particularly like the officer from Toronto, especially since his voice had a whiny tone. He would have told him to fuck off, but one didn't choose one's superior officer. It was the army, you know.

"The mortar shifted again," Ryan said, pointing at the 2-inch mortar in front of them. The mortar's three-foot-long tube rested on an elevating steel bipod attached to a wooden base. A sighting periscope projected a couple of feet above the metal tube. In the four corners there were cord handles his men had used to carry the two hundred-pound weapon into position. The mortar was the latest addition to the Corps arsenal. Royal Ordnance had built it in response to the Germans' deadly 7.58 cm *Minenwerfer*.

Beside it was a stack of fifty stick-type mortar rounds. The metal shafts contained the propellant that sent the round eighteen-pound basketball-size sphere nearly six hundred yards. Each of the spheres was a dirty white with a pink band painted in the middle. The pink band indicated that it was filled with ammonal. A box of Type 80 fuses lay beside the rounds.

There were four them pointed in the same direction. Farther down was the sole 1.57 Vickers mortar. It was a more complex design than the 2-inch ones they were using.

"Well, I want it fixed," the lieutenant demanded. "Or I'll kick your fucking ass."

Paul tried not to give him a sour look. MacKenny happened to be one of those officers who felt you needed to scream at the men to motivate them. On occasion you had to do that to get the men moving. If you overdid it, as Paul had learned the hard way, it lost its effectiveness. Which this particular officer had yet to appreciate.

Paul also knew that the lieutenant wanted to make a good impression on the CO of the mortar detachment. This battle plan was being closely monitored by Lieutenant-General Alderson. The plan had been developed with the objective of damaging the German defences that surrounded Birdcage and to kill their repair work parties. One of the secondary aspects was that Alderson was keen on learning what worked and what didn't work as combined action.

"What the fuck do you want us to do?" asked Bombardier Maclean, who was responsible for setting the fuses.

"Get the damn thing up and we'll slide some wood underneath. That should keep it upright," MacKenny said.

"Okay," Maclean said as he looked at the ground rather dubiously. "It's worth a fucking try."

"We'll give it a go," Ryan replied. He then pointed at the ground under the wooden base. The recoil had driven it into the ground, elevating the mouth of the mortar nearly an inch or so. "The ground is pretty wet and spongy here. We might get a few rounds in, but the recoil will elevate the mortar again."

"I don't care. I want to fire as many rounds as we can before the Germans start retaliating," MacKenny replied before he stalked off.

Ryan sighed as he glanced up at the observation balloons. One of their tasks was to inform the 18-pounders if the Germans started to lob shells in their direction. They were well hidden in the Ploegsteert Woods, but the Germans were pretty quick. He wouldn't be surprised if he didn't hear from them in ten minutes or so.

Once they had resettled the base, he noticed that Bombardier Maclean was scrawling on one of the mortar heads using a yellow chalk stick. "What the hell are you doing?" Ryan asked.

"Oh, just sending Fritzy a message."

"What message?"

Maclean grinned when he lifted the mortar so that Ryan could see what he had written. It read *Happy New Year.*

DECEMBER 31, 1915
PRIME MINISTER'S HOME, GLENSMERE, OTTAWA

Borden woke with a jolt. He groaned in pain when a muscle spasm racked his back.

"What's the matter, Bob?" Laura croaked. His groan had been loud enough to wake her. She needed her rest, since she was suffering from a bad cold.

"My back is killing me," Borden replied through clenched teeth.

Ever since he and Laura had come back from their American vacation, they had been feeling miserable. They had spent the first week in Atlantic City, but they had to stop in New York until the tracks were cleared of thirty inches of snow that had buried the state. They hadn't bothered leaving the hotel until they decided to take in a Broadway evening show. They had been very pleased with their hotel room at the Chalfonte in Atlantic City. The room had beautiful views of the sea. Their daily walks had been invigorating, and he felt more energized. He had been surprised when the hotel staff gave him an invitation to speak to the New England Society of New York City. How they found out where he had been staying, he had no idea.

It might have been a mistake accepting the invitation, since it meant he had to devote some considerable time preparing a speech. When they had returned to New York, just before Christmas, they had been greeted at the station by a New York City detective who had been assigned as their bodyguard. The man hadn't done a particularly good job, since both he and Laura came down with a cold. He managed to make do, especially when Blount came down to give him a hand. His secretary also brought a bunch of messages and memos he had to deal with.

His main concern was Laura, since the cold had hit her hard. On Christmas Day, he was so worried about her that he had to call a doctor. It wasn't until several days later that she was well enough to travel. He could still see the relief on her face when she finally stepped into her home and could sleep in her own bed. Now this!

"How bad is it?" she whispered hoarsely.

Borden tried to roll over, but his muscles locked up on him. "I can't move," he replied. "I think I need a doctor."

Laura blinked at him. He could see her concern and her thought that it must be pretty bad for him to ask for a doctor. She struggled to sit up and put on a robe. She made her way to the bedroom door, using the walls to support herself. Once she had opened the door, she called out weakly, "Marie! Marie!"

Not getting a response, she continued down the hall to find a servant while he lay helplessly in bed.

The story continues in

SHARPENING THE BLADE

In 1916 the Canadians' rough edges were being honed off.

First, in February, there is the tragic loss of the Parliament Buildings' Centre Block by a suspicious fire. Then, in May, Lieutenant-General Alderson's leaked memo damning the Ross Rifle ignites a political firestorm. After the Canadian Corps' disaster at St. Eloi Carters, it doesn't take long for Major-General Sam Hughes to replace Alderson with Lieutenant-General Julian Byng. Within days, the Corps is struck by a devastating blow at Mount Sorrel. In October, Sir Robert Borden tires of crossing swords with his mercurial minister of Militia and Defence issues a *do what you are told* ultimatum! A defiant Hughes quits.

At the sharp end, Major Llewellyn and his men continue to learn the use of the hand grenade, the rifle, and the bayonet as they are grounded in the terrible carnage at St. Eloi, Mount Sorrel, and the maw of the Somme. Gunner Paul Ryan will have to live with the tragic mistake as his shells decimate his own countrymen. Matron Samantha Lonsdale continues to use all her skills to put back the pieces of men torn apart by devastating new weapons. In the fall, Lonsdale is sent to Russia, where she is soon plunged into the Russian Revolution.

By the year's end, they have been sharpened to a razor's edge.

For latest news and updates visit
www.sambiasebooks.ca